like
GRAVITY

Julie Johnson

WORKS BY JULIE JOHNSON

LIKE GRAVITY
SAY THE WORD
ERASING FAITH

This novel is dedicated to everyone who has ever struggled against the weight of gravity, in the hope that one day they will reach the stars.

"I was never one to patiently pick up broken fragments and glue them together again and tell myself that the mended whole was as good as new. What is broken is broken – and I'd rather remember it as it was at its best than mend it and see the broken places as long as I lived."

Margaret Mitchell

PROLOGUE

"Mommy, can I have the pink bubblegum? Please?"
I held up the roll, offering her a glimpse of the round BubbleTape
container clasped in my small hand. BubbleTape was the best
kind of gum; every first grader knew that. Mommy didn't answer.
She was humming, a small smile rounding her lips as she handed
packages of food from our cart to the grocery lady.

I turned my attention back to the bubblegum, crossing
my toothpick-like arms in front of my chest as I eyed the other
options. The checkout line, with all the brightly packaged candy,
was always my favorite part of food shopping.

"Mommy!" I said, louder this time, determined to get her
attention.
"Mmmm, what sweetheart?" she murmured distractedly.
"Can I please get the pink gum tape? All the girls in my
class eat it after lunch."
"Sure, Bee. Here, hand it up to the nice lady so we can
pay for it, okay?"
I stretched my hand above my head to pass the gum to the
grocery lady; even on my tiptoes it was hard to see her face. She
leaned forward to pluck the container from my grasp and smiled
down at me. Her teeth were streaked with pink from her lipstick
and her face was wrinkled like an apple, but she seemed nice.
"And how old might you be?" she asked.
"I'll be seven in a few months," I boasted. "I'm in the
first grade."
"Oh! How wonderful," she beamed. "You must be so
proud," she added to Mommy.
"Oh, yes, of course," Mommy smiled, handing the last
package to the lady.
While Mommy paid, I wandered down towards our packed
cart, peeking into the clear plastic shopping bags and hoping to

3

spot the telltale fuchsia gum container.

"Come on, Brooklyn," Mommy said, steering the cart one handed towards the parking lot. She held out the other hand for me to grab, pulling me close by her side as we walked through the automatic doors and out to our car. I slipped my hand into hers, squeezing tight. Smiling down at me, she gently swung our interlaced fingers back and forth.

The air was thick with August humidity, and my pink Hello Kitty t-shirt seemed to fuse to my skin as we walked through the parking lot. The wheels on our cart weren't working right – they squealed loudly in protest as Mommy wrestled them back onto a straight path.

I giggled at her efforts.

Her fingers remained tight on mine until we reached the SUV. Leaving the cart by the trunk, she scooped me into her arms, tickling my sides relentlessly. I screeched and squirmed in her grasp, loving every bit of her attention.

"So you think it's nice to laugh at Mommy when she struggles with the cart, huh?" she laughed. "Not so funny now, is it Bee?"

"I'm sorry!" I squealed breathlessly, giggling even as the tickle-torture came to an end. She carried me around to the back door and deposited me into my booster seat.

"Oof! You're getting too heavy for me to carry you around," she complained. "Pretty soon you won't have to use the booster at all. You're getting so big." She snapped my seatbelt into place, giving it an extra tug to check that it was safe, and dropped a quick kiss on my forehead.

"I've got to put the food bags in the trunk real quick, but then how 'bout we get some ice cream on the way home, Bumblebee?" Mommy asked, using her favorite nickname for me.

"Yes!" I exclaimed, my mind already busy picturing a chocolate sundae topped with a mountain of whipped cream and rainbow sprinkles.

"Okay, I'll be right back, love." She smiled, ruffling my dark hair one last time before closing the door. She walked back around to the cart and I could hear her humming as she loaded

4

the groceries into the SUV. Suddenly remembering my gum, I twisted around in my seat to face the open trunk.

"Mommy, can I have my bubblegum now?" I called, easing the tight seatbelt away from my throat so I could breathe easier.

When she didn't answer I unbuckled, turned fully around in my booster, and peered through the trunk space to where she stood. She'd stopped putting away the bags and instead stood frozen, with her hands held out in the air front of her. It seemed too still, too quiet without her cheerful humming. She looked scared – and Mommy never looked scared, not even when I told her there were monsters in my closet or under my bed.

Something wasn't right.

I'd just opened my mouth to ask what was wrong when I spotted the man. He stood a few feet away from Mommy, the food-filled cart abandoned in the space between them.

"Give me the keys," he sneered at Mommy, his voice muffled by the black hood covering his mouth. His eyes, the only part of his face not hidden by the mask, glared darkly.

He sounded mean, like one of the villains in my Saturday morning cartoons. I didn't like him, and I could tell Mommy didn't either. Clutching a black duffle bag tightly in one hand, he shifted back and forth from one foot to the other. His eyes kept darting to the liquor store behind him, the one where Mommy sometimes got the bottles of wine she drank with dinner. I wasn't allowed to have it; she said it was a grown-up drink.

Mommy's eyes flickered over to the backseat, and locked on my wide-eyed gaze for a short second. Her head shook slightly back and forth in the tiniest of movements, and I knew she was trying to tell me to keep still and quiet. I wanted to ask what was happening and who that angry man was, but I did as she asked.

"Are you fucking deaf? I said give me the keys! Do I look like I'm fuckin' around lady?" The man was yelling now, striding closer to Mommy and looking angrier than ever. Her eyes broke away from mine as she straightened her shoulders and faced the man once more.

"No," she said, her voice sad.

Why was she so sad?

"Your choice, then," he said, raising a hand up from his side and pointing a gun at Mommy's face. Before I could make a sound, he fired a single bullet into her forehead and watched silently as she crumpled to the cement.

"Stupid bitch," he muttered.

I sat frozen in place, unable to look away from Mommy bleeding in the parking lot, watching with wide eyes as he pried the keys from her hand and slammed the trunk hatch closed.

Racing around the SUV, he hopped into the driver's seat, Mommy's seat, and quickly started the engine. He peeled out of the parking lot without a backward glance at the bloodstained pavement. I turned slowly back around in my booster, trembling with fear and disbelief, and watched as he tossed the gun on the front passenger seat, followed by a duffle bag that was overflowing with crumpled money. Tears blurred my vision and tracked slowly down my face, but I remembered Mommy shaking her head at me and somehow managed to stay quiet.

For her.

Never once did the man look behind him and notice the small girl whose world had just ended, crying in the backseat.

Chapter One

The Barren Moon

The panicked scream that burst from my throat was a tribute to a long-remembered terror – one undimmed by the passage of time. The six year old within me cried out in desperation as I was ripped from the nightmare. The dream had been my nightly companion for fourteen years, a constant reminder of the day everything in my life changed.

As if I could have forgotten.

There was no doubt that the events would remain etched permanently into my memory, an unwanted tattoo I hadn't requested and could never remove, even if the nightmares had stopped. Somehow, though, I knew they wouldn't. If anything, they were getting worse, becoming more vivid and frequent with each passing year.

I wiped the gathering beads of perspiration from my brow, pulled my damp hair up into a loose ponytail, and untangled the twisted sheets from my legs. The small glow from the nightlight beside my bed warded away shadows that otherwise threatened to consume me. Focusing on the warm mellow light, I tried to push the memories from my mind. Although I was well practiced in driving away the nightly terrors, it took more effort than I liked to admit for my mind to settle and my heart rate to stop thundering in my chest like a goddamned cavalry charge.

Dragging a shaky breath into my lungs, I swung my legs to the floor and padded out of my small room. The kitchen's icy linoleum tiles were uncomfortable under my bare feet, and I hurried to pour myself some water from the tap before tiptoeing back to the warmth of my bed.

I sipped my water after slipping back beneath the covers, searching for the book I always kept within reach on my nightstand. Any hopes of more rest tonight were futile; after the nightmare inevitably hit I could never relax my mind enough to sleep. Sometimes I'd get lucky and the dream wouldn't rear its ugly head until near dawn, allowing me a few solid hours of rest. Other nights, like tonight, I wasn't so lucky.

A glance at my cellphone informed me that it was only 2:37 AM, leaving me with almost six hours until my first class of the semester began. *Great way to start sophomore year, Brooklyn,* I thought bitterly. *Overtired and grumpy. Oh, and dark under-eye circles are* so *in this year.*

The near constant bruise-like circles that lined my eyes were usually manageable with the help of some quality foundation. Most people would never notice them at all, and those who did would never discover their origin. Holding people at arm's length was easier and, in the long run, saved everyone a lot of unnecessary hurt and heartache.

I'd never been one to reach out to others for companionship or comfort. Those who gravitated in my social orbit were either blissfully self-involved or simply uninterested in my past. Anyone who pushed me for more was dropped like a bad habit.

I wouldn't really say that I had *friends* – acquaintances, maybe, but not friends. Friends usually wanted to know personal information; they liked to ask questions. And that made friends something I really couldn't afford to keep.

There was one exception to this rule, and that was Lexi. Then again, Lexi didn't follow any of the rules she made for her own life, so I guess I shouldn't have been surprised when she broke all mine as well. She'd spun into my life like a tornado, uprooting everything in her path and creating chaos from the fragile illusion of normalcy I'd tried to reconstruct after my mother's murder. In the second grade, on my first day at a new school, Lexi had declared she liked my blue sparkly backpack, and that we would be friends.

And so we were.

It's rare that Lex doesn't get her way. People are drawn to her as if she exudes some invisible magnetic force, pulling them in and making it impossible to deny her anything. She's tall, with fiery red hair and light blue eyes that constantly glint with mischief. In many ways, she's my opposite.

While she towers at 5'10," I barely hit 5'5" in my tallest pair of stilettos. Her bright copper mane bobs around her shoulders like a halo of light; my dark brown-black loose waves tumble almost to my waist. Her freckled skin glows with pale luminescence; my natural olive tones leave me looking slightly tan even in the heart of winter.

The biggest difference between us, though, isn't detectable if you look only skin deep. Because below the surface, where no one can see, something is broken inside me. Or maybe not broken, but definitely missing.

Hell, maybe I never possessed it at all.

Because its indisputable that Lexi is warm, glowing and vivacious; her eyes dance with that indelible spark of life. Instead, I am cold; empty of that inner glow and utterly unable to make my emerald eyes appear anything but lifeless and guarded. Comparing Lexi to myself was like comparing the sun to the moon: her, a warm life-producing star around which everyone orbits, and me, a solitary, barren moon, brightened only by others' reflected light and riddled with craters.

With a sigh of resignation, I pulled back from the spiral of depressive thoughts I swirled into whenever I compared myself to Lexi. She'd been best my friend – my only friend – from age eight on. We'd even applied to college together and, after a miserable freshman year of on-campus housing and randomly assigned roommates, we were about to be sophomores with our very own hole-in-the-wall apartment.

Our two bedroom, double bath suite took up the entire second floor of an ancient, dilapidated Victorian-style home, which had been roughly chopped up to accommodate student renters. Yes, it was a dump, and yes, the hot water rarely worked properly; but it was ours, and the rent was only $450 a month – far more affordable than some of the swankier new properties littering the student housing neighborhood.

The downstairs neighbors kept to themselves; we'd yet to meet them, and we'd moved in a month ago. Conveniently, we didn't have to cut through their apartment to reach the stairs, as our landlord had constructed a rickety, steep outdoor stairway, leading up to our second floor balcony. Cobbled together with plywood, it probably wasn't the safest entryway, but it served its purpose.

State universities generally draw in all types – jocks, preps, nerds, princesses. With nearly 20,000 undergrad on campus, I'm sure some people felt lost, overwhelmed by the crush of academia. Where others may have felt alone, I reveled in the anonymity. Here, I had no past. No one knew my story. If I felt the urge to vanish into the crowd, faceless and disconnected, no one would even glance up from their own lives long enough to notice. It was the exact opposite of my high school experience, and it was everything I had hoped for when I'd applied.

Crawling down to the foot of my bed, I pushed open the window to let some of the humid Virginia air creep in. The late August night was dark and quiet; the bars had let out hours ago and no one loitered on the street. Most people would be getting up early tomorrow, eager to start the new semester. After about a week of attending every class and taking copious notes, what I called the "good student syndrome" would quickly wear off most undergrads. The end of early-semester diligence generally marked the launch of party season and, consequently, the end of quiet nights on my bar-riddled street.

Taking advantage of the undisturbed night, I scooted slowly off the foot of my bed and out onto the slate roof stretching directly below my open window. The rooftop was nearly flat, wide enough for me to lie with my – albeit short –legs fully extended. Technically, it served to shelter the wraparound porch below from the unrelenting Virginia elements, but in my mind, the roof was created especially for me. It was my special spot, my private nook – the one place where I could block out the rest of the world and feel safe.

Safe.

I guess it shouldn't seem like such an unattainable state. I'm sure it isn't for normal people. But I had accepted long ago that I was not, nor would I ever be, a normal girl. After the incident fourteen years ago, I'd been taken into state custody until my biological father could be notified. My mother had never wanted anything to do with him and, as he was long gone by the time she'd discovered she was carrying me, she'd never tracked him down. I spent the first six years of life believing that it would always be just the two of us – that we didn't need a man to make us a family. And in the years after, I'd started to believe that I didn't need a family at all.

Since she'd never informed him of his fatherly duties, after my mother's death there was some confusion about what to do with me. It took Child Protective Services nearly six months to find the man whose name was listed on my birth certificate. The delay, apparently due to his extended business trip to Beijing, left me stranded for months without a guardian. So, as my mother had no living relatives, I was placed into a group foster home until my father could be bothered to collect me.

Most of my memories from that time are inaccessible to me. I'm not sure whether I forcibly blocked them out or involuntarily repressed them, but whatever the case, that time in my life remains a blur.

Some images are clearer than others; I can almost still hear the sympathetic voices of the social workers and doctors as they explained to me that life as I knew it was over. The all-consuming despair I'd felt at the loss of my mother had never really gone away.

After the incident, I know I didn't speak to anyone for several months. The foster mother I'd been placed with made sure that I ate and dressed each day. A psychologist stopped by several times each week to chart my progress in her small state-issued notebook, assuring me that everything would be okay. But really, what else could she say?

Nothing was okay. I was a six year old ward of the state who'd witnessed the violent murder of the only source of love I'd ever known. I would never be "okay" again, despite the shrink's reassurances.

Throughout the years, I'd seen a never-ending parade of therapists, psychologists, and psychiatrists, all equally eager to get a glimpse inside my twisted adolescent mind. These consultations invariably proceeded the same way – with them prompting me to speak about my "childhood trauma," and me sitting on a slightly uncomfortable leather chair, staring at the clock in brooding silence. After the first few sessions of unrelenting taciturnity, my shrink-of-the-week would inevitably become frustrated, accuse me of burying my feelings, and claim that I would remain "spiritually lost" or "damaged" until I battled some bullshit inner emotional war.

What I *didn't* say, during all those weeks of silence, was that no amount of soul searching would fix my past. There was no magical Band-Aid I could stick on my heart, no special glue I could use to make myself whole again. I had shattered to pieces like a fragile vase on concrete; some fragments could be roughly cobbled back together, but many of my vital parts had simply turned to dust, pulverized and scattered by the first gust of wind.

Leaning back on my hands, I closed my eyes and pulled a deep breath in through my nose. The summer night air smelled of fresh-cut grass and a faint hint of the coming autumn. There was a slight chill in the breeze, rustling the leaves of the maple tree nearest the house and sending goosebumps skittering up my arms. I rubbed them absentmindedly, my eyes scanning from the maple's graceful sloping branches down to the quiet street below.

Shit! What the hell is that? Correction - who the hell is that?

My pulse immediately began to pound in my veins as my eyes confirmed that there was, in fact, someone standing in the dimly lit street.

Watching me.

My muscles tensed up and I froze like a deer in headlights – a naive prey trapped neatly in a predator's lair.

It was definitely a man. Though I could only make out a silhouette, as the nearest working street lamp was a half block away, the shoulders were too broad, the build too tall, to be anything but male.

Or, it was possibly one of the steroid-abusing female swimmers from China's Olympic team, I thought to myself, nearly snorting aloud at the thought. *Yeah, Brooklyn, that's totally probable.*

My brief moment of levity died and an irrational sense of dread commandeered my senses. I remained frozen, unsure whether I should move back inside. Could he see me? Was he *watching* me? Surely it was too dark for the stranger to notice a relatively small girl perched on a rooftop in the dark.

I could see the small glowing cherry of his cigarette flare brighter whenever he brought it up to take a drag. The rest of the street remained empty yet the man continued to lean against his motorcycle, a Harley from the looks of it, seemingly waiting for someone or something.

Clearly, he was not waiting for *me* or watching *me*, I reasoned. I'd never seen him before in my life. Though I couldn't see his face in the darkness, I knew simply by his build, his choice of transportation, and the smoke billowing in his lungs that we didn't exactly run in the same social circles.

Still, I wasn't about to sit outside alone in the middle of the night, dressed only in the skimpy tank top and cotton shorts I'd slept in, when there was a random man lurking in front of my house. It was time to go back inside, preferably without drawing any undue attention to myself.

Channeling my inner Sydney Bristow, I slid my hands back until my fingertips grazed the edge of the windowsill. Very slowly, I moved my body backwards, keeping my eyes trained on the shadowed man. When he had no reaction to my covert movements, I felt the sense of leaden panic ease from my chest. He hadn't noticed me; he wasn't even looking at me.

Bond, Brooklyn Bond.

More confidently, I pivoted my legs and slid them inside the window, my knees sinking into my plush down comforter. I glanced down once more at the man in the street as I began to shift my torso inside, my hands braced against the windowsill.

Through the darkness, I felt our eyes meet. It wasn't as if I could physically *see* his eyes, but somehow I knew they were staring directly into mine.

So much for my theory that he couldn't see me.

I watched as he took a final drag on his cigarette, moved his hand to his forehead, and sent me a mocking salute, as if to acknowledge my departure from the roof. My eyes tracked the movement of his hand, unmistakably identified by the dim glow of his cigarette, and I hastily moved the rest of my body inside, locking the window shut behind me.

What a creep.

Back in the safety of my bedroom, my fear quickly faded. Whoever he was, he was clearly pleased with the fact that he'd managed to make me so uncomfortable simply by loitering. It was probably just some stupid fraternity brother, waiting for his sorority counterpart to stumble outside for a late-night hookup. It didn't have anything to do with me.

At least, that's what I told myself when I glanced out the window a minute later and saw that the motorcycle had vanished completely.

***

A few hours later, I perched on one of our kitchen island barstools and sipped my coffee greedily. *Ah, caffeine. Sweet nectar of the gods.* The weak morning sunshine trickled in through an overhead skylight, illuminating our paint-chipped cabinets and mismatched furniture. My fingers absently moved across the marred countertop, tracing a collection of scratches gouged out by the last decade of tenants.

Lexi shuffled into the kitchen, her red hair still mussed from sleep and her feet stuffed into a pair of hideous green frog slippers.

"Coffee," she muttered.

Lexi was not exactly what you'd call a morning person.

"Already brewed," I reported, hiding a smile behind my coffee mug as I took in the sight of her disheveled bed-head and rumpled pajamas.

"You're a saint," she said, pouring herself a steaming cup and inhaling deeply as the aroma reached her nose.

"I thought we decided to burn those slippers after seventh grade along with your collection of Beanie Babies and N' Sync posters," I observed sarcastically. Lexi simply glared over at me, unwilling to be baited into a response.

"How are you already dressed and perfect? I still have to shower before class at eight. What time is it anyway?" she asked.

"To answer your first question – I've been up all night and had plenty of time to get dressed. And as for the second," I glanced at the digital microwave clock, "It's 6:57."

Lexi grimaced in sympathy at the thought of my sleepless night. Then again, that girl could sleep fifteen hours a day and it probably still wouldn't be enough for her. Her bed was quite possibly her favorite place in the world.

"Wait! *Shit*! It's already seven?" Lexi exclaimed, jumping up from her barstool and nearly upending her coffee in the process. "I'll never be ready in time! Perfection doesn't just happen, it takes *time*, Brooklyn. I guess I'll be late for my first class. Shit!" she cursed again, racing out of the kitchen.

"The professor will probably just go over the syllabus anyway! Nothing crucial," I called down the hall after her.

Not that it mattered; whether she had five minutes or forty, Lexi could pull together a polished look most of us could only achieve with the help of trained makeover specialists. Somehow, she even made bed-head look attractive. Hell, if Lexi went to class wearing those damn frog slippers, half of the female student body would be rocking them within the week.

It seemed ironic that, thanks to my sleepless nights, I had hours to get ready when I rarely needed more than ten minutes to do my hair and makeup. As for picking clothes, I'd never been one to meticulously plan or accessorize my outfits. I usually just threw on my standard combo of jeans, a tank top, and flip flops. As for the rest, after concealing my dark under-eye shadows, dabbing on a touch of mascara and lip-gloss, and letting my dark waves tumble freely, I was ready to go.

I didn't understand what could possibly take Lexi so long. Throughout the years, she'd frequently been frustrated by my utter lack of interest in clothes, makeup, and shopping. As per my best friend duties, I'd served as her dressing-room sounding board for many years as she tirelessly weighed the pros and cons of a particular dress or pair of heels. I drew the line, however, at letting her pick out clothes for me. As a fashion-merchandising major, she was constantly trying to get me to deviate from my boring girl-next-door look, but I didn't see the point. My clothes were just fine, even if they lacked designer labels or avant-garde flair.

I considered pouring myself another cup of coffee, but decided against it. Two cups was my limit – any more and I'd be shaky and on-edge for the rest of the day. Wandering back into my bedroom, I double-checked that I had some empty notebooks and a copy of my class schedule tucked neatly into my backpack.

I'd have three classes today: Criminal Justice, Sociology, and Public Speaking. *Joy*. The university's Pre-Law degree track encompassed a widely varied array of courses, most of which were supremely boring and full of brown-nosing, argumentative lawyers-to-be.

Can't wait. I rolled my eyes. *Sophomore year, here I come.*

***

Lexi offered a running fashion commentary as we walked the three blocks from our apartment to campus. Mostly I just listened and tried to keep a straight face.

"What is that girl *wearing*? That's a plaid skirt!" Lexi whispered, clearly outraged as she unsubtly pointed at the girl walking a few steps in front of us. "It's like Rory stepped right off the set of *Gilmore Girls*!" She shook her head in disbelief.

"You've been watching reruns on ABC Family again, haven't you?" I accused.

"*Psh*, Brooke. Who are you kidding? I own the box set."

"You have so many issues."

"I know, but that's why you *looove* me!" she sang, throwing one arm around my shoulders and propelling me faster down the sidewalk.

"Um, Lex, your legs are each at least six inches longer than mine," I complained, struggling to match her increased pace.

"I know, but I think I see Finn up ahead," she said, peering over Rory's shoulder to catch a glimpse of whatever boy had caught her eye.

Evidently unsatisfied with the view, she tugged me around the plaid-wearing Gilmore and nearly headfirst into a stop sign, refusing to slow down even when I squealed in protest and tried to wrench myself from her grip. She didn't even bother to acknowledge my struggles and, after several more unsuccessful escape attempts, I stopped fighting. Allowing myself to be dragged along, I heaved a martyred sigh and resigned myself to my fate.

"And who, may I ask, is Finn?"

That caught her attention. Her head whipped around so fast I was instantly reminded of *The Exorcist* head-spinning scene.

"What do you mean *who is he*? Do you *ever* listen when I talk? Wait, no, don't answer that," she glared down at me, still walking at a breakneck pace. "He's only the most attractive specimen of manhood on this campus! The star of every sorostitute's fantasies!"

"Sorostitute?"

"Think sorority plus prostitute. Kinda catchy right?" Lexi smiled for a brief second before slipping back on her sternest, most disapproving frown. "Jeeze, Brookie. I know you have zero interest in gossip, but at the very least you need to recognize the drool-inducing men on this campus! They're few and far between."

"Sorry. *Please*, continue describing said specimen of manhood," I requested with considerable sarcasm.

"Well, he's beautiful. And completely unattainable, of course. I mean, he sleeps around, don't get me wrong. But he doesn't stick around. It's a hit-it-and-quit-it deal, from what I hear," she gushed. "He's a senior, he transferred here last year."

Lexi continued to scan the sidewalk ahead of us, hoping to keep her elusive target within sight. Apparently, we were stalkers now. No wonder this boy didn't stick around; if Lexi was any indication, the girls at this school really did *not* understand boundaries.

"That's definitely him, straight ahead," she squealed, her voice at least three octaves higher than normal.

I couldn't see over the heads of the three girls walking

directly ahead of us, and thus was denied a glimpse at Lexi's new obsession.

"What are you going to do if you even catch up to him, genius?" I panted, slightly out of breath.

In lieu of answering, Lexi yanked me sideways, successfully passing the cluster of girls and whipping me into the direct path of an unseen fire hydrant. I pulled back, digging in my heels and trying desperately to slow my pace, but Lexi's momentum made it impossible to avoid the oncoming collision.

Crashing into the hydrant at full speed, the wind was knocked from my lungs and I sailed into the air. I only had enough time to throw my hands in front of my face and squeeze my eyes shut before the pavement rushed up to meet me.

CHAPTER TWO

KARMA POINTS

There was something wet trickling into my eyes and down the side of my face. It was dark. My eyes felt heavy, like they'd been glued shut. I tried to take a deep breath, wincing in pain as air filled my sore lungs.

"Take small breaths, for now. That was a pretty nasty spill you took," a deep voice said quietly, close to my ear.

That's definitely not Lexi.

Experimentally, I took a small breath in through my nose and held it inside my lungs, relieved that there was no sharp burning sensation this time. Releasing the breath, I slowly began to gather my senses. I was still lying on the pavement, judging by the cold hard surface beneath me, but my head was cradled by something soft.

"Can you open your eyes?" the voice asked, huskily imploring me to try.

I slowly pried my eyelids open, allowing a slitted view of the sky to come into focus. Reaching up to brush the damp hair away from my face, I was surprised when my fingers came away covered in blood.

"There's a cut on your temple. It doesn't look too deep; even superficial head wounds bleed a lot. You'll be fine," the voice assured me. "That'll be an impressive goose egg, though."

I tried to sit up, immediately regretting my decision as the world began to spin around me. Hands clamped onto my upper arms, forcing me slowly back down to rest against the broad chest of my rescuer.

"Don't try to sit up. You could have a concussion. You need to stay still until the ambulance gets here."

"Ambulance?!" I croaked, my voice scratchy with panic.

"Your friend, the redhead, is calling for one right now."

"Tell her to stop," I pleaded. "Please, I just need to go to the Student Health center. I don't need an ambulance." I turned my head up, finally meeting the dark eyes of my rescuer. "Please," I repeated, my green eyes staring into the darkest set of blue irises I'd ever seen. They were the deepest shade of cobalt, barely distinguishable from his black pupils. Unusual eyes.

"I don't do well with…hospitals," I admitted, looking away from his penetrating stare.

"Fine. Whatever you say," he agreed somewhat uncertainly, frowning as he cradled my shoulders with one arm. Shrugging out of his black leather jacket, he wadded it into a ball, gently shifted my head off his chest, and laid me down on the makeshift cushion.

I shifted my eyes to follow as he got up, walked over to Lexi, and took the phone from her hand. He spoke rapidly into it, glancing back in my direction several times before hanging up. In my semi-dazed state, I only registered his tall frame and dark hair before letting my eyes flutter closed once more.

"Hey, you still alive down there?" his deep voice chuckled.

I moaned noncommittally in response.

"I'm going to pick you up and carry you to Student Health. It's only a few buildings down from here. Okay?" he asked, not waiting for an answer as he gently hooked his arms beneath my knees and scooped me up like a child. "At least you picked a convenient place to wipe out." I felt his laughter rumble through his body as he carried me along, seemingly unaffected by my weight.

Cradled against his chest, I opened my eyes again to look for Lexi. She was walking directly beside us, her eyes trained on my face. As soon as she saw that my eyes were open the apologies began flowing from her in a torrent, causing my already-aching head to pound.

"Oh my god, Brooklyn, are you okay? I am so, so, so, *so* sorry. I owe you big time. Please don't die. I'll buy you endless Starbucks for a month, as many venti chai tea lattes as you can handle. I promise, I didn't mean to! That hydrant came out of nowhere. And you just went flying! Oh my god, I've never been so scared in my whole life. And you have a cut on your head! Don't worry, it's by your hairline. You can totally cover it with your bangs…Are you sure you're okay?"

I swear she never even took a breath. It might've been impressive if I wasn't bleeding from the head and very possibly concussed.

"I'm sure she'll be better once you stop yammering at her," the guy's voice scolded from above me.

"Oh…right," Lexi whispered, looking suddenly chagrined. "I'm so sorry, Brookie. I'll be quiet now I promise."

"I'm fine, Lex," I mumbled, turning my face away from the bright sunlight and into my savior's shoulder. When I inhaled I got a whiff of his cologne or aftershave, a heady scent of autumn leaves and crisp apples. He smelled like fall, my favorite season. I giggled aloud at the thought, recognizing almost immediately that I was delirious and, in all likelihood, suffering from a concussion.

Suddenly, we were walking up steps and through a set of glass doors. The health desk receptionist took one look at us before calling for a nurse on the intercom, simultaneously directing us toward a curtained-off section of the room. Laying me down gently on a cot, the guy moved my hair away from my eyes and grinned down at me, a dimple appearing in one cheek.

"Well, this definitely fulfills my annual act-of-kindness quota," he quipped. "At least, I *think* helping someone oblivious enough to trip over a fire hydrant will count." His eyes crinkled up in laughter as he joked at my expense.

Rude.

"Careful," I warned, wagging my finger back and forth at him. "Making fun of the injured is a definite deduction of karma points."

"I'll take my chances. You got blood on my favorite shirt, by the way," he said, gesturing unhappily toward the bloodstain now marring the band insignia on his dark grey t-shirt. "I mean, I knew walking and talking simultaneously posed a challenge for you sorority girls, but at least *try* to remember to avoid the hydrants – you know, those red shiny things – in the future. Think you can manage that, sweetie?" he mocked.

In an instant, any gratitude I'd felt toward this stranger vanished, replaced by anger and more than a little embarrassment. Not only had he insulted my intelligence, he'd equated me to, as Lexi would say, a sorostitute!

"Oh, I'm just *so* sorry. Next time I'm bleeding from the head I'll be sure to direct it at someone else!" I snapped, my voice trembling with indignation.

"I'd appreciate that," he bantered back. "Now, as fun as this has been, I really need to go. Watch out for those hydrants, kiddo. Next time I might not be there to save you."

Kiddo?! Who the hell *did this guy think he was?*

"I don't recall asking for your help!" I glared up at him icily. "I'd typically say thank you, but at this point I think I'd have preferred to be left to bleed out in the street!"

"You're welcome," he grinned back at me, again showing off that infuriatingly cute dimple as he retreated backward toward the door. As he turned, he spotted Lexi making a beeline for my cot with a nurse in tow.

"Enjoy your time with the redhead. I don't think I've ever heard someone talk that fast in my life," he noted, one eyebrow quirking up at the thought. "Oh, and before I forget – you owe me a dark grey *Apiphobic Treason* t-shirt. Size large."

With a final wink at me, he spun and walked to the glass entryway, disappearing out into the sunshine before I could even contemplate a comeback. I lay in stunned silence, slowly processing the fact that he'd just sauntered out, leaving nothing but his freaking t-shirt order behind.

What an asshole!

Shock from the accident had worn off several minutes ago; in my anger, I hadn't even noticed that the aching in my head had mostly subsided. The nurse quickly determined that I did not, in fact, have a concussion – just a severely unattractive lump on my temple and a small cut by my hairline. With an efficiency that attested to years of patching up reckless college kids, the nurse cleaned the blood from my face, placed a small bandage over the cut, and sent me promptly on my way to class with an ice-filled compress to reduce the swelling.

My brush with death wouldn't even make me late for Criminal Justice.

Damn.

***

In a rare moment of silence, Lexi and I stepped outside and slowly retraced our steps to the accident site. My backpack, discarded in the rush of activity, lay abandoned on the pavement. As I bent to retrieve it, I noticed a lump of dark material had been roughly shoved beneath the pack. I threw my bookbag strap over one shoulder and reached for the wadded up material, which I now recognized as the black leather jacket.

Shit.

"Finn's jacket," Lexi explained. "He put it under your head as a pillow after you fell."

"After I *fell?* That's the story you're going with?"

"Well, I guess I may have been slightly at fault," she admitted, her cheeks flushing pink.

"*Slightly?* Lexi, are you kidding me? You completely— Wait. Did you just say the boy who carried me was Finn? As in... the Finn you nearly killed me by chasing?" I asked, somewhat shocked.

"Yes," Lexi murmured dreamily. "Isn't he such a gentleman?"

"I could think of a few other choice names for him. Like asshole, doucheb-"

"Brooklyn!"

"What?! He was such a dick to me!"

"He saved your life!" She stared me down indignantly, hands planted firmly on her hips in a show of intimidation.

"Lex, I hit my head. I wasn't exactly dying," I pointed out.

"You are impossible," she huffed. "Only you could be *literally* swept off your feet by the most attractive man on this campus and remain completely unaffected. You know, sometimes I think you're an alien."

She tilted her head and peered down at me through narrowed eyes, as if contemplating the odds that I was, in fact, an extraterrestrial. I simply shrugged and started walking toward campus, knowing she'd soon fall into step.

Lexi had never understood my interactions with boys; it was highly doubtful she'd start now. To me, it wasn't worth making yourself vulnerable for the sake of intimacy. Or worse, letting some boy own a piece of you only to inevitably break it. Most of Lexi's relationships stopped just short of her boy-of-the-month whipping out his package and peeing all over her to mark his territory. And yet somehow, in her mind, this translated to romance.

Then again, Lexi wholeheartedly believed in things like soul mates, true love, happy endings.

I didn't.

Humans aren't meant to be monogamous creatures. Most people would probably disagree, but then, most people would also be overlooking the ever-increasing divorce and infidelity rates. Why anyone would choose to rush into something with a 50% chance of failure was incomprehensible to me.

Personally, I'd prefer to stick with my own definition:

Marriage (noun): betting someone half your stuff that you'll love them forever.

In high school different boys had asked me on dates and, mostly to appease Lexi, I'd gone out with them. But after a while, they'd all realized that I could never give them what they were looking for. I'd never belong to them –never wear their letter jackets, or hold their hands in the hallway, or decorate their lockers on game day – because I'd never be tempted enough to even consider becoming emotionally involved.

I understood perfectly the benefits of pure physical attraction. It always seemed like fate, or evolution, had played a cruel joke on me – I was probably the one girl in the world who didn't want a boy's commitment, yet every guy I dated seemed to expect one from me.

I'd tried to explain this to Lexi many times, but she didn't understand. To her, any prospect of love, no matter how dim, was worth pursuing. Unfortunately for me, her mentality mirrored that of the high school majority, and I'd quickly earned the charming title of "Ice Bitch" from the male population. Or at least from those who'd tried, unsuccessfully, to date me. The girls in my class tended to call me by a slew of even less flattering names, but I didn't really give a shit that they thought I was a slut.

Lexi was still muttering under her breath about my astonishing lack of gratitude toward Finn when we parted ways at the Criminology building. Apparently, as the only girl on campus who didn't turn to putty in his hands, I was a freak of nature destined to die alone with thousands of cats. At least, I'm pretty sure that's what Lexi mumbled as she sauntered off toward the art studio.

Walking into my first classroom, I realized that Finn's leather jacket was still clenched in my right hand. Not knowing what else to do with it, I shoved it into my backpack. It was a tight fit, barely zipping closed with the bulky jacket trapped inside. Examining it, I sighed. I knew by carrying this I'd look like one of the stereotypical freshmen, easily picked out of the crowd by their bulging, textbook-laden bags at the beginning of every semester.

After weighing the pros and cons of *that* unpleasant scenario, I hastily removed my notebooks from the pack, leaving only the jacket inside. *Much better,* I observed, breathing a sigh of relief and settling into a seat in the middle of the large lecture hall.

The rest of my day passed without incident. With the exception of a handful of stares drawn by the bandage on my temple, I was able to fly mostly below the radar. My classes were, as expected, boring reiterations of the syllabus and a discussion of course expectations.

Criminal Justice and Sociology each had several hundred students enrolled and were graded on a bell-curve so they'd be easy A's for me. Public speaking would be a different matter – with only twenty students, the professor made it clear that hiding out in the back row wasn't an option. She'd even forced us to make juvenile folded paper signs, prominently displaying our names on our desks like we were in the second grade. Of course, she immediately noticed mine and decided to torture me in front of the class. It was just that kind of day, after all.

"Your name is *Brooklyn?*" she exclaimed, her voice

artificially interested. "How unique! Is there any significance to it?"

This question was not new to me – year after year of elementary school teachers had wondered the same thing. Somehow, I just assumed I'd escaped it when I got to college. Then again, I also thought I'd escaped bubbly, mothering teachers. Was this simpering woman seriously an accredited professor?

"Oh, yes, I guess there is," I shrugged, uncomfortable under the weighted stares of the entire class. "My mother named me Brooklyn because that's where she and my father met." *Translation: that's where he knocked her up.*

I purposefully gave her as few details as possible, knowing it was best to discourage any further questions about my parentage. Disappointed, she frowned slightly before turning to interrogate someone else. I relaxed, looked at the clock above the door, and proceeded to count the minutes until the end of class.

***

Back at my apartment that night, John Mayer crooned through my speakers as I danced and sang my way around the kitchen, gathering ingredients for dinner. The front door opened and Lexi strolled in, a Starbucks cup in each hand.

"One venti nonfat chai tea latte, as promised," Lexi said, smiling as she handed me the steaming cup. "Forgive me?"

"Forgiven," I agreed, happily sipping my chai.

"What's for dinner?"

"How do you feel about veggie lasagna?"

"Sounds perfect. How's your head?" she asked, grimacing slightly.

"It's fine, I took some Advil and I can barely feel it anymore."

"Great! Because we're going out tonight," Lexi announced.

"It's Monday night. I have two classes tomorrow, Lex; I'm not going out."

"Pleeeease," she whined, making puppy-dog eyes, "There's a band playing at Styx tonight and they're supposed to be amazing! We *have* to go."

"You don't even like going to see bands, and you definitely don't like Styx," I noted, remembering her reaction to the dark, crowded club the first and only time we'd ever gone there. "So who is he?" I inquired casually, between sips of chai.

"Who's who?" she asked, playing innocent.

"*Who* is the guy who talked you into going out tonight?" I said, calling her out on her bullshit. I knew I'd hit my mark when her cheeks flamed to match the exact shade of her hair.

"Okay, fine! You got me," she admitted, not meeting my eyes. "There's this guy in my American Lit class. He may or may not have mentioned being there tonight."

"But why do I have to go with you?" I complained.

"Brooklyn Grace Turner! You know I can't just go alone! You're my wing-woman. Plus, you don't want me walking home by myself, do you?" she begged, batting her lashes at me. "I'll owe you big time!"

"You almost killed me this morning! You *already* owe me, Lex," I reminded her.

"Yeah, but you already forgave me for that! Pleeeease come with me, Brooke." Her baby blue eyes were practically glistening with fake tears.

"Even *if* I agreed to come – which I haven't – there's still the matter of the giant bruise on my forehead."

"The swelling has completely gone down and I'll work my magic on your hair and makeup. No one will even notice, once I'm through with you," she promised.

"Fine," I muttered, knowing I was only prolonging the inevitable by holding out. Once Lexi made up her mind about something, it was nearly impossible to deter her.

"Yes! You are the absolute best," she squealed, throwing her arms around my neck. "You won't regret this, I swear!"

"I know," I agreed, smiling as a thought occurred to me. "Cause you're buying every round."

CHAPTER THREE

SMALL PACKAGES

"What's this guy's name, anyway?" I yelled in Lexi's ear, trying to be heard over the thumping bass.

The band had yet to make an appearance, and Styx pulsed with the computerized sounds of electronic music. The dance floor was mobbed with bodies, and Lexi and I pushed our way through the crush to the bar. The bartender was swamped, racing back and forth to fill drink orders.

"What did you say?" Lexi shouted back at me, smoothing her red bob and adjusting her cleavage before trying to flag down the bartender. Finally managing to grab his attention, she ordered two vodka-cranberries and slapped a ten down on the bar.

"Keep the change," she winked at him when he placed the drinks in front of her.

Handing one to me, she led the way toward the front of the dance floor, as close as we could get to the stage. She turned when we reached our destination, holding her drink out to me in salute.

"Cheers, bitch! To sophomore year," she declared, playfully bumping her cup into mine.

"And to fake IDs," I agreed, laughing. I sipped my drink, refreshingly cold in the damp heat of the club, and looked up as the stage lights began to blink, signaling the band's arrival.

"Finally!" Lexi yelled. "Tyler's the drummer, by the way."

Ah, so that was her mystery American Lit man's name – and it explained our ridiculously close proximity to the stage.

I tugged uncomfortably on the short black lace dress I'd let Lexi to talk me into wearing. I had to admit, though, she'd done wonders with my hair and makeup. My long waves were artfully pinned up around my head, with carefully selected tendrils hanging down to frame my face. As for the bruise,

Lexi had kept her word and made it disappear beneath layers of expensive foundation and bronzer. The dark shadows beneath my eyes, permanent remnants from my sleepless nights, would only be discernible under intense scrutiny.

The stage lights came up suddenly, illuminating the platform and blinding me temporarily. When my vision cleared, I saw four men silhouetted against the backlit stage. Slowly, the full house lights came up, revealing the band members.

My eyes tracked appreciatively up the lead singer's body – starting at the black combat boots near eye-level, up past the black denim-clad thighs, and finally settling on the well-sculpted chest filling out a plain black v-neck. An elegant tattoo neatly cuffed one of his biceps and disappeared up under his shirt – a tribal whorl of indiscernible patterns that immediately captured my attention and had me fantasizing about tracing my fingers along the swirling labyrinth of ink.

"Oh, shit," I heard Lexi mutter beside me; apparently I wasn't alone in my appreciation of the band, and my slow perusal hadn't even reached his face yet. With that thought, I stopped blatantly ogling his shoulder muscles and moved my gaze higher.

I stopped breathing.

Yes, it was certainly an attractive face – more than simply attractive, if I were honest with myself. He was beautiful, with dark eyes, a chiseled jawline, and a wickedly sexy smile playing at the corner of his mouth.

The same mouth that had insulted me less than 24 hours ago.

Because I was looking up at Finn. And Finn was staring straight back at me.

He mostly looked surprised, but undercurrents of amusement and smug satisfaction played out across his face as he recognized me and my palpable discomfort. The asshole had obviously just caught me in the process of slowly undressing his body with my eyes, and he couldn't be happier about it.

Crap.

I'm sure he registered my look of shock and confusion before I managed to break away from his smug gaze, turning to glare at Lexi. She looked just as blindsided as I felt.

"I swear I had no idea he was in the band, Brooklyn! I never would've made you come if I'd known." I'd filled Lexi in earlier while she applied my makeup, rehashing all the patronizing remarks he'd made and ultimately concluding that he was a condescending jerk who didn't deserve any more of my time.

"Maybe he won't notice us," I lied futilely, knowing he'd spotted me immediately.

Finn's voice crackled over the microphone, startling my attention back to the stage.

"Hey everyone, welcome to Styx. We're *Apiphobic Treason*, and we're here to liven up your Monday. Make some noise, people!"

The crowd roared back at him.

"I SAID MAKE SOME FUCKING NOISE!"

The cheers that erupted were even louder than before. His presence alone seemed to make most of the girls in the audience go into heat; they were elbowing closer to the stage, pushing out their cleavage, and screaming Finn's name like he was Tom Cruise or something. And I don't mean that because I think Tom Cruise is attractive – more so because he's a crazy religious zealot, and these girls were acting like a horde of cult-like Scientologist worshippers.

I rolled my eyes at their pathetically transparent ploys for attention.

"Before we begin our set tonight, I just want to issue a little public service announcement on behalf of our beloved university," he drawled sarcastically into the mic. Then, looking down directly at me, he continued, "Apparently the fire hydrants have been really acting up today, so watch where you step as you stumble home tonight."

The audience laughed like it was the funniest thing they'd ever heard. I'm not sure *why* they did, since it wouldn't have made sense to anyone in the club except Lexi and me. Half of them were probably too drunk to notice, and the other half were undoubtedly too busy picturing Finn naked to comprehend his

30

words.

As Finn laughed into the mic at his own joke, I glared up at him. He sent an infuriating wink back at me before turning to the crowd and launching into an incredibly energetic set.

"Well," Lexi said, gulping. "He definitely noticed us."

"Crap."

"Do you want to leave?"

Yes, I desperately wanted to leave. I had no desire to stay here and be mocked, for the *second* time today, by an egotistical jackass. But I was sure that was exactly what he was expecting me to do – run home, too embarrassed by his comments to stay at Styx.

Well, I wasn't about to give him the satisfaction of being right, and I sure as hell wasn't about to let him chase me away. Plus, if I left, Lexi's night would be ruined too. I just wouldn't make eye contact with him again, I resolved. It would be fine.

"No. Screw him, we're staying. Maybe just not, um, so close to the stage," I responded, bracing my shoulders and quickly downing the remainder of my drink. "And I'm definitely going to need another round."

"That can be arranged," Lexi smirked, grabbing my hand and tugging me in the direction of the bar.

We maneuvered our way out of the crowd, which was now writhing along in harmony with Finn's voice. To my surprise, he actually sounded great covering one of my favorite Dave Matthews songs, his raspy voice complementing the lyrics perfectly.

"Tyler looks so cute back there behind his drums. And there's *nothing* bad about a man who knows how to use his hands like that," Lexi sighed in adoration as we reached the bar, angling her body to look back at the stage. "Such dexterity."

"This morning you were desperately in love with Finn," I reminded her, ordering us another round.

"Ugh, lead singers are *so* egotistical. They just want to talk about themselves all the time. Who does that?" she wondered.

"Oh, I can think of a few people," I laughed, raising an eyebrow at her.

"Shut up! I do *not* talk about myself all the time. And that's beside the point! This morning he was beyond rude to me. He actually snatched my phone right out of my hand!"

I continued to chuckle, turning to accept our drinks from the bartender. Holding out a ten, I looked at him questioningly when he didn't take it from my hand.

"These are on the house," he said, smiling at me.

"Oh, thanks," I replied, surprised at the gesture. I took the drinks and passed one to Lexi. "You didn't have to do that."

"I know, but I wanted to. I'm Tim, by the way." He held his hand out for me to shake. He was good-looking – definitely cute enough to distract me from my life for a few hours. Maybe I'd let him take me home when the bar closed.

"Brooklyn," I responded, placing my hand in his.

"Like the city?"

"No, they actually named the city after me," I joked, rolling my eyes.

"Wait," he said, clearly confused. "Are you serious? Is it, like, a family name or something?"

"Thanks for the drink, Tim," I said, removing my hand from his grasp and trying desperately to keep a straight face.

The giggles finally burst out as I walked away from the bar, Lexi in tow. She broke away from her Tyler-induced fangirl adoration long enough to look down at me.

"What's so funny? And why aren't you back there flirting with that bartender? He was cute and you totally could've milked him for free drinks all night."

"He was dumb as a doorpost, Lex."

"Your standards are way too high," she complained.

"Lexi, he thought I was serious when I told him a well-known historical borough of New York City is named after me, not vice versa."

"Okay, so maybe he's not the brightest bulb in the box, but it's not like you're looking for a relationship anyway," she reminded me, fully aware of my dating policies.

"True, but I like them to have at least above a fourth grade vocabulary and reading level if I'm going to have to spend any amount of time with them."

"That's probably a good benchmark," Lexi noted, giggling.

By this time we'd made our way back to the dance floor, a good distance from the stage but still close enough for Lexi to shamelessly ogle Tyler. The set was lively and upbeat, a mix of well-known cover songs and some unknown stuff that I assumed were their originals. Soon, our alcohol had kicked in and we were dancing wildly with the rest of the crowd, mouthing the words along with Finn as he crooned into the mic.

"Craaaaash into me," he sang.

"Craaaaash into me," the crowd echoed.

I looked up from dancing for the first time, taking in the sight of the stage, and immediately felt Finn's weighty stare on me. My eyes locked with his across the sea of people and the breath caught in my throat.

He was attractive, and he knew it. Worse, there was a heartless edge to him that told me he used his face as a weapon, bending the world to his will one sorority girl at a time. It almost hurt to look at him, like staring directly at a solar eclipse – something I knew I shouldn't watch, that could potentially damage me in the long run, but was so beautiful that I couldn't quite tear my eyes away. In that moment, it seemed like he was singing only to me; everyone else faded away as I became enthralled by his eyes, the lyrics, the deep rasp of his voice.

Damn it, he was good. No wonder the sorostitutes didn't stand a chance.

"Brooklyn! Hello! Come back to earth, girl," Lexi laughed, pulling me out of my reverie.

"Sorry," I said, forcing a smile, "I must be drunker than I thought."

"Well, that just means it's time for another round!" Lexi exclaimed, heading off in the direction of the bar before I could protest.

The song ended just as we reached the bar. Over the appreciative roar of the crowd I faintly heard Finn announce that the band was taking a quick break. Tim immediately noticed our return and walked toward us, smiling and ignoring the other girls who were trying to place drink orders.

"Back again?" he said, grinning as if I'd come solely to visit him, rather than get a refill. *Ah yes, Tim, my decision to return was based on an uncontrollable need to see you again. The plethora of alcohol bottles lining the shelves behind you had absolutely nothing to do with it.*

"We need another round," I said, playing along and plastering on a smile. "Two shots of tequila please, with salt and limes if you've got 'em."

"Coming right up, babe."

Babe? Really? There were few things I hated more than pet names. I mentally gagged before turning to look at Lexi.

"How does my hair look? Is it too frizzy?" she whispered quickly.

"It's perfect, as always," I said, briefly scanning her red bob. "Why do you ask?"

"Because Tyler is walking right toward us. Don't look, idiot!" She scolded, smacking my upper arm when I peered over her shoulder to spot the approaching drummer.

"Jeeze, calm down, Lex," I said, rubbing my arm. "You didn't have to hit me so hard!"

Lexi ignored me, suddenly throwing her head back and laughing hysterically in an attempt to grab Tyler's attention. Her loud, albeit false, laughter succeeded in drawing his eyes, and he immediately beelined toward us.

"Lexi, you made it," he smiled, evidently happy to see her.

"Oh, yeah, I mean, Brooklyn wanted to go out so I said I'd come," she shrugged, happily throwing me under the bus in her attempts to appear nonchalant. Tyler's gaze shifted over to me.

"You're Brooklyn, I assume?" Tyler asked.

"Guilty," I said. "And you are?"

As if Lexi hasn't gushed about you ad-nauseam for the past five hours.

"Tyler," he said. "I'm in the band. Drums."

Tim had finally returned with lime slices and a salt shaker, saving me from making any small talk. He poured out four shots instead of the two I'd requested, lining them up in front of us.

"Go big or go home, ladies," he grinned in challenge.

"Tim, we really only wanted the one round," I said, peeved that he was either A) trying to get us drunk or B) incapable of following a simple drink order.

"Oh, come on," he said, "Don't be such a pussy."

Oh, no. He did not just call me a pussy.

I grabbed my first shot, throwing it back and chasing it quickly with one of the lime slices. Placing the empty glass upside down on the bar, I reached for the other shot, fully prepared to throw it in Tim's cocky face. I'd endured more than enough of his bullshit for one night.

As my fingers grazed the shot glass, a hand launched over my shoulder and plucked it from my grasp. I watched, stunned, as the hand carried the tequila around me and out of sight. Confused and slightly pissed that my drink-throwing plans had been undermined, I spun around to confront the shot-thief.

Oh, perfect. This night just keeps improving.

I glared as Finn threw back my tequila. He winced and leaned forward to grab a slice of lime off the bar, completely invading my personal space with his reach. His chest grazed mine as he placed the empty shot glass and lime rind back on the countertop.

"Well, that certainly wasn't Patrón," he complained, still standing far too close for my liking.

"That was my shot!" I said, shocked at his audacity.

"There are two more sitting right there, from what I can see," he noted indifferently.

"Those are Lexi's! And that isn't exactly my point, here."

"It doesn't really look like Lexi is interested in them. In fact, she's a bit preoccupied at the moment." He jerked his head to the side, toward Lexi and Tyler, who were busy making out a few feet away.

"Jesus, that was fast," I muttered.

Finn laughed and I felt it rumble through his chest, which was still pressed against mine. Placing both hands on his midsection I pushed hard, trying to shift him away from me. He didn't budge, even when I put considerable weight behind the shove.

"Back off!" I snapped, exasperated by my inability to move him. "This isn't funny."

"Fine, fine," he chuckled, putting both hands up in a submissive gesture and taking a step back. "It's not my fault you're such a shrimp."

"A *shrimp*? What is this, the first grade?" Rolling my eyes, I turned back to the bar and reached for another tequila shot.

"Are you always so friendly, or am I a special case?" he asked sarcastically.

"What can I say, egotistical jerks really bring out the best in me."

"Ouch, that hurts," he drawled, moving up next to me at the bar and grabbing the other shot glass. "You know, I'm only a jerk because I've been hiding my deep emotional pain. You want to come back to my place and hear about it after the show? I can open up to you, cry on your shoulder, and then afterwards you can comfort me. Preferably naked."

"Does this shit *ever* actually work for you?" I asked, genuinely curious. "Do girls really fall for the emotionally-damaged-jackass ploy?"

"Usually," he laughed, completely unashamed by his methods. "My dashing good looks and endless charm don't hurt either."

"Charm?" I snorted, "HA!"

"I am, in fact, very charming," he insisted. "Most of the time."

"So I'm just – what did you call it? – a *special case*, then?" I laughed, preparing to throw back my shot.

"Wait, don't you want some salt for that? I'll let you lick it off my hand and everything."

"Pass. Who knows where those hands have been?" I grimaced, throwing my head back and letting the tequila burn a path down my throat. A slow warmth was beginning to spread through my body, swirling out from my stomach to fill each limb.

Finn burst into laughter at my comment.

"You're funny," he said, still chuckling, "And you can hold your own. We're going to be great friends, I can tell."

"Friends? I don't even like you."

"Yes you do," he scoffed, tossing back his tequila. "Everyone likes me."

"I can't imagine why."

"So much sass in such a very small package," he laughed, looking down at me.

"Speaking of very small *packages*," I said, glancing at his belt buckle suggestively, "Don't you have a set to finish?"

Ignoring my insinuation, Finn once again leaned forward into my space. I immediately moved away, until my upper back brushed against the bar. His eyes traveled leisurely down the length of my body and then back up to meet mine. Reaching out to touch my temple, he gently traced a finger over the now-concealed bruise.

"Brooklyn," he whispered, his face inches from mine.

"What?" He was unnervingly close, leaving me no room to move away.

"You still owe me that t-shirt," he said grinning broadly, his demeanor switching from smoldering to playful in less than a second.

"You want me to get you a t-shirt for your own band? You can get a new one whenever you want! There's no way in hell I'm paying for it," I growled. "And you just drank two of my shots. So we're even."

"You didn't even pay for those shots," he noted. "So technically—"

"Oh, just shut up."

He laughed, turning away from me and taking a few steps toward the entwined form that was Lexi and Tyler.

"Yo, Ty! We've got a set to finish man," he called. "Break's over."

Tyler broke away from Lexi and shot a lengthy glare in

Finn's direction, finally turning back to whisper something in her ear. Whatever it was had her beaming brightly. She gave him a final, lingering kiss before he walked away.

"Oh, and Brooklyn," Finn called out to me as he followed Tyler to the stage, ignoring the desperate girls flocking around him. "Why don't you get yourself an *Apiphobic Treason* shirt and wear it all day tomorrow to commemorate our new friendship. *Then* we can call it even."

I flipped him off in response. He laughed – as usual, he was completely unaffected by my disdain – shaking his head back and forth as he walked away.

Lexi wandered over, still slightly flushed from her blatant PDA session.

"Well, you two looked...friendly," I laughed.

"Oh. My. God." Lexi whispered, a goofy grin spreading across her face. "I think I'm in love."

"Lexi, you've known the boy for less than 24 hours," I noted.

"Time didn't matter to Romeo and Juliet," she sighed dreamily. "They only knew each other a few days."

"Yes, and look how that turned out -- they both ended up dead. Have we learned *nothing* from history?" I asked incredulously.

"You're such a cynic, Brooke," she said, "One day, someone will break down all those walls you've surrounded yourself with and worm his way into your heart. Then you'll understand."

I chose to ignore that comment. Clearly, Lexi was now a certified love guru. By this point, the band members had regrouped onstage and were preparing to finish their set. I welcomed the distraction, glad for a brief respite in what I was sure to be a night of endless, lovesick Tyler-worship.

"Can we go home now?" I asked.

"What? No! We have to stay for the end of the set, Brooke. Plus, Tyler said he'd see me after the show."

At this point, I was too tired to argue with her. Last night's lack of sleep was finally catching up to me, as were those final two shots. I grabbed her hand and led her back to the dance floor, maneuvering past several drunken couples shamelessly hooking up against the club walls.

After pulling us into the heart of the throng, Lexi and I began to dance. Within minutes, two cookie-cutter blond frat boys had joined us. Mine – either Jason or James, it was hard to hear over the music – snaked one arm around my waist and pulled my body flush against his, grinding his hips into mine. He was cute enough, but I wasn't in the mood to be mauled on the dance floor tonight.

I looked at Lexi with wide eyes, signaling for her intervention. Her eyes flared with understanding and she moved away from her own frat boy, grabbed my hand, and pulled me from Jason-James' grasp. Quickly leading me toward the stage, Lexi tossed a parting wink and goodbye wave over her shoulder in the boys' direction.

"Thanks," I said when we were safely hidden from their view.

"Don't thank me, it's in the wing-woman job description," she said, looping one arm around me. "I'm so happy we came tonight."

"I'm glad you're enjoying yourself."

"Aren't you? What were you and Finn talking about at the bar?"

"Um, mostly we just insulted one another," I said, "I'm surprised you came up for air long enough to notice."

"Very funny," Lexi muttered.

The rest of the set flew by. I was feeling the full effects of the tequila, and everything was slightly fuzzy around the edges. Before I knew it, Lexi was tugging on my arm, waving a hand in front of my face to capture my attention.

"Brooklyn! How drunk are you?" She looked sternly down at me, hands planted firmly on her hips. "We're leaving now, the set's over. Come on," she ordered.

I trailed behind her, one hand loosely clasped in hers, and we were carried along with the crowd as they poured out the club doors and into the night.

"Come on, drunky," Lexi chided as we cleared the exit, leading me around a corner and down a dim alley between buildings.

A few yards into the alley, a side exit door opened into the narrow passageway. Tyler and the other band members were laughing as they walked outside, lugging instruments and stereo equipment into a waiting van.

"Tyler!" Lexi called out, announcing our arrival.

He finished storing his drums in the trunk before turning to greet us, swooping Lexi up into his arms and spinning her around like a child.

"Did you like the rest of the set?" Tyler asked, placing her back on her feet.

"You were so good!" Lexi squealed.

I began to tune them out, leaning back against the cool brick building and closing my eyes. I wanted nothing more than to crawl into my bed and sleep, even if it only was for a few brief hours. Drunk and exhausted, my legs felt almost as heavy as my eyelids, which had begun to drift closed of their own accord.

"You look like shit," a voice said. Cracking open one eye, I took in the sight of Finn standing directly in front of me, an amused smirk on his lips.

"Thanks," I croaked, "That's the look I was going for tonight."

"I meant you look exhausted. And possibly wasted."

I let my eyes close again, trying to shut him out. The tequila thrummed through my veins and I planted my palms flat against the brick to steady myself.

"Don't pretend you know me," I mumbled tiredly.

"Do you need a ride home? I'd guess Lexi isn't leaving anytime soon."

My eyes snapped open in surprise, fixing on his face. I'd come to expect asshole-Finn; I wasn't quite sure what to do with an offer from chivalrous-Finn. I looked over at the van, now completely packed with band equipment.

"Where am I going to sit, the roof?" I asked acerbically. "Also, you've been drinking. I may be wasted, but I'm not stupid enough to climb into a car with you behind the wheel at the moment."

"Relax, I'm not driving. It's Scott's van," he said, indicating the bass player leaning against the driver's side door. "Come on, let's go tell Lexi you're leaving."

"I don't even know you!"

"I'm not a serial killer, Brooklyn. Pinky promise," he chuckled.

He walked over to Tyler and Lexi, who were sitting on the back bumper, intermittently kissing and staring deeply into each other's eyes.

Ah, true lust, I thought sarcastically.

Finn laughed, looking back at me.

Shit, did I say that out loud?

"Not one for PDA, huh?" he asked.

Not really one for affection, generally speaking, I thought, this time managing to keep my drunken ramblings contained.

I just shrugged and shouldered past him, making my way to Lexi.

"Lex," I said, trying to pull her gaze from Tyler. "I want to leave. I'm exhausted."

"Okay," she murmured, not bothering to look up at me, "I'm going to go home with Ty."

"Fine," I snapped. "Whatever. You're really campaigning for friend of the year, aren't you Lex?" My voice dripped with sarcasm.

She finally looked away from Tyler, startled by my harsh tone.

"What the hell, Brooklyn. Don't be a bitch to me just because you're drunk and pissed off. Go home," she said.

"Are you kidding me, Lexi? *I'm* the bitch in this scenario?"

I was livid. How could she even call herself my friend? She was abandoning me to go hook up with some random guy, after forcing me to come out against my will! I'd opened my mouth to really let her have it when a large hand slipped over my lips, effectively silencing me. Finn slowly dragged me around

41

toward the front passenger seat, only removing his hand when I'd stopped trying to squirm out of his grasp and bite his fingers off.

"What the hell, Finn," I snapped, glaring up at him. "Who do you think you are?"

"I'm the guy who just saved your drunk-ass from saying something you'd never be able to take back. She's your best friend, Brooklyn," he said, as if I needed a reminder. "Yeah, she's being selfish tonight. But we all get selfish sometimes, so let it go. You have a ride home; you're not stranded."

"Fine," I sighed, still pissed off but unwilling to fight with anyone else tonight. "I just want to go home." I didn't exactly feel comfortable going with him, but it was my only option thanks to Lexi's abandonment.

"Then let's get you there," he said, climbing into the passenger seat. Scott was already situated at the wheel, tapping out a rhythm on the dashboard as he waited to leave.

"Come on," Finn said, reaching down to grab my upper arms and pulling me up into the van with seemingly little effort. Before I could protest, I was firmly settled on his lap and we were rolling out of the alleyway. I glanced in the rearview mirror as we pulled away; Lexi and Tyler were walking toward a beat-up blue sedan, stopping to make-out every few steps.

I snorted at the sight, too drunk to worry about being ladylike, and heard Finn chuckle in response. I was perched on his knees, my back ramrod straight with tension. His hands moved to stroke the sensitive area on the inside of my elbows, and he gently pulled me back to lie against his chest.

"Relax," he whispered in my ear, "I don't bite – unless you're into that kind of thing, that is."

I elbowed him in the ribs, laughing softly despite myself. Reluctantly, I relaxed into him, letting my head fall back to rest on his shoulder blade. I had to admit, he was comfortable. And warm.

"How did you get to Styx tonight? It's a pretty far walk from campus," he noted.

"We took the bus," I explained sleepily, my eyes closing as my muscles slowly unclenched, releasing a day's worth of tension.

The tequila, my exhaustion, and his radiating warmth joined forces, dragging me under and lulling me to sleep.

***

"Hey, Brooklyn, wake up," Finn's voice whispered, startling me back into consciousness. "We're at your house."

Groggily, I lifted my head from the crook of his neck and looked out the passenger window. Sure enough, we were parked outside the yellowing Victorian.

Finn's arms were wrapped around my torso, holding me to his chest. While asleep, I'd snuggled close to his warmth – which left me in an extremely embarrassing predicament now that I was awake.

"Oh, okay," I muttered, sure my cheeks were on fire. Hopefully he couldn't tell in the darkness of the van. Awkwardly extracting myself from Finn's arms, I turned to Scott.

"Thank you for the ride, I really appreciate it."

He nodded in response.

I threw open the passenger door and scrambled off Finn's lap as quickly as my heels would allow. To my surprise, he jumped out after me.

"What are you doing?" I asked nervously. "You can't come in."

Finn ignored me, turning back to Scott. "Give me five minutes, man. I'll be right back," he said, shutting the passenger door. He looked down at me, frowning. "I'm walking you to your door, smartass. I promised I'd get you home, and I'm not leaving you at the curb dressed like that, as drunk as you are."

"I'm fine! And what is *that* supposed to mean?" I said, indicating my dress.

"Never mind," he muttered, exasperated. "Just come on." He grabbed my arm and led me to the side stairway.

"Do you even have your key?" he asked, doubtfully.

"Yes, of course," I said, turning out of his view so I could retrieve the house key from its hiding spot in my bra.

"Classy," he joked.

"Easier than carrying a purse," I countered without apology, shrugging and starting up the narrow stairway.

I could hear him following me, laughing quietly under his breath as we ascended. Reaching the balcony, I unlocked the patio door and turned to face Finn.

"Thank you for getting me home safely," I said sincerely, somewhat amazed that I was now indebted to such a jerk – or maybe that he was turning out to be not such a jerk after all.

"Not a problem," he said, smiling as though he could read my thoughts.

"This doesn't mean I like you," I decided. "And we're definitely not friends."

"Oh, yes we are," Finn laughed. "I'll see you soon."

"Not likely," I disagreed.

"Think what you want," he said, as if he knew something I didn't. "Goodnight, Brooklyn."

"Goodnight," I echoed, shutting the door between us and making my way, finally, to the comforting warmth of my bed.

Chapter Four

Great Expectations

Tears tracked slowly down my face, dripping onto my pink Hello Kitty t-shirt and marring it with small wet blotches. I watched from the backseat as the man jerked the wheel sharply sideways, my head slamming roughly into the window when the car fishtailed around a corner. I whimpered under my breath, but he didn't hear me.

I tried not to think about the parking lot. About Mommy. But I was scared, and I didn't want to stay back here anymore, and where were we going? And why so fast? I trembled and squeezed my eyes shut, praying silently that it was all a dream. Just a nightmare. Mommy will come in and wake me up any minute.

I heard the sound of sirens behind us, and the bad man said a curse. I knew it was a bad word because Mommy only ever said it when she was really upset or when something got broken, and afterwards she always made me promise never to repeat it.

"Fuck! God dammit!" The man was really angry, and maybe scared too. He was sweating and the car kept going faster, faster, faster.

The sirens were getting closer.

Suddenly, the man started turning the wheel wildly, sending us swerving through traffic. I heard the beeps of other cars and saw a red stoplight fly by overhead as we raced below.

He was going too fast. Mommy never drove this fast.

He was going to hurt me, just like he'd hurt her. I remembered the parking lot – watching Mommy falling to the ground like a rag-doll. She wasn't going to get up; she'd never get up again.

My small hands clenched into fists. This bad man had hurt Mommy.

I was going to hurt him back.

Without another thought, I launched my small body out of my booster seat and used all the strength I had to hit him in the face.

He was surprised; he'd thought he was alone in the car. When my fist cracked across his temple, he yelled and lost his grip on the wheel. The car jolted, and I fell backwards onto my seat, clutching the booster straps tightly.

Something big crashed into the front of our SUV and then we were spinning, drifting in circles. The man wasn't holding the wheel anymore – his arms were covering his face as the front windows shattered and glass flew all around us. My head cracked sharply against my window once more, and this time I couldn't keep from crying out in pain.

When we stopped moving, I opened my eyes. The man was bleeding and covered in glass, but he was alive; he was also looking at me, his expression full of shock and disbelief.

My head hurt. I moved my hand up to touch it and sobbed. When I took my hand away, I saw that it was coated in bright red blood. Like Mommy's blood, in the parking lot.

No, don't think about that. Don't think about Mommy.

The sirens were all around us now. My head ached and I wanted to go home. I wanted Mommy. The man brushed some of the glass shards from his jacket before reaching over to the passenger seat. He cursed again, then found what he was looking for – a gun. The gun he'd used on Mommy.

Grasping it in one hand, he turned to look at me.

"Come here," he ordered, "You're gonna help me outta this mess, okay kid? You help me, I won't hurt you – got it?"

I nodded and released the booster buckles with shaking hands. I tugged on my door handle but it wouldn't budge, and before I could crawl over to try the opposite side, the man had lunged back and grabbed me.

Dragging me over the console into the front seat with him, my bare arms scraped against the glass shards littering the driver's side. I screamed when a huge, sharp piece got lodged in my collarbone, slashing deeply and releasing a torrent of blood.

46

"Shut up!" he growled. His face was bleeding and he was gripping my arm so tightly I knew it would leave behind a big bruise.

I whimpered.

"I said shut up! I wouldn't be in this mess if it weren't for you, you little shit. I was home free, they weren't gonna catch me. You fucked it all up. You made me crash." He shook me roughly and my teeth clacked together from the force. I didn't dare whimper this time, though.

He opened his door slowly, holding me in front of him like a shield.

"I've got a kid here," he screamed to the waiting police officers. "Back the fuck off!"

He slowly eased out of the car, keeping a vise-like grip around my midsection. My feet dangled in the air, unable to reach the ground. I felt something cold and metallic press against my temple.

When we were out of the car, I saw that there were at least ten police cars parked in a circle around us with their lights flashing. The front of Mommy's SUV was smashed in from where we'd hit the highway guardrail.

It was getting harder to breathe; his arm was squeezing too tight around my chest. My lungs burned, my hair was wet with blood, and my pink t-shirt was stained bright red around my left collarbone.

I could hear the police officers yelling at the bad man and him yelling back, but I couldn't concentrate on the words. Everything slowly turned to black as my vision cut out and I faded into dark oblivion.

***

The scream tore out of my throat and I sat straight up in bed, gasping for breath and chilled to the bone. Taking calming breaths, I ran through my typical post-nightmare routine and gradually slowed my pounding heartbeat. A cursory glance at my cellphone informed me that it was almost seven in the morning. Thankfully, the nightmare had held off until dawn this time, allowing me a few extra hours of much-needed rest.

After making a cup of coffee, I grabbed my tattered copy of *Gone With the Wind* and propped open my bedroom window. A cool, early-morning breeze drifted in and I looked around my room for a sweatshirt to slip on before heading out onto the roof. Unable to find one amidst my stacks of unsorted laundry and far too impatient to search further, I swiped Finn's leather jacket from its resting place on my desk chair and pulled my arms through the too-long sleeves. The jacket dwarfed me with excess material, hanging down to mid-thigh, but I knew it would keep me warm outside in the chilly autumn dawn.

Tucking my book under one arm and balancing a precariously full coffee mug, I maneuvered out the window and slid onto the roof. The morning sky was tinged pink with the sun's arrival, and a light breeze stirred the leaves in the arcing branches of the maple. I bent my knees, drawing my legs up to my chest and wrapping Finn's coat snugly around them. Fully cocooned in his jacket, I was enveloped by the scents of rich leather and the crisp apples of harvest-time. Distressed by the idea of Finn invading my senses, I brought the mug to my nose and inhaled deeply, letting the rich coffee aroma push him from my mind.

I took a sip and thought back over the events of the previous night. Miraculously, I'd escaped the typical aftereffects of a tequila binge and was hangover free. My cheeks flamed as I remembered the way I'd fallen asleep on Finn's lap on the drive home. How was it that every interaction I had with that boy left me embarrassed and irritated beyond measure?

People didn't usually get under my skin so easily. In fact, they rarely even made an impression. It disturbed me that a boy I'd known for about a nanosecond could leave me feeling so rattled and vulnerable after a few brief encounters.

Picking up my book, I traced a finger down its broken spine and flipped through the well-worn pages. I'd lost track long ago of how many times I'd read it. There was something about this particular story and the sweeping grandeur of the old south that called to me, allowing me to escape from my own time and lose myself completely within the pages. Books had given me an escape during the long years when I'd needed most to forget;

when I read, Brooklyn disappeared and I became another girl, in different place, at some other time.

The sun crept slowly over the horizon, shooting warm yellow rays down through the abundantly leafed tree boughs and creating a kaleidoscope of shadows on my small perch. Flipping to a random page, I read until my coffee was gone and I heard the front door slam, announcing Lexi's return. Angling my head to the sky, I let the emerging morning sun warm my face and hoped the coming day would be better than yesterday.

***

Wandering into the kitchen, I immediately spotted Lexi sprawled out on our sofa with one arm thrown over her eyes to block out the sun. I deposited my empty coffee mug in the dishwasher and made my way over to her, pulling her feet onto my lap as I sat at the end of the couch.

"How was the walk-of-shame?" I asked, indicating the red dress she still wore from last night. Lexi pulled her hand from her face and propped herself up on her elbows to look at me.

"Actually, he drove me home, if you must know," she said, smiling, "And he said he'd come over tonight."

"So you had a good night, I take it?"

"Good doesn't begin to cover it," she squealed, before launching into an in-depth play-by-play of her entire evening. I sat patiently, listening to her analysis of the things Tyler had said and done for a solid hour before getting up to pour myself another cup of coffee. It looked like I was going to need it with the way this day was headed already.

"I'm sorry I left you," Lexi admitted, "I know shouldn't have but I just really like him, Brooklyn. And I knew Finn would get you home safe."

"You don't even know Finn, Lex," I said, still slightly irritated by her selfishness. "He could've taken complete advantage of the situation."

"He's not a creep! You just haven't given him a chance," she insisted. "You're so hard on people, Brookie. You never let anyone in."

"That's not true!" *Okay, maybe it was kind of true.*

"Brooklyn, I'm your best friend and I still know virtually nothing about your home life or your childhood. And that's okay, because I love you. But you have to let somebody in eventually, or you'll end up alone."

I didn't respond. How had this conversation suddenly turned around on me?

"Thanks, Dr. Phil. I really appreciate it," I snapped. "I'm going to take a shower." I pushed her legs off my lap and stormed out of the room, knowing I needed space to cool down and time to remind myself that she was only trying to look out for me.

Back in my bedroom, I hopped in the shower and stood under the near-scalding water, hoping somehow it could wash away the emotions swirling inside my head.

A few moments later, my phone buzzed on my nightstand as I was pulling on a pair of jeans. I nearly tripped over my own feet in my hurry to answer the incoming call. The screen read *Blocked Number* – I wondered vaguely who it was as I lifted the phone to my ear.

"Hello?" I asked, slightly out of breath. When no one responded I repeated myself, less patiently this time. "*Hello*? Is someone there?"

I could hear someone breathing on the other end of the line, but they still didn't respond.

"Who is this?" I demanded, growing angry as a chill raced up my spine. I could feel the fine hair coating my forearms beginning to prickle in alarm.

The slow breathing continued.

"I know you're there. I can hear you breathing," I pointed out.

Still no response.

"Don't call here again, creep," I hissed into the phone, jabbing at the screen to end the call.

First the nightmare, then a fight with Lexi, and now a disturbing prank caller? If this morning was any indication, it was going to be a long ass day.

***

That evening, I trudged home from campus in a relentless downpour. What had begun as a beautiful sunny day had quickly turned overcast as ominous storm clouds overtook the blue sky. I stepped out of my last class and, as if it had been waiting for me, the sky opened up and sent down buckets of rain that soaked through my jeans and thin t-shirt within minutes. Unequipped to handle the fast-forming puddles, my flimsy sandals continually skidded across the wet sidewalks as I sloshed through the streets. Of all days to forget my umbrella at home, of course it had to be today.

As I hurried around the corner onto my street, I began to sense a presence behind me. It wasn't as if I could hear footsteps following me, since the pounding rain drowned out all sound, but I knew instinctively that someone was walking behind me.

Watching me.

Without stopping, I cast a furtive glance over one shoulder and tried to see who it was. The heavy rain and thick cloud cover had darkened the sky – though I thought I could make out a shadowy form standing still on the sidewalk about twenty yards behind me on the otherwise abandoned street.

Who stands out on the street in weather like this?

I began to walk faster, suddenly eager to get home for more reasons than just the rain. No doubt looking like a drowned cat, I cursed myself for not checking the weather forecast this morning and continued my waterlogged trudge.

As soon as the dilapidated Victorian came into view, I bolted for the stairs and rushed inside, chilled to the bone and sopping wet. Rather than drip water all the way to my bedroom, I immediately peeled the t-shirt over my head and shimmied out of my sodden jeans, leaving them in a damp pile on the kitchen floor.

Dropping my backpack beside the door, I walked into the living room in just my bra and panties and hurried toward my bedroom. My teeth were chattering with cold and my hair was dripping, the long dark tendrils tangled and plastered around my torso. I couldn't get to the shower fast enough, desiring nothing more than to stand beneath the torrent and let the heat gradually sink back into my bones.

A loud, appreciative whistle sounded from the couch and stopped me in my tracks.

"Do you always walk around like that or did you just know I was coming over?"

I knew I shouldn't have gotten out of bed this morning

Finn lounged on my couch, completely relaxed, staring at me with an amused grin on his face. Throwing my hands in front of my chest I tried to cover my most crucial girl-parts, strategically rearranging my hair so it blocked his view of my chest. Miracle of miracles, I was wearing lacy boyshorts, rather than of one of my skimpier sets that left little to the imagination.

"It was raining," I stammered, completely mortified by his presence but damned if I was going to let it show. "What the hell are you doing in my house?"

"I came over with Ty. He and Lexi disappeared into her room, oh—" he glanced at his watch. "–about a half hour ago." He was still grinning at me, clearly pleased with himself.

"Fine. Whatever. I'm going to shower."

"Is that an open invitation?" he asked, waggling his dark eyebrows at me. An involuntary laugh burst from my lips before I could stop it.

"You may well be the cockiest guy I've ever met," I decided, still laughing.

"Thank you," he said with a laugh.

"It wasn't a compliment." I shook my head, exasperated. "You do realize that you're ridiculous, right? And that it's never going to work on me?"

"Sweetheart," he smirked, "It doesn't really matter what you think, so long as the rest of the female student body disagrees." His eyes continued to roam up and down the length of my body, and I promptly flipped him off.

"Ass," I muttered, walking into my bedroom and firmly shutting and locking the door behind me. I wouldn't put it past Finn to simply barge in and hop in the shower with me.

How could anyone seriously be attracted to him? Yes, I admit, he was godly to look at and yes, he had that whole tortured-musician vibe working for him, but his cocky attitude was a complete turnoff.

After a long, scalding hot shower, I padded back out into the living room dressed in my comfiest sweatpants and a tank top. My wet hair hung loose to my waist as I yanked a brush through it, trying to work out the snarls. Finn, still fully at ease on the sofa, didn't even look up from the television as I made my approach.

"You're still here?" I asked, irritated that he was taking up the entire couch. His eyes flicked briefly away from the screen, making a swift appraisal of my sweats, lack of makeup, and wet hair before returning to his show.

"I told you, I'm waiting for Ty," he said. "Are you always so cranky?"

"Only when random boys barge into my home, proposition me, and then take up all the room on my couch," I retorted. "Can you at least scoot over?"

He sighed, as if completely inconvenienced my by request, before shifting his legs off the cushions and onto the floor.

"*So* sorry to disturb you," I said, settling onto the couch with a deep sigh of resignation.

"You should be," he smirked, "I was pretty comfy."

"Ugh!" I groaned, chucking a pillow at his head. "You are beyond obnoxious." He easily dodged my throw before settling back into the cushions, an amused smile tugging at the corner of his mouth. I huffed, exasperated, before crossing my arms over my chest and glaring at him. If he had a superpower, it wouldn't be his singing ability or even his irresistible attractiveness – it would undoubtedly be his ability to piss me off like no one else.

"Don't pout," he mocked, "It promotes wrinkles."

I chose to ignore him, turning my attention to the movie and attempting to relax. To my great surprise, we were able to stop bickering long enough for a comfortable silence to descend. Aside from the occasional giggle or moan emanating from the direction of Lexi's room, the apartment was still and quiet. After almost an hour had passed, I heard the rhythm of Finn's breathing change, growing deeper and steadier with each inhale. Sure enough, when I glanced over he was fast asleep.

He looked peaceful, almost childlike. His angular cheekbones were softened by the fading afternoon light, his dark hair was tousled, his mouth – usually firmly fixed in a condescending smile – was slackened with sleep. I couldn't help but grin at the sight of him, curled up like a young boy with one arm pillowed beneath his head.

Seeing him like this, I could understand why he was so appealing to the hordes of women who constantly trailed in his wake, vying for a minute of his attention. Hell, if he suddenly lost the ability to speak, I'd probably be right there with them. I knew, though, that the sweet sleeping boy before me was an illusion; when he woke, his mouth would quickly twist into a smirk and he'd morph back into an entitled, arrogant jerk. That Adonis-like physique was a total waste when it came packaged with a personality like his.

At least that's what I tried to tell myself.

I shut off the movie and quietly moved from the couch to the kitchen, so as not to disturb him. Grabbing my iPod off the counter, I slipped in my headphones and flipped to a favorite artist. It was nearly impossible for me to cook, clean, or do any kind of housework without music. My stomach growled as I began to gather dinner ingredients. Having skipped lunch earlier in my rush to get to class, I was craving Italian – preferably, some of my homemade chicken parmigiana.

Thirty minutes later, the aroma of freshly breaded cutlets and boiling pasta wafted around the kitchen. I'd made more than a single serving, figuring that Lexi and Tyler would be hungry after…working up an appetite…all afternoon. Laughing softly at the thought, I cleaned up my mess, loading dirty plates into the dishwasher and wiping down the countertops as Bon Iver hummed in my ears. I jumped about a foot when I finally looked up and noticed Finn perched on a barstool, watching me with that unwavering cobalt gaze.

"Jesus! You scared the shit out of me!" I exclaimed, pulling my headphones from my ears. Annoyingly, my heart was racing and my breaths were much shallower than normal. I planted my hands on my hips and frowned at him. "You can't just sneak up on people like that."

"Sorry," Finn yawned, completely unconcerned with my distress. He still looked rumpled and heavy-eyed from his nap. "Is that chicken parm I smell?" He inhaled deeply, clearly appreciative of the smells wafting from the oven. "I think I just fell in love with you."

I chuckled, turning back to the sink and continuing to rinse the dishes. Finn swiped my iPod off the counter, scrolling through my list of artists and occasionally grunting in what I assumed was a grudging approval of my eclectic music tastes.

"Well, I'm definitely surprised," he admitted after perusing for several minutes. "I'd pegged you as more of a Taylor Swift, Justin Bieber kind of girl." I snorted openly at this assumption. "But you *are* missing some crucial bands on here. Namely, mine." he noted.

"When are you going to realize I'm not one of your groupies?"

"Probably never. More importantly, when are we eating? I'm starving."

"We?" I looked at him quizzically, raising one brow. "Who says I'm feeding you?"

"Oh, come on. You're killing me here! It smells amazing and I haven't had a home cooked meal in – come to think of it, I don't know if I've ever had a home cooked meal. My adoptive parents were big into take-out."

His eyes were distant, clouded over as if he was sorting through memories. I glanced at him to see if he was being serious, but I didn't know him well enough to tell. If he was looking for pity from me, though, he'd be sadly disappointed. His childhood, however lacking in home cooked meals it may have been, couldn't possibly have rivaled my dysfunctional upbringing.

Plus, I'd always had very little tolerance for people who used the shitty hand they'd been dealt by life as a perpetual crutch. Or worse, as an excuse for their later failures. I think the empathy gene may have skipped a generation with me – then again, taking my father into account, it may have been simply nonexistent in my family lineage.

Finn broke from his reverie and turned his pleading, puppy dog stare on me.

"Come on, please?"

I was saved from answering as the oven timer chimed, signaling that dinner was ready. With a sigh, I retrieved two plates from the cabinet and heaped them high with big portions of pasta, sauce, and cheese-covered chicken. I slid one across the kitchen island toward Finn and took a seat on the stool beside him.

He immediately dug in, showing gusto for food unique to college men, and we ate in companionable silence for several minutes. Finishing in record time, he let out a belch and happily patted his protruding stomach.

"Will you marry me?" he joked. "Because that was delicious. Where'd you learn to cook like that?"

"Well, there are these new things called *recipe books…*" I smiled teasingly, swirling strands of pasta around the tines of my fork. "Really, anyone can cook. You just have to know how to read and follow basic directions."

"So you taught yourself?"

"My father wasn't around much. I had nannies, but they didn't typically stick around long enough to teach me anything."

"I bet you drove them away with all that sass, you little troublemaker." He smiled at the thought.

"Not exactly." I said, grabbing his empty plate and stacking it on top of mine. "My father usually screwed them and when he inevitably grew bored, he'd hire a replacement. They tended to last longer when he was traveling abroad for business."

Keeping my tone flat and indifferent, an ability I'd acquired after years of self-discipline, I hoped to discourage any more of Finn's questioning – or worse, his pity. I carried our plates to the sink, rinsing them off and loading them into the dishwasher. Transferring all of the leftovers into a Tupperware, I placed it in the fridge where Lexi would be sure to find it if she ever emerged from her bedroom. When I looked up at Finn, he was staring at me with an indecipherable look in his eyes.

"What?" I snapped defensively. This was exactly why I

didn't talk about my childhood.

"Nothing," he said, looking away. "That just sounds... lonely, I guess."

I shrugged, having no other reply to offer him. I didn't want to talk about my past, especially not with a guy I barely knew. I was trying to think of a way to change the subject when Finn, to my surprise, did it for me.

"Come on," he said abruptly, grabbing my hand and towing me from the kitchen.

"Let go of me!" I squealed, attempting to tug my hand from his grasp. "I'm not going anywhere with you."

"You've got real trust issues, you know that right?" Finn said without breaking stride and continuing to drag me along in his wake. "We're going to get dessert. You'll thank me later – take my word for it."

"I'm not sure your word is worth much of anything," I grumbled, grudgingly allowing myself to be towed along.

"Ouch," he said. "I don't know how much longer my ego can take this abuse."

"Well, considering its massive size, it should take more than a few of my insults to chip away at it."

We were both laughing as we stepped out onto the patio and made our way down the stairs. Though the rain had stopped, moisture lingered heavily in the air and the setting sun peeked out from behind dark clouds, staining their edges pink and orange in the fading light. Reaching the bottom of the steps, Finn made his way over to a black motorcycle parked in the driveway behind Lexi's sedan. He looked down at me warily, as if anticipating an adamant refusal to ever ride such a deathtrap.

I bit my lip to hold back a laugh and nimbly plucked the keys from his hand. Slipping on the too-large helmet, I straddled the bike, pulled out the choke, and started the ignition. I easily shifted into neutral before turning to look at Finn, who was staring at me open-mouthed.

The look of absolute shock on his face was priceless; I finally lost control and a stream of giggles escaped my lips. Sliding the helmet visor down, I shifted into gear and sped out of the driveway, leaving him in the dust.

Finn's Ducati handled a bit differently than the vintage ones my father kept in our garage at home, but I soon adjusted to its controls. It had been several years since I'd ridden. Many nights during my high school years, when I'd been desperate to escape my father and his large, soulless house, I'd snuck into the car hanger and taken one of his many toys for a drive. Sometimes, I'd take the Lamborghini, the Bentley, or the vintage Aston Martin, but on the nights I'd craved rushing wind and dangerous speeds, I'd always preferred the motorcycles.

I did a lap around my block before pulling back into the driveway. Finn hadn't moved. His face was still frozen in a mask of surprise as I whipped off the helmet and handed it back to him, laughing.

"You...I...What...just happened?" He stammered, gazing down at me with a mix of admiration and astonishment. "Am I dreaming? 'Cause you just fulfilled one of the all-time top male fantasies. Except typically by this point in my dream, you'd be naked."

"Sorry to disappoint," I laughed.

"You just keep surprising me," Finn said, shaking his head. "You're so different from what I expected."

"What does that mean, exactly?" *What had he expected?*

"Never mind. Now, can I hop on, or are you planning to drive and completely emasculate me on my own motorcycle?"

I laughed and slid backwards, making room for him to take over the controls. Hesitantly, I wrapped my arms around his torso as we raced into the autumn night. The sun slipped below the horizon and the fallen maple leaves, stirred into a fluttering vortex by our tires, settled onto shadowed streets.

CHAPTER FIVE

TOO PERCEPTIVE

The anniversary of my mother's murder loomed before me. It was unavoidable, creeping up on me each year and casting my already gloomy world even deeper into shadows. Like standing at the base of an impossibly tall skyscraper, I could crane my neck in any direction trying to avoid it, but in the end the imposing steel-glass tower would dominate even the sun's presence and obstruct my view of the sky completely.

My nightmares were always worse during the weeks leading up. Their intensity left me shaken and weak, effortlessly transporting me back fourteen years to become the blood-soaked six year old in a crumpled SUV. Some nights I dreamed about the hospital, instead: doctors and nurses conferring in hushed tones, the whirring of machines, too many wires and IVs hooked into my pale, broken body to count. It got harder to slow my racing heart and release the viselike pressure in my lungs – more difficult to shove the memories back into the dark recesses of my memory.

Functioning on even less sleep than usual, I doubled both my caffeine intake and my sassiness. Lexi tried to pry information from me about my unexpected late-night motorcycle ride with Finn, as well as give me a detailed account of her latest Tyler sexcapades, but I lacked any patience to indulge her. I could barely tolerate some of her stories in my most rested state, let alone after a sleepless night. The dark circles lining my eyes were a perpetual testament to my lack of sleep, but Lexi didn't seem to notice or heed their warning to give me space.

Truthfully, I didn't want to talk to Lexi about Finn because I knew I'd never hear the end of it. She'd overanalyze and make it a much bigger deal than it was. And though I might admit to *myself* that I'd been taken aback by the night I'd spent with him, I would never share that fact with Lexi.

Finn had surprised me. He drove off campus for almost an hour without saying much of anything or giving me any indication as to where we were going. My ever-cynical mind had just begun to wonder if this drive into the darkening woodlands was a ploy to kill me and stash my body where it would never be found, when Finn pulled off the winding road and out onto a highway lookout point. He hopped off his bike and walked to the thin, rusted guardrail, where he could look down at the lazily flowing river just discernible in the growing dusk. I dismounted and followed him warily.

"Why are we here, Finn?" I asked, curious and slightly confused about our location. This was the last place I'd expected a leather-clad, tattooed bad boy to spend his nights. There were no other cars on the road, no streetlights, and no signs of civilization; this place had been neglected for years, if the corroded rail and cracked pavement were any indication.

"Shh," Finn whispered without looking back at me. "Do you hear that?"

I couldn't hear much of anything except for the buzzing of a nearby mosquito, eager to make a meal of me, and the faint trickling of water as it flowed over the mossy stones in the riverbank.

"What am I supposed to be hearing?" I asked skeptically.

"Nothing," he said, turning to glance at me as I joined him at the railing. "Just the quiet. I come here to think sometimes. Clear my head."

I looked away from him, trying to process that bit of incongruous information. I didn't really want to know that there were other sides to the beautiful man standing next to me. I wanted him safely in the box labeled *Narcissistic Assholes* I kept in storage in my mind. He certainly wouldn't lack for company in that particular box.

But now, he wasn't really fitting, no matter how hard I tried to close the lid on him. I couldn't entirely merge the asshole he pretended to be with this guy quietly enjoying the tranquility of nature. The vapid self-obsessed typically don't appreciate much except their own reflections in the mirror. He, on the other hand, was complicated. And I didn't like complicated; I liked my mental storage boxes – clearly labeled, organized, and easy to handle.

Though unspoken, it was clear that we weren't leaving until I'd satisfactorily appreciated his river vantage point. I studied the view from our perch, which hung about thirty feet above the riverbank, and had to agree that it was calming – soothingly beautiful in a way that only the outdoors can be. The ceaseless flow of the inky river numbed my mind and as I focused on my surroundings, I quieted the relentless worries racing around my head. For the first time in weeks, I wasn't focused on the approaching anniversary of my mother's death; my mind was blissfully clear.

There was no light out here except that cast by the nearly full moon and the stars above, infinite in number and even more beautiful than they appeared from my rooftop at home. After a few minutes of silent appraisal, I began to understand why this place was so special to Finn.

It was his rooftop.

That abruptly led to another thought – why had he brought *me* here, to his sanctuary? He barely knew me. How could he know I'd even enjoy something like this? I certainly couldn't imagine him taking one of his bimbo-groupies all the way out here.

"Why did you bring me here?" I whispered, reluctant to break the quiet that had descended on us. He looked over at me, his dark eyes trapping mine immediately, almost hypnotically. Long seconds dragged by as his gaze burned into mine, unblinking; I wanted to look away, to break from the intensity of that look, but somehow I couldn't. His eyes flashed briefly down to my mouth before returning to stare into mine. I gazed back guardedly, trying to discern his intentions.

I thought he wasn't going to answer me at all, but after several more heartbeats he cleared his throat and finally fractured the silence.

"I just knew you'd get it," he said, shrugging and finally moving his penetrating stare back to the river below. "You get *me*."

I didn't like his answer. It implied a level of understanding, of closeness, that we didn't share. He didn't know me; no one did – not my closest friend and certainly not my father. Finn was dangerous, I decided. Perceptiveness was not a quality I encouraged in those I spent time with.

I grew uneasy, the tension I'd cast off when we'd first arrived slowly creeping back up my spine and reclaiming its viselike grip. Finn seemed to sense my growing unease, suddenly pointing down the riverbank to divert my attention.

"Fireflies," he said, drawing my gaze to the glowing orbs darting through the grassy fronds that lined the banks. A small smile curled one side of his mouth up as he watched the phosphorescent bugs light up the sky. "They'll be gone soon."

"Why?" I asked.

"They're only ever out in the summer months. This is probably one of their last nights, it's getting too cold." A soft laugh slipped between his lips. "I used to catch them in glass jars when I was a kid, just to look at them up close for a few minutes before letting them go. I'd sit out in the field behind my house all night, waiting for them to appear. Sometimes they didn't. But when they did, it was like magic, you know? Like a sign that there was something more out there for me, and maybe if I was patient enough I could have it."

I watched the lightning bugs in silence for a few minutes, unsure of what to say. I was stunned that he was opening up to me; I hadn't asked him to, nor did I intend to reciprocate. I didn't do the whole heart-to-heart, lets-bond-over-our-troubled-childhoods thing. But I *was* curious.

"I wouldn't have pegged you for a nature lover," I said, eyeing his tattooed bicep.

"Less about nature than it was about escape, Brooklyn. I'd imagine you'd understand that better than most." He leveled that intense stare at me again and I quickly looked away. This boy saw infinitely too much about me, and I'd barely said a word about myself.

We didn't speak again as we made our way back to Finn's bike, and I couldn't help but feel that something had changed between us, as we stood together watching the fireflies glowing one final time in the dying heat of August. As I slipped my arms around his waist, I knew, without a doubt, that I would have to stay far, far away from him after this night. I could handle the carefree, bantering Finn I'd encountered before, but the guy who'd brought me here was an entirely different creature. I didn't know how it was possible, but he could read me, see me, in a way no one had ever been able to do.

Finn kept his initial promise of dessert, driving back toward campus and pulling into a small homemade ice-cream parlor a few minutes from my house. We licked our cones on picnic benches outside, and he effortlessly slipped back into the funny, overly-sexual lead singer he'd been before our time at the lookout point. We bantered easily and laughed about Lexi and Tyler's evolving relationship, pushing aside any memories of the charged interaction we'd shared in the darkened woods. It was surprisingly fun; Finn was easy company, as charming as his heartbreaker status required him to be. But I couldn't quite forget the look in his eyes as he'd watched the fireflies in the darkness, no matter how hard I tried.

He dropped me off at home shortly after, giving me a friendly hug and making inappropriate jokes as I walked toward the house. It was almost as if he sensed my disquiet and was trying to calm me, like I was some skittish wild animal he'd pushed beyond its comfort zone.

Too perceptive, I thought for the hundredth time that night.

I waved cheerily from the stairs, pretending everything was fine between us before firmly shutting the door behind me and letting a shaky breath of relief rattle from my lungs. Finn Chambers was the worst kind of wonderful —charming, attractive, funny, and painfully intuitive.

And I intended to avoid him like the plague.

***

I spent the next two weeks doing everything in my power to stay away from Finn. When he'd approach me on campus it was tricky, but not impossible, to escape any kind of interaction. Avoiding eye contact and ignoring him wasn't enough, though –

the guy really couldn't take a hint, and proceeded to try to speak with me every time we crossed paths. I'd had to resort to slipping into the girls' bathroom, dodging into empty classrooms, and even mingling with groups of random passerby to evade him.

On the few occasions he managed to confront me face to face, I'd formulate an immediate excuse and practically flee the scene. And my excuses were always flimsy at best; I'm pretty sure he knew I was lying when I told him I had to pick up Lexi from tennis practice, in light of the fact that she's never voluntarily stepped foot onto any sort of athletic arena in her life. Oh, and he definitely knew I was bullshitting him when I claimed to be late for work – my nonexistent job certainly helped to solidify *that* alibi.

My lack of sleep was definitely interfering with my cognitive abilities. Either that or the intensity of his dark eyes was causing my brain to short-circuit every time he came within a ten-foot radius, thus eliminating any deceptive skills I once might have possessed.

Considering he hadn't even existed in my life until a few short weeks ago, he suddenly seemed to be everywhere I looked. I remained convinced that eventually he'd accept my tireless evasions as an indication that we weren't friends and simply lose interest in me. After a few weeks, I knew my strategy was finally working when I literally stumbled headfirst into my problem on my walk to class, not paying attention as I shot off a quick text to Lexi about our Friday night plans.

"Oh my god, I'm sorry," I said, steadying myself on the arm of the guy I'd obliviously barreled straight into. "I'm such a ditz, I–"

The words died on my tongue when I looked up into a set of deep blue eyes – eyes so uniquely expressive they could really only belong to one person – and realized my mistake. I hastily stepped backwards out of his personal space, suddenly uncomfortable and dreading anything he might say. Something flickered in Finn's eyes as he looked down at me, but it disappeared too quickly for me to process.

He didn't say a word. He simply stepped out of my path,

half-bowing with a mockingly chivalrous sweep of his arm, as if to usher me along. I avoided his eyes, walking as fast as my short legs could carry me away from his presence and, strangely, from the guilty pangs clenching like a fist around my heart. The guilt both confused and terrified me.

I hadn't done anything wrong. What right did he have to look so hurt? It wasn't like we were friends. We were strangers, really.

And yet, the way he'd looked at me revealed that he'd been wounded when I'd shut him out of my life. I didn't understand it, or him, or the feelings of regret coursing through my veins – and frankly, I didn't want to. So, I did what I did best – compartmentalized my emotions and moved on.

I knew I was doing the right thing by staying away from him. He was a risk I couldn't afford to take, and I assured myself he'd soon forget all about me. After all, he had plenty of adoring fans to keep him company in the meantime.

At least, after two solid weeks of dodging him, he finally understood that we would never be friends. As I walked home, I realized that I'd likely just experienced my last ever encounter with Finn. I tried to remind myself that it was what I'd wanted, pushing the small voice screaming *You're such an idiot, Brooklyn* as far from my consciousness as possible. I could deal with any amount of regret, if it meant I was safe in the end.

***

The anniversary of her death finally arrived. I was exhausted from the nonstop nightmares that had taken up residence in my head for the past two weeks, but I knew I needed to escape this day and be alone. I borrowed Lexi's car and ditched my classes, hoping a long drive with no particular destination might do something to calm my mind. It was a futile hope, but I clung to it in desperation.

The annual sympathy card, no doubt selected and signed by one of my father's secretaries, had been delivered with the morning mail. I'm not sure why he bothered to have one sent; we'd never done anything to commemorate her death in the past, even when I'd lived with him. When I was little, I'd spend the day crying each year, sometimes begging him to talk about my mother – how they'd met, what she was like, anything to keep her picture unfaded in my memory. But he wouldn't, or couldn't, speak of her and eventually I stopped asking him to.

I drove until Lexi's car ran out of gas, pulling off to fill up in a nameless town full of faceless people. It was ironic that everything seemed to blur together today, as if I were moving too fast to process any details, since each minute dragged by like an hour and each hour passed like a day.

My weeks of nightmares had assured that the memories boiled just below the surface of my consciousness, and today I didn't bother to push them under, as I would've on any other day. Instead I reveled in them, letting them wash over and consume me as I relived each horrifying detail of her death and its aftermath. When my eyes blurred and I could no longer see the road before me, I pulled over and finally allowed myself, just this once, to be weak.

I was never more grateful for Lexi's self-absorption – she hadn't even questioned my need for her car or asked where I was going. I'd never discussed my past with her though we'd met only months after my mother's murder, when I'd moved across the country from California to live with my father. I couldn't talk about her death, and Lexi hadn't ever pushed me to.

I'd always loved her for that.

By the time I was able to pull myself together, night had fallen. Wiping the wetness from my tearstained cheeks and puffy eyes, I drove home on autopilot. I felt hollow, like a shell of my normal self. Everything inside me had been wrung out and all that remained was the jumble of skin and bones that looked and sounded like Brooklyn – the emptied husk I allowed the world to see.

As I wound through the hushed streets of my neighborhood, my headlights illuminating the growing darkness, my thoughts drifted to my mother's killer. It was rare that I allowed myself to think about Ernest "Ernie" Skinner, inmate 91872-051 in San Quentin California State Prison, but tonight I was too emotionally drained to push the thoughts away. His face, the face that haunted my memories and filled my nightmares, had long been burned into my brain as a symbol of the life that had been ripped from me.

I still remembered his words from the day of the crash with startling clarity. How his bloodshot eyes, glazed over from the cocaine thrumming in his veins, had stared into my face as if memorizing every small feature.

I wouldn't be in this mess if it weren't for you, you little shit. I was home free, they weren't gonna catch me. You fucked it all up! You made me crash.

A shudder passed through me as I saw myself at age six, trembling on the witness stand as I gave the testimony that condemned him – sealing his fate with a twenty-five year prison sentence and overturning his appeals for a lesser sentence. The hate blazing in his eyes as they led him away in chains and an orange jumpsuit was directed solely at me, as if he could incinerate me with the force of his glare alone.

Thankfully, he had ten more years to rot in prison. I didn't let myself think about what might happen on the day he was finally released back into society.

I pulled into the driveway next to the old Victorian and tried to collect myself before going inside. Even Lexi, in all her egocentrism, would see through my facade of normalcy if I walked in with tear-glazed eyes and smeared mascara. Flipping down the overhead car mirror, I touched up my makeup and schooled my face into what I hoped would pass as my trademark mask of cool indifference.

It would have to do, for now.

CHAPTER SIX

ALMOST-MOMENTS

At some point during my shower, I'd decided that tequila was the best way to forget the crushing sadness and grief I'd been suffocating beneath all day. Hair wet and face scrubbed clean of all traces of my earlier tears, I hopped up on the kitchen counter and poured myself a shot. As it burned warmly down my throat, a nagging voice in the back of my mind suggested that alcohol wasn't really the best way for me to deal with my multitude of issues. I quickly silenced that voice, throwing back two more shots in rapid succession.

When Lexi walked in several minutes later, I was feeling the best I had in weeks. I couldn't forget that today marked the fourteenth anniversary of my mother's death – it was indelibly imprinted in my soul, ingrained in my DNA – but the tequila helped to dull the pain lancing through my chest and blur the edges of memories I didn't want to see anymore.

"Ooh, we're drinking!" Lexi exclaimed, swiping the tequila from my grasp and taking a swig straight from the bottle.

"Give it back, Lex," I said, reaching out a hand. "I need it more than you do," I added, muttering under my breath as I reclaimed the bottle and poured a fourth serving for myself. Lexi cheered in support as I threw back the shot.

"What's this, by the way?" I asked, the tequila burning in my throat as I picked up the sheet of paper lying on the countertop next to me. It was an invoice for E.S. Electric, an electrician based in Charlottesville, according to the document. I wasn't aware that we'd needed any rewiring done, and I sure as hell hadn't requested it.

"Oh, this guy came by today," Lexi said, snatching the bottle back from me and taking another gulp. "Our landlord sent him. He said he had to fix our wiring or something. Don't even ask me what he did – I don't speak engineer."

"Electrician," I corrected.

"Whatever!" Lexi rolled her eyes.

"Wait, our landlord sent him? The same landlord we had to practically take to court when our toilet broke, because he was so unwilling to fix it? The very guy who didn't seem to care that the locks on our doors and windows didn't lock when we first moved in?" I stared at her in shock. "Are you trying to tell me that he voluntarily fixed something and we didn't even have to complain about it for six months first? And he *paid* for it, too?"

"That's what I'm telling you," Lexi grinned at me.

"Well, if that doesn't call for celebratory shots, I'm not sure what does," I giggled, reaching out again for the tequila.

Within the hour, Lexi and I had finished off half the bottle and were unabashedly twirling around the kitchen, slurring our words as we serenaded each other along with the radio's latest hits.

"Lets go out!" Lexi squealed, hauling me towards her bedroom and pushing me down on her bed while she beelined for her overflowing closet. Too tipsy to argue, I clutched the tequila bottle to my chest like a lifeline and watched her shimmy out of jeans and into a slinky pink halter dress.

"Put this on!" She tossed a bright red scrap of material at my face, followed by a pair of spiky black peep-toe stilettos that nearly took an eye out as they careened past my face and landed on the bedspread.

Maybe if today hadn't been what it was, and if I hadn't already had too much tequila coursing through my veins, I might've resisted Lexi's demands. Then again, it was hard to deter her even in my most sober, mentally-stable mindset.

My head swam as I stood up and removed my jeans, swaying into the wall as I tried to tug off my sweater. Lexi laughed at me when she caught sight of my struggles in the mirror of her vanity, where she was applying makeup with the speed and ease of a professional. By the time I'd managed to pull on the strapless red dress, which was so short on me it must've been a shirt on Lexi's tall frame, she'd finished applying her makeup and began attacking my face with a multitude of brushes and powders.

Fifteen minutes later, we were in a taxi on our way to the bar. In my less-than-sober state, I didn't think to ask Lexi where we were headed. I knew I shouldn't have been surprised when we pulled to a stop outside Styx, given Lexi's newfound love interest, yet I was still shocked that she'd bring me back here. By the time I'd managed to formulate any kind of objection, Lexi had tossed a twenty to the driver and yanked me from the backseat, leaving me standing openmouthed as I watched the cab's taillights disappear around a corner.

"Lexi, you've got to be kidding me," I said, spinning around to face her and nearly falling flat on my face as my heels caught the pavement. *Note to self: pivoting in five-inch stilettos while intoxicated is highly inadvisable.*

Lexi laughed at me and shrugged, clearly unapologetic. "The band is great, the drinks are cheap, and it's not like you even have to talk to Finn. Jesus, Brookie, you make it seem like the boy is some kind of obsessed stalker who steals your used tissues and photographs your every movement," she rolled her eyes at the thought. "Seriously, he's probably forgotten you by now. I mean, have you *seen* the boy? He's not exactly hurting for attention."

Ouch.

As bitchy as Lexi had sounded, I had to agree that when she laid it all out there like that, my actions over the last two weeks *did* seem a little ridiculous. It was probably presumptuous, arrogant even, to assume I'd so much as crossed his radar – let alone that he wanted to be friends with me. I'd likely been avoiding him for no reason at all. Suddenly, I felt as brainless as one of his drooling groupies.

"Damn, I hate it when you're right," I complained, linking my arm through Lexi's as we bypassed the crowd waiting to get in and approached the bouncer.

"Billy!" Lexi squealed in greeting, placing a swift peck on the cheek of the obscenely muscular man guarding the door. I had no idea how Lexi knew him, but he immediately pulled aside the velvet rope to allow us inside. Lexi blew him a kiss as we cut the line and disappeared through the doors. I waved playfully at the line of club-goers still awaiting admittance, and their answering groans of complaint were quickly drowned out by an amplified voice that sent chills racing down my spine.

My eyes immediately found Finn onstage. Damn, he looked good. A tight black t-shirt put his well-built chest on display. Low-slung dark jeans graced his hips, and his dark hair fell messily over eyes I knew to be the darkest shade of midnight blue. I couldn't deny that he was attractive, wishing for the hundredth time that I could simply sleep with him without any emotional complications. I tried to remind myself that he was dangerous, that I couldn't get involved, that sex wouldn't be enough for him – he'd want to *know* me.

Then again, he'd slept with all kinds of sorority fangirls without forming any sort of attachment – wasn't I being conceited in assuming he'd treat me any differently?

Lexi shook me from my drunken mental ramblings, leading me to the densely packed bar. We wheedled our way to the front of the line, heedless of the pushing bodies and close-quarters. It was no great surprise to see Tim bartending again, and he recognized me as soon as I approached.

"Brooklyn," he said, smiling. *At least he remembered my name.* "What are you lovely ladies drinking tonight?"

"Two Long-Islands, please," I said, smiling flirtatiously. Maybe I'd get a free round out of him. I knew it was shameless and under normal circumstances I'd probably feel bad for encouraging him, but this guy was an ass and I was too drunk to care anymore. Unsurprisingly, he passed me the drinks and refused my money. I grinned in thanks, turning back to Lexi and passing her one of the glasses.

"Cheers, bitch," she said, clinking her glass to mine and heading to a small alcove off to the side of the dance floor where several private tables had been set up. Most of them were occupied, but we managed to find an empty one near the back of the section, relatively far from the stage. Lexi, of course, was disappointed by our location, but I took comfort in knowing that I wouldn't have to deal with Finn tonight, since he likely wouldn't spot me back here. It wasn't a huge club – we were only about

50 feet from the stage – but he rarely broke eye contact with the swarm of scantily clad girls writhing at the front of the crowd.

I sipped my cocktail and let myself appreciate the timbre of Finn's voice as it flowed over me. It was seductive, deep and slightly rasping as he sang into the microphone. I remembered the first time I'd heard his voice, semi-conscious after my spill on the sidewalk. Even then, when I hadn't known him, his words had resonated sultrily in my mind.

Lexi and I chatted idly and observed the frenzied crowd as we finished our first round, only breaking off when Lexi felt the need to comment on a particularly outrageous outfit or to cheer for the band between songs. We'd laughed ourselves through two rounds and nearly into tears when the band announced they were taking a half hour break. Despite Lexi's earlier assurances that I had nothing to fear from Finn, when she went to find Tyler I excused myself and made my way to the bathroom in the back corner of the club. It was far from the bar and the stage – a perfect place to wait out the intermission and avoid awkward encounters.

To my surprise, the bathroom was nearly empty; like Lexi, the other female club-goers must've been enticed by thoughts of seeing the musicians on their break and opted to hold their bladders. I'd never seen a bar restroom so deserted, and I appreciated the quiet as I attempted to touch up my smudged makeup in the mirror.

I was drunk. I knew I shouldn't have let myself get to this level – I usually stayed in control – but tonight was an exception. I was far too sad to be responsible; too hurt to dwell in the memories. I'd needed an escape, and tequila had given me one.

An added benefit: the effects of the alcohol had fully numbed the pain I was sure would otherwise be crippling my feet from the skyscraper high heels Lexi had forced me into.

I giggled at the thought as I stumbled into a stall, hiking my micro-dress up over my hips and emptying my bladder. I hovered over the toilet as I peed, precariously balanced on my stilettos, and heard the door swing open as someone entered the bathroom. Flushing quickly, I readjusted my dress and walked to the line of sinks.

I'd just finished washing the soapy bubbles from my hands when I felt the tingling weight of someone's gaze on my neck. Looking up abruptly in the mirror, I saw the reflection of a man standing a few feet behind me. I immediately screamed, spinning around too fast on my heels and grasping the edge of the sink to catch myself from falling.

"Jesus, could you have screamed any louder?" a voice drawled calmly.

I slowly righted myself and forced my gaze up to meet Finn's eyes. They were twinkling with mirth, undoubtedly amused by my fright.

I was going to kill him.

"JESUS FUCKING CHRIST, FINN," I yelled, striding forward and shoving his chest with all the strength in my arms. He didn't even shift off balance, which only served to incite my anger further. "WHAT THE FUCK ARE YOU DOING IN HERE?" I demanded. He opened his mouth to reply, but I cut him off. "This is the LADIES room, Finn. Are you a lady?"

He was struggling to hold in his laughter now, shaking his head in answer to my question as a grin tugged at the corner of his mouth. The dimple in his right cheek was out in full force and, despite how adorable it was, at the moment I had an urge to smack it right off his face.

"Then what the hell are you doing in here?" I demanded, narrowing my eyes at him and planting my hands on my hips. Finn took several steps toward me, following as I backed away from him into the bank of sinks. When I had nowhere else to go, he propped his arms on the wall around either side of my body, effectively caging me in. The laughter was fading from his eyes, his irises darkening as they filled with unnamed emotions.

"You've been avoiding me," he stated, holding my gaze. "I want to know why."

It was a statement, not a question – one that demanded an answer. I didn't have one to offer him, though, so he was shit-out-of-luck if he thought he could intimidate me into explaining.

"I'm not avoiding you, Finn. I just don't like you," I glared up at him, raising my chin haughtily and refusing to back down despite his proximity. "And gee, cornering a girl in an abandoned bathroom is *definitely* the way to get her to want to be around you." I practically sneered at him. He just smiled.

"Brooklyn, we both know you're lying," he whispered, his mouth grazing my earlobe. "And neither of us is leaving until you tell me why you've been pretending I don't exist."

"I'm not lying!" *I might have been lying.* "And could your ego *be* any bigger? Seriously, how do you even live with yourself?" I was slurring a little bit. Damn. Of all the possible times that this conversation could've occurred, of course it had to happen while I was wasted.

"You're deflecting," he said, "Just tell me, 'cause I'm missing my break for this."

"Ah, yes, precious time with your groupies is going to waste. All the more reason to leave me alone!"

"You know, I thought you were cute when you were mad, but you're even cuter when you're jealous," he grinned cockily.

"And *you* are delusional." I decided I'd had enough, pushing at his chest to get him to back away from me. I was absently noting how firm his chest muscles were beneath my fingers, my drunken mind conjuring up images of him shirtless, when he suddenly snatched my hands firmly in his grasp. His large fingers fully encompassed mine, his grip steely as his dragged me up tighter against his chest. We were fully plastered together, every part of our bodies perfectly aligned. In my heels, the top of my head was nearly level with his mouth, and my emerald irises were mere inches from his blue ones.

We stared at each other for several long seconds, my eyes moving unchecked between his dark gaze and the full lips nearly touching my forehead. I felt my breaths quicken and recognized the telltale desire pooling in my stomach.

Shit. The tequila was wreaking havoc on my self-control.

Finn's eyes widened infinitesimally as he looked down at me, seemingly as affected by our closeness as I was. He angled his head toward mine, moving further into my space as he brought our lips dangerously close together.

"We shouldn't do this," I whispered against his mouth,

74

knowing it was far too late to stop whatever was about to happen between us. Worse, knowing that I didn't *want* to stop it.

"Shh," he breathed, his lips grazing mine as his hands moved up to tangle in the loose curls at the base of my neck. Just as our lips finally brushed with a gentleness I hadn't thought Finn capable of, the bathroom door banged open, slamming against the wall with a smack loud enough to shatter the almost-moment we'd just experienced. We quickly sprang apart as three girls stumbled in through the doorway.

"Ohmigod! You're Finn! Ohmigod!" The blondest of the three began bouncing up and down in excitement, her surgically-inflated cleavage nearly spilling out of her top as she completely dismissed my presence and honed in on the lead singer of her fantasies.

I avoided looking in his direction, cursing myself for what I'd almost allowed to happen. I assured myself it was only because I'd been drunk, only because my guard had been down after the shittiest day of my year. It wouldn't happen again. Ever.

I squeezed around the trio of fans, nearly running in my haste to get out of the bathroom and away from his presence.

"This isn't over, Brooklyn," I heard him call after me as I fled.

***

"Remind me never to listen to you again," I said, sliding back into my seat across from Lexi. "And to kick your ass."

"What did I do this time?" Lexi grinned impishly, sliding my Long Island iced tea across the table. I took a fortifying gulp, hoping it might erase what had just happened in the bathroom.

"Remember how you assured me that Finn had absolutely no interest in me whatsoever?"

"Maybe?" Lexi's eyes widened in anticipation; whatever she'd been expecting me to say, it wasn't this.

"Well, he just cornered me in the bathroom. And tried to stick his tongue down my throat."

"And you didn't let him?"

"Lexi! Jesus. I don't even like him."

"Who cares? He's gorgeous." She said, looking at me like

I was crazy. "And since when do you care about liking the boys you sleep with? We both know you don't do relationships. Neither does Finn. The way I see it, this could be absolutely perfect."

"It'll get complicated. It always gets complicated."

"Sweetie," Lexi sighed. "Finn doesn't commit. He's a serial dater – if you can even call what he does *dating*. You're clearly into each other and you're both attractive, so just screw and get it over with. Then you can walk away, like you always do. A clean break."

Lexi made it sound so simple, so easy. At that moment, I wanted to cave in. After the scene that had just played out between me and Finn in the bathroom, I doubted I would be able to resist again. The truth was, I wanted him. I'd wanted him since the first time I'd laid eyes on him.

Sex with no strings had never been a problem for me before. I'd never let emotions get in the way with any of my relationships; as soon as I felt that things were getting too intense, I'd broken them off. Maybe it wouldn't be any different with Finn – I'd just have to be more careful than usual. He had a way of getting under my skin like no one else. He saw things in me no one else seemed to.

I'd have to hold him at arms length. I might consider sleeping with him, but I'd certainly never consider trusting him.

"I don't think so, Lex," I said, my voice unconvincing even to my own ears.

"Mhmm," Lexi hummed placatingly, not believing a word of my protests.

I chose to ignore her, turning back to the stage to watch the band members prepare for their second set. Finn looked completely normal, laughing at something Tyler was saying and clearly unaffected by our interaction in the bathroom. It was silly to have thought I'd ever mean anything to a boy like that. I was just another piece of ass to him -- only, unlike his groupies, I offered a challenge because I didn't spread my legs on command. He was interested in the chase, nothing more. For some reason that realization struck me like a heavy blow to the chest.

Ignoring the pang, I took another sip of my drink and

refocused on Lexi, who was, as usual, blabbering about Tyler's many virtues.

"And the drummer really is the one who holds the whole group together, you know? I mean, without Ty, they'd be nowhere. So—"

Lexi broke off mid-sentence, her eyes wide as she caught sight of something behind me. Before I could turn around, I was lifted from my stool and dragged back against an unfamiliar chest. Two beefy arms encircled my waist, holding me so tightly that even attempting to fight was useless.

Not that it stopped me from trying like hell to escape. My stilettos propelled wildly in the air, trying to make contact with a shin or, ideally, the body part several feet higher and infinitely more precious to my attacker.

"Calm down, baby, I'm just messing with you. I know how skittish you can be." Abruptly, the hands released their hold on me and I fell several feet to the ground, losing my balance and nearly landing face-first on the sticky club floor. One massive hand shot out and caught my arm just in time, halting my descent and hauling me face to face with my assaulter – Gordon O'Brien.

Gordon had been a mistake, one induced by too many tequila shots at a frat party last spring. He was a football player here, supposedly a good one, but I couldn't be sure considering I'd never actually attended a game. One of those guys you could tell had been raised with money and bred to believe in his own superiority, he was good looking in a clean-cut, Ralph Lauren model kind of way. The attraction stopped there.

Gordon was the quintessential jock from every high school movie I'd ever watched and rolled my eyes at – always the first to make fun of the nonconformists who refused to bow down to his clique of followers. If there'd been lockers at college, he would've been the one stuffing freshman into them.

He also seemed to have a problem with rejection. After our drunken hookup, I'd fled the scene as quickly as possible. Though he'd tried to contact me numerous times since, I'd always turned down his offers for a repeat performance. Four impossibly long minutes of a sweaty behemoth grunting on top of me had been enough Gordon to last a lifetime, thank you very much. There wasn't enough tequila in the world to convince me otherwise.

"Aren't you gonna give me a proper hello?" He said, lips pursed in a seductive expression I'm sure he'd practiced in the mirror.

"Hello, Gordon. Goodbye, Gordon," I said, spinning around to face a wide-eyed Lexi and my table. I heard the band launch into their first song, a Bon Iver cover I loved.

"Not so fast, Brooklyn." His hands wrapped around my upper arms tighter this time, with enough force that I knew I'd likely have twin bruises tomorrow. He gradually increased the pressure as he pulled me back against his chest once more, causing my eyes to water in pain. Lexi, recognizing that this situation was more than I could handle, hopped off her stool and made a beeline for the door, no doubt in search of Billy the bouncer.

"Let go of me, asshole," I demanded through clenched teeth. My arms were aching and my breaths were getting shallow. I didn't like to be casually touched by anyone unless I was in control of the situation, and this had far exceeded my limits.

"Brooklyn," he whispered, his mouth in my ear and his rapid breathing hot against my neck. He was excited by this, by hurting me; he was sicker than I'd originally given him credit for. "Why can't you be nice to me, baby? You were *so nice* last spring. Don't you remember?" He shifted suddenly, and I could feel his erection pressing against my lower back.

I looked desperately for Lexi, but didn't see her anywhere among the crowd. Everyone else in my vicinity seemed conveniently occupied – either too intoxicated, scared, or self-absorbed to get involved. Finn's voice filled the air around me, singing lyrics about running home and former lovers. I tried to focus on it but all the sounds from the club were quickly dimming. Everything seemed somehow distant now, blurred around the edges. Gordon continued to whisper to me, but it was no longer his voice I heard in my ear. It was another voice, a voice I'd tried to forget for fourteen years.

78

I'll fuckin' kill her. Don't you fuckin' come any closer or she's dead.

A gun pressed against my temple. A grip so tight I couldn't breathe. Blood, so much blood. Yelling police officers. Wailing sirens.

Put down your fuckin' guns or she's dead.

I couldn't get a breath into my lungs. Gordon was still talking, but I was long past hearing. My eyes squeezed shut as I tried to make it all go away. Distantly, I thought I heard the abrupt sound of the music cutting off, but I wasn't sure of anything at that point. My head was spinning from a lack of oxygen.

Then, as suddenly as it had taken hold, Gordon's grip was simply gone. I crumpled to the floor and didn't even attempt to stand up this time, knowing I was out of commission. Hearing the unmistakable sound of fists meeting flesh, I lifted my head enough to see Finn straddling Gordon, repeatedly punching his face.

"Don't you ever fucking lay your hands on her again." Finn snarled. Gone was his normally playful grin; he was feral, his brutality fully unleashed on the writhing linebacker beneath him. Though Gordon was bigger by at least thirty pounds, Finn was clearly faster and more skilled.

"You hear me, fucker? If you so much as *think* about talking to her again, I swear it'll be the last thing you ever do."

Gordon moaned in response, unable to form words.

Abruptly, Finn stopped raining down punches and the rage cleared from his face. He leapt off Gordon, who didn't look like he'd be getting to his feet anytime soon, and was at my side faster than I'd have thought possible.

His arms hooked beneath my knees and around my shoulders as he scooped me into his arms, not unlike he'd done the first day we met. I immediately turned my head into his shoulder, blocking out the rest of the world as he carried me out of the club.

When we reached a truck in the parking lot, he opened the door and climbed up onto the front bench seat without ever loosening his hold on me. When the door shut behind us, he continued to cradle me in his arms, his mouth pressed into my hair. It was silent except for his occasional murmurs.

"You're okay, Bee. You're okay. I've got you. Just breathe."

I was still hyperventilating. With conscious effort I tried to slow my breathing.

"That's good, Bee. You're alright now."

My hands were fisted in his t-shirt in a death-grip and I was shaking with repressed sobs. I wouldn't cry. If I cried now I might never stop.

Time passed – it could have been minutes or hours. Finn didn't seem like he was in any hurry to leave; he didn't push me, or tell me to stop crying, as any other boy would have. He simply held me and let me breathe.

Eventually, I stopped shivering and felt the panic dissipating from my system. My voice was nearly unrecognizable when I tried to speak, a cracking, shaky whisper that surely belonged to someone else.

"What…" I cleared my throat before trying again. "What happened?"

"You had a panic attack," Finn said simply, as if that explained everything.

"But…you were on stage?" My voice was unsure, seeking clarification.

"I saw that asshole gripping your arms and then I saw your face. I had to get him off you."

"So you just leapt off the stage mid-song?" I said incredulously, my voice sounding more like my normal self. "Jeeze, do you have a flair for the dramatic or what?"

"You must be feeling better if you're back to insulting me already," Finn said. I could hear the smile in his voice and felt the tension drain from his arms.

"Thank you," I whispered, not sure what else to say.

"Don't thank me. Believe me, it was a pleasure to hit him. That guy is a total tool."

Silence descended once more. I could've – should've – moved out of his embrace, but I didn't. I felt safe here, cocooned in this warm pair of arms, somehow far removed from everything that had just happened. It was a good feeling – one I couldn't remember experiencing since I was a little girl.

I didn't want to break the silence between us, but I felt I owed him an explanation of sorts. With anyone else, I would have brushed off what had happened, but Finn would see through any lie I spun. I was better off saving my breath and telling him at least a semblance of the truth.

I forced myself to move out of his embrace and sat on the seat beside him. Making sure no parts of our bodies were touching, I turned to face him. If his eyes had held any pity, I might have simply climbed out of the truck and walked away, but they were carefully guarded against any visible emotions. I took a deep breath and began.

"I'm sorry if you're looking for some sort of explanation. I can't really give one to you." I swallowed nervously. "He grabbed me too tightly, and sometimes that triggers my panic attacks. I don't like strangers touching me. I can't handle being confined in a grip like that. That's it." I looked at him, waiting for some kind of reaction. "Thank you for helping me," I added, almost as an afterthought.

He was quiet for a long time.

"Okay," he said.

"That's it?" I asked. "No questions? No demands that I explain?"

"Brooklyn, you're not the kind of person who reveals anything she isn't ready to. So I'll wait. As long as it takes, I'll wait. Because when you're ready, you'll tell me." He sounded so confident, as if it were inevitable that I'd one day lay my soul bare to him.

"You might have to wait a long time," I said doubtfully. "You might be waiting forever."

He shrugged, as if the prospect didn't bother him. "I've already been waiting my whole life."

"What's that supposed to mean?" I asked, my eyes narrowing in suspicion.

He just smiled a sad sort of smile, ignoring my question as he turned to put the key in the ignition. The engine flared to life and we began rolling out of the parking lot.

"What about Lexi?"

"She's with Ty. Don't worry."

"And your set?"

"There'll be other shows," he shrugged.

With anyone else I might have demanded to know where we were going, but all my fight was used up. I was exhausted, emotionally drained and ready for this hellish day to finally be over.

"My mother died fourteen years ago, today." Was that my voice, saying that? Out loud? To Finn, of all people? I was losing it.

He looked over at me, surprised. Of course he was. After all, hadn't I just told him that I didn't do explanations? That he'd have to wait forever?

"Death sucks," he said. "It never really gets easier. People say bullshit clichés like 'time heals all wounds' to comfort themselves. But anyone who's experienced real grief knows that it never goes away – you just get better at lying to yourself, at covering up the signs, at faking normal."

He spoke from experience; he'd lost someone too. It was comforting, in a twisted way, to know that there was someone who'd felt the loss I did and was still standing. I wasn't alone in my ceaseless battle with grief.

I didn't say anything else as he drove me home – I don't think he expected me to. When we pulled up outside my house, I hesitated before reaching for the door handle.

"Whose truck is this?" I asked, realizing that since we weren't on his motorcycle, we must be in someone else's car.

"It's mine, actually. I use it when the weather's bad or when I have to move the band's gear before gigs."

"Oh," I said, wondering how a college boy could afford not only a motorcycle but a relatively new truck as well. "Well, it's nice."

"Thanks. Hey Brooklyn?"

"What?"

"Just for the record, we're officially friends now. Once you get into a fistfight for someone, there's no going back."

I smiled. "Figures, you'd want something in return. I suppose chivalry really is dead after all," I said teasingly. "I've never had a male friend before."

At my words, a strange expression flashed across his face, but it was gone too quickly for me to process. His grin was back, and I almost thought I'd imagined the dark look.

"Well, I don't exactly do the female friendship thing myself, so it'll be new for both of us," he said.

I hopped out of the truck and turned around to say goodbye, but Finn was already jumping down from the driver's seat. Coming around the truck, he grabbed my hand and towed me to the stairs leading up to my apartment.

"What are you doing?" I asked, rolling my eyes. "You don't have to walk me to the door."

"As your friend, it's my duty to get you home safely. Its also my duty to point out that you are the most stubborn, pigheaded girl I know."

"Thanks, *friend.*"

"Anytime."

We reached the top of the stairs, and I unlocked the door. Turning to face Finn one last time, I did something that surprised even myself.

Standing on my tiptoes – a feat, I might add, in stilettos – I twined my arms around his neck and tucked my face into the hollow of his throat. His chin came to rest on the top of my head as his arms wrapped around my waist. Standing this way, we were like two puzzle pieces rejoined. A perfect fit.

A content sigh slipped from my lips as he held me. Friends hugged, right? This wasn't crossing any boundaries. This feeling of utter security, of safety, was a perfectly normal reaction to a friend. *But*, a small voice in the back of my head nagged, *even on the rare occasions that Lexi and I had hugged, I'd never felt this way. Crap.*

"Thanks again," I whispered, slowly lowering my feet and unwinding my arms from his neck. I turned quickly to the door, not wanting to look into his eyes – afraid of what I might see there. "Goodnight."

"Goodnight, Bee." I heard him say quietly, as I closed the door between us. I watched him walk down the stairs, climb into his truck and drive away. My legs weakened and I slowly slid down to the floor, bracing my back against the door and curling into a ball. A glance at the illuminated microwave clock informed me that it was 12:03 AM.

The anniversary was finally over. *What a day.*

Chapter Seven

Bad Jokes

I pressed my fingertips into the black leather upholstery and tried to ground myself. It was a nice chair, expensive – the kind I imagined might litter the office of a wealthy businessman like my father. It surprised me, this chair.

Most shrinks I'd visited in the past had offices designed to inspire feelings of comfort and an idyllic home life. They'd been stuffed with bookshelves, packed with knickknacks, and always had a conveniently placed box of tissues within reach. I'm not sure who decided that "troubled youths" like myself would prefer such an environment; if anything, it was a slap in the face, reminding me in no uncertain terms that my father's modern, uncluttered mansion would never be anything like a home.

Psychiatrists – at least those I'd had the misfortune of knowing – didn't typically go for the modern look; it was too clinical, too sterile to foster any false sense of camaraderie. So far, by her furniture selections alone, Dr. Joan Angelini had surpassed my expectations and was flying in the face of convention. Then again, nothing about this situation was conventional, considering she was the first shrink I'd ever sought out voluntarily.

For the tenth time in as many minutes I fought the urge to bolt for the door, reminding myself this torture was self-inflicted. She wasn't some state-issued doctor, checking up on me at my father's or the court's behest; she was sitting there analyzing me strictly because I'd asked her to. I'd actually handed over several hundred dollars – and a small piece of my soul – and *requested* this torment.

And for what? One little panic attack had me running scared.

"Aren't you supposed to ask me questions?" I demanded, crossing my arms over my chest and glaring at the woman in front of me. She was in her late forties and stylishly dressed, her blonde hair coiffed in an elegant chignon and her blouse pressed to perfection.

"Is there something in particular you want me to ask you?" she replied with practiced indifference, unruffled by my irritable nature.

"Well, I'm not paying you to stare at me for sixty minutes."

"Brooklyn, you sought me out. Why? What made you decide to come here?"

"I had a panic attack last night."

"Okay, that's nothing to be too concerned about. Nearly everyone experiences a panic attack at one point or another. Was this your first one?"

"No." I took a deep breath, and prepared to unload fourteen years worth of pent up dysfunction on this woman. I just hoped she could handle it – it was her job, after all. "I've been having them sporadically since I witnessed my mother's murder at age six. The drug-addict who killed her took her keys and drove off. Apparently he was so high he didn't realize there was a little kid in the backseat."

I watched Dr. Angelini's eyes widen – not even shrinks could hide every emotion – and the flurry of her pen assured me she was documenting each detail. I kept my voice impassive as I offered her the facts – and nothing more.

"I hit him in the face and he let go of the wheel. We crashed. He grabbed me and used me as a human shield during a shoot-out with the police, but I don't remember much of that. I think he held me so tight I passed out. I remember losing a lot of blood and not being able to breathe, though."

"What triggered the panic attack last night?" she asked.

"Some asshole in a bar grabbed me from behind and lifted me off the ground," I said, absently rubbing the bruises hidden beneath the sleeves of my jacket. "I couldn't breathe. I heard sirens and *his* voice in my head."

"His?"

"Ernie Skinner. The guy who killed my mom."

"So you're saying the attack triggered a memory?"

"I think so," I shrugged. "I've never really *tried* to remember much about that time in my life. In fact, I've done everything in my power to avoid it."

"And now?"

I looked her in the eye. "Now, I think I want to remember."

Dr. Angelini smiled for the first time since I'd walked into her office.

"That's a start, Brooklyn."

***

I walked through the door of my apartment and tossed my keys on the kitchen island. My meeting with Dr. Angelini hadn't been as bad as I'd been expecting – for some reason, I'd opened up to her in ways I hadn't with any of my other shrinks. Maybe I just hadn't been ready to talk about it before now.

Lexi wasn't home, which didn't surprise me; she was spending most of her spare time at Tyler's apartment these days. I didn't mind being alone, though. I'd learned self-sufficiency at age six.

Walking into my bedroom, I immediately noticed two things: Finn's unreturned leather jacket still hanging from a hook on my closet door, and a bouquet of flowers lying on my bedside table. They definitely hadn't been there this morning when I'd left for my appointment with Dr. Angelini and, to my knowledge, Lexi hadn't been home all day.

I quickly crossed the room and looked at the flowers. They weren't in a vase and their only adornment was a black satin ribbon, which held the bouquet together. The flowers themselves were unusual – a dozen black roses. There was no card with them, nor was there any indication as to how they had arrived in my bedroom. The hairs on my neck instantly stood on end and despite the warmth of the day, goosebumps flourished across my skin.

Someone had been in my room.

I whirled around and scanned the space for intruders, an umbrella clutched in my hand as a makeshift weapon. I checked under my bed, in the bathroom, Lexi's room, the kitchen, and the living room. I wasn't an investigator, but I figured I'd watched enough episodes of CSI to know what to look for. Nothing seemed to have been disturbed; there were no mysterious footprints in the carpet, the doors and windows were all locked and didn't look tampered with, and not a magazine was out of place. It was as if the flowers had simply materialized.

Returning to my room, I scooped up the bouquet and tossed it into the small wastebasket next to my desk. As I released the stems, sharp thorns tore at my hands. I winced as several drops of blood fell from my fingertips, landing on the black petals in the trash bin and staining them crimson.

All kinds of red flags were going up in my mind as I thought about the flowers. Who had left them? How had they gotten into my room? What did they mean? *Who gives someone black roses with the thorns still attached?*

I wrapped a tissue around the worst of the scratches to stop the bleeding and pulled open my laptop. A quick Google search told me exactly what I wanted to know.

Black roses, which do not exist in nature, are most often used to symbolize intense hatred or death, though they can also mean farewell, rejuvenation, rebirth, or the return from a long journey in which one did not expect to survive. In folklore, black roses are a foreshadowing of death on the horizon; a person who comes across this ominous flower is likely to suffer their demise.

Death.

Someone was sending me roses as a harbinger of my coming death. My heart beat faster at the thought and I felt the walls closing in around me. My mind began to flip through a list of people who might want me killed, or at the very least scared. Gordon came to mind immediately. After the beating he took last night because of me, he might want revenge.

Another possibility, a suspect infinitely more deadly than Gordon, lurked in the recesses of my mind, but I didn't dare examine it yet. I didn't want to even consider *him* an option. Plus, he was safely locked up in San Quentin. If he'd been paroled, I would have been notified.

I pulled out my phone and quickly dialed Lexi's

number. When she didn't pick up on the first try, I hung up and immediately redialed. She eventually answered, sounding slightly out of breath.

"Brooklyn? Is everything okay?"

"Lex, have you been here at all today?"

"No, I've been at Ty's since last night. What's going on?"

"There was a bouquet of black roses sitting on my bedroom table when I came home just now. The apartment was locked. I don't know where they came from."

"Did you say black roses?" Lexi whispered, a tremor in her voice.

"Yes."

"I went through a big roses phase when I was helping my sister plan her wedding floral arrangements. Black roses aren't good, Brookie. They usually mean—"

"Death," I cut her off. "I know."

"What are you going to do?" she asked.

"I think I'm going to call the police," I said, feeling paranoid and foolish but not knowing what else to do.

"I'll be right there," she said, disconnecting the call before I could protest.

Within minutes, the front door opened and Lexi's running footsteps could be heard as she made her way to my bedroom. Throwing open my door, she launched herself onto my bed and wrapped her arms around me. I was so stunned that I didn't even have time to return her hug before she was pulling back to examine my face.

"Are you okay?" she asked, concern flickering in her blue eyes.

"I'm fine," I shrugged. "Just a little freaked out I guess."

"Where are they?"

I nodded in the direction of my trash can, and Lexi leapt off my bed to investigate the sinister bouquet. After a few minutes, she returned to sit on the bed.

"There was no note?"

"No."

"Have you called the police yet?"

"I was waiting for you," I lied. Truthfully, I'd nearly talked myself out of calling. It was probably just a stupid prank. Creepy? Yes. Life-threatening? No. Plus, what could the police do at this point?

"Brooklyn Grace Turner," Lexi glared at me, easily seeing through my lie. "We are calling them. Right. Now." She whipped out her cellphone and dialed the non-emergency number for the local police. As soon as it began to ring, she offered the phone to me.

"Charlottesville Police Station, how can I help you?"

"Um, hi. My name is Brooklyn Turner and I'm calling to report... I guess we've had a break in."

"You guess?" The man sounded exasperated. "Ma'am, if this isn't a serious call I'm going to have to hang up."

"Well, I came home this afternoon and there was a bouquet of black roses sitting in my bedroom. I have no idea how they got there, nor does my roommate. The apartment was locked. And there was no note."

"I'll send someone over to check it out and talk to you. What's the address?"

After rattling off our street name and house number, I was assured that an officer would arrive shortly. I handed Lexi's phone back to her and she quickly grabbed my arm and towed me into the living room.

To my surprise, Tyler and Finn were sitting on our couch, talking quietly. Their conversation stopped and they both looked up as we entered the room. My eyes met Finn's and quickly skittered away. I had no idea what to say to him after last night. Before I could move further into the room, Finn was on his feet and standing in front of me, his hands gently clasping my forearm and examining the smattering of dark bruises that Gordon's hands had left behind.

I looked up into his eyes, which had clouded over with rage. Seeing the anger there, I tried to tug my arm from his grasp but he held fast.

"I'll kill him," he growled through clenched teeth. I'd never seen him so furious and I definitely didn't like it.

90

"I'm fine, Finn. It's no big deal, so please relax."

"No big deal? Are you kidding me, Brooklyn?" Finn dropped my arm and began to pace around the living room. "He put his hands on you. You have fucking bruises! Please explain what part of that is not a big fucking deal!" He was yelling now, running his hands through his hair in exasperation. Abruptly, he turned back to face me.

"It is *never* okay for someone to put his hands on you like that. Please tell me you know that."

"I do," I said somewhat meekly. I hadn't realized how much the sight of my bruises upset him. "But really, they don't hurt anymore. And you took care of him last night."

"I'd like to do a lot more than mess up his pretty face," Finn muttered, evidently contemplating Gordon's murder. To calm him, I placed both of my palms against his cheeks and turned his face toward mine. He startled, clearly surprised by my touch, but as soon as his eyes met mine he seemed to relax.

"Thank you for last night," I said, holding his gaze. "I don't know what I would have done if you hadn't been there."

He pulled in a deep breath and closed his eyes. "You don't need to thank me."

A knock sounded loudly at the door and I dropped my hands from Finn's face. Lexi pulled open the door, revealing a middle-aged police officer with a beer-gut, a graying beard, and a receding salt-and-pepper hairline.

"I'm Officer Carlson. I'll be taking your statements and looking around the place for any signs of a break in. Can one of you tell me what happened?"

Lexi got the officer a glass of water and I sat on the couch with him discussing the flowers and their mysterious arrival. After jotting down my statement in a small black notebook, he followed me into my bedroom and examined the bouquet lying in my wastebasket.

"Well," he drawled, scratching his protruding belly, "It'd have been better if you hadn't touched them, of course, but I can take them back to the station and see if we can lift any prints off 'em. It's doubtful, though. Flowers aren't exactly ideal for fingerprinting." He snorted, evidently amusing himself.

Glad they sent out Charlottesville PD's finest to help me through this ordeal.

After bagging the flowers and taking a cursory glance at the front door lock, Officer Carlson left. He promised to let me know as soon as they had any answers about the break in, but I certainly wouldn't be holding my breath. I closed the door behind him and walked slowly to my bedroom, ignoring the identical looks of concern plastered on Lexi, Tyler, and Finn's faces. I needed to be alone.

Propping open my window, I slid out onto my rooftop and curled my knees up to my chest. I pillowed my arms on top of my knees, laid down my head, and closed my eyes, trying to regulate my breathing. Somehow, even my rooftop didn't feel safe today. The creepy flower delivery had me more rattled than I wanted to admit – not to myself and certainly not to the three people inside on my couch.

In fact, the only time I'd felt safe in weeks was when Finn had swooped in like a freaking knight in shining armor and carried me away from Gordon and the panic-inducing crowds at Styx last night. I wasn't sure why he had such a calming effect on me. I'd never needed anyone to save me before, and I definitely didn't want to need someone now.

I was alarmed to recognize how much I enjoyed Finn's company – how often he made me laugh, how I'd find myself smiling against my will in his presence, how he'd forcefully reacted to seeing me hurt. Despite all that, I wasn't sure he felt anything for me, other than desire to add me to the long list of bimbos he'd screwed.

I'm not sure how much time passed as I sat out on the rooftop. Dusk had begun to descend and the sun crept ever closer to the horizon. I heard the sound of my window sliding open, and Finn's muffled curse as he maneuvered his tall frame through the small opening. I didn't turn my head to acknowledge him as he settled in next to me.

He was on my rooftop. Lexi had never even been out here with me. I should've felt violated or incensed at his intrusion into

92

my private space, but somehow it felt right to have him here. He'd shared his highway lookout point with me, after all.

I waited for him to speak, but he remained silent. After a few minutes, he slipped his leather jacket, which he must've found hanging in my room, around my shoulders and wrapped an arm around me. I hadn't realized how cold I was until his warmth was pressed against my side.

"Want to hear a bad joke?" Finn asked.

I turned my head to look at him and cocked one eyebrow. Was he being serious? He didn't exactly seem like the comedian-type.

"I'll take your silence as tacit approval," he said, pausing to collect his thoughts. His eyebrows pulled together as if he were deep in thought. "What do you call a pony with a cough?"

I looked at him blankly.

"A little hoarse!" Finn laughed, evaluated my less-than-amused expression, and became contemplative once more. "Hmm, no luck with that one. Okay, why couldn't Dracula's wife get to sleep?"

Again, I failed to give him a reaction.

"Because, Brooklyn, she was up all night with his *coffin*." He sighed dramatically. "That one was obvious! If I didn't know better, I'd think you weren't even *trying* to answer these."

When I still didn't laugh, Finn rolled his eyes. "Jeeze, tough crowd. Okay this is my last one. Mostly 'cause I don't know any more jokes. Baby, do you play Quiddich?"

I think my mouth fell open in shock. He couldn't possibly be making a Harry Potter joke…could he?

"'Cause you sure look like a Keeper to me," he finished, smiling broadly.

I couldn't help it -- I burst into laughter. "You like Harry Potter?" I asked incredulously.

"What kind of question is that?" Finn asked, his cheeks flushing slightly pink with embarrassment. "Everyone likes Harry Potter," he grumbled. "Don't you?"

"Well, yeah. I've just never heard a guy admit to it before." I dissolved into giggles at his obvious discomfort.

"Seriously, where did you get those jokes? They're pretty terrible, just so you know for any future attempts at cheering up sulking girls."

"Oh, believe me, I know how bad they are. My little sister taught them to me a while back, though, and I can't seem to forget them. Plus, they made you laugh...eventually." His eyes crinkled up as he grinned playfully at me.

He was gorgeous all the time but seeing him like this, so boyish and lighthearted, made him even more attractive. My heart seemed to turn over in my chest as I took in his profile: the chiseled jawline, his perpetually messy dark hair, that freaking adorable dimple, and those stunning cobalt eyes. I leaned into his side and pressed a feather-light kiss to his jawline, settling my forehead into the hollow of his throat before he had time to react.

"Thank you. Again." I laughed. "It seems like I'm always thanking you for something these days."

Finn kissed the top of my head and shrugged. "What are friends for, right?"

Hmm. So we were still just "friends" in his eyes. I pocketed that little nugget of information away for future dissection.

"So you have a little sister?"

"Step-sister, technically. I was adopted when I was ten."

"Oh." I wanted to know more, but was afraid to ask. If he told me his story, would I be obligated to tell mine?

"Yeah, my biological parents died when I was eight. Car crash. I spent a handful of years in foster and group homes before my adoptive parents found me. They saved my life." His tone was reflective – there was no sadness in it, just a contemplative acceptance of his past. I didn't apologize for his loss, because people had been telling me how sorry they were for fourteen years, and it had never changed a damn thing for me.

"I—" I broke off, cleared my throat, and tried again. "I spent some time in a group home too." Turning my face into the crook of Finn's neck, I blocked out the world and my voice dropped to a whisper. "Eventually, my biological father came and took me home with him. I'm not sure why he bothered; its not like

94

he had any interest in raising me."

We fell into silence for a time, watching as the stars slowly began to emerge in the darkening sky. We'd both left things unsaid, but it didn't feel strange. It was oddly comforting to know that he had things he wasn't ready to share yet either.

"It's nice up here," Finn whispered. "Peaceful."

"Yeah," I murmured, closing my eyes and thinking my rooftop had never felt so safe. I put the flower incident out of my mind, and tried to savor the feeling.

Finn and I eventually made our way back inside, joining Lexi and Tyler for pizza and a stupid Will Ferrell movie that was on TV. It was a blissfully normal ending to a horrible day.

CHAPTER EIGHT

WORTHWHILE FEARS

The next week was remarkably boring. It was a refreshing change after the drama of my panic attack and the appearance of the sinister bouquet. Lexi and Tyler were still attached at the hip, but were spending more of their time at our apartment. I think they were worried about leaving me alone, which was sweet but completely unnecessary.

I filled my days with homework and classes, and occupied my nights by knocking some books off my lengthy TBR list. I didn't see Finn at all, and I tried to convince myself that it didn't bother me. I did, however, see Dr. Angelini again. I told her about the flower incident and how Finn had cheered me up with corny jokes afterwards.

"You've mentioned Finn several times now. Is he someone you're interested in romantically?" Dr. Angelini asked.

"I don't date," I responded instantly.

"That wasn't my question, Brooklyn."

"He's different," I said, struggling for the right words. "When he looks at me, it's like he sees past all the bullshit barriers I've put up and gets a glimpse of the real Brooklyn – the one nobody knows. The one even I forget exists sometimes."

"How does that make you feel?"

"Scared shitless, if I'm being perfectly honest," I said with a grimace. "That can't be healthy right?"

"Well, in my experience, it's usually the things we're most afraid of that end up being the most worthwhile," Dr. Angelini said, a small smile curving her lips.

"That's deep, doc," I teased, falling silent as the weight of her words washed over me. "The thing I'm most afraid of is forgetting her," I murmured.

"Your mother?"

"Yes. I have a few photos of her, so I can still see her face when I want to. But the little things – how she smelled, the sound of her laughter – those are the things I feel slipping away."

"What is it you remember most clearly about her?"

"Singing. She was a musician. I don't have many memories without her humming under her breath as she composed a new melody in her head. We used to sing together."

"Do you still sing?"

"Only in private, and only when I'm feeling particularly masochistic. I have an old guitar I found in an antique store a few years ago. I taught myself to play in high school, thinking it might make me feel more connected to her memory."

"Did it work?" Dr. Angelini asked.

"I don't know," I answered honestly, shaking my head back and forth. "I never really pursued it."

"I think you should."

"Excuse me?" I asked.

"I think you should find a coffee house or a karaoke bar or even a street corner and perform. Just once, to see how it feels. In fact, that's your assignment before you come back to see me."

"You're giving me homework?" I asked, incredulous. "You're my shrink, not my professor."

Dr. Angelini smiled placidly. "Your time for today is up, Brooklyn. I look forward to hearing all about your musical debut at our next session. " She stood and ushered me into the hallway, closing the door firmly behind me. I stared back at her closed door, my mouth hanging open in shock.

This was going to be a disaster.

I wasn't sure if my time at therapy was helping or not, but for once in my life I had someone I could discuss my problems and my twisted history with. I could talk freely because it was confidential and Dr. Angelini wasn't a friend – she was just doing her job. I didn't burden her and she didn't judge me.

And while I was dreading getting up on a stage and singing in front of a crowd, I knew Dr. Angelini wouldn't have recommended doing it unless it served a real purpose. Shockingly, I trusted her.

Our discussion of relationships had me thinking about sex as I drove home from my appointment. It had been months since my last random hookup, far longer than I typically lasted between boy-binges. Sex was the ultimate mind-numbing escape, reserved for situations where tequila alone couldn't block out my emotions.

I couldn't help but wonder if my sudden prudish tendencies had something to do with a certain new male *friend*, who sang like an angel and told jokes any five year old could top. I dismissed that unwelcome thought, pulled into a nearby liquor store parking lot, and began making plans for a much-needed Friday night out with Lexi.

***

"Lex?" I called, walking into our apartment and dumping two grocery bags full of ingredients onto the kitchen island. I could hear music thumping from her speakers, an auto-tuned pop track I'd never heard before. Lexi and I didn't exactly share the same taste in artists.

She emerged from her room, hips gyrating in time to the beat as she crooned the lyrics into a hairbrush.

"Could you be any more cliché?" I asked, giggling at her as I removed several bottles of tequila, margarita mix, and two fresh limes from the grocery bags.

"Margarita night?" Lexi squealed, dropping her pseudo-microphone and pulling the blender down from a cabinet.

"Yeah, I was thinking we could head over to The Blue Note in a little bit."

"The karaoke bar?" Lexi asked, her nose wrinkling in confusion. "But you don't ever want to go there."

"I thought we could change it up tonight, try somewhere new."

"Works for me," Lexi said, always agreeable to a night of debauchery. She was firing up the blender with our first round of margaritas in two minutes flat.

After a brief cheers, I left the kitchen and headed into my room to prepare for the night. Picking an outfit was the least of my worries; I somehow had to convince myself that singing onstage in front of a crowd of random strangers wasn't going to be a total train wreck. Sipping my margarita, I hoped a bit of liquid courage would keep me from backing out at the last minute.

Finn's jacket still hung on the hook by my closet – he must've left it here after the night of the flower delivery. Before I could talk myself out of it, I crossed the room, grasped the supple leather in my hands, and held it up against my face. Inhaling, I could detect the faintest aroma of falling leaves and crisp apples – that uniquely autumnal, masculine scent Finn seemed to carry everywhere he went. Ignoring the pang in my chest, I dropped the jacket onto my bedspread and scolded myself for acting like such a girl.

The truth was, I missed him. I'd gotten used to him being around, and not seeing him for over a week was a slow form of torture. I wouldn't seek him out, though. It wasn't in my nature to chase after anyone's affection.

After changing into a sparkly fitted grey blouse, dark skinny jeans, and a pair of black high-heeled leather boots, I pulled my guitar from a long-neglected back corner of my closet. It was out of tune; it had been months since I'd last played.

After making some adjustments, I strummed a few chords experimentally. For an old guitar, it had a nice sound. I smiled as I began to play the opening melody of one of my favorite songs, singing under my breath as I reached the chorus. Enthusiastic applause greeted me as soon as I trailed off; Lexi was standing in my doorway, watching with rapt attention.

"Does this mean you're going to play tonight?" She squealed, clearly excited by the prospect.

"I was thinking about it." I didn't mention Dr. Angelini's assignment, as that would've required me to tell Lexi that I was seeing a psychiatrist.

"Ohmigod! Brooklyn, I don't know what inspired this but I'm so happy you're going to play! I've been telling you for years, you could be a professional with pipes like yours."

"I don't know about that," I said, strumming softly. "My mom was a singer, you know."

"No, I didn't know," Lexi sighed. "But that's because you never talk about her. I wish you would."

That had my attention. "You do?" I asked, surprised.

"Of course I do, Brooklyn. You're my best friend." She walked over to sit beside me on the bed. "I know I can be selfish, believe me. But I also know that my self-absorption is the only reason you've let me stick around this long. I figured out a long time ago that if I pushed you, I'd lose you." Her eyes filled with tears as she looked at me. "And I can't lose you, Brookie. But sometimes I wish you'd let me – or *anyone* – in, because you can't keep it all locked up inside forever. Nobody's that strong."

I was shocked speechless. I wanted to shake myself for being so blind. Lexi wasn't ignorant, self-obsessed, or totally uninterested in me. In fact, she'd figured me out long ago, understood how I functioned, and decided to stick around anyway. For the first time in years, I felt the telltale signs of tears prickling at my eyes. Placing my guitar next to me on the bed, I reached over and pulled Lexi into a hug.

"I'm kind of an idiot, huh?" I asked her after a few minutes.

"It's okay. I'm kind of a vapid narcissist. So it all evens out in the end," she giggled through her tears. "Great, now I'm going to have to completely redo my makeup! If you have any more sentimental bullshit to unload, now is the time. I refuse to redo it again after this." Lexi winked at me as she hurried out of my room, no doubt headed for the numerous beauty products littering her vanity.

I rolled my eyes and felt a smile spread across my face. I had a best friend who actually gave a shit about me. And I was ready to kick some musical ass.

***

By the time Lexi and I walked into The Blue Note, open mic night was well under way. A boy wearing a dark fur vest and white leather pants wailed into the microphone on stage, accompanied by a willowy girl with shoulder-length dreadlocks who occasionally beat her tambourine in time with the chorus. I immediately felt like I'd been transported back to the 1970s; it was painful to watch.

Lexi stifled a giggle as we sat down at a small round table

near the back of the room. I settled my guitar case on the ground by my feet and surveyed the club. It was dark in the audience, the only light cast by flickering jar-candles that had been placed on each tabletop. Dim halogen lamps illuminated the stage, creating a halo around a solitary stool and microphone stand.

Lexi headed to the bar to grab our drinks while I staked out our table; more people poured in through the front door with each passing minute, and the seating was limited. The club may have felt intimate, but was bigger than it had appeared at first glance. There were probably close to a hundred people scattered around the different booths and standing at the bar.

Watching as the room quickly filled, I began to reconsider coming here. Maybe performing wasn't such a good idea after all. I could always try a coffee shop or – what had Dr. Angelini's other suggestion been? Oh, right. A street corner.

Lexi arrived back at our table just as the next act stepped up on stage. A girl dressed in all black, covered in tattoos, and flaunting multiple facial piercings approached the mic. It was no great surprise when she began screaming out the lyrics to an angst-ridden Alanis Morissette song.

Sipping the lemon drop martini Lexi had gotten for me, I decided this wasn't the right venue for my debut. I wasn't nearly angry enough at the world to fit in amongst these performers. Nor did I have a fur vest or dreadlocks.

"Guess what?" Lexi exclaimed, a huge grin spreading across her face.

Oh shit. I knew that look. I felt a leaden weight drop into the pit of my stomach, dread mounting in anticipation of whatever she was about to tell me.

"What did you do?"

"While I was up getting our drinks, I may or may not have signed you up to perform! Isn't that great?" She was giggling uncontrollably at this point, no doubt amused by the murderous expression thundering across my face.

"Lexi! Why would you do that to me?" I whined.

"Because I knew you were about two seconds from bailing as soon as we walked in and saw Sonny and Cher up there—" she nodded in the direction of the hippie couple who'd just left the stage, "—reliving their seventies glory."

I didn't respond; I hated when she was right.

Thankfully, several more acts were called to the stage before my name was announced, giving me time to gulp down my martini and slightly calm my ragged nerves.

"Let's give it up for Brooklyn, everybody!" The MC was a blur as I walked to the stage and settled onto the stool, holding my guitar to my chest like a lifeline. My feet didn't quite reach the ground, so I propped them up on the bottom rung. Lowering the microphone stand so it was level with my face, I looked out at the crowd. The dark room was a blessing; I couldn't see anyone's faces. It would almost be like I was back in my room, playing alone.

Almost.

"Hey, you guys, I'm Brooklyn. I've never done this before, so cut me some slack, okay?" There were some appreciative chuckles from the audience, helping to put me at ease. "I'm going to sing one of my favorite songs for you tonight. This is *Blackbird* by The Beatles."

I strummed the opening chords easily. I'd been playing this song for so many years it was ingrained in my soul, a melody my fingers had memorized long ago. And though I had the upmost respect for The Beatles, I couldn't help putting my own spin on the song.

I'd slowed it down to fit the acoustic atmosphere, raised it up an octave, and tried my damnedest to infuse my voice with all the emotions that the lyrics conveyed. Hope, sadness, love, rebirth: this song embodied them all.

The crowd faded away as I sang about learning to fly with broken wings, losing myself to the music. Of all the songs in the world, I'd always felt that this one fit me best. The lyrics gave me hope that maybe I wasn't the only one who'd been shattered by death and loss and sorrow. That maybe everyone's a little bit broken inside.

As a little girl, I remember watching *Peter Pan* one night with all the other foster kids in the group home. The other children, most of whom were too old to be entertained by Disney, were making fun of the movie or ignoring it altogether. I alone sat quietly, transfixed by the scene where Peter chases his shadow around the room and tries to wrestle it back into compliance before Wendy finally sews the damned thing to his shoe. That scene had always resonated strangely with me, and after a time, I'd come to see my grief as a sort of disobedient shadow. I'd dragged a wraith of misery around for fourteen years and damned if it didn't kick and scream the whole time, refusing to be ignored.

I was tired, so tired, of fighting my shadow every minute of the day. My grief had become a living entity, personified by years of self-blame and incarnated by my refusal to confront it. Like Peter, I'd chased my specter for years and repeatedly forced it into submission in a never-ending battle of wills. Too often, though, the grief broke free – and I broke down.

Singing on that stage, I wouldn't say I felt my mother's presence, or saw her spirit or anything ridiculous like that. It was more like a surge of warmth filled my veins and made my heart expand – like a moment of clarity as I realized she'd be proud to hear me carrying on her legacy.

It was closure.

I felt like I'd been drowning in my grief for years and hadn't even realized it. Like I'd been gasping for breath for so long I'd become accustomed to barely breathing at all. And now, I'd been thrown a life-ring and hauled ashore and given a chance to live again. I imagined my grief, that phantom of perpetual misery, finally settling inside my heart. It no longer tugged at its tether, or rattled the bars of its cage – it simply took a deep breath of acceptance as it dissipated into me and finally, finally gave up the fight.

I smiled as I gave myself over to the feeling, completely surrendering to the music as it flowed from my lips and fingertips. I heard my mother's voice in my head.

There's a song for every feeling, Bee. Every tear, every smile, every heartbreak and every victory. Music ignites the soul and strips us bare. It's our very essence. Even if you have no one else to turn to and you feel all alone, remember that you can always find comfort in ballads and melodies, serenades and love songs.

I knew my shadow would never fully leave me – that's not how grief worked. What had happened to me as a little girl had changed me, altered me on a chemical level, forged me into the woman I was becoming. But maybe it wouldn't fight me so damn hard from now on. Maybe it would take up residence inside my soul – a scarred, clouded part of my essence – and let me breathe unhindered.

Strumming the last note, I opened my eyes, growing nervous as I took in the utterly silent crowd.

Was I that bad? Jeeze, I didn't even get a sympathy clap.

Then, to my utter surprise, I saw people getting to their feet and applauding wildly. Catcalls sounded from the bar area and I thought I heard Lexi screaming from somewhere in the back, but it was hard to tell over the rest of the cheers. Grinning, I hopped down from my perch on the stool, slung my guitar over one shoulder and waved to my new fans.

"Thanks, guys!" I called, walking off the stage to make way for the next performer. As I stepped back into the crowd to head for my table, I was immediately engulfed by a swarm of people eager to congratulate me on my performance. I laughed when several asked me where I performed locally, as they were eager to catch my next show.

I eventually made my way back to Lexi, who was jumping up and down in excitement. Squeezing me so tight I could barely breathe, she screamed in my ear.

"You were freaking amazing! Oh my god, Brooklyn. You could've heard a pin drop in here during your performance and I swear I saw a few people crying. You're a rock star!" she exclaimed. Releasing me, she turned to face the people seated in the audience around us. "MY BEST FRIEND IS A FREAKING ROCK STAR!" She screamed at the top of her lungs, entirely too loudly for such a relaxed venue. I smacked her on the arm.

"Quit it, Lex! You're embarrassing me. Not to mention yourself," I laughed.

"I'm declaring myself your official musical agent," she

said, eyes distant with thoughts of our future fame and glory.

"Lexi, don't you think you're getting a bit ahead of yourself? You do realize that I'm still going to become a lawyer, right?"

Lexi snorted, grumbling under her breath about wasted talent and missed opportunities. Oh well. Singing had always been just a hobby and though it recently may have become a therapeutic outlet, I doubted it would ever transition into a path to stardom. As exhilarating and enlightening as my performance had been, I didn't see it going anywhere professionally.

A familiar, deep voice rasped into the microphone, immediately catching my attention. Butterflies erupted in my stomach as my eyes drank in the sight of the beautiful dark haired man sitting on the stool I'd just vacated. His eyes scanned the room restlessly, as if seeking someone particular in the dark crowd.

"Well, I don't think I'm going to be able to top that last performance—" *Did he mean mine?* "—but I'll do my best. This song is dedicated to a friend I worried I'd lost for good. For a long time I thought it was impossible that this person might still exist out there," he paused, clearing his throat and running a hand through his hair – a sure sign he was nervous. "But I'm happy to say that sometimes we get second chances in this crazy life. Sometimes the things we lose are returned to us. Sometimes, we're lucky. So, yeah, enough of my bullshit ramblings. This is *The Scientist* by Coldplay."

Finn's voice was hauntingly beautiful as he sang along with his acoustic guitar. He'd never looked more attractive, but I could tell by just a glance that something was wrong. There were circles under his eyes dark enough to rival mine before my daily Sephora-intervention; it was clear he hadn't been sleeping. He looked utterly worn out and it set me on edge immediately.

As the lyrics washed over me, I wondered about his strange song dedication. Who was he talking about? It was probably irrational for me to feel jealous, considering there was nothing remotely romantic between Finn and I. He'd made it clear on more that one occasion that he was strictly my friend and, with the exception of a drunken near-kiss in the bathroom at Styx, he'd never even implied that he found me attractive.

The man-whore doesn't even want you. Talk about an ego-bruiser.

I wasn't too proud to admit that his lack of attention over the past week had stung. I hadn't heard from him at all, and I couldn't help but be reminded of the way I'd avoided him at the beginning of the semester. Oh, how the tables had turned. How the mighty had fallen. *How many more clichés can I use in a row?*

I was getting a taste of my own medicine – *okay, that was the last one, I promise* – and, unfortunately for me, it was the disgusting store-brand, grape flavored liquid cough syrup my foster mom used to shove down our throats when we couldn't sleep at night.

It was obvious that Finn had chosen this song, one that cried out for redemption and second chances, purposefully. It was equally unobvious *why* he'd chosen it. The lyrics were clearly an apology, a plea for someone's forgiveness – and I was near-desperate to figure out whose. Somewhere along the line, he'd started to matter to me.

Evidently, the feeling was not mutual.

But he'd been there for me last week after my breakdown. Granted, his jokes were so pathetic they could barely be considered consolatory. Still, if he needed someone to talk to, I would try not to be a coldhearted bitch for at least five minutes and offer him some comfort. I would be his friend.

As soon as he stepped off the stage, women with too much makeup and too few clothes surrounded him. They reminded me of the seagulls that would swarm any flyaway scrap of food on the California beaches my mother had so often taken me to as a child. She'd called them *rats-with-wings*, laughing as she'd tossed yet another potato chip into the sky to increase their rabid fervor. Come to think of it, Finn could probably throw a dirty sock into this swarm of girls and they'd kill each other in the animalistic race to win it.

He was laughing, in his element as he soaked up their attention. The sadness that had been etched onto his face as he performed had retreated back behind his eyes and that trademark panty-dropping smile. Or maybe I'd been seeing things.

I rolled my eyes and turned back to Lexi, who was watching me closely.

"You like him," she said, surprise written across her face.

"No I don't," I snapped, forcing a laugh as if she was ridiculous to think such a thing. "And we've already discussed this, haven't we?"

"No. We talked about you sleeping with him and tossing him aside, like you do all the others. Not that there have even *been* any others lately – but we'll get back to that later." She stared at me, as if trying to decode my brain with just the power of her eyes. "You *like* him. As in, you care about him. I never thought I'd see the day." Her voice was laced with something like awe as she continued to look at me.

"I don't know what you're talking about, Lex. You know better than anyone that I don't do relationships or commitments or even emotions."

"Then why haven't you been with anyone else since you met him? Explain that!" She stared at me, triumphant.

"You know, you're right. It has been too long," I said, pushing back my seat and standing up. "I think I'll go find someone to go home with right now."

Sadness and regret instantly flashed in Lexi's eyes. "I'm sorry I mentioned anything, Brookie. Stay with me," she pleaded. "Don't do this again."

"Take my guitar home for me, 'kay?" I tossed over my shoulder, ignoring her as I turned to head for the bar. A quick glance toward the stage assured me that Finn was still busy with his adorning fans. With one blonde on each arm, he certainly wouldn't be in need of my friendship tonight. I mentally scoffed at my earlier thoughts of comforting him; clearly, I'd been mistaken.

When I reached the bar, I singled out the guy who'd be taking me home within thirty seconds. It was a talent I'd possessed for years: one glance told me everything I needed to know about a person.

My bedmate for the night was an easy mark. He was at the bar laughing with two male friends, which told me he was laid-back and likely single. He was drinking a beer, so he was probably straight and wouldn't be so hammered that he'd have any problems performing in the bedroom. His light green plaid button down was casual, but showed off the muscles in his broad back and mirrored the color of his irises.

I could have him back at his apartment, naked, within the hour if I played this right.

Approaching slowly, I made sure to ignore him as I walked up to the empty barstool next to his and leaned over the bar. I waved in the bartender's direction to signal that I was ready to order, then pushed my dark curls over my shoulder in a gesture designed to appear impatient. If my approach alone hadn't caught plaid-shirt boy's attention, the fragrance of my shampoo would do the trick. I bought it on special order and it smelled like apples and cinnamon – something that, apparently, attracted boys like crack. I think its male-enticement abilities would be surpassed only by bacon-scented shampoo, and I was pretty sure John Frieda didn't make that.

When the bartender reached me, I ordered a bottle of Sam Adams and paid him quickly. Turning around, I faced the stage and leaned back against the bar, taking a deep pull on my beer. I could feel the weight of plaid-shirt boy's gaze on my profile as the cool bottle rested against my lips and I swallowed slowly. The tip of my tongue lightly traced the glass rim, and I hid a smile as I heard him clear his throat roughly and shuffle his feet.

"Hey, I'm Landon," he said, moving in front of me. "You were pretty amazing up there earlier." He held out a hand for me to shake, smiling in a friendly, *I'd-like-to-see-what-color-your-panties-are* kind of way. His blond hair was lightly tousled and his eyes were gorgeous up close – green with flecks of hazel throughout.

Perfect.

"Brooklyn," I said, smiling flirtatiously and placing my hand in his. This was going to be even easier than I'd expected.

"Don't you know it's not good to drink alone, Brooklyn?"

He laughed.

I sidled a glance at him, winking. "Good thing you're here to keep me company then." He grinned and I downed the rest of my beer.

Two beers – courtesy of Landon – and thirty minutes later, I was feeling buzzed and ready to leave. I was anxious to get away from Lexi's accusations and Finn's flock of women. I'd purposefully avoided looking in his direction, then immediately scolded myself for doing so. If I couldn't even watch him flirting with other girls, he was even deeper under my skin than I'd realized before. I needed Landon to help push Finn from my mind as soon as possible. Maybe then I could finally get back to normal.

Part of my mind was screaming at me, even as I allowed Landon to lead me toward the exit.

Is this the person you want to be, Brooklyn?

Do you really want to go back to being the guarded, selfish, self-preserving whore you were a few months ago?

What about all the progress you've made with therapy and Lexi and Finn?

Just thinking his name had me pushing away that annoying inner voice and snapping back to reality. It was suddenly easy to lace my fingers through Landon's and follow him to the exit, once again eager to leave.

Near the club door, Landon bumped into a table of his fraternity brothers and stopped briefly to talk. He introduced me, laughing and blushing as his brothers made crass and utterly unoriginal comments about him "getting lucky" tonight. I rolled my eyes and waited impatiently for him to move on.

When nearly five minutes had passed, I tapped Landon on the shoulder and told him it was time to leave. Turning toward the door, I cast one final glance behind me and, to my dismay, locked eyes with the one person I'd been determined to avoid.

I grinned halfheartedly at Finn, but felt the smile drop off my face as I registered the anger in his eyes. His dark blue irises were steely with rage as they glared at Landon, who'd just placed his hand on my ass in an attempt to usher me out. When I didn't move, Landon leaned down and kissed my neck.

"Come on, babe, I thought you wanted to go?" His breath was too warm and smelled like beer; it made my skin crawl. There were no butterflies, or chills, or stuttering heartbeats – just an intractable sense of wrongness. I ignored the feeling, pulled my neck away from Landon's lips, and tore my eyes from Finn's.

He'd ignored me for an entire week, and now he was furious that I was leaving the bar with someone? Well he could go to hell, as far as I was concerned. Either he had some kind of multiple personality disorder, or I was missing some crucial information.

"Yeah, I'm ready. Let's go," I said, setting my shoulders determinedly and ignoring the ache in my chest as I allowed Landon to pull me through the exit.

Thankfully, it wasn't a long walk to Landon's apartment. He lived about three blocks from the club, in the same neighborhood as me. I tried to remind myself how hot he was as we stumbled through his front door, his lips fused to mine. When his tongue entered my mouth, I responded on autopilot, unable to engage on a deeper level. Groaning in frustration – which Landon no doubt assumed was passion – I pulled off his shirt and ran my hands over his chest.

His six-pack was a chiseled work of art. If I'd met him months ago, I'd have gladly spent the night tracing my tongue along each indentation in a show of my appreciation. But tonight, I wasn't going to waste any time. I needed him to clear out my mind.

Lexi used to say that I treat sex like a trip to the masseuse or the chiropractor – like a romp between the sheets was nothing more than a good back stretch or spine cracking. I'd always laughed when she'd said it, but deep down I knew it was true. I'd used sex to scratch an itch, nothing more.

Until I'd met Finn, and started to care.

I knew instinctually that sex with him would be different. I also knew that what I was doing with Landon right now couldn't hold a candle to the fantasies I'd had about being with Finn, let alone compare to what actually sleeping with him might be like.

110

My grey tank top hit the floor, followed quickly by my bra. Landon's hands cupped my breasts too clumsily and roughly to even remotely turn me on. He was slobbering on my neck, murmuring between openmouthed kisses.

"You're so fucking hot, baby."

"Don't call me baby," I said immediately, muscles tensing under his touch.

"Okay." The slobbering continued as I stood unresponsive, my hands at my sides. "You're so fucking hot."

His hands reached for the button on my jeans, and I knew I had to put a stop to this before he went any further. Glumly, I admitted defeat – his touch couldn't drive Finn out of my mind any more than alcohol or denial could.

I was screwed. And not in the literal, good sense of the word.

"Landon, stop."

To his credit, he did stop immediately. Some guys probably would have been assholes about it – complaining or even trying to force me to continue. But Landon was understanding when I told him I needed to leave.

"It's cool," he said, grinning and running a hand through his messy blond mop of hair. "You ever change your mind, though, you know where to find me."

I laughed as I put my clothes back on and said goodbye. He wasn't a bad guy. I knew he'd be a good boyfriend to someone someday – just not to me.

Thankfully, the walk home was short. I hadn't worn a jacket to the bar and the temperature had dropped in the hours since I'd left my house. I rubbed my arms with my palms, trying to work some warmth into my limbs as I turned onto my block. To my surprise, a familiar black pickup truck was parked in front of my house.

I approached cautiously, noting that the truck was still idling and that Finn was probably sitting inside. I'd stopped just short of the passenger window when I heard the engine cut off abruptly and the driver's side door flew open.

Finn rounded the front of the truck in a blur, grabbing me by the arm and planting my back flat against the passenger door before I could even formulate a protest. He glared at me, his face mere inches from mine. A muscle worked in his jaw as he tried to get control over his anger.

"What do you think you're doing? Let me go, Finn," I glared back at him, tugging my arm from his grasp. "I don't know what the hell your problem is, but I'm going to scream if you don't back off."

"You don't know what my problem is? That's perfect," he barked out a laugh, but there was no humor in it. His hands ran through his hair in frustration. "You. *You* are my fucking problem, Bee."

He was calling me *Bee* again. He'd only done it once before, so I'd dismissed it – but here he was, using it again. No one ever called me Bee. It had been my mother's special nickname for me. I decided to let it go, for now; it seemed I had to pick my battles tonight.

"What the hell does that mean?" I asked, incredulous.

"Did you fuck that guy tonight?"

"That is absolutely none of your business! Now let me go!"

"NO!" Finn roared in my face, his anger reaching a new high. "I can't let you go. I can't. And believe me, I've tried really fucking hard. It's impossible – *You're* impossible." He blew out a harsh breath, and some of the anger cleared from his face. He seemed defeated, suddenly. "I didn't know how hard this would be. I wish I could say that if I'd known, it would have made me stay away from you. But I can't, 'cause I know that's not true. There's literally nothing that would've keep me from coming back to you once I'd found you."

I had no idea what he was talking about at this point. His eyes were wild with a desperate intensity I'd never seen before, and he looked like a man close to his breaking point. Honestly, he was starting to frighten me, and I was dangerously close to delivering a swift kick to his balls and making a getaway.

As I was contemplating escape options, he startled me by

112

gently cupping my face in his hands. Anger shifted to tenderness so rapidly I couldn't pinpoint the exact moment it had happened. His blue eyes pierced mine with a look of steadfast resolve, as if he'd suddenly made a decision about something, and I had the overpowering urge to run far, far away from whatever he was about to say.

"I stayed away from you all week, trying to convince myself that I didn't need you. I knew I should stay away from you, that I shouldn't pursue this. But then I saw you leaving with that douchebag at The Blue Note and I lost it. I can't even—the thought that—" He broke off, unable to even say the words. "Did. You. Fuck. Him." He ground each word out, as if it caused him physical pain to expel them.

"No," I said, glaring into his dark blue eyes. "Not that it's any of your business. I can fuck whoever I want, Finn. You certainly do."

"I haven't been with anyone since I met you."

What?!

I pushed my shock aside and scoffed. "Yeah, right. And even if that's true, why would I care? It's not like I give a damn who you're fucking."

In a flash, the anger was back. "Don't do that. Don't trivialize what's between us. Don't think you can pretend with me. Your little indifferent act might work with everyone else in your life, but I see through it. And you know what I see, Bee?" He paused, leaning in so close our noses grazed. "I see fear. You're scared shitless that you feel something for me, 'cause *god for-fucking-bid* you actually had to let down those walls you've built around yourself and let me in."

My mouth gaped open like a fish as I tried to conjure a response, a denial, even a laugh – anything to steer this conversation into safer waters. My mind was reeling, though, and I couldn't form a single sound. I simply stared at him, adrift in a state of shock. Years of shutting out my emotions had left me utterly incapable of processing his declaration, let alone how I felt about it. Maybe Finn recognized this about me, though, because he continued to speak, undeterred by my silence.

"Since the second you woke up in my arms on the sidewalk that day, it was only a matter of time until we got here, to this moment. We were inevitable. You know it. I know it."

"You barely know me. And if you did…you might not like me so much any more. I'm sure you've heard my reputation…" I swallowed my embarrassment, looking anywhere but at him.

"It doesn't matter, Bee."

"But–" I protested.

"Look, I can't fucking explain it, okay? I'm no good at this. All I can tell you is that it feels like the most natural thing in the world for me to be near you – like I was put on this earth just to breathe your air and tell you how beautiful you are. To make you laugh at my dumbass jokes, and hold you in my arms when you're sad. And I don't want to control you, or own you, or change you. I just want *you*, no matter who you are or what your past is. I don't care about the other guys, or anything that happened before we got together, because all that shit made you *you*." He inhaled deeply. "Being near you, Brooklyn…it's like breathing. I don't have a choice about it; I just have to do it or I know I won't survive very long."

His eyes were so startlingly earnest as he spoke the words, there was no way I could doubt the truth behind them. I'd thought he was done, but apparently he still had more to say; when he continued speaking, his tone had gentled and his gaze had grown serious.

"Even when I'm not with you, I can feel myself being drawn wherever you are, like a goddamned physical tether connects us. And it's not going away; if anything, it's getting stronger the more time I spend with you."

He swallowed roughly.

"I've never felt anything like this before, and I *know* you feel it too," he said, his voice low. "It's undeniable – like a magnetic force. Like gravity. And it's not something I can control, or change, or stop. It just *is*."

His eyes softened as he recognized the raw fear in mine. "Don't be scared, Bee. Don't you know I'd never hurt you?"

"I know that," I whispered, realizing it was true as soon as the words left my mouth. He'd been protecting me since the day we met. From fire hydrants, from Gordon, even from myself.

He slowly leaned toward me, resting his forehead against mine and closing his eyes. "I don't think I can stay away from you anymore," he admitted quietly, exhaling a breath and trying to shake off some of the tension in his shoulders.

"Then don't," I said simply, my mouth twisting up in a smile as his eyes popped open. His blue eyes stared into mine for a fraction of a second, evaluating whether or not I was serious, and then his mouth crashed down against mine.

His lips were demanding, his tongue tracing the seam of my lips and seeking entrance almost immediately. He backed me even more firmly against the truck, his body pressed flush against mine. My hands found their way into his unruly dark hair and I pulled him closer, standing on my tiptoes to reach him.

He smelled deliciously of fall again, and tasted even better. I grumbled a complaint when his mouth left mine to trail kisses along my jawline and down my neck. He laughed at the sound, a dark sexy chuckle that nearly set my panties on fire with want. Needing more, I hooked a leg around his waist and tried to pull him closer. He must've shared my thoughts – his hands immediately cupped my ass as he lifted me from the ground, allowing both my legs to wrap around his waist as he held me pinned against the truck. Tugging on his hair, I managed to get his lips off my neck and back on mine.

Usually when I kissed someone new for the first time, there was an adjustment period – a few fumbling moments spent learning how his mouth moved and adapting to it.

It wasn't like that with Finn. It was like our mouths knew each other, like my lips had been designed to fit exclusively with his. I wasn't a religious person; I didn't believe in past lives or reincarnation. But if someone had asked me in that moment if I'd ever lived before, I would've said yes, because I must have known Finn before this lifetime. Kissing him was like coming home after an impossibly long journey – one so long I'd not only forgotten what home looked like, but that it even existed in the first place.

Our mouths explored, a passionate melding of lips and

tongues and teeth. I wanted to drink him in, to bottle him up and carry him around with me so I'd never be without this feeling again – this sensation of completeness, of utter *rightness* – that made me ache with the need to laugh and weep and lose myself in him.

I gasped when I shifted in his arms and felt the strength of his arousal through his jeans. Finally seeming to realize that we were in a compromising position in the middle of the street, Finn pulled his face away from mine and looked into my eyes as he tried to slow his breathing. His eyes were dark, hazy with desire and surely matching the look in mine.

"We have to slow down," he whispered, kissing my forehead.

I groaned in response.

Laughing, he set me down on my feet and wrapped his arms around me. My arms twined around his neck and my head nestled into the crook of his neck. A feeling of contentment filled me when his chin came to rest on top of my hair, and I thought back to the first time we'd hugged like this. I remembered thinking how well we fit together, like two missing puzzle pieces. After tonight, that feeling was only amplified.

"Come on," he said, detangling our limbs. "Let me walk you to your door." I opened my mouth to protest, but he cut me off. "Don't even try. I'm walking you to your damned door, Bee."

We walked quietly up the stairs, stopping outside my patio door.

"You could come in, you know," I said, stretching up onto my tiptoes to plant a kiss on his lips. Finn groaned and pulled away.

"My self-control is hanging by a thread, here. Please don't tempt me."

"Fine," I shrugged and turned to the door, not wanting him to see that his denial confused and hurt me. No one had ever turned me down before. "Your loss."

"Hey," he said, spinning me back around to face him. Tilting my chin up, he forced my eyes to meet his. "Believe me, I want nothing more than to stay with you. I want you pretty fucking desperately, if I'm being honest. The fact that you'd even doubt that is crazy."

Suddenly, appallingly, my eyes were filling with tears. "Maybe I am. Crazy, that is. I'm fucked up, okay? You don't know the first thing about me. And if you did, you'd probably just run." I tried to break away from the grasp he had on my face, but he held firm. "I can't give you what you want. A– a relationship. Even if I wanted to, I can't make you any promises," I hiccupped.

Finn leaned in and slowly kissed each teardrop from my cheeks. "First of all, I don't want to hear you call yourself crazy, or fucked up, or anything like that ever again. Secondly, did I ask you to make me any promises? No." His eyes radiated sincerity and warmth. "Nothing has to change. Well, other than the fact that I'm going to be kissing you as often as you'll let me, because your mouth is amazing. Seriously, I may have to go home and write a song about it. We'll play it at our next show; I'll call it *Ode to Brooklyn's Orifices*. It'll be an instant Top-40 hit, just you wait."

I deteriorated into giggles – he was so ridiculous. "I hate you," I sighed, my laughter gradually subsiding.

"Impossible," he grinned, pressing a chaste kiss to my lips and watching as I opened the door to my apartment. "I'll call you tomorrow."

"I'm sure that's what you tell all the girls," I teased.

His face turned serious. "Bee, there are no other girls. There's never been anyone real for me except you." A wistful expression crossed his face. "It's always been you."

My heart stuttered in my chest at his words and I gripped the doorframe to keep myself steady.

"Goodnight," I whispered, overwhelmed.

"Goodnight, Bee." He winked at me before turning to walk down the stairs. I closed the door and brought a hand up to trace my slightly swollen lips, the only tangible proof I had of what had just happened between us. Otherwise, I might've dismissed it as some kind of misguided fantasy.

Could I do this? Could I get involved with Finn and remain emotionally detached? He said he wasn't going to stay away from me anymore, and I didn't want him to. He was my friend and all I knew was that I'd missed him this past week. But could I sleep with him without letting all my walls come crashing down? I felt like I'd been asking myself that question for months as Finn and I slowly circled each other. And now that we'd finally collided, I still wasn't sure what my decision would be.

Sure, I was getting better – going to therapy, thinking about my mom and facing up to my past. That didn't mean I was *normal*, and I was certainly not well adjusted enough to give myself to another person in a committed relationship.

I needed to sort out my own shit before I could even consider taking a leap like that. As if that wasn't enough of a hurdle, I also doubted I would ever get to a place where I could be fully honest with Finn about my past – and he was too pushy to ever be content with being left in the dark. This relationship was a disaster, a ticking time bomb waiting to explode, even in theory.

I was confused, and I definitely needed time to think about everything. I was also too tired to deal with the gamut of emotions battling for my attention.

Channeling Scarlett O'Hara, my all-time favorite literary lady and clearly a formative influence on my development, I decided I couldn't think about the Finn situation right now – I'd think about it tomorrow.

After all…*tomorrow is another day.*

Chapter Nine

Bare Walls

I was afraid of the top bunk. It was too high off the ground.

At home, I'd had a pink bed – Mommy always called it my princess bed. She'd painted my bedroom to look like a scene from one of my favorite fairytales, and the walls were covered with princesses and fairies and knights and even a magic castle. The ceiling was painted with stars and clouds and a green sparkly dragon. Every night, she'd read me stories before bed, and I would stare at my walls and pretend I was skipping down the paths of an enchanted forest, or locked high up in the tallest tower of the castle. Sometimes, Mommy and I would read a new story and afterwards she would get out her paintbrushes and add to my walls.

I wondered if another little girl was sleeping in my princess room now.

I looked up at the chipping paint of the gray ceiling in my new room, stained with brown and green splotches. My foster mother didn't know how to paint castles or stars or dragons.

The house was quiet. I'd been lying in my bunk for hours but I couldn't sleep. I was scared of what I knew I'd see when my eyes drooped closed. I missed my room. I missed Mommy. I missed bedtime stories and the way she'd always sing as she painted.

Slipping quietly down the bunk bed ladder, I adjusted the too-long sleeves of my pajamas and padded out into the hall. I shared a bedroom with three other girls, but they were all older than me and they snored and drooled and thrashed as they slept.

I moved down the hallway on my tiptoes, trying not to make any noise. My foster mother got mad when she caught us out of bed at night, even if we'd had bad dreams. I'd been here for a few weeks now, but I'd learned the first night that there would be no bedtime stories or soft hands to tuck me in.

When I reached the back door, I pushed it open cautiously; I knew from coming here almost every night that it would squeak if I moved it too fast. I stepped out onto the porch, my bare feet cold on the uneven wooden planks. Sitting down on the steps that led into the backyard, I propped my head in my hands and looked up at the sky. There were no stars, here. No green sparkly dragons, either. Just clouds and swirling darkness.

"You shouldn't be out here, you know."

I startled, my head whipping around to peer into the dark corner of the porch where the voice had come from. It was a boy's voice, deeper and rougher than my own. I curled in on myself, frightened as I watched him emerge from the shadows.

"You don't have to be scared of me," he said, sitting down on the step next to me. Close but not too close. "But you shouldn't be out here. It's late and it's cold."

I stared at him.

"You're the one who doesn't talk," he stated, looking down at me.

I nodded.

"I just got here a few days ago," he sighed sadly. "I can't sleep either."

I looked up at the sky again, seeking a star, but there were still none behind the clouds. The boy didn't seem like he wanted to hurt me. He was older by a few years, probably nine or ten. I was surprised he was even talking to me. Most of the older kids didn't want to spend time with the "little mute freak."

"Are you scared?" he asked softly. When I looked over at him, there was no teasing in his eyes – only kindness and maybe some sadness too. He understood. He hadn't asked what I was scared of, but it didn't matter – fear is fear.

I nodded slowly.

"Want to hear a story?" he questioned, his voice unsure.

I felt my lips turn up in a small smile. I nodded again, turning to look at him.

"Okay," he took a deep breath, his forehead scrunching up as he thought about where to start. I doubted his story would be as good as Mommy's, but any story was better than none at all.

120

The boy looked up to the dark sky before he began.

"Once upon a time, there was a beautiful princess named Andromeda. When she was born, her parents, the king and queen, were so proud of her beauty that they bragged she was the most beautiful girl in their kingdom, in their country, in the entire world."

The dark haired boy looked over at me to make sure I was following his story. I watched him quietly, enthralled by his words. It had been weeks since someone had talked to me – really talked to me. The therapist visited each week, but she didn't say much; she just asked too many questions that I had no answers for.

"When the sea nymphs heard what the King and Queen were saying about Andromeda's loveliness, they were enraged; until now, they'd always been the most beautiful creatures in the land, and they weren't ready to give up their title. The jealous nymphs begged Poseidon, the god of the sea, to send a terrible monster to Andromeda's homeland and to destroy the kingdom."

I perched on the edge of my seat, my eyes wide as I watched the boy and listened to his fascinating tale.

"The evil sea monster destroyed towns and killed villagers, and the King and Queen were desperate to end the suffering of their people. They asked an Oracle – the wisest man in the kingdom – how they could stop the monster's violent attacks." *He gazed up at the clouds overhead.* *"The Oracle told them the only way to end the violence was to sacrifice their beautiful daughter Andromeda to the sea monster."*

I gasped.

"They had no choice, if they wanted to save their people. So, they chained her to a rock in the middle of the ocean and left her there – alone and defenseless. When the monster appeared, with its razor sharp teeth and evil red eyes, Andromeda knew she was going to die."

The boy looked over at me, his blue eyes intense.

"Suddenly, out of the sky, the hero Perseus appeared, flying on his winged horse Pegasus. He took one look at the beautiful Andromeda, fell instantly in love with her, and killed the evil monster before it could even touch her." *The boy*

smiled softly. *"The princess was reunited with her parents, who were thrilled to have their daughter back. The very next day Andromeda and Perseus were married, and from that moment on they lived happily ever after."*

The boy fell silent, his tale over. I'd never heard a story like that before, and I was fascinated. Mommy had never told stories about sea monsters, flying horses, nymphs, or gods!

I had so many questions that I wanted to ask this boy – where he'd heard such a tale, and whether he knew any more like it. I wanted to thank him for sharing his strange story, but I still hadn't spoken to anyone since Mommy had...

I reached up and touched the cut near my shoulder. Though it was wrapped with bandages and the doctor had put stitches in it, it still hurt. It didn't bleed anymore, at least. The rest of my cuts and bruises had faded; it was the only mark I had left to remind me of that day.

I turned back to the boy and caught him staring at me.

"You should go to bed. Your name is Brooklyn, right?"

I nodded, climbing to my feet. The boy stood too, and he seemed shocked when I reached out and grabbed ahold of his hand. I squeezed tightly, hoping it was enough to tell him what I couldn't say out loud.

Thank you.

He glanced down at my small fingers wrapped around his and gently squeezed back.

"You're welcome."

I smiled my first real smile in weeks and disappeared back into the house, leaving the strange lonely boy in the dark.

***

I woke with a start.

I'd never had such a vivid dream about my time in foster care before. It caught me off guard, startling me with its clarity. Sure, I'd had vague memories of the boy who'd told me stories at night. But nothing had ever been that specific. It had felt so real – like I'd really been there, standing on that porch in the darkness.

I absently ran a finger over the jagged scar on my collarbone. It was barely noticeable anymore, just a faint line of lighter pigmentation. The slightly raised, permanent mark of my past was the only physical remnant I carried from that terrible day. Thankfully, my emotional scars weren't nearly as visible.

I bunched my down comforter around me more securely as I stared up at my plain white ceiling, instead envisioning a swirling canvas of cyan and cobalt, dotted with brilliant yellow stars and a luminescent jade dragon. I'd nearly allowed myself to forget the fairytale world my mother had created within the four walls of my tiny childhood bedroom. The dream had brought it all back.

Suddenly, the walls of my room seemed too bare. I had no pictures, no posters, not a single work of art – just plain white walls as unadorned as the day I'd signed my lease. They'd never bothered me before, or maybe I just hadn't noticed the bleak, impersonal nature of my living space. My clothes hung neatly in my closet, meticulously arranged by color and season. My laptop sat on a clutter-free desk. My carpet was vacuumed and there were no piles of clothes or discarded papers anywhere. It looked like a ghost lived here, leaving no footprint as she moved through life.

And after all, wasn't that who I'd become? A girl with no family, no true friends, no emotions to speak of. Had I let myself disappear? Had I forsaken that little girl who'd believed in fairytales and happily ever afters?

Yes. Because it had been easier.

But I wouldn't do it anymore. I would find that little girl again, somehow. I would take back my life from the apparition I'd become.

For the first time in years, I was thankful for one of my nightmares. And as I closed my eyes and drifted back to sleep, I smiled.

***

I awoke the next morning near dawn, feeling more refreshed than I had in weeks. After making coffee, I sat on the roof and studied for a few hours. I had several exams coming up, and between Finn, therapy, and mysterious flower deliveries, I hadn't had much time to focus on my classes.

When ten o'clock rolled around, I walked into Lexi's room and grabbed the picture frame I was looking for from her desk. One pedicured foot dangled over the side of her mattress and a fuzzy halo of red waves quickly disappeared as she yanked her fuchsia comforter up to block the light I'd let in. Growling, she blindly threw a pillow across the room at me, evidently pissed I'd woken her up. I laughed and closed the door gently on my way out.

Looking down at the picture in my hands, I smiled. It had been taken last year at a Halloween party. Lex and I had dressed up as Mario and Luigi, and we looked carefree and happy in the photo – smiling so hard our lopsided black stick-on mustaches threatened to fall off our faces.

Returning to my room, I opened a drawer in my desk and moved aside several neatly stacked spiral notebooks. At the bottom of the drawer, I finally found what I was looking for. Two small, faded photos of my mother were all I had left. They were timeworn and tattered, but they were precious to me. She looked beautiful in them – young and incandescently happy as she grinned at whoever had taken the photos.

One was a portrait of her alone, leaning into the wind on a pier in California. Her arms were thrown up as she raced through the salty ocean spray toward the photographer. The second was a photo of the two of us. I was young, probably three or four, and she held me suspended in her arms. She was looking at me with the pure, unadulterated love only a mother can give, and I was looking back at her like she was my whole universe. Because she had been.

Tears filled my eyes, but they were happy. I'd been loved – I had the proof right here in my hands. And it had been neglected that drawer, gathering dust, for far too long. Dashing the moisture from my eyes, I grabbed the three photos I'd collected and made my way to the driveway. I hopped into Lexi's car and drove straight to the closest photography store, where I knew I could have the prints enlarged and enhanced.

After explaining exactly what I wanted, I left the photos in the capable hands of the shop owner and headed across town to Andler's, the only local mom-and-pop hardware store that was still in business. Most of the others had crumbled under financial strains in the recent recession, unable to compete when a national chain home improvement superstore had opened just outside of town. I wasn't much for DIY, but whenever I needed to buy replacement light bulbs or duct tape, I'd head to Andler's. I liked to think I was supporting the little guy.

Considering the early hour and the fact that it was Saturday morning, I was unsurprised to find that I was the youngest customer in the shop by at least three decades. I was also the only female.

As I walked in, six male heads swiveled around and performed a frank assessment of me. Equally quickly, they dismissed me and returned their attention to the items they were purchasing, undoubtedly assuming I was a lost sorority girl who'd wandered in by accident. I typically would've been peeved, but a glance down at my attire had me swallowing my indignation; my candy-apple red, plunging v-neck, emblazed with the words *Surrender Dorothy* in black script across my chest, was a far cry from the plaid lumberjack look most of these men were sporting. The wedged strappy red sandals and slim black capris I was wearing probably weren't helping my credibility as a DYI'er either.

I obviously hadn't given much thought to appropriate outfit selection when I rushed out this morning.

Head held high, I wandered further into the quiet store, looking for the paint section. It took me a few minutes, but I eventually found the colors I'd been searching for amidst what seemed like thousands of cardstock sample palettes. I grabbed the two I needed and made my way to the front counter, where a thin, balding, taciturn man of middle years was mixing paint.

"Can you mix me a gallon of each of these, please?" I asked, handing over the two paint samples and attempting to subtly shift my shirt higher to hide the cleavage he'd begun to eye rather enthusiastically. His fingers lingered on mine as he took the cardstock from me, and I suppressed a shudder. The man, whose nametag read Hank, leered at me with a suggestive smile that was missing more than a few teeth before disappearing into the back room. Presumably to mix my paint. Or to grab some zip ties and rope that he could use to restrain and abduct me. It was pretty much a toss up, at this point.

I was mentally calculating the probability of my being able to outsprint Hank in my flimsy – but oh so cute – wedges when he reappeared, a can of paint in each hand. When he told me the total, I tossed a few bills down on the countertop and hurriedly grabbed the paint can handles. I headed for the door, not even waiting for my change in my hurry to get away from Hank's ogling, the less than friendly customers, and the uncomfortable store atmosphere.

"Come back again real soon, sweetheart!" Hank called after me as I used one hip to prop open the door.

"Not on your life," I muttered under my breath. So much for my plan to support local small businesses. Next time, I was totally going to Home Depot, with its brightly lit aisles and plethora of cute employed college boys in orange aprons, eager to fill my every need. Okay, maybe not *every* need. But at least those that involved paint and hardware.

I finally managed to swing the door open, elbowing my way outside and struggling to balance both the paint and my purse while extracting my car keys. I was looking down, cursing under my breath, when a large hand closed over mine and grabbed both cans of paint before I could even react. Startled, I jumped about a foot in the air and my purse dropped to the pavement, exploding on impact and sending everything, from tampons to my cellphone, flying in different directions. I watched forlornly as my favorite lip gloss rolled under my car and out of sight. The puddles riddling the parking lot all contained various forms of indistinguishable goo and piles of trash, insuring that I would never again be putting that tube anywhere near my lips.

"Well, at least you didn't scream this time," a familiar husky voice chuckled from behind me. Every muscle in my body tensed with anger and I froze, still facing the car. "But seriously, Bee, we need to work on your reflexes if you're going to pee your pants in fear every time I approach you. It's either that or you start wearing adult diapers, and I don't think that's going to work for me." His voice was threaded with amusement.

I turned, exceedingly slowly, to face him. Or, more accurately, to glare at him. I unleashed my iciest look, the one typically reserved for ass-grabbers and would-be rapists who got a bit too friendly on the dance floor.

Of course it had no effect on him.

He stood there, grinning like an idiot at me, looking more gorgeous than ever. His eyes crinkled, alight with humor and something less-easily defined. His toned arm muscles were on display as he held the paint cans aloft, the tattooed skin of his right bicep standing out prominently. I remembered the first time I'd seen the inky whorls that encased his upper arm – how I'd wanted to trace my fingers along the swirling patterns. Followed by my tongue.

Brooklyn! Pull it together. Jesus Christ.

I took a harsh swallow to banish those thoughts and refocused on how pissed I was, hoping like hell he hadn't recognized the lust that had undoubtedly just flickered across my face.

"Well, maybe if you would stop SNEAKING UP ON ME," I yelled, launching myself into his space so I was nearly pressed against him and stomping one wedged sandal with indignation, "I wouldn't scream or drop all of my things or lose my FAVORITE LIP GLOSS. I *loved* that lip gloss, Finn. And now, it's in a gutter. A sticky, gooey, gutter. And why are you even here? Why are you *always* here? Are you stalking me or something?"

His lips twitched with amusement and I could tell he was trying desperately not to laugh. "Did you just stomp your foot at me?" he asked, shoulders shaking with barely-contained mirth.

I glared at him and jerked my chin higher. I would *not* let him embarrass me. I would *not* back down. And I definitely would *not* continue to fantasize about kissing him until I ran out of air and passed out in his arms.

Shit.

"I don't think I've ever seen anyone over the age of five do that," he choked out, breaking down at last and throwing his head back to laugh at me. I smacked him hard on the arm, pivoted, and bent to retrieve some of my scattered belongings.

Finn was wiping tears from his eyes and still chuckling when I felt him squat down beside me. Then it was my turn to hold in the giggles, as I watched Finn Chambers – campus' very own mythical sex god and legendary badass – scooping up my tampons and shoving them into my purse like they were on fire or dripping with arsenic. When everything – with the exception of one tube of Sexy Mother Pucker – was back in my purse, we stood up and faced each other.

I was still muttering under my breath about rude boys and the loss of my gloss, when Finn stepped forward into my space and tilted my chin up so I was staring into his eyes. Words died on my tongue, my brain frazzled into static, and all I could think about was last night. My legs wrapped around his waist as he pressed me into the side of a pickup truck, his lips roaming down my neck, his mouth kissing away the tears that tracked down my cheeks.

His eyes captured mine and held, the smoldering desire I saw burning in them telling me that he was thinking about last night too. One hand slowly lifted to stroke my cheek, his fingers skimming lightly over my cheekbone in a soft, almost reverent caress. The other hand threaded into my long ponytail and, with a gentle tug, he pulled me closer. I went willingly, my anger long forgotten.

His head lowered until his forehead was resting in the crook of my neck. He inhaled deeply, then let out a groan. "God, you smell incredible. Like cinnamon and apple pie. It should be illegal to smell the way you do."

I let out a breathy laugh, which cut off sharply when I felt Finn's tongue trace slowly up my neck. I shivered when his lips reached my ear and he tugged at the lobe with his teeth. His hands moved to my hips and he walked me slowly backwards until I was pressed between his body and the side of Lexi's car.

"What is it with you and cars?" I breathed teasingly.

His head lifted abruptly from its lavish appreciation of my earlobe and he stared down at me, eyes suddenly serious. "It's got very little to do with cars, and everything to do with you. Doesn't matter where – I'm always going to want you, Bee. Every time I see you, it takes everything in me not to drag you against the nearest wall and taste that perfect pink mouth of yours." His hooded gaze dropped to my lips.

His words sent another shiver through me, and I had a sudden realization that if he was this sensual in a public parking lot, he would be a different creature entirely if – okay, *when* – we got behind closed doors. My thighs clenched together at that thought and I squirmed a bit under his heated gaze.

"My very own caveman," I drawled in a perfect, much-rehearsed Southern drawl that would make Vivien Leigh proud. He smirked roguishly and then, before I could react, his mouth captured mine.

His hands gently cupped my face with a tenderness that belied the demands of his lips. My mouth parted on a gasp and his tongue sought mine immediately. I began to respond to his kiss, my hands twining up to grip his broad shoulders. When my tongue stroked gently against his in return, Finn groaned and pulled away, his breathing labored. Resting his forehead against mine, his blue eyes were full of tenuously-leashed passion.

He closed his eyes and pulled a deep breath in through his nose, trying to calm himself. I smirked, enjoying the effect I'd had on him, and he stepped back to put a few feet between us, as if our close proximity was too tempting for him to remain in control.

"What's with the paint?" he asked, voice rough as he gestured toward the forgotten paint cans by my feet.

"I'm going to paint my bedroom," I responded with a casual shrug, as if it was no big deal, something I did every week. As if I were one of those girls – like Lexi – who spent hours on Pinterest looking at recipes, crafting ideas, and the 99 ways you can "upcycle" old newspapers into your very own fashion line. I had never and would never be that girl – planning my imaginary wedding twelve years in advance and picking out color palettes for my dream house. *Never*.

Finn raised a questioning eyebrow at me but didn't comment on my sudden desire to redecorate.

"Do you have rollers?" he asked.

I stared at him blankly for a minute, then looked away a bit sheepishly when I realized that, in my hurry to leave Andler's, I'd forgotten to grab paintbrushes and rollers. I guessed I'd be making that trip to Home Depot after all.

"No," I said, crossing my arms defensively over my chest, mentally daring him to make fun of me. There would definitely be no more make-out sessions if he did, and I made sure my glare told him exactly that.

He smiled as if he could read my thoughts and, for once, didn't tease me.

Smart choice.

"What about brushes? Coveralls? Painter's tape? Drop cloths? An edger? Primer?" He continued to rattle off paint supplies – none of which I had purchased – until I couldn't even remember them all. I looked at him perplexedly, a bit taken aback. *Who knew painting required so many materials?*

"Okay, so maybe I forgot a few things," I mumbled, not looking at him. His muffled laughter brought my eyes back to his face.

"I'll meet you at your place in a few hours," he sighed. "I have to go grab some supplies."

"I don't need your help," I snapped automatically, trying to cover the flash of anxiety that had streaked through me at his words. "You're not my boyfriend. And I'm not going to fuck you as a reward, if that's what you're thinking."

"I helped Ty paint his bedroom last month and, shockingly, I didn't fuck him after," he growled menacingly. His eyes, which had been filled with warmth only seconds ago, were now flinty with anger. "And no, I'm not your boyfriend. But last time I checked, I was your friend. Friends help each other out – especially when one *friend* doesn't know her ass from her elbow when it comes to painting."

"Okay," I agreed, casting a caustically acquiescent smile up at him. "You can help."

"You are the most infuria–" he broke off and took another calming inhale. It seemed he had to do this at near-constant intervals when he was around me. "I don't know why I bother," he muttered.

"Because of my sparkling personality?" I asked, laughing a little at his blatant frustration with me.

"Somehow, I don't think that's it," he said dubiously. "I'll be at your house by two."

I nodded in acceptance. He was right – I *didn't* know my ass from my elbow when it came to home improvement. I could use all the help I could get.

"What are you doing here anyway?" I asked, glancing around the near-empty parking lot. His bike was parked a few spaces down from Lexi's car.

"I was headed to the diner," he said with a nod in the direction of Maria's, the tiny breakfast place that abutted Andler's and hadn't been redecorated since the early 1970s. The retro feel gave the restaurant character, though, and it was a popular venue for hungover coeds after a long night of partying. Their pumpkin pancakes were legendary during the fall season.

My stomach rumbled at the thought and, with a final longing look cast at the restaurant, I glanced back at Finn. If he weren't there, I would have happily treated myself to a short stack, smothered in whipped cream and syrup. As it was, I'd have cut off my left foot before going in there now and eating with him in front of half of the student body. If I did, I might as well paint a sign across my ass that read "FINN CHAMBERS TAPPED THIS LAST NIGHT," given all the gossip our morning appearance together would prompt.

If we were going to get involved, I wanted a signed contract – possibly in blood – stating that no one would find out about us. My reputation was tarnished enough without adding a tryst with Finn to the list.

His lips twitched in amusement as he evaluated me.

"Don't suppose you want to get pancakes with me?" he asked, a knowing smile playing out across his face.

"No!" I blurted, my fast response a dead giveaway of my

horror at the suggestion of such a date-like activity. "I mean, I have errands to run," I muttered, more subdued.

"*Right*," he said, lips curled up in a sexy dark smirk. I wanted to pounce on him and punch him at the same time. He was fully aware of the effect he had on me. He was tying me up in knots – and he was enjoying it, the smug bastard. "I'll just go enjoy my pancakes alone, then. See you in a few hours." He winked, then turned and walked into Maria's, leaving me hungry for more than just breakfast. I slumped back against Lexi's car, drained from the interaction.

Crap.

I shakily loaded the paint cans into the trunk and got behind the wheel. Taking a steadying breath, I determined not to let Finn get under my skin. Maybe I'd let him under my panties later, though.

Damn, I'm such a slut.

I felt like an emotional yo-yo, rejecting Finn one minute and kissing him the next. I wanted to slap some sense into myself. Instead, I did what I did best and pushed the thoughts from my mind. Starting the engine, I pulled onto Main Street and headed across town to the grocery store. I had to pick up some things to make dinners for the week, refill my birth control prescription at the pharmacy, and make it back to the photo store to pick up my prints all before Finn got to my apartment at two.

A glance at the clock on the dashboard informed me that it was already past noon. I stepped on the gas pedal, speeding Lexi's car through several yellow lights in my haste. I did *not* want him to beat me to the house. Something told me that having Finn Chambers unsupervised in my bedroom wasn't a good idea.

***

I was steering my cart down the aisle of the grocery store, gathering items for the week, when my cellphone rang.

"Hello?"

The only answer I received was in the form of heavy, disturbing breathing.

"Stop. Calling. Me." I growled into the phone. "Is this Gordon?"

More breathing.

"I don't know who the hell this is, but if you keep doing this I will call the police. Got it, sicko?"

The breathing stopped for a minute and I thought the line had gone dead, but a quick glance at the screen showed it was still connected. Just before I hung up, I heard what sounded like faint laughter from the other line.

It wasn't the gleeful laughter of a twelve year-old prankster with nothing better to do for amusement; it was a sinister laugh, menacing and full of dark promise. The laugh of a man I didn't know and definitely did not want to know.

I disconnected the call and stood frozen in the middle of the grocery store. This was the second call I'd received. Then there was the deadly flower arrangement that had been delivered to my room. Could they be connected? Who wanted to scare me this much? It could be Gordon, but I doubted he would take things this far. And he probably didn't possess enough brainpower to break into my apartment without leaving any traces behind.

I placed a quick call to the police station, asking for Officer Carlson. When he answered, he halfheartedly assured me that while they had done everything in their power to discover who'd dropped off the flowers, they had no answers for me at this time. After telling me to take extra precautions in locking my doors and windows, and to call if any more suspicious deliveries appeared, he hung up. I'd considered telling him about the phone calls, but quickly decided against it. It wasn't like there was anything he could do to help; I somehow doubted that the paunchy, doughnut-loving officer had ever solved a case in his career.

I didn't want to think about my phone stalker right now. I had enough on my mind, what with the dead-sexy man arriving at my house in – I glanced at my cellphone – less than an hour.

Crap!

Phone call forgotten, I rushed to the front of the store, paid for my groceries, and was on my way to the pharmacy within minutes. Grabbing my prescription, I headed to the photo store which was, thankfully, located in the same plaza. My photos were ready, and they looked perfect. I'd had them enlarged onto big 24x36 inch canvases that would adorn my newly painted walls. I thanked the shop owner countless times before paying and lugging the three large photo canvases to the car, where I laid them gently in the backseat. Smiling, I raced home, eager to beat Finn there and start redecorating.

Though it was well into the afternoon by the time I'd gotten all of the food put away, Lexi was still sleeping soundly in her room. I wasn't surprised. If napping were a sport, that girl would take home Olympic gold every time.

I lugged both cans of paint and all three blown-up photos into my bedroom and cast an assessing glance around the room. The only pieces of furniture were my desk, chair, bedside table, and bedframe. I struggled to maneuver the heavy oak desk into the hallway for several minutes until Lexi appeared in my doorway, coffee mug in hand and eyes wide.

"What are you doing?" she asked, her gaze moving from the displaced furniture to the cans of paint.

"I'm redecorating."

She stared at me like I'd said I was planning to tattoo a swastika on my forehead and join a cult that worshipped Cabbage Patch dolls. "Excuse me? I must have misheard you. I thought you just said that you, Brooklyn Turner, were redecorating your room. The same girl who told me that I was forbidden, on pain of death, from putting up wallpaper and cute decorations in the living room."

I rolled my eyes. "You were going to paste a wall-quote that said *Live, Laugh, Love* in magenta, five foot tall lettering across the wall over our couch. You seriously didn't anticipate me vetoing that idea?"

She harrumphed in frustration, taking another sip of her coffee and realizing she wasn't going to win this argument.

"So how was your night with the Ken doll?" she asked, switching gears. "Was it everything you dreamed of and more?" She snorted into her mug.

"Sarcasm is *so* not your strong suit, Lex," I said, smiling. I turned back to the desk and began yanking it toward the door once

134

more. "And actually, nothing happened with Landon. I walked home."

"What?" she exclaimed, surprise evident in her voice. "Why the change of heart?"

I sighed. "Are you going to help me move this desk?"

"Only if you tell me what happened with Landon."

"Bitch," I muttered. "Fine. I just wasn't into it, okay? He was hot, but I couldn't clear my mind enough to enjoy it."

"Clear your mind of what? Or, should I be asking *of who*?" she pressed.

I spun around to glare at her. "Before you even start, this has nothing to do with Finn," I lied.

"Oh, you are so full of shit! Brooklyn Turner has a crush! I can't freaking believe this!" She squealed, dancing into my bedroom and slinging an arm over my shoulder. "I've been waiting *years* for this to happen. And this is perfect! I've always dreamed of us dating best friends! Ohmigod! We should all go to this party tomor—"

"LEXI!" I yelled, cutting her off before she could start planning our double wedding, thus inducing one of my panic attacks. "There is nothing going on between Finn and I. We're friends. F-R-I-E-N-D-S," I spelled out emphatically, hoping she'd listen to me for once.

"You let all your *friends* pin you against the side of their truck and kiss you like that?" Finn's deep voice asked from the doorway.

God dammit. Was the man incapable of just announcing his presence like a normal person?

I groaned.

Lexi spun around, spied him leaning casually in the doorway, and squealed happily. I think she actually may have started jumping up and down in delight, but I was too busy looking around for a rope to hang myself with to be sure. The small digital clock on my desk read 2:05 – he was right on time, so I couldn't even be mad at him for eavesdropping.

"You bitch! I can't believe you were selling me that 'just friends' bullshit!" she smacked my arm and glared down at me.

135

"Haven't you heard of knocking?" I snapped, ignoring Lexi and blasting an icy stare in Finn's direction.

"I *did* knock. No one answered," he said, glaring back at me. His voice was calm but his eyes were stormy as they pierced mine.

Nope, he definitely wasn't happy about my 'just friends' comment.

"You. Me. Details. Later," Lexi demanded, still glaring at me. Turning to Finn, a sunny smile crossed her face and she sighed. "Be patient with her. She's emotionally retarded."

I let out a mortified groan and Finn tried – and failed – to hold in his laughter as Lexi wandered into the hallway and disappeared. When she was gone, a thick silence descended on the room. A charge seemed to build in the air as Finn and I stared at each other, the laughter dying slowly from his eyes. He took a step toward me into the room and I immediately stepped back, maintaining the space between us. A dark look crossed his face and his eyes narrowed.

Striding across the room, he was in front of me in seconds. I'd backed up until I was flush with the wall, with nowhere further to retreat, and he immediately caged me in with his arms.

"Let's get something straight," he whispered, tone dark with something possessive and slightly scary. "We are *not* just friends. We have never and will never be just friends. So stop twisting this around in that head of yours and making it into something it's not."

"You said nothing had to change," I said defiantly, unwilling to accept his words.

"I've always wanted to fuck you. You've always wanted to fuck me. Nothing's changed as far as I can tell," he said, a smug smile crossing his face.

"I don't want to fuck you! You are the cockiest, most conceited, arrogant asshole I've ever met. I wouldn't sleep with you if you were the last man left on earth and we were singlehandedly responsible for repopulating the plan—" My tirade was abruptly cut off as his mouth descended on mine.

I responded to his kiss instantly, eagerly, in complete

136

contradiction to my words.

Fuck! What was I doing?

I reeled back and before I could stop myself, my hand shot out and slapped him across the face. I froze, stunned at my own actions. It was like my hand had acted independently of my brain. My face was a mask of shock, my eyes saucer-wide as I stared at the blooming crimson mark on his cheekbone. I hadn't intended to hit him; I'd just been so desperate to put a stop to the kiss – to take back some control.

Breathing hard, I was still mere inches from Finn's face. He looked equally surprised, but his face quickly morphed into something darker. "Just for that, I'm going to make you beg for it before I'll kiss you again," he vowed, rubbing a hand back and forth along his cheek.

"You're going to be waiting forever."

"I've heard that before," he said, a small smile turning up the corner of his mouth. I suddenly remembered another conversation we'd had, after he'd saved me from Gordon, when I'd told him he'd be waiting forever for answers about my past. He'd simply looked over at me and whispered, *I've already been waiting my whole life.*

I still didn't know what that meant.

"I'm sorry I slapped you," I murmured, lifting a hand to trace the red splotch on his cheek. His hand came up to cover mine, holding it gently against his face. "I really am emotionally-challenged sometimes," I reluctantly admitted.

"Sometimes?" Finn lifted a skeptical eyebrow at me.

"Okay, fine, all the time," I grumbled. "Can we paint now?"

"Sure," he agreed, stepping out of my space. As I walked around him to reach the desk, I lifted up on my tiptoes and uncharacteristically pressed a soft kiss to the angry red handprint on his cheek. I felt him smile as I pulled away and began tugging on the desk.

Thankfully, Finn was a lot stronger than me, and he made quick work of moving all my furniture out into the hall. My bed was too big to move, so we pushed it into the middle of the room, stripped it of its bedding, and spread one of the drop cloths Finn had brought over it. He'd also brought over several rollers, white primer, painting tape, and white coveralls that he insisted we both put on.

"You can't paint in that," he said, indicating my red v-neck and capris. I'd already traded my wedges in for a pair of ratty old tennis shoes.

"Fine," I said, grabbing the coveralls, a tank top, and cotton shorts before heading into the bathroom to change. After slipping on the tank and shorts, I stepped into the massive white suit. It had been designed for an adult male, and it was ridiculously large on my small frame. The sheer amount of fabric dwarfed me, with at least a foot of extra material hanging down past each hand and gathering over my feet. I haphazardly pushed up the sleeves and struggled to zip up the front of the coveralls. As soon as my hands fell to my sides, the extra fabric tumbled back down and covered my hands.

This was useless; I wouldn't be able to maneuver my arms, let alone paint an entire bedroom. I trudged back out into the bedroom, concentrating on not tripping over the extra material around my feet. Hearing the sound of Finn's choked laughter, I drew to a stop and slumped my shoulders.

"This isn't going to work," I said, windmilling my fabric-swathed arms in circles in the air. "I look like an idiot."

"You're adorable," Finn said, a soft look in his eyes as he took in the sight of me swallowed up by the enormous coveralls. "Come here," he whispered, crooking a finger to beckon me over to him.

Crossing the room, I stumbled on the bunched fabric and fell forward. Finn's arms shot out and he caught me before I hit the ground, steadying me with his large hands resting on my shoulders.

"Let's fix you," he said, squatting down in front of me and deftly rolling each long pant leg into a cuff I wouldn't trip over. He repeated this with the extra material of each sleeve, making sure I had full range of motion before releasing me. A funny feeling built in my chest as he adjusted my sleeves so

138

painstakingly. There was something intimate about him dressing me, something that went beyond *just friends* or even *friends with benefits*. I looked down at the top of his head and realized something that floored me.

Finn really cared about me.

Not just in friendly way, or an *I'd-like-to-know-what-color-your-panties-are* way. He actually cared.

And it didn't feel impossible, or ridiculous, or even terrifying. To be honest, it felt pretty damn nice.

CHAPTER TEN

FINGER PAINTING

We painted.

I turned on The Civil Wars, an indie duo whose music we both enjoyed, and we covered the walls with primer. The repetition of my roller-brush striking the wall was soothing, and I could feel myself relaxing with each passing minute, finding comfort in the monotony and mindlessness.

Finn began to sing along with the male vocal part and before long, I'd unconsciously picked up the female versus. We sang and painted until there were no more walls left to prime and the CD player had fallen silent after the final track.

"I didn't know you could sing until I saw you up there on stage last night. I thought I was hallucinating at first," Finn laughed, breaking the silence that had descended on us.

"I don't really," I replied, turning in a slow circle to see if we'd missed any spots with the primer. We'd have to wait awhile for it to dry before we could start covering it with the blue shades I'd picked out.

"That's not what it sounded like last night, or just now," Finn noted skeptically. "You've got talent. Why not use it?"

"Singing is something I do just for myself. I don't do it for the applause, or the audience, or the spotlight," I tried to explain. "It's an outlet for me, I guess."

Finn nodded. This, he could understand.

"Why were you there?" I asked. It hadn't escaped my notice that he had his own band, with real fans and scheduled performances; he didn't need to be singing at an open mic night. "It's not exactly Styx."

"Styx is great for when I'm playing with the guys, blowing off steam," Finn said, walking over to lean against my draped bedframe. "But sometimes, when I need a reminder of what's important in my life, I need to play alone and reground myself. Music's one of the only things that can clear my mind. "

"One of? What else works?" I asked, genuinely curious.

"Sex." One side of his mouth curled up in a dark smirk, and he waggled his eyebrows at me playfully. "Don't suppose you want to help me out with that method?"

I glared at him, but there was no heat behind it. His smile became a full-fledged grin, complete with dimple.

"What's all this about? The sudden urge to paint?" he asked, switching topics abruptly and gesturing at the whitewashed walls.

"I needed a change," I said, shrugging. "I looked around this morning and realized how bare my walls were – how empty it made my life seem."

Finn set down his brush and pulled off the paint-spackled plastic gloves covering his hands. Making his way over to my desk, which sat in the hallway just outside my bedroom door, he gently lifted up one of the canvases I'd had printed earlier – the photo of Lexi and me in costume – and examined it.

"You look happy here," he said, smiling as he looked at the photo. Picking up the second canvas, the one of my mom on the pier, he stilled and his face grew serious. "This is your mom?" he asked quietly.

"How'd you know?"

"You look like her," he said. "The eyes, the smile – on the rare occasion you show yours – even the hair. They're the same."

Warmth erupted in my chest at the thought that I might look a little like my mother. I wasn't like her in other ways – not artistic, or forgiving, or kind. I didn't possess her open heart or her capacity for love. But if I looked like her on the outside, maybe it meant that buried deep down beneath my cynicism, trust issues, and jaded bitchiness, I had a little of her within me after all. Maybe, if I looked for hard enough, I could find pieces of her inside myself.

Finn had moved on to examine the third picture, and he looked sad as he took in the sight of the little girl I'd once been, wrapped in my mother's arms. His eyes shifted to me, where I leaned against my bedframe watching him.

"You don't talk about her." It wasn't a question.

"No."

"I didn't talk about my parents for a long time."

"What changed?" I asked, genuinely curious.

"I met you."

That threw me for a loop. "What do you mean, *you met me?*"

"You were the first person I ever really talked to about my parents' death."

My mind was reeling. How could it be that Finn had never discussed his parents before the other night on my rooftop? Granted, I never really talked about my mother either, but he seemed far more adjusted and normal than I ever hoped to be.

"Do you want to – need to? Talk, that is?" I asked, taking a hard swallow to calm my breathing. Jeeze, I was terrible at this. I didn't know the first thing about properly dealing with my own grief, let alone other peoples'.

"Do you?" He turned my own question around on me, pinning me in place with the weight of his intense stare.

Did I?

"I don't know. Sometimes, I think that if I don't talk about her, it will be like she never existed at all. Like she's just some figment my psyche conjured, or an imaginary friend I dreamed up during my childhood. And other times, I think I'd rather not remember anything about her at all, because then it wouldn't hurt so damn much. I'd be free, normal, just like any other college girl. Worried about normal things like boys and homework and whether I'll be invited to the Sig Ep party next weekend.

"But I don't think about those things. I think about death, and loss, and heartache. I wonder why people bother to fall in love, when they know from the start that they'll be separated one day – whether by infidelity or distance or death." I took a deep breath, slightly shocked I'd just admitted all that out loud. "I've never had the luxury of being normal, Finn."

"Normal is boring, Bee. It's not something I'd wish for you." He crossed the room to me, bringing one hand up to gently trace the line of my jaw. "Grief is a kick in the chest. It steals your breath, hits you so hard you think you'll never stand back up again. And it's not just because you're grieving death or heartbreak or loss – you're grieving change. You're grieving the life that might have been, if it hadn't all gotten fucked up along the way."

His other hand joined the one holding my jaw, so he was cupping my face in his hands. I closed my eyes and turned my cheek to rest in one of his palms.

"You could spend forever thinking about the things you'll never experience with your mother – infinity contemplating the memories she won't ever be a part of. But at some point, you have to let the life you should've had go, and start living the one you've got," Finn whispered.

Tears spilled out from under my lashes and he caught them with his fingertips before they could fall. Ignoring the fact that I was a paint-splattered mess, he cradled me against his chest and his lips came to rest in my hair, bringing me comfort as I trembled in his arms.

"Let go, Bee," he whispered.

And I did.

After a time, my tears subsided and I became very aware of the fact that I'd just had a full blown meltdown in Finn's arms. I wanted to run. A month ago, *would've* run; I'd have bolted as fast and as far away as possible. But now, I just moved a step back out of the circle of his arms and wiped the residual tears from my eyes.

"I don't know what's wrong with me. I'm not this person. I've cried more in the past two months than I have in the last fourteen years combined," I said, forcing a laugh. "I'm sorry for falling apart like that."

"You don't have to apologize."

"I think the primer is dry enough for us to paint on now," I said with a sniffle, walking over to the paint cans resting in the corner of my bedroom. Finn followed, quiet for once, and crouched down beside me as I shook up the dark blue paint. He grabbed the lighter shade of blue and, after shaking it thoroughly, he used a screwdriver to pop open the lid.

"So, I was thinking we'd paint the walls the sky blue color, and then make the ceiling the navy, dusk color," I said, explaining what I'd envisioned when I'd picked out my color scheme. "Like the sky at nightfall."

"Bringing the view from your rooftop inside," Finn murmured intuitively.

"Something like that," I said, smiling softly at him. It was weird how well he understood my messed up brain – like we were on the same wavelength all the time.

We painted the walls first. The light cerulean I'd picked was perfect, like the cloudless sky on a crisp fall afternoon. It took nearly two hours, long enough for us to listen through two more full albums. We sang together again, and I could feel the tension and residual sadness from my breakdown melting away.

Being with Finn was as natural as breathing. He didn't demand anything of me, didn't want me to be anyone other than myself. The time passed quickly, and I was silently grateful for his bossy insistence to help; it would have been a much longer process if I'd had to do it all on my own.

While Finn made a trip back to his house to pick up a ladder so we could paint the ceiling, I wandered into the kitchen, threw together some grilled cheese sandwiches, and grabbed a bag of corn chips. It was well past dinnertime; dusk had fallen outside, and we'd been working hard for hours. The least I could do was feed the boy, after everything he'd done for me today.

We took a dinner break when he returned with the ladder, but quickly resumed painting. Lexi had vanished, assumedly to Tyler's apartment, and I'd never been more aware of the fact that I was completely alone with Finn, in my bedroom. Granted, it was more of a disaster site at the moment, but still – standing in an enclosed, semi-dark space with Finn Chambers and my bed was nearly more than I could take.

Don't think about him naked.

Definitely don't think about both of us naked.

Definitely, definitely don't think about both of us naked in my bed.

The more time I spent with him in that room, the harder it was to focus on the task at hand. Being this near to him for hours and completely unable to touch him was torturous for me, yet he seemed completely unaffected. Maybe I was the only one who felt the growing tension between us, filling the air with unspoken promises and unvoiced desires.

He painted with a single-minded determination I couldn't match, evidently intent on finishing the project before the day ended. My arms were aching, my feet were sore from standing all day, and I'd been ready to call it quits hours ago. Between the darkness of the room, the hours of manual labor, and the exhausting battle I was having with my inner hussy – who wanted nothing more than to tackle him and show my eternal gratitude for all he'd done – I was ready to drop.

"Take a break," Finn suggested quietly.

"Am I that obvious?" I asked. I thought I'd been successful at hiding my growing exhaustion, but apparently he was more attuned to my body than I'd realized.

"Brooklyn, you're swaying on your feet. The ceiling is practically done, all that's left to do is touch up the edging. Lie down," he ordered, yanking the drop cloth off my bed to expose my comforter. I moved toward the bed in a daze, truly exhausted. It was past ten – we'd been painting for nearly seven hours.

"Wait," he said, dropping the edger he was holding and walking over to me. I stilled, several feet away from my bed, and watched his approach. He had a smudge of indigo paint on his forehead and another by his jawline, places he'd likely touched absentmindedly with his paint-covered hands. His dark hair was sticking up in wayward clumps and it looked slightly sweaty; for some reason, I found that incredibly sexy. He was usually so put together, so self-assured – Finn looking like a bit of a disheveled mess was something I'd bet not many people had witnessed.

I smiled at the thought.

"You'll ruin your bed if you get in like that," he whispered, coming to a stop inches from me. He reached out a hand and tugged the front zipper of my coveralls, dragging it down so slowly the breath caught in my chest. I don't know how he made stripping me of baggy painting clothes into something sensual, but I shouldn't have been surprised. This was Finn, after all – he could make just about anything sexy.

Except Crocs. No one *can make Crocs sexy.*

When the zipper reached the end of its downward journey, Finn lifted his hands and pushed the material from my shoulders. It slid off quickly, pooling around my feet in a white and blue-splattered cloud and leaving me in only my tank top and shorts.

"Step out," he murmured, taking one of my hands in each of his and guiding me toward him. My heart fluttered in my chest and I felt a swarm of butterflies explode into flight in my stomach. Staring up into his dark eyes, my hands found their way up to rest on his broad shoulders.

His eyes were hooded, and I immediately saw the desire that swirled in their depths. My hands slid from his shoulders around to the front of his coveralls, the residual paint on them leaving blue streaks in their wake. When my fingers found the zipper, they trembled.

Finn leaned down slowly and pressed a kiss to the hollow of my throat. My hands began to move, drifting downward and dragging the zipper along with them. As my fingers traced slowly down across his stomach, I felt the muscles there contract and an involuntary puff of air slipped out from between his lips.

When there was no more tread left in the zipper, I slid my hands lightly back up to his shoulders, taking my time to graze each taut muscle of his abs and chest as I went. His head lifted from the crook of my neck and he stared down into my eyes as I gently shoved the material of his coveralls off his shoulders. His eyes darkened even further, the cobalt irises nearly disappearing into the black of his pupils.

The material dropped around his feet, revealing a tight black v-neck and faded gray jeans that looked like they'd been washed a million times and fit him like a dream. He was utterly still, watching me. Waiting to see what I'd do next.

"Step out," I whispered, echoing his earlier command.

At my words, he took one stride forward and was on me, invading my space completely and hauling me up against

146

his chest. His mouth crashed down against mine and I lifted up automatically onto my tiptoes, determined to meet his kiss head on. I poured all my pent up frustrations from the day into that kiss, letting my lips tell him in no uncertain terms what I'd never admit out loud – that I'd been suffering without his touch for hours and wouldn't, couldn't, stand another minute without his hands on my skin.

He groaned into my mouth, a sound that made me want to do cartwheels around the room because it told me he'd been suffering too – he was just better at hiding it, apparently. His hands were everywhere, skimming from my hips up my sides, just grazing the undersides of my breasts before moving away to explore the small of my back. His fingers lightly traced the exposed skin between the edge of my tank top and the elastic of my thin cotton shorts, and mine were fully ensconced in the unruly hair at the nape of his neck.

His lips were relentless, his tongue unhesitant and proprietary as it entered my mouth, like he was reclaiming something that was already his. I tugged at his hair, trying to pull him even closer – to deepen his crushing kiss.

I wanted more.

His hands slipped beneath my tank top and traced along my spine, sending shivers radiating through all my limbs. I'd never felt like this – so out of control in my need to possess someone. And I'd certainly never before wanted to be possessed in turn. But right now, I had to push all of my normal hang-ups about sex from my mind, because Finn was invading my senses completely and using up all my brainpower. When he was in my head, there was simply no room for anyone, anything, else.

I wasn't a virgin by a long shot. I liked sex, a lot – it was my drug of choice, after tequila. But this was different. It was all-consuming. A need like I'd never experienced rushed through my veins and demanded more of him. His hands moved again, and then my tank top was on the floor and I was standing before him in just my bra and shorts.

Thank goodness I'd had foresight enough to put on my cute lace bra set from Victoria's Secret before I got dressed this morning.

"Beautiful," Finn whispered, gazing down at me and dragging his thumb across my bottom lip. Before he could move it away, I gave it a playful nip with my teeth and then traced my tongue lightly along the pad.

He let out another throaty groan, and pulled me against him again so my nearly bare chest aligned with his. My hands slithered down his sides and found the bottom hem of his shirt, yanking it up impatiently when I realized I was too short to lift it over his head.

He chuckled darkly and bent slightly at the waist, lifting his arms so the shirt could slide free. I carelessly tossed it next to me with no regard for my aim, and watched as the black v-neck sailed into a pan of cerulean paint.

"That's the second shirt of mine you've ruined," he grumbled in my ear, pressing kisses along my jawline.

"I'm sure I'll think of a way to make it up to you," I breathed, gasping as his mouth moved over a particularly sensitive spot beneath my ear.

Before I could react, I was lifted into the air, cradled in Finn's arms as if I weighed no more than a feather, and gently laid down on one of the paint-splotched drop cloths covering my hardwood floor. I could feel the slightly tacky wetness of the paint sliding over my bare back as he laid me down, but I quickly forgot about that as he settled over me, with one arm braced on either side of my head and his legs straddling mine.

He kissed me again, and I leaned up into him so our chests were touching, skin to skin. My hands wrapped around his back and I explored the solid muscles there, tracing their fluid movements with the tips of my fingers. I used my grip on his back to leverage myself, sitting up beneath him. He rose with me, leaning back on his knees and somehow never disengaging his mouth from mine as we moved.

We kneeled eye to eye, our breathing ragged as we stared at one other. He stilled as his eyes flickered down to notice the light scar that marred my collarbone, and his eyes clouded over with more emotions than just lust; something darker, harder, scarier filled his eyes as he saw the mark my childhood had left behind, but it was tempered by a tenderness that made my heart turn over. He was angry that someone had hurt me. He didn't know who, or what, or when it had happened, but I could tell from the storm raging behind those gorgeous cobalt eyes that he hated the idea of me bleeding for any reason.

Someone examining my imperfections so closely should have embarrassed me, and likely would have – except it was Finn. He didn't look at me with pity or disgust; he didn't flinch away or ask probing questions. Instead, he leaned forward and gently kissed the scar, as if tracing it with his lips would make it vanish, and take away the painful memories it was a permanent tribute to.

I wanted to cry. None of the guys I'd slept with in the past had ever even noticed my scar, let alone tried to kiss it better for me. A pang of longing lanced through my chest, one I didn't understand and didn't want to overanalyze at that moment – not when there was a beautiful, half-naked Finn kneeling inches away.

Taking him by surprise, I launched myself at his chest and we toppled roughly backwards. He landed on his back with me sprawled half across his body, my hands planted on his shoulders. Our shift had upset one of the paint pans we'd used earlier, and there was a sudden rush of cerulean liquid leaking across the drop cloth and onto our tangled limbs.

I laughed as Finn realized what had happened, dipping my right hand into a paint puddle near his head and then splaying my fingers wide across his bare chest. When I pulled my hand away, there was a perfect blue handprint over his heart, like some crazy tribal war paint. I giggled at the surprised look that came into his eyes, but my laughter cut off abruptly as they narrowed in a promise of retribution.

"Don't," I half-begged, trying to hold in more giggles as I watched him examine his decorated chest. His eyes shifted to mine and in a flash he was sitting up, with my legs straddling his lap. We were pressed close, nose-to-nose.

"Oh, you asked for it," he said, smiling roguishly as one hand snuck around my back and unhooked my bra with a quickness that could only be achieved with years of practice.

I was so preoccupied with my disappearing bra, I hadn't noticed what his other hand was doing until it was too late. As his right hand tugged each bra strap down the lengths of my arms and threw it to the floor beside me, his left – dripping paint – trailed across my collarbone and between the valley of my now exposed breasts.

I watched, mesmerized, as his long fingers deftly swirled the paint in blue patterns across my skin. His fingers streaked down to my stomach, circling gently and drawing a perfect blue ring around my bellybutton. I would have laughed if I hadn't been so unbelievably turned on.

This gives a whole new meaning to finger-painting.

My own fingers dipped back into the paint by my sides, and I began to paint his body in whorls of color as I explored in turn, creating a labyrinth of blue that matched my own.

His fingers felt like fire as they trailed along my skin, burning a path from my stomach down to the top of my shorts. My hands stilled on his chest and my belly fluttered as his fingertips slid under the elastic, following the band around to the small of my back. With his hands hooked half inside my shorts, he pulled me flush against him. I felt the air leave my lungs in a whoosh as the apex of my thighs brushed against his arousal for the first time – even through his jeans, I could feel how hard he was for me. A sound that might've been a moan escaped before I could stop it.

I'd never been this out of control before; sex had always been a well-choreographed dance, a predetermined sequence of actions with an established conclusion. This was different – it was wild, spontaneous. Finn wasn't playing by any of my rules; he'd abandoned the steps altogether.

And I loved it.

My hands trembled as I reached for the button of his jeans, and he captured them within his own, halting their progress.

"Hey," he whispered, using his nose to nudge my face up so we were looking into each other's eyes. "We don't have to do this, you know."

I waited a beat, seeing the sincerity radiating from his

gaze and knowing that if I asked, he would wait as long as it took for me to be ready.

"We really do," I said resolutely, reaching for the zipper of his jeans again.

"I was hoping you'd say that," he grinned against my mouth; I couldn't respond because he was kissing me again.

Within seconds, he'd rid me of my shorts and panties, and I was struggling to pull his jeans and boxers down his legs. He kicked them off impatiently, and then he was on top of me again, his mouth fused to mine. With one knee, he gently nudged my legs apart and settled in the space between them.

I knew, at that moment, that my life was about to change irrevocably. I saw the change coming – I was standing in the middle of the tracks watching as the train bore down on me. I could've jumped the track. I even could've tried to outrun the damn thing, knowing it was futile but still intent on making an attempt at escape.

I did none of those things.

I looked at Finn and I knew that this would change everything, not just between us, but for me as a person. For years, I'd used sex as nothing more than an avoidance tactic – a way to shut out my grief and bury the hurt. It was an escape; with my body engaged, my mind was, for once, at rest.

This was different – I knew it in my soul, deep in the marrow of my bones, in the essence of my very self.

Finn's words from earlier came back to me.

At some point, you have to let the life you should've had go, and start living the one you've got.

He was right.

Now, as he gently traced my face with his fingertips – no doubt leaving blue streaks along my cheekbones – I realized I was ready to start living.

I leaned up and kissed him, trying to tell him this with my lips.

He'd always been good at reading my mind.

I gasped as he slid inside me, all thoughts fleeing as I tried to acclimate to the feeling of him. As he rocked into me, eyes locked on mine, I met him thrust for thrust and spiraled slowly toward oblivion, my world going fuzzy around the edges. The only thing in focus was the paint-covered man above me, who was staring into my emerald eyes with a look of rapturous incredulity, as if he couldn't quite believe this was happening.

My own mind swirled with the same turbulent ecstasy, reeling at the intimacy of the moment. I almost wanted to look away from his eyes, to break the emotional connection between us, to go back to pretending that this didn't mean anything. But I couldn't – Finn wouldn't let me. And more importantly, I wouldn't let myself.

With our eyes mirroring thoughts neither of us had ever voiced, we let the world disappear and fell utterly into one other.

We were covered in paint – a living, breathing form of art – entwined and breathless and caught up in each other. Spackled in blue from head to toe, a masterpiece of limbs, we lay tangled together on my floor and for a single moment in time, the individual creatures called Finn and Brooklyn ceased to exist. We simply weren't *them* anymore – we were one form, one being, connected in the most primitive of dances. Our defenses obliterated in an elegant give and take, an equal exchange of breaths and caresses and thoughts and vulnerabilities, that would alter everything.

Afterward, we stayed wrapped around each other without speaking – as if we both feared what might come next and didn't quite know how to break the silence. It had been intimate – shockingly so. I'd never experienced anything like this before, so I didn't really understand the protocol. Typically by this point, my clothes would be halfway back on and I'd be edging slowly toward the door, preparing for a swift departure and leaving no forwarding address in my wake. But for now, I just let Finn hold me in the circle of his arms and tried not to tense up or bolt.

I'd never cared much about what a guy might be thinking after sex – usually, I'd simply assumed he was happy to have gotten some action and didn't want to talk any more than I did. But in that moment, I'd have given up caffeine for a month – *okay, not a month, that would be torturous... maybe a week* – to know what was running through Finn's mind.

I really didn't want to be *that* girl – you know, the one who can't even enjoy her post-orgasmic bliss because she's so busy dissecting what the sex *means*, or how this *changes* things? The post-coital, over-analyzing, neurotic mess?

Crap. I am so becoming that girl.

And what were we supposed to do now? *Cuddle?* The thought was so incomprehensible, so foreign, that I didn't know what to do with it. So, per usual, I pushed it from my mind and decided not to think anymore. I tried to force my body to relax into Finn's chest and let my eyes drift closed.

They quickly shot back open when I felt Finn's chest rumbling beneath my cheek. Was he *laughing*?

Full-blown chuckles were now escaping from him.

The bastard was laughing!

I propped myself up on an elbow and glared down into his face.

"You're *amused* by this?" I accused scathingly. No guy had ever laughed after having sex with me. Left pathetic voicemails and staged "accidental" run-ins at places he'd known I would be? Yes. Laughed at me? No. I was good in bed – this was unheard of.

His laughter abated somewhat, and he managed to gasp out, "Yes, the amount of overanalyzing that's going on in that mind of yours right now is highly amusing. If your brain is about to implode or something, a warning would be nice."

"Excuse me?" I glared at him some more. He stopped laughing and brought one hand up to graze my temple, his blue eyes tender as they met mine.

"I can literally feel you freaking out and getting ready to make a run for it," he said, rolling over onto his side so we were lying face to face.

"How?" I didn't like the fact that he could read me so well.

"Because every muscle in your body is tensed and your face looks exactly like mine does after I sleep with a girl and am trying to think of the most-effective, least-dramatic way to extract myself from her bed."

I smacked him on his arm and jerked my head out of his grasp, refusing to meet his eyes after that comment. Was that really what my face looked like? Worse, was that the look on *his* face right now? I couldn't look at him – I'd happily live in the dark, never knowing the answer to that question so long as it meant that particular insecurity wasn't confirmed.

"Brooklyn," he said, turning my reluctant face back to look at him. I tried to fight his grasp, but denying him anything was nearly impossible when those cobalt eyes were locked on you. "You wouldn't make it two feet before I hauled you back in here with me."

"This is ridiculous! It's *my* room!" I huffed. "If anyone is leaving, it's you."

"Bee, do me a favor?" Finn asked, ignoring my complaints. "Stop thinking."

I opened my mouth and prepared to ream him out. The cocky asshole had not only brought up all the other girls he'd nailed in the past when we'd *just* had sex – which violated just about every girl rule on the planet – but also was spot-freaking-on about my impending freak out – which violated just about every *Brooklyn* rule on the planet. I hated that he was right.

Before I could get out even a single word, however, he leaned in and kissed me firmly – a no-nonsense, deliberate kind of kiss that told me he knew everything that was going on in my mind and didn't give a shit about any of it. The kiss was shorter than I'd have liked; just as I was beginning to kiss him back, he broke away and pressed a quick peck to my forehead.

"Look at us," he murmured, eyes full of mirth as he slowly examined our paint-covered bodies. I glanced down at the smears of paint that coated our limbs and couldn't help but laugh. Small round blue fingerprints spackled his forearms, marking the places I'd gripped; there were smudged handprints around my hips and thighs where he'd held my body against his.

"A work of art," he whispered, tracing one blue fingertip along the curve of my breast.

My eyes met his and I suddenly couldn't breathe,

seeing the emotions his held locked away in their depths. It was remarkable how expressive they were, how rapidly they could fluctuate from playful to sensual to tender, and right now, they were full of a look so soft, so *loving*, I nearly had a panic attack at the sight of them.

It wasn't a look you gave a one-night stand. It wasn't a *just sex* look. It was a *forever* kind of look. Desperate to return to safer waters, I slid off his chest and began to stand up.

"Come on," I said, grabbing his hand and trying to pull him up with me. With a sharp tug, he pulled me back down and I sprawled across his chest with a squeak of protest.

"Where do you think you're going?" he asked.

"Well, jeeze, caveman – I *was* going to suggest we take a shower and clean each other up..." I drifted off. "But if you'd rather stay here alone, that's fine with me, I guess." I grinned mischievously at him, our faces only inches apart.

He sat up faster than I would've thought possible and abruptly scooped me into his arms, stalking toward my bathroom door. I laughed at his impatience as he roughly yanked open my shower curtain and stepped into the tub. Within seconds the water was pouring down on us, and I gasped at both the frigid temperature and the torrents of blue paint that were pouring off our skin and swirling down the shower drain.

"Finn! Turn the lever! It's freezing!" I ordered, shivering as the arctic water fell on us. "No turn it to the left! Jesus!"

He was laughing, cradling me to his chest with one arm and fiddling with the shower controls with the other.

"This is supposed to be sexy," I grumbled, giggling at the ridiculous situation. "In the movies, the water is never too cold, the shower is always big enough for two, and they're never covered in so much paint that the bathtub will have a slight blue sheen for eternity."

Finn finally found the right lever and the water began to warm up. His other arm returned to hold me against him, and his lips grazed mine. I could feel every contour of his hard body pressed against me, and suddenly realized that we were, in fact, very naked. I stopped talking as his lips captured my mouth, and after a few tantalizing moments he pulled away to stare down at my dazed expression.

"You were saying?" he whispered, amused.

I couldn't remember my own name, let alone whatever nonsense I'd been spouting less than a minute before. Clearly, I had no idea what I was talking about – showers with Finn could never be anything *but* sexy.

Putting me down to stand on my own feet, he gently scrubbed my skin clean with my apple-scented body wash, removing every trace of paint from my body in a slow, sensual perusal. After he'd shampooed my hair, painstakingly massaging each dark curl until I was nearly purring like a kitten, I forced him to bend down so I could return the favor and wash his unruly mop. We reluctantly emerged from the shower only when our skin was no longer spackled cerulean and the water had run so cold I'd started to shiver.

Finn shut off the water and grabbed one of my large fluffy green towels, swathing it around me like a shroud before scooping me up into his arms and carrying me out of the bathroom. He unceremoniously dropped me onto my bed and slid in behind me. Pulling the comforter up over us, Finn adjusted my body so we were spooning, my back pressed fully against his front and every curve of our still-wet bodies perfectly aligned.

"Are we seriously *spooning* right now? Finn Chambers *spoons*?" I teased.

Finn was silent for a full minute, breathing quietly into my damp hair, and I again found myself wishing I could know what he was thinking or even just see the expression on his face. When he finally spoke, his voice cracked with restrained emotion.

"Finn Chambers doesn't spoon unless it's with Bee Turner," he whispered, so quietly I nearly didn't hear him. I couldn't help it – my heart turned over in my chest at his words. He made me feel special, like all of this was a first for him as well. Like he wanted me for something more than just my body.

When he said things like that, it was impossible to push him away – even though a big part of me still wanted to. Normally, I'd have put up a fight about a guy trying to spoon with

156

me – it was far too coupley, too affectionate, for my taste. In the past, I'd never have even brought a guy back to my apartment, let alone allowed him to sleep in my bed afterward. I'd always specifically chosen to follow guys to their places for sex, rather than bringing them here.

I hadn't wanted them to know where I lived, what my room looked like. I hadn't wanted them to know *me*, in any way except that most basic, physical way two people *can* know one another. As a general rule, I'd done everything possible to discourage future interaction and affection.

At the moment, though, I was too tired and far too satisfied to argue with Finn about our sleeping arrangements. Silencing the small part of my brain that was shrieking about boundaries and the dangers of commitment, I smiled and closed my eyes. Melting into Finn's warm embrace, I was asleep within minutes.

Chapter Eleven

Narcissistic Asshole

Stepping out onto the porch, my small hand slipped into his larger one immediately. He was there on the steps, just like he'd been every night since the first time we'd met – the night he'd told me the legend of Andromeda.

My eyes sought his, and when they met I was comforted for the first time all day. He was the only thing that made the group home bearable; when he told me stories or simply held my hand and talked to me, I could forget about the older girls and their teasing comments. I could forget about the bad man, the police officers, the hospital, and even about Mommy.

It's not that I wanted to forget her. I just missed her so much – too much. When he told me stories, though, I could pretend it had never happened. When I left my room, scared after a nightmare, he was always there to make me feel better. On those nights, he'd tell me silly stories, tales to make me giggle or smile, and I wasn't an orphan anymore; I was back in my princess room, surrounded by brave knights and magical fairies. I was in a world of magic and happy endings, where things like murder and death were impossibilities. Where mommies didn't get taken away to heaven when their little girls needed them.

"Hi, Brooklyn," he said, a small smile in his sad eyes.

I didn't reply, I simply looked up at him. I still wasn't speaking – not to my foster mother, not to the other kids, not even to the lady who called herself a "therapist" and came twice a week to see me.

I knew they wanted me to. Sometimes, the adults got angry at me – even though there were smiles on their faces, I could see the frustration in their eyes and hear it in their voices when they talked to me. The other kids didn't get angry – they just got mean.

Except for him.

He never yelled, or teased, or tried to get me to talk.

He just let me listen to his stories, hold his hand, and forget. Sometimes we'd just sit in the darkness, staring into the backyard or up at the night sky together.

"Brooklyn, look," he whispered, pointing into the dark, toward the tall grass at the bottom of the steps.

I looked at him questioningly; I didn't see anything unusual in the yard.

"Fireflies."

I turned back and peered into the night, trying to catch a glimpse of them. I'd only seen them once before, at the beginning of the summer. Mommy and I had gone on a picnic at our favorite park one night, and when the sun had started to go down we'd seen hundreds of the glowing bugs flying all around us. Mommy had laughed and said maybe they were really fairies, like Tinkerbell, and if some of their fairy dust fell on us we could fly away too.

Mommy had flown away, after all – but she hadn't taken me with her.

The boy started to tell me a story about the time the hero Perseus killed a monster named Medusa – a woman so ugly her hair was made from snakes and her gaze turned people into stone. I liked to listen to the sound of his voice. He was still a boy, but his voice was deeper than the other foster kids voices – slightly raspy and so different from Mommy's. Her voice had sounded like music all the time, whether she was singing or talking or shouting.

I waited until he'd finished his story, watching the fireflies as they weaved between the tall grasses. When he fell silent, I looked up at him expectantly.

"What?" he asked me, as if he didn't know exactly what I wanted.

He knew, he just wanted me to ask for it. I stared at him, waiting – just like I had every other time he forgot to say the ending.

"Oh, all right," he sighed. "'And so, after Perseus beheaded Medusa, there was celebration throughout the land and everyone lived happily ever after.' Happy now?" The boy rolled his eyes at me.

I was *happy. Stories weren't finished without the happily ever after, everyone knew that. Mommy had always said it was the most important part of any fairytale.*

I smiled.

"Real life isn't like the stories, Brooklyn," the boy said, the sad look back in his eyes. Sometimes when he was telling me a story, his eyes would lose that look – but it always came back eventually. "There aren't any white knights or glass slippers or second chances," he whispered into the night, not looking at me. "People don't wake up after eating poisoned apples. They don't live again after an evil witch curses them. They just die."

I looked at the boy with the sad blue eyes, and I saw it – he wasn't a kid anymore. Whatever had happened to him, whatever brought him here to live in the foster home, had made him stop believing in happily ever afters.

I wanted to tell him that I understood. I recognized the sad look in his eyes – I'd seen it in my own every time I looked in the mirror. I knew why he thought this way; he was protecting himself.

Sometimes, it was easy to feel sad or angry about what had happened to Mommy, but then I'd think about all the fairytales she'd told me. In all of those stories, the princesses had moments when they'd thought they would never get their happy endings, or that the bad guys would win. But eventually the dragons got slayed, the princes came to the rescue, and the princesses did *get their happily ever afters.*

I wanted to tell him that Cinderella hadn't believed either, until her fairy godmother showed up the night of the ball. And of course Snow White would've stayed dead, if Prince Charming hadn't believed in the power of true love's kiss.

I wanted to make him believe we could have happy endings again, even in a world without mommies or daddies to take care of us.

Mommy used to tell me, "Bee, a very smart man named John Lennon once said, 'Everything will be okay in the end. If it's not okay, it's not the end.' Remember that, sweetheart. Tuck it away and keep it with you when you're having a bad day."

160

Then she'd kiss my forehead and hug me, her long fingers lightly tickling my sides and coaxing a laugh.

I slipped one hand back into his and squeezed.

"You can call me Bee," I whispered, my voice trembling as I used it for the first time in months.

It wasn't what I'd wanted to say, but it was a start.

His head whipped around at the sound of my voice and when he looked down at me there was surprise, not sadness, in his eyes.

"Bee," he whispered back, smiling.

***

"Bee," Finn whispered, shaking me awake. "Come on, love, wake up. You're trembling. I think you're having a nightmare."

I peeled open my eyes and looked up at him. He was leaning over me, beautiful in the faint moonlight trickling through the window at the end of my bed. His hair was tousled, his voice was rough with sleep, and his tired eyes were slowly clearing and coming alert. Our limbs were still entwined; in sleep I'd turned over to rest my head on his chest, with one arm thrown across his abdomen and my right leg hooked up over his thigh. He had one hand looped around my back, holding me tightly against his side, and the other resting on my hip.

I was typically an active sleeper. My nightmares were always vivid and I'd toss and turn while caught in their throes, waking up with my sheets a tangled mess around my legs. It seemed that tonight with Finn, though, I'd been happily immobile, pressed against his warmth until he'd woken me.

When my gaze met his, a soft look replaced the anxiety that filled his eyes and the lines of tension started to ease from his face.

"Hey," he whispered, bringing a hand up to touch my cheek. "You okay?"

I thought back to my dream – it hadn't been frightening, just confusing. I wasn't sure where these memories were coming from, or why they had started to reemerge now, so many years later. Maybe between my therapy sessions with Dr. Angelini and playing music again, I'd stirred things that I'd been repressing for over a decade. While I was happy to be regaining some memories from that fuzzy time of my life, it was still an unsettling experience; it felt like my mind was unraveling like a spool of yarn, revealing long-buried people and events I hadn't even known existed. Finn had been right – I *was* trembling.

"Hi," I whispered back.

Finn brushed a curl back from my face and tucked it behind my ear. "Was it a nightmare?" he asked.

I nodded, not wanting to explain or knowing how to begin to.

"Do you want to talk about it?" The gentle look in his eyes told me that I could've shared anything with him at that moment, even the story of my mother's death and the twisted path my life had followed ever since. But I knew, once I told him, the soft look would leave his eyes – replaced by sympathy or, worse, pity.

I shook my head no. I wasn't ready to see that look in his eyes. I didn't think I'd ever be ready for that.

"Okay," he said, leaning down to kiss my forehead gently. I snuggled into his side and felt his arms tighten around me. When his hands started to wander down my body and his mouth found mine, I allowed my mind to go blank and forgot all about my strangely vivid dreams. And as Finn made slow, achingly sweet love to me, the boy with sad eyes, who'd given me the happy endings he was far past believing in, disappeared from my mind altogether.

***

When I woke, the first thing to enter my consciousness was the pungent, unmistakable scent of paint fumes. Cracking open an eye, I saw that it was already midmorning and bright rays of autumn light were streaking across my bedspread. The second thing my bleary mind registered was the fact that I was still naked, and Finn was no longer in bed next to me.

So he left. That's good – great, even. It's what I wanted all along.

Isn't it?

162

My inner voice sounded unconvincing even to myself, and I couldn't quell the disappointment that was beginning to bloom in my chest like a cancer – a sharp pain radiating quickly from my heart out through my limbs.

I was an idiot.

Sex with Finn had been so different for me – more intimate and so far removed from what I'd experienced in the past – that I'd simply assumed he'd felt it too. Apparently he hadn't. Maybe last night had been nothing to him; maybe *I'd* been nothing to him. No different from any other girl he'd – *how had Lexi termed it so eloquently?* – hit-and-quit.

This is fine. This is better, in fact. Now, things can go back to normal and I'll forget all about the emotional, tear-ridden months I've had with Finn in my life. I'll go back to having fun *– who wants to cry all the time, anyway? He's just a boy, nothing special. It isn't like he took my virginity, for god's sake. This will be no different from any of my other hookups. Snap out of it, Brooklyn.*

They were paltry consolations, but they were all I had left. I clung to them desperately, my lifeline in a storm – unwilling to be dragged out into the endless ocean of my disappointed hopes. Breathing deeply into the pillow I clutched tightly to my chest, tears immediately prickled my eyes as Finn's scent washed over me. I wondered how many other stupid girls' empty pillows had smelled like the warm breeze of an early fall day, and how long they'd waited to wash them after he'd left. A day? A week?

I groaned at the ridiculous thought. I was being such a *girl* – what the hell was happening to me?

Don't get me wrong, I was fully aware how hypocritical it was for me to feel this way. After all, hadn't I pulled this exact maneuver on countless one-night-stands of my own? I was the expert at it; so good, I could probably teach classes at the university– *How to Escape Your Awkward Morning-After: Avoiding the Coyote-Ugly and Sneaking Out the Window 101*. I had no right to expect anything different from Finn; in fact, I was naïve for thinking it could have ever meant something more to him than just sex. He was Finn Chambers, after all.

Two months ago, I would've balked at the idea of sex meaning anything other than the mind-cleansing fulfillment only an orgasm can deliver. Now, here I was, brought down by the idea that sex *hadn't* been meaningful – that I'd been nailed-and-bailed on.

Damn, karma really is a snaggletoothed, hairy bitch.

I took another deep breath, through my mouth this time, and decided to stop being a whiney, pathetic, doe-eyed little girl. I had things to do, like finish painting my room.

When memories of painting with he-who-must-not-be-named began to play through my mind in vivid high-definition color, I did my best to shove them way down into my triply-reinforced mental box labeled *Narcissistic Assholes*. He finally fit in the box, I realized with a despondent, detached sort of acceptance – a pyrrhic victory if there ever was one.

Flipping over onto my back, I startled when I caught sight of the deep blue ceiling above me. When I'd finally fallen asleep, utterly wiped out after Finn and I had finished *getting acquainted* for the third time, the ceiling was an unadulterated shade of midnight. Now, it was littered with a galaxy of white stars, so detailed and painstakingly crafted that they must have taken several hours to hand paint.

Finn.

As if thinking his name had conjured him, my bedroom door swung open and Finn strolled in, looking annoyingly bright-eyed and cheerful, clothed once-again in his paint-spattered coveralls. *He* clearly hadn't just undergone a slightly embarrassing, utterly dismaying spiral into the land of self-doubt and rejection.

Crap.

Propped up on my elbows, a sheet covering my chest, I warily watched him enter, unsure what to expect.

"Sleeping Beauty awakens," he said, smiling crookedly at me and coming to a stop at the end of my bed.

He was still here. He hadn't left at all.

My heart stuttered in my chest, then started to race at what felt like twice its normal rate. The walls of the *Narcissistic*

164

Asshole box started to rattle, then buckle violently, the wood straining under the pressure until the top exploded off altogether and Finn *freaking* Chambers escaped back into the forefront of my mind. I mentally acknowledged that he'd never fit in that damn box again – not that he'd ever really belonged there in the first place.

I should've been angry that he'd caused my minor – *okay, major* – freak out, but I was overwhelmed by equal parts giddiness that he was still here and paralyzing terror at the undeniable attachment I felt for him. Anger had to take the back burner, for the moment – I could only handle one mental breakdown at a time, pre-caffeine fix.

Covering up my extreme internal distress, I aimed for nonchalant indifference – rolling my eyes at him and flopping backwards onto my pillow, my gaze alternated between the painted universe of stars and the mind-fuck of a man before me. He looked completely at ease and self-assured, as if it were the most natural thing in the world for him to be waking up in my apartment and doing god knows what while I was still asleep.

"How long have you been awake?" I asked somewhat grumpily. I was unprepared for this conversation, for this day, without first having my coffee. My brain didn't even begin to function normally until after cup number two. In fact, that debilitating pain that had lanced through my chest when I'd thought Finn had left me? Maybe it had just been caffeine deprivation.

One could only hope.

"A few hours," he said, shrugging and walking closer to me. Leaning over the bed, careful not to get any paint on my comforter, he kissed me. Though our mouths were our only point of contact, it wasn't the gentle good morning peck I'd anticipated. Finn's kiss was consuming, near-painful in its irrefutable desire – a reminder of what last night had been, and a promise of more nights to come.

"How did you sleep?" he asked, pulling away.

I tried to slow my breathing so I didn't sound like an asthmatic who'd just run a half-marathon when I answered him. I

165

cleared my throat and pulled a deep breath into my lungs, praying I wasn't as transparent as I felt. For fuck's sake, I was nearly panting.

"Like the dead, apparently," I said, glancing up at the ceiling. "I didn't even hear you do all this."

"I was quiet. Stealthy. Some might even say ninja-like," he grinned down at me, his cobalt eyes warm on mine.

"Who? Who might say that?" I asked, raising one eyebrow.

"Me."

"It doesn't count if you're the only one saying it," I grinned back at him and rolled my eyes at his ridiculousness. "And I was so tired I could've slept through an earthquake."

"Is that you admitting I wore you out last night?" he asked, waggling his eyebrows suggestively.

"Cocky."

"Confident," he countered, dropping a light kiss on the end of my nose. I wrinkled it at him in response, watching as he made his way back to the ladder in the corner of my bedroom. "So, do you like it?" he asked, voice deceptively casual as he gestured up at the stars on my deep blue ceiling. Despite his blasé tone, I thought I detected a nervous undercurrent in his question, as if he were genuinely worried about my reaction.

"I love it," I whispered honestly, looking anywhere but at him. It was enough that he could hear the emotion making my voice crack roughly; I didn't need him to see the moisture clouding over my eyes as well. This gesture was more than anyone had done for me in all the years since my mom died, and I was overwhelmed by it.

It was as if he'd somehow dipped into my memories and known exactly how my childhood walls had been painted; like he'd sensed that this would be the perfect addition to my new bedroom. It was uncanny how well he seemed to know my tastes, to recognize and anticipate my likes and dislikes – almost as if he were innately attuned to my every thought and feeling.

When I was confident that my tears were under control, I turned back to look at him. He was standing at the base of the

166

ladder, staring straight at me. I knew he could read my face like an open book, watching as I struggled to weather the storm of emotions brewing within me. Thankfully, he didn't push me to talk about it.

"I'm glad you like it, princess," he replied, a small smile twisting up one side of his mouth.

"Princess?" I asked. The only time I'd ever heard the nickname "princess" used, it was said sarcastically or condescendingly. Finn said it affectionately, though – a sincere, reverent endearment I wasn't sure how to process. He grinned at me, failing to elaborate any further. Apparently, I was going to have to drag it out of him.

"Why *princess*?" I didn't think he was making fun of me, but considering how off base some of my assumptions about Finn had been in the past, I decided it was safest to simply ask him.

"You look so small in that big white bed of yours, swallowed up in all those pillows and fluffy blankets. And when you were sleeping, with all that dark hair spilling across your pillow, and your face so peaceful…You were beautiful. You *are* beautiful." He swallowed roughly, eyes intense as he stared at my face like he was committing every feature to memory. "Angelic. Like some unattainable fucking fantasy I dreamed up."

He left the ladder and approached the bed, leaning down so his mouth brushed the shell of my ear. I shivered, and felt his lips curve into a knowing smile as they brushed against the lobe. "You are, without question, the most beautiful girl I've ever seen, Bee," he whispered. "Sometimes, I look at you and wonder if you're even real. Girls like you aren't supposed to exist in real life – you're the stuff of legends and bedtime stories. So, no, I don't give a shit if you think it's lame as hell – you're *my* princess."

Okay. He could call me princess. He could call me whatever he wanted if he kept talking to me like that.

I didn't say anything. Instead, I threw back the covers, hurdled out of bed, and slammed my frame against his. When my bare legs wrapped around his waist, my mouth found his and my hands slipped into his hair as I let my body do the talking.

Much later, we emerged from the shower and Finn took

his time drying me off, using a towel to gently wipe every droplet of water from my body. We'd once again had to scrub ourselves clean of blue paint, as our earlier activities on my bedroom floor had gotten unintentionally creative and we'd ended up looking like aspiring Blue Man Group members. Again.

Finn finally allowed me to leave my bedroom and I greedily consumed half a pot of coffee as soon as I entered the kitchen. He laughed at me, taking only a single cup for himself and downing it black.

Yuck. What was coffee without cream and sugar!?

Lexi was still at Tyler's apartment, so it was just Finn and me. I shouldn't have been surprised that there was no morning-after awkwardness, but I was. I guess, despite everything Finn had said and done in the past twenty-four hours, I was still insecure about where this whole thing was heading. I could finally admit to myself that yes, I had definite feelings for him. And yes, the sex had been off-the-charts amazing – better than I'd ever imagined sex could be. But I still was nowhere near ready or eager for a relationship. The idea of Brooklyn Turner, irrefutable "Ice Bitch," as someone's girlfriend was laughable. The idea of being the girlfriend of someone like Finn Chambers, however, was downright scary.

"Stop," Finn ordered, shaking me out of my reverie.

"Stop what?" I looked at him, confused.

"Overthinking us."

Us?

He set down his empty cup on the kitchen island and made his way around to the stool I was perched on. Bringing one hand up, he lightly smudged a finger across the tension lines that were pulling my eyebrows together.

"Princess, can I ask you something?"

I nodded reluctantly, automatically anticipating the worst.

"Did you have fun with me last night? This morning?"

I nodded again, waiting to see where he was going with this.

"Well so did I. In fact, I had more damn fun last night than I've had in a long, long time. So please don't get all wiggy

168

and female on me. Don't twist this around into something bad, because what we've had these past few days is beautiful. You know that deep down, princess. And if I know you the way I think I do, then I bet it scares the ever-living hell out of you."

I took a deep breath, met his eyes, and nodded again. His crinkled up in amusement.

"I don't mind the silent treatment," he grinned. "If I'd known sex was all it would take to stop you from being so sassy all the time, I'd have made my move a lot sooner. Give the girl an orgasm and she's finally complaisant."

"*Complaisant*? Did you get that off your word-of-the-day calendar, caveman?" I smiled, jabbing a sharp elbow into his stomach. He let out a small *oof* as I connected, though my arm probably took most of the brunt from colliding with his steely abs. I fought the urge to rub feeling back into it, not wanting to look like the weakling I totally was.

"You'll have to come over to my apartment and see," he said with a wink. I'd never been to Finn's apartment – I hadn't really allowed myself to think about the fact that this god-like specimen of man actually had a bed and a toothbrush and maybe even a damn word-of-the-day calendar somewhere out there. The thought was staggering.

"Maybe sometime," I murmured noncommittally.

"After my show tonight," Finn countered decidedly. He hadn't invited me or asked if I would be going – he simply informed me that I'd be there, as if my plans for the night were predetermined without any necessary consent on my part.

Overbearing caveman.

Casting a look at the microwave clock, he winced. "Speaking of, I have to get going. It's already past three and we have a rehearsal before the set. We go on at nine."

"At Styx, right?" I confirmed unnecessarily. *Apiphobic Treason* rarely played at any other venues on campus because Styx was one of the few places that could accommodate such a big crowd. On a good night, their shows drew in over two hundred people.

Finn nodded, then leaned down so our faces were aligned

and brought up both hands to cup my face. Staring into my eyes, he shook his head back and forth so our noses grazed lightly before tilting his head and giving me a light kiss goodbye.

"I'll see you tonight, princess," he whispered against my lips.

"If you're lucky, caveman."

"Oh, I'm lucky, all right," he returned cockily, eyes twinkling as he no doubt remembered how very *lucky* he'd gotten both last night and this morning. I rolled my eyes as I watched him walk out of the kitchen, but even my exasperation with him was starting to feel forced. If I were being honest with myself – which, let's face it, was a rare occurrence – I'd have to admit how happy I was feeling at that exact moment. *I* was the lucky one – and "lucky" was definitely not something I'd ever considered myself before now.

My heart literally fluttered in my chest as I heard the distant click of the front door closing, marking Finn's departure. He'd only just left, but I already found myself checking the time and counting down the hours until his show tonight, when I'd see him again.

I barely recognized this girl I was becoming, and I knew it was all because of Finn.

What in the hell have I gotten myself into?

Chapter Twelve

Cliff's Edge

"And you have no memories of this boy other than those from your dreams?" Dr. Angelini asked.

If I'd been expecting her to express shock or even mild surprise at my revelation of the sad-eyed boy in my dreams, I would have been sincerely disappointed – her face was utterly unresponsive as she leveled me with her clinical stare.

"I don't have many clear memories from my time in the foster system," I admitted. "Until now, it's mostly been fuzzy images. Sometimes, a particular smell or taste would trigger a vague memory, but nothing has ever been this vivid before."

"When you say vivid—" Dr. Angelini began, seeking clarification.

"When I have one of the dreams, it's like I'm six years old again, reliving things in real-time. It's so real – more real than almost anything I've ever felt."

My mind reeled through a series of images: the hands of two lost children clasped tightly; a swarm of fireflies meandering through untamed bracken; the dark night sky, swirling with stars far beyond our reach.

I looked away from her unflinching stare, steering my gaze out the large windows over her shoulder. She had a great view – I wondered absently whether she ever took the time to enjoy it. It was hard to imagine Dr. Angelini looking anywhere other than inside the skulls of her patients.

"Do the dreams upset you?" she asked.

My eyes drifted back to her face, which, unsurprisingly, was blank of any true emotion. Despite her unruffled serenity, I could see the alertness in her eyes and knew that she was highly focused on everything I was saying. The mind hidden beneath that smooth blonde chignon was constantly analyzing and evaluating, picking apart everything I said and inferring the things I'd purposefully left out. More than once, I had to remind myself that this torture was self-imposed – that it was *good* for me.

"Sometimes," I admitted. "But not because of what happens in them. It's more upsetting because I feel like I don't even know my own mind. I suddenly have all these memories I never knew about, just locked away in my subconscious – it makes me wonder what else I've forgotten or blocked out."

"The human mind is a complex thing, Brooklyn. Even after decades of research and despite the revolutionary development of brain imaging machines, we still are virtually no closer to understanding how the brain functions, let alone *why* it works the way it does."

I nodded in agreement; I'd taken Pysch 101 freshman year – none of this was news to me.

"And memory is one of the most mysterious and complex mental processes of all," she continued. "We really don't know how the brain stores and recalls information; all we *do* know is that memories are rarely brought to the surface randomly. Typically, there is a trigger of some kind, which creates a mental association between a current sensory stimulus and one that has been stored away in the mind."

"So, you're saying that something I'm experiencing now is unearthing my memories of this boy?"

"It's possible," Dr. Angelini postulated noncommittally.

Damn shrinks and their inability to give a definitive answer to a single question.

"Do you want to remember?" she asked. "Or would you rather these memories remained buried?"

"It's got nothing to do with whether I *want* to remember or not," I said. "I have no control over it."

"Brooklyn, have you ever considered that maybe you're simply remembering now because you're finally ready to?" she asked.

I didn't know the answer to that question.

We moved on, spending the remainder of the session discussing my performance at The Blue Note and my painting

172

project. I didn't mention Finn's role in the whole process, nor did I tell her that we'd finally crossed the boundary of friendship.

There was still a significant part of me that didn't want to admit anything had changed between the two of us. There was also a smaller, yet equally vocal, part of me that was afraid if I admitted our relationship out loud to Dr. Angelini, I would jinx the entire thing, and it would fall apart before it had ever had a change to fall fully together.

As I stood to leave, Dr. Angelini rose from behind her desk and stilled me by placing one manicured hand lightly on my forearm.

"For what it's worth, Brooklyn, I think you've shown tremendous progress in the past few months," she said, her eyes detachedly compassionate in a clinical sort of way. "The fact that you're finally opening up and allowing yourself to embrace the past is extremely brave, not to mention exceedingly more healthy than your previous coping strategies."

"What, doc, you didn't approve of the meaningless sex and tequila binges?" I asked playfully, uncomfortable with the serious turn our conversation had taken.

She was being complimentary – supportive even – and it instantly made me uneasy. I knew I was being cynical, but in my experience, people were rarely genuine and sincere compliments were few and far between. Since I'd also never been on the receiving end of many – my father hadn't exactly been Brady Bunch material – I was wary of the look in Dr. Angelini's eyes, which could easily be classified as pride.

"Brooklyn," Dr. Angelini said, pulling me back to the present. "Even *you* didn't approve of your sexual activities or alcohol abuse." One sculpted eyebrow lifted sardonically from behind her square-framed Chanel glasses as she stared at me.

"How do you figure that, doc?" I asked.

"You wouldn't be standing here in my office if you did."

***

After the session, I headed to Maria's and ordered two Greek salads – dinner for Lexi and me. Thankfully, no one I knew was in line so I didn't have to make small talk. There were few things I hated more than idle chitchat: the inane volley of meaningless words, nothing more than fillers in an otherwise uncomfortable silence.

One of the many things I failed to understand about so-called "normal" people was their inability to just enjoy the quiet. Were they so afraid of others' judgment that they felt it necessary to prattle on indefinitely, in hopes of keeping the conversation superficial and safe? Or was it that they were afraid to look, even for a short time, into the depths of their own mind – to *truly* examine their own thoughts –for fear they wouldn't like what they saw?

I didn't know.

All I *did* know was that nine out of ten people I encountered had no concept of the value in simply sharing a silence. And I guess that was kind of a shame for them, because there was a certain kind of purity, intimacy even, in just sitting with someone and not feeling the need to speak at all.

One of the only people I'd ever felt that with was Finn.

I hadn't heard from him since he'd left my apartment several hours ago, but I was glad for the time alone. He knew me well enough to understand that I needed space enough to process everything that had happened between us last night – but not so much space that I had time to talk myself out of becoming involved with him altogether.

Even though Finn hadn't said it in so many words, I was relatively sure he wanted "us" to be more long-term than a single sleepover. It was his actions that spoke to me the loudest – his feather-light caresses as he'd made love to me, the constellation of stars he'd hand-painted on my ceiling the next morning, even his stupid "princess" pet name. They all pointed to one thing: a relationship of some kind.

I knew I'd freak out if I over-analyzed it, so I wasn't letting myself think about it at all. Well, that's not entirely true – I was thinking about the *sex*, I just wasn't really concentrating on the *relationship* aspect of things…Possibly because I was so focused on how good the sex had been. And how long I had to wait until we could do it again.

174

A quick glance at my watch showed that it was quarter past six, and Finn's show would likely go until nearly midnight. I groaned inwardly; six hours seemed a lifetime away.

After paying for our salads, I hurried out the door and headed home. I sent Lexi a quick text telling her I was on my way, and she replied instantaneously.

Here anxiously waiting 4 dinner and details. Hurry up! :p

Great, so I was walking into an ambush.

I hadn't been naïve enough to hope that Lexi would simply forget to ask about Finn and I, but I *was* hoping to avoid it for a little longer. I couldn't skirt the topic with her like I had with Dr. Angelini – Lex already knew something was going on between us. But that didn't mean I had to give her all the details, right?

Who was I kidding?

This was *Lexi* – she'd tie me to a chair and shoot bamboo slivers under my fingernails until I gave her a detailed play-by-play of each minute I'd spent with Finn. The girl was annoyingly persistent when she wanted something; I'd always thought a career with the CIA as a terrorist interrogator might've been a better fit than fashion merchandizing.

Stepping through our front door, I set down the bag containing our salads on the kitchen island and looked around warily for her. Right on cue, I heard her bedroom door fly open and slam against the opposing wall, followed by the sound of bare feet rushing across the hardwood floors. I watched as she came into view; rounding the hallway corner at full speed, her red hair whipping around her face, she skidded to a halt directly in front of me.

"Tell me," she demanded, slightly out of breath.

"Okay, okay, let's eat dinner and then I will. Calm dow—"

"No!" Lexi cut me off. "You will tell me *immediately.* I have been your best friend since the *second fucking grade* and this is the first time you've ever had anything remotely romantic happen to you. I have been totally gypped in the friend department until now! " Lexi huffed, as if my lack of previous relationships was a direct attack against her.

"Gee, thanks Lex!"

"Oh, shut up, you know what I mean," she said, smacking me lightly on the arm. "Can't I be excited, Brookie? All I've ever wanted was to see you happy."

I snorted. *Yeah, like that's her* only *motive here.*

"Oh, fine!" She glared at me, but I could tell she was trying not to laugh. "I also happen to be excited about the prospect of double dates. So sue me!"

I started laughing and she immediately joined in, throwing her arms around me and squeezing me tightly for almost a full minute.

"Um, Lex?"

"What?" she asked, her arms still wrapped around my torso.

"Cant...breathe..."

"Oh!" Lexi gasped, releasing her hold at once. I gratefully gulped oxygen into my lungs. "Sorry," she muttered. "Sometimes I forget how little you are."

I rolled my eyes and turned to pull our salads out of the bag. As I grabbed silverware and plates, Lexi grabbed a bottle of ginger ale from the fridge, poured some into two tall glasses, and topped each off with a healthy dose of vodka and grenadine.

"Dirty Shirleys," she said, smiling in anticipation as she stirred ice into the glasses and handed one to me.

"Cheers," I said.

"To best friends and boyfriends," Lexi toasted with a wink at me.

"And really great sex," I added, giggling into my glass as Lexi snorted ginger ale out her nose.

"Details. Right. Now," Lexi demanded, dabbing her face with a napkin.

I took a big swig of my drink – I was going to need it for this conversation.

***

Several hours later I'd consumed half a Greek salad and three and a half Dirty Shirleys, and Lexi was staring at me with her mouth gaping open. I'd just finished telling her everything

176

about Finn and me, from the night I'd bailed on Landon, to painting my bedroom together, and, of course, the marathon sex we'd had afterwards. She'd been silent throughout the entire story, her only expression one of ever-building astonishment as she absorbed every word that left my mouth with rapt attention.

When I'd finished she didn't speak for a long time, and as the minutes slowly ticked by I began to grow uneasy. Then, abruptly hopping down from her stool at the kitchen island, she wandered from the room without a word to me. I followed her because, well, what else was I supposed to do?

Lexi turned down the hallway to our bedrooms, bypassed her own door, and threw mine open without hesitation. I waited in the doorway, watching as she entered the room and spun in a slow circle, taking it all in. After Finn had left this afternoon I'd spent some time cleaning up the brushes and paint-covered drop cloths, pushing my furniture back into place and, lastly, hanging the canvas images on the wall opposite my bed. Offset against the sky blue paint, the photos looked beautiful.

Lexi made her way over to them, stopping to examine each one individually before lightly tracing her fingertips across the three smiling faces enlarged on canvas; her own, then mine, and finally, my mother's.

The faces of my family.

Lexi turned away from the images and, when her eyes found mine, they were filled with unshed tears.

"Brookie," she whispered, her voice cracking with emotion.

"Look up," I said, nodding toward the ceiling.

She did as I told her; tilting her head back to examine it, her eyes widened in surprise, then wonder. As she took in the constellation of stars overhead, I saw the floodgates finally break open and watched as tears cascaded down her face. She didn't move to wipe them away; she simply let them fall as she pivoted in a slow circle, staring up at the beauty Finn had created for me with a simple paintbrush.

I would have hugged her, but I knew from experience that Lexi would only cry harder if I tried to comfort her. Right now, she simply needed quiet time to process her thoughts – so that's exactly what I gave her. I didn't leave my spot in the doorway or try to speak to her, and within minutes her tears had dried up. She moved to sit on my bed, looking overwhelmed and slightly shell-shocked. I couldn't really blame her – I'd felt that way for most of the day.

Turning from the room, I walked back to the kitchen, grabbed both of our drinks, and carried them back to my bedroom. Without a word, I handed Lexi her glass, and she gulped down a fortifying sip. She'd barely said a word, with the exception of my name, for the past three hours. That had to be some kind of record, considering Lexi typically had more trouble staying quiet than most hyper five-year-old children.

I should have known it wouldn't last long.

Her blank expression began to morph, an unmistakable shit-eating grin spreading across her face. "He did this," she said, gesturing up at the ceiling.

I nodded.

"You let him stay the night," she noted.

"Yeah," I shrugged, taking a sip of my drink.

"You like him," she continued, her smirk still in place.

"Yeah," I shrugged again, taking an even bigger gulp of my Dirty Shirley.

"You like, really, *really*, like him," she squealed, clapping her hands together and beginning to bounce up and down in her seat. I decided that not responding to her was my safest course of action at this point. Any more confessions and she might spontaneously combust.

"You want to go on dates with him, and let him hold your hand, and have little baby BrookFinns – FinnLyns? – with him!"

Well, that escalated quickly.

I stared at Lexi in semi-horror and fought to control the instant nausea that had gripped me as soon as those words left her mouth. I never wanted children. I couldn't – wouldn't – bring a kid into a world like this one.

Not ever.

But unless I wanted those three Dirty Shirleys I'd

consumed to have an encore appearance, I needed to get control of myself. I shoved away my near anxiety attack and reminded myself that Lexi had been joking.

"*FinnLyn*? Did you seriously just combine our names?" I asked, forcing a laugh.

"I like BrookFinn better," Lexi murmured contemplatively. Her eyes were glazed and distant as her mind conjured images of terrifying things – bridesmaid dresses and houses with white picket fences and squirming babies with dark hair and cobalt eyes. I shuddered and tried to ignore her, only just resisting the urge to cover my ears and yell *la-la-la-la* over and over again until she left me alone.

"You're lucky you even have names that mesh. This girl Kylee in my American Lit class is dating a boy named Kyle – total disaster."

"*Totally*," I agreed, snorting into my drink.

"No need to be sarcastic, Brookie," Lexi said, snapping out of her white taffeta dreamland and leveling me with an evaluative stare.

Uh oh. I knew that look.

"You have to look epically hot tonight," she decided. "Boy, do I have my work cut out for me."

"Bitch!" I protested, smacking her on the arm.

"Oh, shush, I was just kidding," Lexi said. "You're not *that* bad."

I glared at her. She giggled.

"You're beautiful, and you know it," Lexi rolled her eyes at me like *I* was the ridiculous one, before blowing me an air kiss which I pretended to swat away from my face. "I'm still pulling out the big guns, though."

I quirked an eyebrow at her, scared to ask what Lexi's "big guns" entailed.

"The Dress," Lexi said, as if that explained everything.

"That really doesn't clarify anything for me, Lex."

"Just trust me. When you see The Dress – actually, when *Finn* sees the dress – everything will be clear as day."

When she grabbed my hand and pulled me toward her

bedroom I didn't put up a fight, mostly because I was drunk but also partly because Lexi was right – I did want to look hot tonight. For the first time in my life, I actually cared about impressing a boy.

Lexi led me into her room and immediately knelt down to retrieve a sleek box wrapped in ornate white and gold paper from the space beneath her bed. She handed it to me, an excited grin plastered across her face and her eyes twinkling with anticipation.

"What's this?" I asked, hesitantly taking the box from her.

"Early birthday present," Lexi shrugged. "I was saving it for next week, but tonight calls for epic, and The Dress is *epically* epic."

I stared down at the box in my hands, then back up at my best friend. Setting the present gently on her bed, I closed the distance between us and wrapped my arms around her tall frame.

"Love you, Lex."

I felt her stiffen with surprise, then sigh as her body relaxed and her arms came around me. "Love you too, Brookie." She whispered, squeezing me tightly. "Now open your goddamned present!"

I laughed, pulling away and grabbing the box. Tearing away the wrapping paper eagerly, I opened the lid and found The Dress nestled in a cocoon of white tissue paper.

Lexi had been right – it *was* epic.

The Dress was a deep emerald green, nearly the exact shade of my eyes, and strapless, with a daringly low sweetheart neckline that would make the best of my cleavage. It had a tight bodice-style top, intricately embroidered with small beading around the edges, which would fit my body like a glove from the waist up. The bottom half of the dress was short – the skirt would only brush the tops of my thighs – but it was made of a gauzy, flowing material of the same deep green shade, that would float out around me as I walked.

I loved it instantly.

For the first time I was grateful to have a best friend studying fashion, and as I clutched The Dress to my chest I lifted my eyes to look at Lexi.

"The Dress is freaking epic. *You* are freaking epic."

"I know," Lexi agreed, smiling hugely. "Now sit your ass down so I can do your hair and makeup."

I rolled my eyes and did as she said.

***

When we stepped through the doors of Styx, Finn and the band were already well into their first set and the place was so packed with people it must've been well over the fire marshal's legal capacity. My eyes cut straight through the pulsating crowd, landing immediately on Finn.

Dressed in a dark grey t-shirt and distressed jeans, he was leaning toward the audience with both hands wrapped around the microphone stand. His eyes were closed as he sang the final note of a Red Hot Chili Peppers song, his face chiseled and beautiful under the bright stage lights.

God, he was hot.

It was clear I wasn't the only one who thought so; his resident fangirl skanks were in attendance by the dozens, pressed tightly against the stage and flashing their girl-bits at him every chance they got.

Retract claws, Brooklyn.

I tore my eyes away and did a quick scan of the room. When my gaze passed over the bar, I noticed Gordon and several of his hulking football teammates drinking beers. He'd noticed our entrance and was staring straight at me, his eyes narrowed and his mouth twisted up in a cruel smirk. Our eyes locked briefly before his gaze lowered to travel the length of my body, so slowly and thoroughly that my every hair stood on end in discomfort.

I hoped he wasn't stupid enough to approach me, after what had happened last time. If Finn had to pull him off me again, I wasn't sure he'd be able to stop himself before sending Gordon to the ER.

Or the morgue.

I kept my face expressionless, knowing that assholes like Gordon got off on scaring and manipulating women. While mentally projecting a *go-fuck-yourself* his way, I steered Lexi toward the opposite side of the bar, as far from him as we could get. Finn had launched into a new song, and I focused on his voice rather than Gordon's foreboding presence.

I squared my shoulders. I was wearing The Dress, I'd had fantastic sex with a guy who was so amazing it scared me, and my best friend was quite possibly the coolest girl on the planet – nothing, not even Gordon Asshole O'Brien, was going to ruin this night for me.

After a few rounds at the bar, I was almost able to forget about him completely. Lexi and I were buzzed and happy, dancing on the fringes of the dance floor with drinks in hand as we watched the band – or, more specifically, the drummer and lead singer – play through their set.

Every once and a while, I'd see Finn's gaze sweeping through the crowd as if he were searching for someone. My airway felt constricted as hope warred with fear within me; more than anything, I wanted it to be *me* he was looking for in that sea of faces. Several times, I refused Lexi's attempts to drag us closer to the stage, where Finn would be sure to spot us; I wasn't ready to have my fears confirmed, one way or the other.

When the band announced they'd be taking their first break, I watched as Finn, Ty, Scott, and Trent – the final band member who I'd yet to meet – hopped off the stage and were immediately swarmed by groupies. I tried to reel in the unfamiliar, unfounded jealousy I was feeling. Finn wasn't my boyfriend; sure, we'd had great sex – but we'd never talked about what that meant. We'd certainly never said anything about exclusivity or labels.

Finn was slowly making his way toward the bar; I could just make out his form amid the crowd of girls hanging off him. I'd never felt this way before, never *cared* this much before, and for a moment I stood rooted to the ground, watching him and feeling like I'd been kicked in the stomach by a steel-toed Timberland boot. Lexi's eyes were swinging from me, to Finn, then back to me, her expression both sympathetic and wary of my reaction.

Suddenly, I had the strong urge to slap myself across the face. Who was this girl, standing in the shadows and watching a guy she had feelings for get mauled by slutty groupies? Who was

182

she, waiting on the wings because she was too afraid to step out and face the music? I sure as hell didn't recognize her.

She wasn't the person my mother had been. And she definitely wasn't the person my mother had raised me to be. Closing my eyes, I could almost hear the whisper of her words in my ear; I could nearly feel the warmth of her body pressed to my side as we lay in my childhood bed looking up at my fairytale ceiling.

Brooklyn, some people live their whole lives standing on the cliff's edge, waiting for some guarantee that when they finally take that leap into the unknown, there'll be a safety net there to catch them. But those people, Bumblebee? They never really live. *They watch as their lives pass them by, waiting for something that doesn't exist.*

Because you'll never be a hundred percent sure of anything. You'll take chances on people, and they'll hurt you. You'll try some things, and you'll fail at them. And that's okay, Bee – that's life. You can't stop living it because you're scared. You can't wait on the cliff's edge forever, just because it's safe.

You have to jump.

I had to jump.

Suddenly, before I had time to think about what I was doing, I was moving – pushing through the crowd to get to him. I unapologetically elbowed my way through the swarm of girls, ignoring their sharp squeals of protest and finally breaking through the circle surrounding Finn. I came to a stop about a yard away from him.

His eyes met mine immediately, as if he'd been waiting for me to materialize from the crowd at any moment. We both stood frozen with several feet between us and simply stared at one other. As our gazes locked, emerald clashing with cobalt, I felt it again: that indescribable force that seemed to tug me in his direction whenever we were close, like two magnets held only centimeters apart – their attraction irrefutable and infinite. The look in his eyes told me two things: firstly, that he felt it too, and secondly, that it *had* been me he was searching for in the crowd all night.

Jump.

I took one step in his direction and then, so fast my mind hadn't even registered that he was moving, he'd closed the distance and was there in front of me, a breath away.

"Princess," he whispered, a hand coming up to stroke the side of my face.

"Caveman," I breathed back, leaning into his touch.

I felt his smile against my lips the instant before his mouth was on mine, our arms twining around each other simultaneously. I clung to him tightly as our mouths devoured one another, as if it had been months rather than hours since we'd last been together. His hands were everywhere: tangling in my hair, caressing my shoulders, sliding down my back to rest on my hips and pulling me tight against his front so every line of our bodies melded together.

And as I lost myself in his touch, I didn't care about the other girls or the fact that we'd never talked about labels or feelings or terms. Because he was Finn, and I was Brooklyn, and in that moment nothing else mattered.

I was home.

I'm not sure how long we stood there, locked together in our own little world, before the catcalls and whispers of the crowd around us broke into my consciousness.

"I think he just got you pregnant," Lexi's voice called from somewhere behind me. My lips broke away from Finn's and I twisted to look over my shoulder at her.

"I mean, seriously, that was the hottest thing I've ever seen," she continued, her expression reflective. "I may have had an orgasm just watching."

Tyler, who was standing by her side, burst out laughing and pulled her into his arms.

"Lex," I said, giggling. "You need to get out more."

I detangled my hands from where they were wrapped around Finn's neck and looked up into his eyes.

"Hey," I said, smiling.

"You came," he grinned back at me.

"I told you I would."

184

"I know," he shrugged. "I just figured you'd have found a way to talk yourself out of this by now."

"Well, fine," I huffed. "I'll just leave if that's what you were expecting,"

I tried to pull away from him. His arms, still wrapped around me from our kiss, didn't buckle or even loosen as I struggled against his hold.

"Stop fighting me, princess," Finn said, his voice low. "It'll be a lot easier for both of us if you quit running away from this and inventing reasons to be mad at me."

"I'm not running and I'm not *inventing* anything," I snapped, even though I kind of was.

"Bee."

"What." I barked the word, staring at his chin so I wouldn't have to see the look in his eyes.

"I'm happy you came."

I sighed and, just like that, the anger I was trying so hard to hold onto slipped away. Anger was easy – I could deal with rage, or hate, or indifference. It was these new emotions, the ones I was too afraid to even put a name to, that I was struggling to cope with.

Lifting my eyes, I met his gaze, which was warm and full of amusement.

"This isn't going to be easy, you know," I told him.

He raised an eyebrow. "This?"

"Us," I choked out, nearly stuttering over the word.

He smiled and the dimple in his right cheek popped out.

"The good things – the things that are really worth it – usually never are," he replied, hooking one arm around my shoulder and steering us toward the bar. "Now let's get a drink."

"Or five," I added under my breath, swallowing nervously.

Finn laughed and squeezed me a little tighter as he led me toward the stools where Lexi and Tyler were sitting.

CHAPTER THIRTEEN

FREE FALLING

Finn and Tyler were back on stage, whipping the crowd into a frenzied state as their second set of the night progressed. They'd spent their break laughing at the bar with Lexi and me, and – not that I'd ever admit it to Lexi – it had been so much fun I was actually looking forward to the possibility of double dates in the future.

After they left us to go perform, Lexi and I had claimed a small high-top table on the outskirts of the crowd where we had a prime vantage point for ogling the band and watching the writhing people on the dance floor. We were giggling at the sight of a stumbling-drunk couple sloppily making out against a thick ceiling support column, when Finn's voice cut through the noise of the club and immediately caught my attention.

"Alright, alright, alright!" Finn yelled into the mic. "You guys enjoying the show?"

The crowd screamed their approval.

"We're gonna slow it down a bit now, so bear with us. This next song is really important to me, 'cause it says everything I never seem to be able to find the right words for." Finn smiled as he looked out over the crowd, his eyes coming to rest on me. "This one goes out to my special girl – she knows who she is." He winked at me.

There was a collective sigh from the females in the audience; it was obvious that 99.9% of them believed he was talking about them.

"And, actually, I'm gonna need her help to sing it," Finn told the audience. "She's probably going to kill me for doing this, so I'll need your help getting her up here. Let's give her some encouragement! Make some noise for BROOKLYN!" He held his arms out at his sides and waved them up and down, pumping up the crowd's volume to an ear-splitting decibel.

"You call that loud?" Finn yelled into the mic.

The crowd roared even louder. This was unprecedented; never once in *Apiphobic Treason*'s history had they ever called someone from the audience up on stage.

"Come on, princess, get your ass up here!"

He was laughing into the microphone, undoubtedly amused by the look of murderous rage that was beaming from my eyes. I began vigorously shaking my head back and forth so he would understand that there was no way in hell I was getting up on that stage.

"He means you, dummy!" Lexi shoved at my arm. "Go!"

I looked at her in horror. "I'm not going up there! Whose side are you on?" I yelled, appalled.

"Finn's!"

Traitor!

By this point the crowd had started to turn around, curious about the identity of Finn Chamber's "special girl." Then, the chanting began – a slow-building crescendo of my name, called out in unison by the nearly three hundred people.

"BROOK-LYN, BROOK-LYN," they chanted relentlessly, the room vibrating with the sound.

Whoever was working the stage lights located me in the crowd – Finn had probably tipped them off beforehand so they'd know exactly where I was standing – and I suddenly found myself illuminated on all sides by a spotlight.

Well, there goes my plan to escape unnoticed out the back door.

"Come on, princess, don't be shy," Finn's voice teased, booming through the speakers at me.

"BROOK-LYN, BROOK-LYN, BROOK-LYN," the crowd screamed.

"Go!" Lexi cajoled, giving me a push from behind and sending me toppling off my chair in the direction of the stage.

Fuck.

I moved through the dense crowd, the spotlight following my every step, and club-goers parted around me like I was freaking Moses navigating the Red Sea. I kept my eyes locked on Finn's as I neared the stage, and felt Lexi's presence hovering close behind me, her hand clasped tight around mine.

Traitor or not, the girl always had my back.

As we ascended the stairs and found ourselves on stage, Lexi leaned forward so her mouth brushed my ear. "Thank *god* I took the time to curl your hair. And you wanted to wear it up in a ponytail, of all things! Can you *imagine*?!"

Her voice was teasing and affectionate, full of the reassurance I so desperately needed to calm the nervous butterflies swarming in my stomach. My nerves eased slightly as I laughed at her ridiculousness, and I sent her a warm look as she gave my hand a final squeeze of support. She winked as we parted ways, dropping my hand so I could make my way to Finn while she went to stand by Tyler's drum kit.

The warmth immediately faded from my expression as I turned to look at Finn. He was waiting for me, unbothered by my wrath, with one hand outstretched. I slipped my hand into his and dug my fingernails harshly into his palm.

He didn't even bother to flinch, the bastard.

"What the hell are you doing, Finn!" I whispered, careful not to project into the microphone. He winked at me, then turned to face the crowd.

"Ladies, gents, here she is – I give you Brooklyn Turner, everybody! Make some noise for her!"

Great, he was ignoring me.

The crowd, however, was not; from the loud, appreciative catcalls and male yells I heard emanating from the audience, it was clear that The Dress was not only appreciated, but a very welcome change from the all-male entertainment Styx usually boasted. I couldn't help but smile a little.

"Now, like I said earlier, this song is special to me and Brooklyn. You might even say it's our song," he said, grinning at me. "Right, princess?"

"We don't have a song," I muttered, appalled. I really didn't like where this was headed. "We aren't even a couple!" In spite of my growing alarm, I managed to keep my voice low enough that the microphone didn't project my protests across the club. Finn ignored me, throwing an arm around my shoulder and hauling me close to his side.

"We can't hear you!" a voice shouted from the crowd.

"Yeah, what'd she say?" another yelled.

"She agreed with me," Finn told the crowd, his body moving with suppressed laughter. "So, without further ado, for our first performance as a couple...this is *Home* by Edward Sharpe and the Magnetic Zeros!"

Couple? What the...what?!

Before I could protest or even fully process the bomb he'd just dropped on me – and approximately three hundred random strangers – Scott, Trent, and Ty started playing the intro notes. My cue to sing was approaching too rapidly to move or think or even breathe – all I could do was react.

Thanking my lucky stars that – due to countless practice runs in my shower – I knew all the words to this song by heart, I took a step out from under Finn's arm and grabbed the mic stand. If I was going to do this, then I was going to do it right; you just can't half-ass a song like "Home."

Looking out over the screaming crowd, I forgot to be mad at Finn. My mind cleared completely, and all that was left was the feel of the microphone gripped in my hand and the utter rush of adrenaline coursing through my veins.

Then even that was gone; I was empty of everything except the lyrics, and I was singing my heart out.

Finn and I traded off verses seamlessly, as if we'd practiced this song together millions of times. In reality, we'd only sung it once – when it played yesterday as we'd painted my bedroom.

The song's tone was playful, and we laughed as we sang and circled each other on stage, eyes locked on one other rather than the audience. Despite the lightness of our performance, the lyrics conveyed a deeper and infinitely more meaningful message. I didn't fail to notice what Finn was telling me by selecting this particular song.

Home.

It's wherever I'm with you.

It was a strong statement to make to anyone, but it was especially powerful for me – a girl who hadn't had a true home for most of her life. His choice hadn't been accidental; he knew better than anyone what my life growing up had been like. The bits and pieces I'd revealed had painted him a pretty good picture of my childhood, even if he was still missing some of the more vital details.

So him choosing this song? It wasn't a coincidence, or an oversight, or a mistake.

It was a declaration. It was an assurance I'd never before been offered. It was a promise that, even though I didn't have a traditional home with two loving parents, a white picket fence, and a golden retriever in the front yard, it didn't matter.

He would be my home.

It was in that instant I fell in love with him.

I know people always talk about love like it's a realization you have one day – a sudden moment of clarity where you realize you've been slowly falling in love with that person for days or weeks or months. People talk like it isn't really *falling* at all, but instead, a gentle recognition that you've already hit the ground.

It wasn't like that for me.

It wasn't a slow epiphany, or an awareness that I'd floated down into love weeks ago, without ever realizing it.

It was as sudden as a flashflood, as violent and terrifying as diving headfirst off the side of a skyscraper. I hadn't fallen; No, I was *free-falling* – spiraling down into an abyss and waiting for the ground to rush up and meet me.

I didn't even bother to brace for impact, because my landing was inevitable. Gravity was pushing me down, speeding my descent. Faster, faster, faster, I crashed down into love, with no hopes of ever pulling myself back up the side of building to safety.

When the pavement below came into view, canvased in a sidewalk-chalk tableau of broken hearts and crushed expectations, I waited for the forthcoming pain of impact. My arms didn't flail, my legs didn't bicycle the air. With detached acceptance, I anticipated the hit; the splintering of bones, the splattering of flesh and marrow on concrete as love – that horrible, destructive, immovable force – destroyed every atom and particle of my being.

So, when that inevitable crash happened – when I landed so hard against the realization I that loved Finn, it stole my breath and nearly made me stop singing – I was shocked that no parts of me shattered.

My bones didn't break, my lifeblood didn't spill, my heart wasn't pulverized. Instead I felt the telltale crumble of every wall I'd ever barricaded my heart with, as they fractured to dust against the ground.

When the debris settled, and I found myself standing unharmed at the bottom of an impossibly tall skyscraper, I realized that I'd done it.

I'd jumped. And, more importantly, I'd survived the fall.

The walls I'd so meticulously constructed to keep everyone out had cushioned my fall and were now simply gone, as though they'd never existed in the first place.

I loved Finn Chambers – I freaking *loved* him – and there wasn't a single barrier left to keep him out of my heart.

My face must have registered awe or fear or a mixture of both, because when I snapped back into reality I realized that Finn was looking at me strangely, with questions alight in his eyes. Thankfully, even during earthshattering realizations like the one I'd just experienced, I liked to think I could keep a pretty good poker face. Since I'd never even stopped singing, it was likely that Finn and Lexi were the only ones who'd recognized the glazed look of panicky joy in my eyes.

With a wink of reassurance in Finn's direction, I turned back to the crowd and finished out the song with a secret smile on my face. When Scott and Ty played the final notes, I grinned as the crowd at our feet jumped up and down, applauding madly and yelling their approval. Finn waved to the crowd before grabbing my hand and tugging me toward him. Heedless of the hundreds of people watching us, he pressed his lips to mine and gave me a searing kiss.

The catcalls, if possible, grew even louder.

"Brooklyn Turner, everybody!" Tyler yelled into the mic he used for backup vocals, his voice breaking Finn and me out of our private moment. I tried to move away, but Finn didn't let me get far; keeping his arms locked firmly around my lower back, he rested his forehead against mine. He didn't even bother to look at the crowd – he had eyes only for me.

"You are so amazingly talented it actually stuns me," he said, his gaze intense. "This is what you're meant to be doing with your life, Bee."

"Singing?" I asked, incredulous.

"Yeah," he whispered, pulling back so he could kiss my forehead. "Just promise me you'll at least think about it. Deal?"

"Deal," I whispered back, pressing my lips against his to seal the agreement. When we pulled apart, Finn turned back to the crowd, keeping one hand locked with mine.

"Can't you see why I'm crazy about this girl?" he asked the audience, holding our joined hands over my head and twirling me in a slow circle. There were cheers from the men in the audience; the fangirls, however, were uncharacteristically quiet.

I'm could almost hear the sound of thousands of hearts breaking all across campus as girls texted, tweeted, and blogged the news that Finn Chambers was officially, inconceivably, off the market. The girls nearest the stage were either staring at me with thinly veiled jealousy and hatred, or looking longingly at Finn, as if at any moment he'd announce that it was all a big joke and call them up onstage instead.

I waved at them cheerfully as I walked off stage with Lexi at my heels.

Bitchy? Maybe. Satisfying as hell? Definitely.

Lexi and I were the recipients of more than a few judgmental looks as we made our way to the bar to grab another round. We decidedly ignored them, paid for our drinks, and walked back to reclaim our small table near the stage.

"Girl, if you don't lock that shit down, *I* will. That boy is so fucking hot, every girl in this room would kill to be you right now," Lexi said, her light blue eyes wide as she stared at me across the high-top. "In all seriousness, though, watch your back.

Some of these bitches wouldn't bat an eyelash as they sliced your throat with a lethally manicured fingernail and left your body to rot in the dumpster outside."

"That's comforting, Lex. Thanks so much."

"I try," she grinned.

"I think I love him," I blurted.

Lie. I totally knew *I loved him.*

"Yep." Lexi nodded sagely. "You were a goner the minute that boy sauntered into your life."

"He doesn't saunter," I pointed out, sipping my drink.

"You're right. You were a goner the minute he scraped you off the pavement when you fell over that fire hydrant."

"After I *fell?*" I asked. It seemed Lexi and I remembered the events of that day very, very differently.

"Yep," Lexi giggled.

I shot a glare in her direction.

"You love him," she sighed happily, a dreamy look drifting over her face.

"Lex," I said, warningly. Admitting it out loud was one thing; discussing it casually over drinks was another.

"I know, I know," she grumbled. "You don't want to talk about it."

"I'm going to run to the bathroom," I told her, rising from my seat. I needed to clear my head. "Be back in a second."

"Want me to come?" she offered, her eyes fixed on the stage.

"Nah, stay here and guard the table. I won't be long."

"Mmkay," she murmured, practically drooling as she watched Tyler perform a kickass drum solo. I cast a final look at Finn, who was fully engrossed in his performance, his eyes closed in concentration, and I felt my heart swell with so much feeling I thought my ribs might crack under the strain.

Tearing my eyes away, I turned and headed for the back hallway where the bathrooms were located. As I pushed open the door to the women's room, I froze in the doorway when I saw that all of the stalls were occupied, with several girls waiting in line. Every head swiveled to look at me as the door swung open, and I abruptly realized that I would never be able to think surrounded by so much female hostility.

Allowing the door to swing closed again, I turned my back to the bathroom and glanced down the dim hallway. The walls were dingy, covered in peeling gunmetal gray paint and a myriad stains whose origins I had no desire to discover. A single bare, flickering light-bulb swung from a wire on the ceiling, and the hallway's other two doors offered passage either into the men's room or out into the narrow alleyway running adjacent to Styx.

It wasn't exactly an environment suited to finding one's inner Zen.

In under a second my decision was made and my feet were moving, carrying me toward the door to the alleyway. I needed to breathe the night air, to see the ever-present night sky and regain an iota of control over the parts of me I felt spiraling wildly.

The door was constructed of heavy, soundproofed metal and, judging from its worn, rusted appearance, it didn't appear to see frequent use. It squealed on its hinges as I pushed it open, flecks of rust falling like ashes into the dim alleyway beyond. At my feet was a lone cinderblock, pushed against the wall as a makeshift doorstop. Leaning down, I used one hand to grab it and dragged it over to prop open the door.

Yellow light from the hallway spilled out into the alley, illuminating a small section of the otherwise dark passage. Stepping through the doorway and down two concrete steps, I acted on an instinct so deeply ingrained I couldn't quite remember its origins; my head tilted back, gaze lifting to the night sky, and as the stars swam slowly into focus, I was overcome with a feeling of infinite calm.

I'd craved the grounding serenity of the stars for as long as I could remember; the vastness of the galaxies above had always made my problems seem somehow smaller or more manageable – whether it was from my perch on the Victorian's rooftop, from the French-style balcony off my bedroom in my father's estate, or from a dilapidated porch stoop in a long-forgotten foster home. Now, thanks to Finn, I could even see the stars from my bed as I looked up at my ceiling. The thought made me smile into the dark night.

I leaned back against the cool brick wall opposite the club door, head tilted up to the constellations above. With an efficiency born from years of practice, I rattled off their names in my mind.

Andromeda.

Pisces.

Aquarius.

Pegasus.

Eventually, I felt my mind clear and allowed my eyes to droop closed. The minutes ticked by as I listened to the muffled music leaking out the propped door into the alley, trying to work up the courage to go back inside. It wasn't that I was scared to see Finn. In fact, it was the opposite; I was so eager to be alone with him, it was taking every modicum of self-control I possessed not to storm back on stage and forcibly drag him to my apartment.

My eyes flew open at the unmistakable sound of the heavy metal door slamming shut with a resounding boom that shook me to my very core. Even more startling was the sudden quiet, as if the darkness had thrown a thick woolen blanket over every sound – the music, the laughter, the chatter of rowdy patrons as they bought drinks. It was all gone now, leaving me alone in the utter stillness.

And the dark.

Every trace of calm in my system had fled along with the light, and my mind was abruptly full of panicked thoughts that pinged around the inside of my mind faster than I could keep up with.

Did someone close the door, or was it the wind?

Are you an idiot? There isn't any wind, Brooklyn.

Okay, so someone closed it.

Did they know that I'm out here?

Shit, does anyone *know that I'm out here?*

Or, worse…is someone out here with me*?*

I forced myself to stop thinking along those lines before I induced a full-blown panic attack. My eyes, unadjusted to the sudden darkness, reeled wildly as they searched for something, *anything*, in the pitch-black alleyway. Every muscle in my body tensed as I prepared for an attack of some kind. I took stock of the situation, my hands curled into fists and my body poised on the balls of my feet as I prepared to take off at a moment's notice.

I had two options: either feel my way back toward the door and try to open it – which I wasn't even sure was possible, given the fact that I hadn't seen a doorknob on the outside – or follow along the wall I was leaning against until it led me to the street in front of Styx. The alley was probably only a hundred feet long – it would have taken me no more than a few seconds to find my way out under normal circumstances.

Now, however, with only my hands and ears to guide me, my feet strapped into a pair of Lexi's highest heeled sandals, and fear coursing through my veins, I knew it would take me much longer to reach the street. Especially if I was bumping into dumpsters and wading through refuse the entire way.

I cursed my own stupidity. I'd broken every rule in the *Girls Who Don't Want to Get Murdered at College* handbook by going outside alone and not bringing Lexi or even my cellphone with me on this asinine escapade.

I decided my chances of prying open the heavy door were better than attempting to navigate a garbage-filled cobblestone alley in five-inch stilettos. With my luck, I'd probably end up tripping over a hobo or falling headfirst into a dumpster.

Taking a tentative step forward into the darkness, I kept one hand planted against the wall behind me, the brick surface rough beneath my palm. Despite the faint light cast by the stars above, the alley remained too dark to make out any shapes at all. Initially, I'd been optimistic that my eyes would adjust to the shadows, but after nearly a full minute had passed with little change, my hopes had dwindled.

Without my sight, my other senses were all on high alert; I could smell the cloying stench emanating from the dumpsters and, if a mouse had scurried anywhere within a half-mile radius, I was sure I'd have heard it. So with each passing minute that the alley remained utterly quiet, I grew more confident that I was alone.

196

I felt some of the tension uncoil from my shoulders. Though I was still uneasy about the situation, I was beginning to think that the door slamming closed was the work of a jealous fangirl, rather than some kind of creeper-rapist-monster-zombie.

More assuredly, I took another step forward into the darkness, taking me farther from the wall at my back and leaving only the fingertips of my left hand on the bricks. I was reluctant to relinquish that final tactile connection to the world, irrationally worried that, if I did, I might find myself lost in the darkness.

The alley was relatively narrow; standing directly in the center, I thought I might be able to reach both walls with my arms extended out to either side. Anxious to reach the doorway and get back to the safety of the club, I swung my right hand out into the darkness, hoping that my fingertips would strike the cool metal of the door, or the hard concrete of the steps.

They didn't.

Instead, they came into contact with something infinitely scarier.

Something that made my heart seize in my chest and my lungs constrict with a sudden loss of air. Something that froze the blood to ice in my veins.

Because that thing my fingers had grazed?

It was a man's chest.

Chapter Fourteen

Fight or Flight

I screamed.

It was a shriek of desperation – a shrill, ear-piercing wail born of sheer terror. It was helplessness personified, echoing forlornly off the walls of the alley. And even as the scream left my mouth I knew, deep in my bones, that it was futile; no one would ever be able to hear it over the thumping music inside the club.

My last thought, before his hands clamped down on my shoulders in an unbreakable vise-grip, was that I was no better than the dumb sorority girls I'd constantly mocked. I'd played right into his hands.

Whoever *he* was.

People always talk about our innate human fight-or-flight instinct. Supposedly, some people just have *it* – that will to live, to escape, to carry on in spite of the fear. And others simply don't. They lack that burning desire to survive above all else.

It's said that these moments in our lives, those split seconds in which we must decide whether to stand and fight or turn-tail and flee, define us as who we really are.

I'd always thought that was a crock of bullshit.

Of course, possessing the will to live is important – vital even. It can make the difference between life and death, between taking one more breath or succumbing to a quick end.

But so can a pair of five-inch stiletto heels.

Afterward, I'd often wondered, with a sense of morbid curiosity, whether things would have gone differently had I been wearing different shoes; had the ground had been paved, rather than cobbled; had the light cast by my favorite constellations above had been just a little bit brighter, so I might've seen him standing there in the dark with me. Biding his time. Waiting for me to make my move toward the door.

Would it have changed things? I guessed I'd never really know.

The scream died in my throat, turning to a gasp of pain as his grip cut harshly into my bicep muscles and he lifted me onto my tiptoes. Struggling against him, I used all the strength in my arms to try to free myself. I could feel my muscles weakening, my energy waning the longer we grappled. His breath puffed warm on my face – short, quick bursts of air that betrayed his excitement.

He was enjoying this.

He started to move then, steering me backwards with the ease of a master puppeteer pulling the strings of a hapless marionette. I had no control over my body as he closed in, trapped between the brick wall at my back and the monster pressed harshly against my front.

When he crushed his body to mine and I felt the undeniable hardness between his legs, my stomach began to churn with nauseating anticipation at the thought of what he planned to do to me. I knew then, with startling clarity, that if I didn't fight back I was going to die here in this alleyway – but not before I suffered a fate almost worse than death.

"Let—" I cried out, tugging at my arms. His hold was unshakable.

"Me—" I tried my legs next, kicking out with my stilettos but never quite managing to make contact with his shins.

"GO!" I screamed, my voice nearly cracking with hysteria as I thrashed in his hold. His grip was too tight, though; I could feel it coming, just like it had with Gordon in the club all those weeks ago. The overwhelming anxiety, crashing like a wave through my system and taking away what little control I was still in possession of. Sapping my will to fight.

I could see it now, played out in my mind in perfect, high-definition color and surround sound: I was going to have a panic attack and then, defenseless, he'd be free to do whatever he wanted – beat, rape, kill me. Here lies Brooklyn Turner, campus casualty and veritable afterschool special.

I wasn't going to let that happen. I wasn't ready for my life to be over – not when it was finally getting good.

Taking deep breaths and trying desperately to quell the overwhelming anxiety and fear that had taken hold, I did the only remaining thing that I could think of – a last ditch effort, really. I cocked my head back as far as it would go, and head-butted his face with as much force as I could muster. My forehead smashed into his nose, and I heard a sickening *crunch* as we made contact. Something wet – I assumed it was blood – poured from his nostrils in a torrent and dripped onto my forehead.

I'd broken his nose.

He let out a muffled curse, and, for a small fraction of time, his grip loosened enough for me to escape. I didn't waste my opportunity; as soon as my feet settled on the cobblestones, I ducked low and scurried out of his reach.

Knowing that he couldn't see me in the dark, I remained crouched, moving as quickly as possible without making too much noise. Though every instinct in my body was screaming for me to run, to sprint to safety as fast as my legs could carry me, I knew I had to be smarter than that. In such a confined space, even the smallest sound would give me away.

I slowly crept away, wincing with each step as my stilettos clicked mutedly against the cobblestones. Heart and mind racing, I tried to block out the questions that were rattling around my mind. I didn't have time to wonder who he was, or why he was doing this. It didn't matter right now – the only real thing, in this moment, was survival.

Quiet, don't move too fast.
Don't let him hear you.
Breathing too loud, take smaller breaths.
Hands on the ground, palms spread flat for balance.
Step, wince, freeze, listen.
That's it. Slowly, slowly.

I was gaining ground. He was behind me, floundering in the dark as he searched. I could hear his ragged breaths and sense his presence in the shadows several yards away. I could also sense his fury, fully unleashed at having lost me.

I knew if he caught me again, he wouldn't show what little restraint he had before. He was angry now, uncontrolled – a real wildcard. If I had any chance at all of living through this, I couldn't let him find me in the darkness.

It was the cobblestone that did me in.

One loose stone, warped enough to set me off balance. When my weight shifted forward, the stone beneath my heel slipped and before I could catch myself, I was careening forward, face-first onto the ground.

I felt the skin tear away from my elbows and knees as I slid across the rough-worn cobblestones, small pebbles and grime from the alley floor biting into my shredded skin. My temple cracked painfully against the cool stony surface hard enough to make my head spin dizzily, and a tiny, involuntary cry escaped my lips.

Immediately, I clamped my mouth closed to stop the sound, biting my bottom lip hard enough to draw blood. *Please, please, please*, I chanted, a mantra in my head. *Don't let him have heard me.*

For one suspended moment in time my ears strained to hear his movements, but it was utterly quiet once more in the alley. His ragged breathing had been silenced. I could almost picture him, standing stock-still as he tried to locate me in the shadows – listening just as hard as I was, as he crept ever closer.

I knew I had to move; yet, I remained frozen, lying on my stomach and paralyzed with indecision. Would the sounds produced by my movements only draw him closer? Was I better off simply making a run for it in my heels? Or, did I stay on my stomach and try to crawl my way out?

Before I could make any kind of decision, the choice was ripped from me.

Fists closed around my ankles, dragging me backwards. My hands, sprawled as they were on the ground in front of me, desperately scrambled for something to hold onto. My dress rucked up around my waist as I was towed by the ankles, the rough alley floor scraping my bare thighs raw within seconds. As he dragged me back, I managed to grab onto a shard of loose cobblestone, protruding slightly upwards – likely a piece of the cracked stone I'd tripped over. My fingernails nearly lifted from their beds as I tugged at the disrupted rock fragment, but it finally came loose in my hands.

I had a weapon.

He stopped dragging me, his hands moving up from my ankles to grip the base of my thighs, where my dress had ridden up. His grip wasn't rough, it was very nearly gentle – more akin to a lover's caress than a murderer's sadistic clutches.

I shuddered, fear and disgust overtaking me for a moment, before they were pushed out – overridden by an intense, all-consuming rage at this man, this stranger, who was going to take everything from me.

I wasn't just angry; I was enraged, I was incensed.

I was *furious*.

Bending my right knee, I curled my leg up and sent a powerful kick in the direction of my attacker. In my first stroke of luck all night, my stiletto landed a perfect blow to what I believed was his face, and his hands released me instantly. If the howl of pain he emitted was any indication, I'd caused some significant damage.

I was absently wondering if I'd punctured one of his eyes with the sharp heel of my shoe, when I snapped to my senses and sprang to my feet. Throwing out one hand so I was touching the brick wall, I ran flat-out, ignoring the burning pain in my ravaged knees. The wall beneath my hand was my only guide, keeping me upright as I sprinted for the faint light emanating from the end of the alleyway.

I could hear him behind me, cursing and noisily clamoring to his feet. Then, the pounding of his footsteps echoed in the night as he charged after me, gaining ground with each passing second.

I was getting closer to safety. I could finally make out the street at the mouth of the alley where people were waiting to get into Styx, faintly illuminated by the yellow streetlights overhead. As I ran, I stumbled twice on loose cobblestones and nearly fell over. I would have been a goner, had I not had one hand on the wall to catch myself. My other hand was preoccupied, still tightly clasped around the stone shard I'd pried from the ground.

He was faster than me, even with the injuries I'd inflicted.

I desperately wanted to stop and take off my stilettos, aware they were slowing me down, but I was too afraid to pause even for a moment. I knew that each time I'd tripped, I'd lost a bit of my lead, and he was going to catch me again if I didn't do something to slow his progress. Though I could see people ahead on the street, I knew there was still a good chance that they wouldn't be able to hear my screams from this distance – or, worse, that they wouldn't help me, even if they did hear my cries.

When I sensed he was close – less than ten feet away, if my perception was accurate – I twisted and hurled my sharp piece of cobblestone in what I thought was his general direction. I heard a *thud* as it made impact, and I prayed it had hit him in the head – or at least somewhere painful.

If I could just make it out of the alley, out of the dark, I'd be safe. He wouldn't be stupid enough to follow me into a crowd of people.

I hoped.

I sprinted for the street with every ounce of energy I had left in my body. Legs throbbing, lungs aching, head swimming with the effort, I ran until my vision clouded with black spots.

I didn't listen for him behind me. I didn't scream for help. I didn't even breathe.

I just *ran*.

Finally, miraculously, I broke through the entry of the alleyway and onto the semi-populated street. My legs gave out and I collapsed to my knees, my hands outstretched to brace my fall. Down on all fours, I lifted my head to look at the crowd of people standing in line for the club.

They stood there in their party clothes, looking down at me with their mouths hanging open in shock. Their faces were a kaleidoscope of emotions, ranging from confusion, to disbelief, to horrified comprehension.

I supposed, with my torn dress and bloodied knees, that I did look a bit of a mess.

"Help me," I whispered, just before my limbs gave out completely and I crumpled to the pavement. "Please…help me."

That's when everything went black.

***

It was the drone of approaching the sirens that pulled me up into consciousness.

One cheek pressed to the cool pavement, I cracked open an eye and looked skyward. Two girls, both wearing too much makeup and clothed in identical painted-on dresses, were staring back at me with worried expressions on their faces. At least, I thought they looked worried – it was a little hard to tell, beneath all that foundation and bronzer.

From the looks of it, they were standing guard – in their platform pumps, no less – over my prone form. Apparently, they'd also called the police and an ambulance.

"Are you okay?" one of the girls asked, her eyes wide as they scanned down my body, coming to rest on the once glorious Dress, which was now in tatters. I ignored the questions in her eyes.

Was I *okay*? No.

I was horrified, traumatized, stunned – she could pick her poison.

I didn't know if I'd ever be *okay* again.

"Yes," I croaked out, with a cough. My throat felt raw, whether from screaming or sprinting, I didn't know.

"The ambulance is on its way," the other girl informed me, as if I couldn't hear the ever-increasing wail of the siren. "We didn't know what else to do."

They looked uncertain, as though they thought I might be angry with them for calling in the cavalry.

"You did the right thing. Thank you," I whispered, in a tone I hoped conveyed how appreciative I was. "Really."

I didn't get to tell them anything else or even ask their names, because the ambulance had arrived and, all at once, I was surrounded by a sea of paramedics and police officers.

With quiet efficiency, the paramedics rolled me over onto my back and examined my scraped legs and arms. None of the wounds were deep enough to require stitches, so they applied a stinging antiseptic and wrapped the worst of them tightly in white gauze. I think they tried to tell me some things or maybe ask what

204

had happened to me, but I was adrift in my own private bubble; their voices sounded far away, muffled as though they were speaking to me through a clear Plexiglas wall.

I tuned in enough to catch a word every once in a while.

"…….*in shock……..possible head trauma…….multiple contusions…*"

After they'd checked my pupils by shining a glaringly bright pen light directly into each eye, there was more muffled conferencing between paramedics. Something they'd seen in my pupils' response must've worried them, because in no time at all, they'd wheeled over a stretcher and gently lifted me onto it.

"…*Jane Doe….attacked…..concussion….*"

When my back gently hit the cushion, I automatically looked up to the stars.

Andromeda.

Pisces.

Aquarius.

Pegasus.

I closed my eyes and tried to shut them out, to turn off the images that seeing them had triggered, but it was too late.

A door slams. It's dark, so dark I can't even see my hand in front of my face. Utterly quiet, hopelessly alone. My hand touches a foreign chest. His bruising grip on my shoulders. Tight, so tight. I gasp in pain. Screams no one can hear echo in the night. I'm cornered. I'm helpless. I'm going to die.

The sounds of a struggle snapped me back into the present. My eyes followed the loud voices, until I found him in the crowd. He looked frantic to get to me, his face flushed red and his deep blue eyes flashing dangerously as he screamed at the duo of police officers restraining him. He was gesturing toward me, clearly trying to explain something to the officers, when his eyes locked on mine and he realized that I was conscious.

"Bee!" Finn screamed, his voice cracking, broken. "Tell them to let me through, Bee. Tell them, princess. They won't let me get to you."

Still floating in the numbness of my aftershock, I stared at him, mesmerized by the haunted look on his face. He appeared nearly unhinged with worry at my condition, as though the strain of what had happened to me was more than he could bear. He almost looked as if he'd been the one alone in that alleyway, when a monster had slithered from the shadows.

I wanted to tell him that it was okay – that *I* was okay. I wanted to take that tormented look out of his eyes. I didn't do that, though. Instead, I turned my head away from him, not wanting to see that expression on his face anymore and too preoccupied with my own demons to spare any thoughts for his.

Maybe I can stay like this forever. Comfortably numbed to the world. Adrift – quite possibly unhinged – but safe. Alone in my bubble. Untouchable. Maybe it's better this way.

As much as I wanted to hold onto my detached catatonia, I knew it couldn't be healthy. And it was probably a one-way ticket to a padded cell and a lifetime supply of all-you-can-eat Jell-O.

It was then that I realized there was a paramedic speaking to me in a low, soothing tone, her mouth close to my ear. Turning my eyes to her face, it was as if an un-mute button had abruptly been pressed; all the sounds came rushing back, nearly overwhelming in their volume.

Sirens wailing. Police radios crackling. Curious onlookers whispering. A man's voice, yelling my name.

"Can you hear me, sweetie? We need to know your name, so we can take care of you."

"Br—Brooklyn," I stammered out, my voice sounding fragile. Clearing my throat I tried again, "Brooklyn Turner."

"Okay, Brooklyn, that's good. I'm Shannon." She stared into my eyes searchingly, looking for answers to the mountain of questions that had piled up in however long had passed since I first emerged from the alley. "Do you remember what happened?" she asked me.

I nodded.

"That's good, Brooklyn," Shannon smiled encouragingly.

"I was…I was attacked," I whispered, at once a confession and a plea for understanding. Her eyes were a warm brown, like melted caramel, and at the moment they were filled with sympathy and worry.

"The police officers are going to have some questions for you in a little while, do you understand?" Shannon asked me. "Your injuries are minimal. You have some scrapes that will need fresh bandages and antiseptic daily, but nothing too serious. They shouldn't leave scars, but you'll have some pain and discomfort for the next several days. You may have a broken rib, and your forehead is slightly bruised, as are your upper arms.

"You also need to be aware of the fact that you have a minor concussion. It's important that you stay awake for the next hour or so, and when you do eventually go to sleep for the night, someone needs to wake you every few hours to check your condition. Do you have anyone who can help take care of you? Your parents?"

I shook my head.

"What about a roommate? A boyfriend, maybe?"

My eyes left her face and once again found Finn in the crowd. He was still facing off with the police officers, trying his damnedest to get to me, but he seemed to be losing hope. The look of dejection and defeat on his face would've brought my to my knees – had I been standing and had my knees not already been ripped to shreds, that is.

"Officers," I called out, with as much strength as I could suffuse into my voice; I hoped it would be enough for them to hear me over the noise of the sirens and the gathering crowd. "Please, let him through. He's my boyfriend."

The officers – one of whom I recognized as Officer Carlson, the semi-pudgy policeman who'd investigated the break-in at my apartment – turned to me and nodded. Dropping their arms to allow Finn to pass, he was at my side in an instant. His arms folded around me gently, as though he was afraid I might shatter if he touched me too roughly.

Bringing his forehead down to rest against mine, he stared into my eyes. His own were brimming with unshed tears.

"You're gonna tell me what happened," he whispered roughly. "Everything. Every detail. And when you're done, I'm gonna find the fuck who did this to you and make sure he never sees another goddamn sunrise."

His words were vengeful, but his hands were gentle as they came up to cup my face. When he pressed his eyes closed, trying to regain control over his emotions, a solitary tear slipped out from beneath his eyelid and tracked down his face. I leaned forward to kiss it off his cheek, and his eyes sprang open to look at me once more.

"Are you okay?" he asked me.

I nodded.

"You scared the fucking shit out of me, you know that?"

I nodded again, my eyes locked on his.

"I saw you leave for the bathroom. Sang two whole songs, and you still hadn't come back. I knew something wasn't right – I could feel it. So I stopped playing, found Lexi, and asked her where the hell you were." His eyes pressed closed again and I saw the tic of a muscle in his cheek as he tried to temper his anger. "She had no idea. She was too busy eye-fucking Ty to even notice you'd been gone for way too long."

"She didn't know," I whispered, coming to Lexi's defense. I'd been the idiot who'd gone outside alone, without my cellphone. This was all on me. "It isn't her fault, it's mine."

"She should've fucking known better," he snarled, clearly not willing to forgive Lexi tonight. I decided to let this battle go. For right now, Finn needed someone to blame – someone to take out his anger on. His frustration with her would fade once the police found whoever had attacked me. At least, I hoped it would.

"Finn," I whispered. "I need to talk to the police. Give them my statement."

"I'm staying with you," he told me, his tone leaving no room for argument. I sighed. I hadn't exactly wanted him to hear all the gory details, but I had no fight left in me. I'd used it all up in that alleyway.

When Officer Carlson and the other policeman – a thin man with a graying beard and an avuncular manner who introduced himself as Officer O'Callahan – approached, I sat up slowly and Finn moved to stand by the side of the stretcher. He kept his fingers laced with mine, giving my hand reassuring squeezes whenever my voice faltered or I struggled to find the

208

words to explain what had happened during the attack.

When I reached the point in my tale that I had to describe my attacker's sexual arousal, Finn's grip grew dangerously tight. I could tell, without even a glance in his direction, that he was waging an internal battle to keep his composure – warring with his instincts to lash out in rage. He somehow managed to remain silent so I could finish giving my statement. The policemen listened with stony faces, their expressions hardened by years of experience with victims whose fates were far worse than my own.

When I was finally done speaking, feeling shaken from reliving every moment of the attack, it was my turn to answer questions. They pelted me with query after query, wanting to know about the most minute, seemingly inconsequential details. To their disappointment, and my own frustration, I didn't have answers to many of their questions.

Did he have any distinguishing marks or characteristics?

It had been so dark; I didn't know.

Could you estimate his age?

Maybe somewhere between twenty and forty?

I couldn't be sure.

Did he mention any kind of motive?

He hadn't said anything, even when I'd broken his nose or smashed my high heel into his face.

Do you believe this is related to the break-in incident at your house last month?

It was possible, I supposed.

Can you think of anyone who would want to harm you?

Finally, a question I could answer.

"There's this guy. Gordon O'Brien. He's threatened me before." I swallowed tightly, talking around the large lump in my throat. "I think he gets off on scaring girls. And he was definitely at the club tonight – I noticed him when I walked in."

"When you say that he's threatened you in the past, what do you mean?" Officer Carlson asked.

"He grabbed me roughly the last time I bumped into him at Styx – he lifted me clear off the ground," I explained. "I pleaded with him to stop, but he wouldn't. I ended up having a panic attack right there in the club."

"And you didn't report this incident to the police?" Officer O'Callahan chimed in sternly, disapproval apparent in his tone.

"It's my fault," Finn jumped in, his face cloudy with rage and regret. "I thought I'd handled the situation. Apparently I hadn't."

Officer Carlson raised one eyebrow as he turned his attention to Finn. "And how exactly did you 'handle' the situation?"

"I punched him in the face, sir," Finn answered, never one to beat around the bush. I actually thought I might've detected a note of pride in his voice.

Officer Carlson looked as if he were fighting a smile. Officer O'Callahan chuckled outright, evidently amused by Finn's forthright nature.

After asking a few more questions I couldn't answer, taking down all the information we knew about Gordon, and promising that they would be in touch as soon as they had any leads, the police officers left to go examine the alley more thoroughly. Apparently, as soon as they'd arrived on the scene, the officers had checked the alleyway to see if my attacker was still lurking in the shadows.

Unsurprisingly, he hadn't been.

Now, they explained, a forensic team would comb the crime scene looking for any kind of evidence that could help them discover his identity: blood, fabric from his clothing, even finger and footprints left behind on the cobblestones. I might have to go down to the station at some point to answer more questions, but for now I was free to go.

Before I could even make a move to hop off the stretcher, Finn was once again standing in front of me. He whipped his t-shirt over his head, leaving him bare-chested in the crisp autumn night air.

"Arms up," he ordered softly.

"But you'll get cold—" I began to protest, but stopped when I saw the look on his face. Resistance was definitely futile, and truthfully I was grateful that I wouldn't have to walk to the parking lot while exposed and indecent, with my tattered dress on display for the crowd. Obediently, I lifted my hands toward the sky and allowed him to slip the faded grey shirt over my head and arms.

Ignoring my protests, Finn swept me up into his arms and insisted on carrying me to his truck. As soon as we moved out of the protective shield of police and paramedic vehicles, we were surrounded by curious onlookers. Finn's glare kept them at a distance and, for the most part, they gave us wide berth as we made our way to the parking lot where Finn had left his truck.

There was no keeping Lexi away, though.

She didn't speak as she trailed us through the crowd, somehow keeping pace with Finn's quick strides. I could see traces of tears on her face, her normally light blue eyes watery and rimmed with red. She was quiet, even when our eyes locked, but I could see the apology in her gaze.

I winked at her, to let her know that I was okay and that I didn't blame her. If anything, I was grateful that Lexi hadn't been in that alley with me; if she'd been hurt, I would have been devastated.

It *was* eerie, though – the strong sense of déjà vu that filled me as Finn cradled me in his arms, with a remorseful Lexi hovering by his elbow. Just like the first day we'd met, before I knew what a big part of my life he would become. He was just some random guy then – a jerky prick who'd insulted and angered me beyond measure.

And now I was in love with him. Life was funny that way.

The ride to Finn's apartment was a blur. Finn was silent, lost in his own thoughts, and I kept my forehead propped against the cool glass of the passenger window, allowing my mind to blank as I watched the hazy orbs of the streetlights speed by. In seemingly no time, we'd pulled into the driveway of a modest two-story condo.

To say that this was not what I'd been expecting of Finn's place was almost certainly the biggest understatement of the century. Semi-reformed slut that I was, I'd been in the houses, apartments, and bedrooms of more guys than I ever wanted to count. I'd been primed for the worst – beer cans littering the front lawns, overgrown hedges, chipped paint, and a stoop that was falling apart.

What I was *not* expecting was a beautifully tended front lawn, pristine whitewashed shingles, and a front porch complete with several flowerboxes – each of them overflowing with cheerful, multicolored blossoms.

This was Finn's house? I actually had to pinch myself because I was nearly positive that I'd stepped into a parallel universe. Or maybe I'd hit my head so hard on those cobblestones that I was actually in the hospital experiencing some kind of weird, coma-induced hallucination.

Whatever it was, though, was no match for the shock I felt stepping inside the condo itself. Absent were the typical posters of bikini-clad girls on motorcycles and sports cars. There were no stray beer cups on the counter, nor was there a mountain of empty pizza boxes piled four feet high next to the trashcan.

"So, this is my place," Finn explained nonchalantly, as if it were totally unsurprising that he lived in a beautiful condo with marble countertops, a kitchen island, and a refrigerator so large I could probably fit my entire body in the freezer compartment.

I continued to spin in slow circles, taking in his uncluttered, minimalist space. The couch was low-slung, elegantly crafted in black leather. Both the coffee table and entertainment system – which housed an unfathomably large flat-screen television and numerous game consoles – were constructed of a sleek, dark wood. The place screamed effortless wealth. Hell, it even *smelled* like cultured masculinity.

Yep, I'm definitely lying in a coma somewhere.

"Bee?" Finn's voice sounded uncharacteristically nervous. "What do you think?"

"You have coasters."

"So?" Finn asked, a baffled look crossing his face.

"*Coasters*, Finn."

"I don't understand," Finn muttered, glancing from me to the coasters with a wary look in his eyes.

"You also have copper sink faucets," I pointed out.

"I guess?" Finn shrugged, looking at the sink like he'd never even noticed it before.

"You're rich," I said accusingly.

"And that's a problem because…?" Finn asked. His eyebrows were raised so high on his forehead they'd nearly disappeared beneath his messy hair.

Abruptly, I collapsed onto his leather couch. It was obscenely comfortable. *Of course it is*, I thought bitterly. *It probably cost more than my rent.*

"Bee, you've got this scary look in your eyes right now," Finn said, kneeling in front of me so he could look into my eyes. "What is this about? Why does it matter that I have money?"

"It doesn't," I snapped.

"Is this about your father?" Finn asked quietly.

"No!" I practically yelled in his face.

Defensive much? Way to play it cool, Brooklyn.

Finn looked at me skeptically.

"Fine. Maybe it's a little bit about him," I sheepishly admitted. I squeezed my eyes closed. "I'm sorry. I'm already so emotional from earlier, and then I walked in here and it was just… not what I was expecting, I guess. I felt like I was back at my Dad's house, and that place…" I took a deep, steadying breath. "It's the last place I ever want to be when I'm feeling vulnerable."

"That's understandable," Finn said, leaning in to brush a soft kiss across my lips. "But don't take it out on Henry."

"Henry?"

"My couch," Finn said, lovingly petting the leather next to my thigh.

"You named your couch?" I snorted. "That's sad."

"Don't disrespect Henry like that," Finn glared at me with mock-indignation.

"You are way too attached to an inanimate object," I said, rolling my eyes.

"Just wait till you meet Betty," Finn said, pulling me to my feet.

I raised one eyebrow in question.

"My bed," he grinned, waggling his eyebrows at me in return.

"You wish!" I smacked him playfully on the arm. "As if I'd get into bed with some weirdo who names his furniture."

"You don't like my jokes, you don't like my condo…Is there anything you *do* like about me?" he said, laughing.

"Nope!" I giggled.

With a fake-angry growl, Finn lifted me into his arms and carried me to the bathroom, careful not to put pressure on any of my injuries. It felt blessedly normal to simply laugh after a night like tonight. For that brief moment in time, I was free, buoyant with laughter and able to forget the fear and uncertainty. It was good to know I even still possessed the ability to laugh, after what had happened.

Our playful mood again turned somber once Finn set me down, the bathroom tiles cool beneath my bare feet. I'd abandoned Finn's grey t-shirt along with my stilettos earlier in his truck and I never wanted to look at the damn shoes again, if I could help it. I couldn't decide if they'd been my salvation or my downfall in the alley, and thinking about it too much made my head spin.

I barely had time to take in the beautiful bathroom, with its recessed cabinetry, pedestal sink, and sunken tub, because my eyes glided over the mirror and caught on the image of the tattered, war-worn girl reflected back at me.

The Dress was ruined – stripped of its intricate beading, the once-flowing skirt now a shredded rag, the bodice torn and dirty. Angry purple bruises already darkened the skin of my bare shoulders, where my attacker's hands had gripped so tightly. The skin of my palms, elbows, knees, and thighs had been rubbed raw, leaving throbbing, gaping red wounds behind.

But it was my eyes that fixated me the most. They looked huge, far too large for my face. Owl-like emerald orbs, glassy with shock, fear, and, worst of all, recognition.

Because I knew this girl in the mirror – this broken-down shadow, full of terror and uncertainty. I'd been her once before, seen this look gazing back at me from her deep green eyes. Years may have gone by, but I'd know her in a heartbeat, no matter how much time passed.

Scared. Traumatized. Alone.

There was one crucial difference, now, though.

This time, there was a boy reflected in the mirror too, standing behind the girl with his hands wrapped lightly around her waist. His steadfast blue gaze held trust, protection, and something that looked a lot like love.

I wasn't alone anymore. Not this time.

Leaning back into Finn's chest, I closed my eyes and felt the tears finally gather in my eyes. I couldn't stop them; I didn't even try. I just let Finn hold me as I wept for the horrible thing that had happened to me, and for all the other even more terrible things that so easily could have.

When the tears slowed, I opened my eyes and once again met the gaze of the girl in the mirror. Now, her face was splotchy, her makeup was running down her face in black smears, and her eyes were red-rimmed – but at least most of that haunted look had faded from her expression.

"What are you thinking about?" Finn asked gently, his gaze finding mine as I stared at our entwined reflection.

"How much I hate pretty criers. Seriously, those girls just release one glistening tear without ever smudging their mascara or getting all red-faced? Utter bullshit," I forced a laugh, trying to lighten the mood.

"Come on," Finn said, rolling his eyes as he guided me toward his walk-in shower. It was large enough for at least four people, enclosed by a wall of opaque glass blocks. After turning on the water, Finn returned to me and carefully unzipped The Dress. Letting it fall to my feet, he knelt down in front of me and I placed my hands on his shoulders to steady myself as I stepped out of the pooled fabric. Finn tossed it into a nearby trashcan without a second glance.

Bye, bye, pretty dress.

Still kneeling at my feet, Finn pressed a soft, warm kiss to my belly button. His hands moved lightly over my ravaged skin as they tugged down my underwear and unclasped my bra, leaving me naked before him. I felt ugly, exposed – bruised, broken, and laid bare in a way I'd never been.

When I moved my hands to cover myself, Finn stopped me. Interlocking our fingers, he began the painstaking process of kissing every scrape and bruise on my body, as he'd done with the scar on my collarbone the first time we'd slept together – as if his mouth could take away some of the hurt that had been inflicted.

He might not have been able to remove my injuries, but he did eventually erase any insecurities I'd felt. After he'd attended to each cut, he stripped off his own clothes and guided us inside the shower. The warm water was soothing against my skin, the dirt and grime that had coated me rushing off in brown-black torrents.

Finn poured some of his body wash onto a wet washcloth and carefully scrubbed my skin clean. He took his time, insuring that no traces of the alley were left behind on my body. Afterward, he shampooed my hair and the sensation of his strong fingers massaging my scalp was so relaxing it nearly put me to sleep. With each passing second, I could feel fatigue creeping into my bones, the weariness from my physical injuries as well as the mental strain of the night threatening to overtake me.

Just as my knees began to buckle, Finn wrapped one arm around my shoulders to support my weight and used his free hand to shut off the water..

Grabbing two large fluffy black towels from a rack on the wall, he wrapped me in one and looped the other around his own waist. He held my hand and led me, stumbling and bleary-eyed, from the bathroom and into his bedroom – which, under normal circumstances, I would have been beyond curious to examine.

Right now, however, I didn't even glance around as I followed Finn to the massive bed that dominated the room. Collapsing onto a plush grey down comforter, I vaguely registered Finn climbing in next to me and pulling the sheets up around our bodies.

I was asleep before my head hit the pillow.

CHAPTER FIFTEEN

MISSION ACCOMPLISHED

"See that star, Bee?" the boy asked, pointing at an especially bright one in the night sky above our heads. My gaze followed the direction of his finger. When I found it, I smiled; I was getting better at picking out constellations every night.

We were sitting on the stoop again, and the night was colder than usual. It was well into November, now. I'd been here at the foster home for nearly three months, and winter was coming fast. I had to bring the thin blanket from my bed with me when I came out onto the back porch each night.

I hoped I wouldn't still be here at Christmas time.

"It's pretty," I whispered, my lips forming the words but barely any sound escaping. The boy heard me though, looking away from his star to stare over at me. Though nearly a month had passed since that first night I'd told him my name, he still always looked happily surprised whenever I spoke to him, like he'd just opened a really awesome Christmas present or gotten a triple fudge sundae with his favorite ice cream flavors.

Maybe it was because I still wasn't talking to anyone else.

"That star is part of a constellation called Cassiopeia," the boy said. "See those four stars, shaped like a sloppy W?" He pointed from one star to another, tracing a map of the constellation with his finger.

I squinted, at first unable to see it. To me, the stars looked like a glowing, jumbled mess – sort of like the tangled strands of Christmas lights Mommy pulled down from the boxes in the attic when it was time to decorate the tree each year. It was hard to imagine ever picking out a pattern from within the chaos.

But then, as if something clicked in my mind, I did see it.

Cassiopeia: *a lopsided, w-shaped mess of stars, shining so brightly I wondered how I'd never noticed it before.*

"Remember the legend of Princess Andromeda?" the boy asked.

I nodded. I'd loved that story – it was the first one he'd ever told me.

"Cassiopeia was the queen – Andromeda's mother. All the characters from that story have their own constellation: Pegasus, Perseus, Andromeda, Cassiopeia... They're all up there."

I watched, fascinated, as the boy pointed out cluster after cluster of stars.

"Show me another one," I demanded quietly, enthralled.

"Okay," the boy said, a look of concentration crossing his face. *"See that one? That's Pisces. It's supposed to look like two fish swimming but I think it looks more like the letter V."*

My eyes followed the direction he was pointing and, though this one was harder, I eventually found it. When it popped into focus I smiled a real grin for the first time in months.

"How do you know about these?" I asked, my voice filled with awe.

"My dad taught me about them." The boy's voice was sad.

I decided I wouldn't ask him to show me any more tonight, not when he sounded so upset. But I knew tomorrow night, I'd ask again. And the next. And the one after that.

I'd ask until he ran out of stars.

My fascination wasn't exactly new– I'd always loved to look at the sky, especially after Mommy had painted stars on my ceiling. But now, they seemed enchanting, mysterious, and nearly irresistible. It was like he'd opened up a whole new world to explore, and I wanted – needed – to learn everything about the constellations floating in the darkness far above me.

"Bee, can I ask you something?" The boy's voice interrupted my thoughts.

I nodded, tearing my eyes from the stars to look at his face.

"Why me?" he asked, his voice quiet and his eyes turned away from mine.

"What do you mean?"

The boy swallowed roughly, his small Adam's apple

jumping in his throat like he had a gumball stuck down there. I
almost giggled as I watched it bob up and down but his voice had
sounded so serious, I held it in.
      "Why do you talk to me and no one else?"
      I was silent for a while, thinking about his question. The
truth was, I didn't even fully know why I felt so comfortable with
him and not the doctors or psychiatrists or the other the foster
kids.
      "I guess..." My voice faltered. "I guess it's because you
make me feel safe."
      "Safe?"
      "Yeah." I shrugged my shoulders, looking up at the sky.
I knew the boy was staring at me, but I couldn't look back at him
just yet. "At first, your stories...they reminded me of my mom. She
loved fairytales. She'd tell me one every night before I went to
sleep."
      The boy didn't answer. After a minute of silence, I felt his
larger fingers wind through mine as he laced our hands together.
      "Tell me a story," I whispered, squeezing his hand tightly.
"One with a happy ending."
      "Okay, Bee," the boy said, returning my hand squeeze.
Taking a deep breath, he began.
      "Once upon a time..."
                              ***

      I woke to the sound of a guitar strumming softly. It was
still nighttime and moonlight was streaming through the skylights
overhead, illuminating the soft, down comforter I was wrapped
in. After a brief moment of disorientation, I realized that I was in
Finns' bed.
      I closed my eyes as it all came rushing back at once: the
attack, my escape, talking to the paramedics and police officers,
all the helplessness and the fear. I began to tremble, hugging the
blankets closer around my body.
      I forced myself to think of the good things that had
happened tonight instead: the look on Finn's face when we
sang together on stage, my realization that I loved him, the way
he'd cleaned me up and cared for me when we got back to his

apartment.

Once I'd gotten the shaking under control, I opened my eyes and looked around the room for Finn. He wasn't hard to find.

Dressed only in a pair of faded, unbuttoned blue jeans, he was sitting on a chair facing a window on the other side of the room with his guitar balanced on his lap. I'm not sure he was even aware that he'd woken me, his playing was so soft. I vaguely recognized the tune he was strumming, but I couldn't put a name to it until he began singing quietly.

The melody was haunting, the words unforgettable.
Brooklyn, Brooklyn, take me in....

As he reached the chorus, the lyrics pleading for me to take him in and give him shelter, I finally remembered the name of the song and my eyes filled with tears.

He was playing *I and Love and You* by the Avett Brothers. And it was perfect.

When his voice trailed off with the final words, the *I love you* hanging in the air like a specter, it was utterly silent in the room except for the sound of our quiet breathing. I felt like an intruder – like I'd witnessed something he might not have wanted me to see.

Did I pretend to be asleep? Act like I hadn't heard him, like his words hadn't reached into my chest and grabbed me by the heart? I wasn't sure.

Before I could decide, his voice cut through the silence.

"How's your head?" he asked, his shirtless back still turned to me.

Well, I guess this means he knows I'm awake.

"It's alright," I whispered.

He rose from the chair, setting down his guitar and turning to face me across the dark room. The sight of him made my breath catch in my throat. His hair was a mess, as if he'd been running his hands through it over and over. Bare chested, his muscles and tattoos had never looked more prominent – and he'd never looked sexier. With half his face in shadow and the other half illuminated by an errant moonbeam, he was otherworldly gorgeous, like some kind of dark angel sent to save and destroy me all at once.

220

He approached the bed with his lithe, inherently graceful stride, and I couldn't tear my eyes from him. I was entranced by the way he moved toward me, fixated by the fluid way his muscles contracted beneath the skin. His eyes were intense on mine when he reached the side of the bed, stopping three feet away – just out of reach. I wasn't sure what he was waiting for, but I could see the indecision in his eyes and I didn't like it.

"I need to tell you something," his voice sounded more serious than I'd ever heard it. I instantly felt a cold sweat break out across my body, my heart beginning to hammer in my chest as my mind raced with possibilities.

"What is it?" I asked. "Did the police call?"

Finn expelled a harsh breath through his lips and dragged his hands up through his hair; whatever it was, he definitely didn't want to tell me about it.

"Finn?" I prompted.

He finally met my eyes. They were burning with frustration, anger, and sympathy. My heart rate increased even more.

"Officer Carlson called. They checked out Gordon's alibi," he took a deep breath, and I watched as his hands curled into fists. "It's airtight. They say it couldn't have been him."

Finn smashed his right fist angrily into the palm of his left hand, his face cloudy with rage and his eyes far away; it wasn't hard to guess exactly whose face he was imagining that fist smashing into. In fact, part of me was worried that he was seconds away from tracking down Gordon and extracting his own vigilante version of justice.

"Come here," I said, stretching out a hand to him. When his fingers twined through mine, I gave his hand a sharp tug, catching him off balance and sending him stumbling forward toward me onto the bed. After regaining his balance, he settled in next to me, though his expression remained distant with thoughts of Gordon and revenge.

"Finn," I said, snapping a finger in front of his face. His eyes flew to mine. "You can't kill him, caveman. Haven't you heard? Pretty boys like you don't do well in prison."

His lips turned up in a small, involuntary smile. I was getting to him.

"You'd end up with a 350-pound roommate named 'Tiny,' who'd totally take the top bunk and make you his bitch."

His eyes narrowed, but I could tell he was fighting a laugh.

"Oh, hey, do you know what prisoner's use to contact each other?" I asked him.

He raised one dark eyebrow at me skeptically.

"*Cell* phones. Get it?" I elbowed him in the stomach for emphasis.

The dimple popped out, and I knew I had him. Soon, his small smile turned into a grin, and then to full blown laughter as he processed my pun.

"And you said *my* jokes were terrible…" he gasped out, trying to catch his breath.

"Whatever," I shrugged. "Mission accomplished."

"And what mission would that be?"

"Well, since you haven't yet left to go kill Gordon, I'd say my efforts to detain you are succeeding."

"I don't know about that," he muttered, the smile fading from his expression. "That guy better pray he doesn't cross my path. I've been thinking about it all night."

"Well, I'll just have to take your mind off him then," I said, abruptly sitting up fully in the bed and allowing the comforter to fall down around my waist. Finn had evidently forgotten about the fact that I was completely naked beneath the covers; his eyes immediately fixed on my breasts and I watched with more than a little satisfaction as his eyes dilated at the sight of them.

"Mission accomplished," he echoed softly, moving closer to me on the bed. Reaching out his hands, he gently palmed my breasts, and I nearly moaned at the sensation of his guitar-calloused fingers against my skin. Arching into his touch, I closed my eyes and felt the whisper-soft brush of Finn's lips across my own.

When he captured my mouth with his, need flared hotly

222

between us. While he used his hands on me, I trailed my own down the planes of his muscular chest, delighting in the feel of his rippled abs against my fingertips. Pulling my mouth away from his, my eyes sprang open and I began to trace my fingers along the tribal whorls of ink on his bicep and shoulder. When my fingers had fully navigated the maze of his tattoo, I lowered my mouth to the design and began to follow the same path with my tongue, as I'd long wanted to do.

Finn growled low in his throat, evidently enjoying my exploration of his body art. When I'd finished with his arm, my mouth traveled up over his shoulder and collarbone, down the slope of his chest, and finally to his stomach, leaving a trail of damp, open-mouthed kisses behind. As my lips neared the waistline of Finn's jeans, he gently reached down and pulled me back up to eye level.

After a lingering, fierce kiss, he stared into my eyes. "Are you sure you want to do this?" he asked.

I knew what he meant. After what had almost happened to me tonight, it was probably odd that I felt this consuming need to be with Finn. I didn't want to overthink it, though. I didn't want to think *period*. I just wanted to feel.

I looked into Finn's eyes, hoping my answer was apparent in their depths. "I'm sure," I said. "I want you to erase him, Finn. I need you to."

At my words, a tender look came into his eyes. "I will, princess. I promise."

Kissing me sweetly, he used his hands and his mouth over every part of me, eradicating any thoughts of my attacker from even the darkest corners of my mind. When he finally rid himself of his jeans and braced himself over my body, Finn stared down at me as if he'd never seen anything more beautiful.

"I love you, Brooklyn," he breathed, as he slid slowly inside me. "I always have."

I gasped, both at the feeling of him and at his words. Wrapping my arms and legs around him as tightly as I could, I matched his rhythm. We were perfectly in sync, moving together as one, and I could feel something building inside me, more powerful than anything I'd ever experienced.

He loves me.

My hips lifted to his, faster and faster as we climbed toward release.

He loves me.

My fingernails dug into his back as I tried to press us even closer.

He loves me.

My back arched off the bed and a scream built in my throat.

When I exploded into my orgasm, I cried out so loudly I would have been embarrassed if Finn hadn't been right there with me, yelling my name as he came. Together, we climaxed into a powerful, passionate release that I knew, for however long I lived, I'd never forget.

Afterward, Finn pulled me up to lie against his chest so he wasn't crushing me or putting any weight on my injuries. With his warm, strong arms wrapped around me, I was safe. I was loved. And I was happier than I could ever remember being.

"I love you too," I whispered, smiling against his chest. His body went utterly still beneath mine, and I heard the breath catch in his throat at my words. One of his hands cupped my chin and he tilted my head back so I was able to see his face.

"Are you sure?" he whispered, staring into my eyes. "Because once you tell me you love me, that's it, Bee. You're mine. And I'm not ever giving you up."

"Hmmm, well in that case…." I teased, grinning playfully up at him.

He did *not* appreciate my joke; his face remained utterly serious as he waited for my answer.

"Oh, you idiot!" I smacked his arm. "Yes, I love you. Do I need to get it tattooed on my ass and sign a binding legal document, or will a verbal confirmation be enough?" I rolled my eyes.

"You're a smartass," he said, grabbing my hips and settling me on top so I was straddling him. "But I love you anyway."

224

I had just enough time to see that adorable dimple pop out in his right cheek before his lips were again on mine, so fierce it felt like he was branding me as his, and he was slipping back inside me.

***

"So, a lot has happened since our last session."

Dr. Angelini's normal tone of self-possession and composure was slightly ruffled today. I couldn't really blame her, I supposed; it probably wasn't every day that one of her patients divulged about a slew of recovered dream-memories, a near-fatal sexual assault in an alleyway, and a foray into a first-ever healthy romantic relationship – all in one sixty-minute session, I might add.

Just unloading all the details of everything that had happened in the last week had eaten up most of our time together. I wasn't sure how much psychoanalyzing she could possibly get done in twenty minutes, but I didn't peg the good doc as a quitter.

"How are you feeling about the attack?" she asked. "You mentioned you spoke with the police again this morning."

"They say it's not Gordon," I shrugged. "And I don't really know what I'm feeling. Is there a right emotion for this situation that I *should* be experiencing? Because, except for the hour right after it happened, when I cried, I've been feeling generally normal. I'm not scared to go out at night, or walk to my car alone. I don't want to board up my windows and isolate myself for the next several decades with twenty-seven cats," I explained. "I feel like me – just with some extra cuts and bruises."

"There's no singular right or wrong emotion, Brooklyn. You don't necessarily need to feel traumatized, simply because you've experienced a trauma." Dr. Angelini stared at me across her pristine glass coffee table. I vaguely wondered how she kept it so clean; there wasn't a coffee ring or a fingerprint smudge on the damn thing.

"Brooklyn, are you still with me?" Dr. Angelini asked, one eyebrow raised in question.

I nodded, forcing myself to stop the thought process concerning her Windex-ing habits and focus on her words. They *were* costing me several hundred dollars per hour, after all.

"I think it's also possible that, because this isn't the first trauma you've experienced, you may be slightly desensitized to risky or potentially life-threatening incidents," she continued.

"So I'm numb to danger," I mused, miming karate chops in the air as I slayed invisible enemies. "Does that count as a super-power?"

"Brooklyn," she scolded, her voice stern. "Please take this seriously."

"I am! It was a joke," I scoffed. She was overreacting, big time.

"I do admit that your desensitization to trauma could be an asset in certain threatening situations, such as when you needed to defend yourself in that alley and keep your wits about you," she explained.

I nodded, sensing a big "but" coming.

"But," *There it is.* " It may also be a detriment, because it can make you reckless. You have no real sense of fear, and you're completely unafraid to push the boundaries of your personal safety – whether it's with casual sexual encounters, excessive drinking, or going out into a dark alleyway alone, with no viable forms of communication at hand."

I thought about her words for a moment. I guessed there was some truth to what she was saying, but it wasn't exactly something I would be able to fix. As I saw it, I'd been fucked up for so long it was no longer a changeable trait, but an ingrained part of my nature. Sure, I could get better at managing my fucked-upedness, but – let's face facts here – I'd never be completely normal.

"I don't suppose there's a magic pill you can prescribe to fix this little problem of mine, right?" I joked.

"You don't need medication, Brooklyn. Just keep your cellphone with you next time," Dr. Angelini smirked.

I laughed. "Did you just make a joke, doc?"

"Definitely not," she denied, inducing an eye roll from me almost instantly. "Now, I want to discuss your dreams in the few minutes we have left. Have you had more since we last spoke?"

"Yes, and they seem to be getting more frequent; they've pretty much taken the place of my regular nightmares – which is okay, cause my nightmares sucked and I look way better sans the dark under-eye circles."

If I didn't know better, I'd think Dr. Angelini was holding back a laugh.

"I've dreamed about the foster home and the boy three nights this week," I continued. "And I think you're right about them being triggered memories – there's no way my dreams would be that specific if they hadn't actually happened to me at some point. So now I guess all I have to do is find their trigger."

"I don't believe it's something you should necessarily be actively searching for. When your mind is ready, you may simply remember naturally," Dr. Angelini shrugged delicately. "And as I've said before, there's no exact science to how our memories work, Brooklyn. My advice would be to live your life and not dwell too much in the past. It sounds like, for the first time in a long while, you're really enjoying just being in your present."

"You're right," I agreed, smiling wistfully as I thought of Finn. "I finally have something that makes me excited to get out of bed in the morning."

Our time was officially up, and we'd barely even scratched the surface of everything that had been going on in my soap opera of a life. Dr. Angelini stood and ushered me to the door, reaching out at the last second to press a business card into my hand.

"This has my personal cell number on it. I don't usually give it out to patients," she explained. "But I want you to know that I'm always here if you need me, Brooklyn – even if it isn't for a scheduled session."

It was clear that her concern for my welfare extended beyond that of a normal doctor-patient relationship, and her maternal gesture made my heart ache. I wondered whether Dr. Angelini had kids and a family of her own; she didn't wear a wedding ring, so I assumed she wasn't married, and she didn't exactly give off a motherly vibe. I was suddenly struck by the thought that she might be a little bit lonely too.

Somehow, that endeared her to me further.

Though I was definitely not a hugger – and I got the sense that Dr. Angelini wasn't either – I tentatively wrapped my arms around her petite frame and lightly embraced her. She startled at first but recovered quickly, her arms coming up to squeeze me equally hesitantly. After what was perhaps the most awkward hug in the history of mankind, I detached and took a hasty step out of her space.

Clearing my throat, I did my best to dismiss the uncharacteristic display of affection I'd just initiated as no big deal. "Well, thanks doc. I can't make any promises that your number won't end up in a newspaper ad for a phone-sex hotline, though," I teased.

"Well, Brooklyn," she grinned the most genuine smile I'd ever seen from her, pushing me out into the hallway. "I suppose if that happens, I can't promise that I won't recommend you for a lifetime of institutionalization in one of Virginia's finest state asylums."

I laughed as I walked down the hall, turning to toss a goodbye over my shoulder. "See you next week, doc."

"Until then, Brooklyn," she returned, and I could hear the smile in her voice.

Maybe it was sad, because I was paying her and all, but I was pretty sure my shrink was one of the best friends I'd ever had.

Or, maybe I was crazy after all.

CHAPTER SIXTEEN

BLINDSIDED

A week passed quietly, and I had the luxury of acting like I was a normal college student for a brief span of time. There were no more attacks, mysterious deliveries, or asthmatic phone calls. I went to my classes every day, which remarkably seemed only to be growing more boring and unchallenging as the semester progressed and my professors lost any of their prior academic verve. I completed my homework each night, which took me an hour at most, and occasionally I pulled out my textbooks and forced myself to study until my eyes were drifting closed; memorizing the names and details of every major Supreme Court case over the last five decades is enough to put anyone to sleep. Mostly, though, I just tried to take Dr. Angelini's advice by enjoying the blissful ease of living in the present.

In time, my bruises faded, then disappeared completely. The scrapes took longer, but each day Finn helped me apply antiseptic and change their bandages; he was also a firm believer that his *kiss-it-better* approach had real healing properties, and he insisted on running his mouth over each of my injuries at least once a day.

I think it actually had more to do with him getting me naked, but I wasn't exactly complaining.

The police had completely ruled out Gordon's involvement in my attack, leaving me slightly unsettled and more than a little confused about the identity of my mystery attacker. I'd been so ready to believe it was him – to tie a neat little bow around the case and remove all of the unease that came with knowing the person who'd tried to rape – or maybe even *kill* – me that night was still walking around, a free man.

Apparently, Gordon had been occupied – quite publically – at the exact time I was battling for my life in the alleyway, with his tongue stuck down the throat of a cheerleader in full view of numerous Styx patrons. There was no way it could have been him, unless he had a super power that allowed him to be in two places at once.

Somehow, I doubted that was the case.

Since the attack, a constant air of unsettlement had lingered around me, and I was left with the distinct feeling that I wasn't a good victim – not that there was anything *good* about being a victim, but rather that I wasn't processing my trauma in the normal, healthy way. I thought a lot about what Dr. Angelini had told me, and was forced to accept the fact that I was probably walking through life more than a little numb from everything I'd experienced in my relatively short twenty – nearly twenty-one – years on the planet.

Twenty-one: one of the biggest rites of passage for any young adult, especially on a college campus. Somehow, it held no appeal for me. I hadn't actually celebrated a birthday in years and I didn't plan to even mention this one's arrival to Finn.

Maybe a part of that was because I'd had a fake ID since I was seventeen. Or maybe it was because I'd never enjoyed or even understood the concept of birthdays. They had always seemed rather pointless to me – just another meaningless demarcation of life's value; society's way of portraying our heedless march toward the grave as some great gift, rather than an inevitability.

I mean, when you really think about it, aren't birthdays just an opiate for mortality? Our way of saying, *Congratulations! You've survived yet another year in this mess we call life. Here's a piece of cake and a few balloons for your trouble.*

I'd probably felt differently as a kid. Back when my mother was alive, birthdays had been the highlight of my year – filled with color and laughter, frosting and presents. Piñatas strung up in the backyard if the weather was nice. A slightly lopsided pink princess cake, frosted to perfection. Presents piled high on the kitchen table. My mother's voice soaring above the rest, as the partygoers chorused in time…

Happy Birthday, Dear Brooklyn…

Those days had come to a quick end after she'd died. I

couldn't remember my seventh birthday. I knew it had been spent in the foster home, but like so many of my memories from that time, it was locked somewhere deep and unnavigable within my psyche.

Dr. Angelini told me that I couldn't force the memories to reveal themselves, but that hadn't stopped me from trying. When I'd close my eyes and turn my thoughts inward, I could sense the memories there – as if they were hidden in the shadows of my mind behind a thick gauzy curtain. The answers I wanted lurked just out of reach, and sometimes I even thought I'd caught a glimpse of one behind that opaque mental drape – a flash of color, a faintly reminiscent scent, a vaguely familiar face.

I wanted to reach into my head and tear down that curtain. Hell, I would've taken a crowbar to my memories to pry them out, if I'd thought it would do me any good. But, since that didn't seem like a viable option, they remained frustratingly inaccessible to me.

I'd taken a biology course during my first semester of college – an odious and inescapable science breath requirement – and I remembered the days I'd spent hovering over the microscope, turning dials and adjusting light intensities as I tried to bring the microorganisms on my slides into view. The other kids in my class hadn't batted an eye at the task, effortlessly illuminating their samples. Try as I might, though, I could never get the damn thing to focus.

Sadly, looking into the contents of my own brain was strangely reminiscent of those infuriating days in the biology lab.

Finn would have understood – if I'd told him, that is. I think he knew there was something going on with me, something more than just the attack or Gordon's supposed innocence.

He would have been kind. Sympathetic. Helpful, even.

But how do you tell the person you love that you don't even know your own mind? That there are parts of yourself, aspects of your soul – your innermost thoughts and memories – that you've blocked out or simply forgotten? That your brain doesn't function normally – and that maybe it never will?

Things were good between us – great, actually. I was

happy. Even more shockingly, I seemed to make Finn happy too. And, perhaps selfishly, I didn't want to undermine that happiness. I didn't want him to look at me differently, to treat me differently. So I held back.

At least, that's the reason I gave myself to excuse my nondisclosure.

Because, just maybe, if I were really being honest, there was the inescapable fact that I wasn't ready to face the dark questions that had begun to swirl through my mind – a violent maelstrom of suspicion and foreboding and inconceivable possibilities.

Sometimes the mind puts things together in an instant; a hundred pieces of the puzzle that have been lying scattered across the floor suddenly snap together like magic and the whole picture comes swiftly clear. Until that moment of clarity, though, you stare at those goddamn pieces so long they begin to blur out of focus, feeling like you must be missing those vital pieces that hold all the answers.

The truth was, on all those quiet nights of normalcy, my mind had begun to wander over all of the things that had been happening to me recently. I stared at all those pieces of the puzzle, lying on my carpet with seemingly no connectable edges or even a discernable pattern amongst them. I thought about the things I'd dismissed as nothing at the time, shrugged off as no big deal or stuffed down into the corners of my mind that I avoid looking at too closely, for fear of their contents.

But I couldn't ignore the fact that there had been entirely too many strange incidents lately to be merely coincidental. Not anymore.

I'd sat on my rooftop looking up at the stars – late autumn constellations had always been my favorite, though I wasn't sure why – and thought about the attack. And then, almost involuntarily, my mind shifted to examine all the anonymous phone calls I'd received.

Then, the eerie sensation I'd experienced more than a few times of being watched as I walked home or made my way across campus alone.

Then, the bizarre and still-unexplained black rose delivery – an apparent harbinger of my death.

Then, finally, things I'd never even spent a second thought on began to pop into my head, as if my brain were making quantum leaps from one seemingly random occurrence to another, too fast for me to keep up or consciously seek out the next part of the puzzle.

Snap, snap, snap, the pieces flew together, and a picture began to form…

The time I'd come home from class about a month ago to find the books on my desk slightly askew, as if someone had bumped into the furniture and accidentally knocked them out of place.

The way my appointment book, where I'd meticulously scribed all of my academic assignments, social invitations, and random thoughts, had disappeared right out of my backpack while I was in the student center killing time between classes a few weeks ago.

And, lastly, a man standing in the dark, leaning against his motorcycle and smoking a cigarette. Watching me as I sat on my rooftop in the pre-dawn hours of a chilly August night.

Could it all be connected?

Alone, none of these instances seemed like a big deal, but *together*? If I looked at the whole picture, if I considered them as one linked series of events, rather than single, isolated incidents…

The puzzle, though still missing some vital sections, was beginning to come together as a single, clear image: Someone was stalking me. Watching me. Trying to hurt me.

Was I crazy and overreacting? Was I paranoid?

Probably.

But once I'd opened my eyes to the possibility that this was all the work of one individual, one person who might want to hurt or scare me, I couldn't *unsee* the connections my mind had forged. I couldn't escape the ever-building, unshakeable belief that I was in danger. I could feel it in my bones, like a sixth sense or some innate defense mechanism; every atom in my body was screaming at me to run, hide, take shelter somewhere far away.

I didn't know what – *who* – I was supposed to be running from, but from that moment on, I began to live my life waiting for the other shoe to drop. Finn knew; he could read me too well. We were lying in my bed one night, about a week after the attack. The sheets were a tangled mess around our bodies and he was strumming his guitar softly, humming under his breath as he played.

"You okay?" he asked when his fingers had settled into stillness.

"Fine," I lied, staring up at the painted stars on my ceiling.

"You can tell me, you know." He set aside his guitar, rolling over so we were lying face to face. "Anything."

"I know," I leaned in to kiss him softly, possessively, as was becoming my habit. I'd never had the opportunity to be soft, unhurried, with someone before; never experienced that gentle intimacy and familiarity of routine. It was so new, to kiss just for the sake of kissing; a kiss that leads nowhere, with no further intentions than to meet that person's lips with your own, simply because you can.

"I'll tell you soon. Promise," I assured him. There was no use lying and pretending that everything was fine. He'd see straight through me, as he always had.

His brow furrowed and he opened his mouth, as if in preparation of saying something important. He stared at my face so intently I began to grow uneasy. After a small infinity of silence, though, his mouth snapped closed and he swallowed roughly, his eyes as distant as his thoughts.

Whatever he'd been about to tell me, he'd evidently decided to keep to himself. And as much as I would've liked to pry the thoughts from his lips, I knew that would be utterly hypocritical. After all, I was keeping my own secrets – who was I to force him to share his own before he was ready?

"I have a surprise for you," he said instead, reaching over to grab an envelope from the nightstand. The playful light came back into his eyes and the tense moment passed as soon as he placed it in my hands.

Finn's "surprise" consisted of two tickets to the

Charlottesville County Fair, an annual mecca of amusement rides, food stands, and carnival games that passed through the area for two weeks every November. The passes were for tomorrow – my birthday.

He'd known, without me ever mentioning a thing. I shouldn't have even been surprised.

"Lexi?" I asked, arching an eyebrow at him.

He laughed. "Yeah, she did me the honor of informing me that my girlfriend is a bit birthday-phobic. But I already knew it was your birthday." His voice was smug.

"How?" I asked skeptically.

He shrugged, grinning in an infuriatingly cute way. "I know everything."

I narrowed my eyes at him, but couldn't hold onto my mock anger when he pounced on me and began assaulting my sides with relentless tickle torture. I writhed on the bed, desperate to escape and borderline hyperventilating at his onslaught. Only when tears were leaking from the corners of my eyes and my threats had escalated beyond simple bodily harm, to promises of fatal retribution did he release me.

"I...hate....you," I gasped for breath between each word, rolling as far away from him on the bed as I could get.

"Liar," he laughed, rolling on top of me so I was pinned beneath him.

I glared at him, my chest still heaving as I pulled in gulps of air.

He looked down at me and kissed the tip of my nose.

"Happy Birthday, Bee," he murmured, before his lips descended on mine and I forgot all about being mad at him.

***

"Come on," I begged.

"No."

"Finn!" I huffed.

"Absolutely not."

"Pleaseeee." I tried out my best pleading puppy-dog eyes.

"Nope."

"But it's my birthday."

"You hate your birthday."

Clearly, my attempts to appeal to his soft side weren't working.

"I didn't realize I was dating such a sissy," I scoffed, changing tactics. When in doubt, threaten the manhood; they crumble every time.

"Did you just call me a *sissy*?" He asked, incredulous. "I thought we were celebrating your twenty-first birthday, not your fifth."

"HA! If anyone's a baby, it's you. You're the one who won't even go on the Ferris wheel!"

"I don't do heights." The finality in his tone was unmistakable.

"Wow, I'm seeing a whole new side to badass Finn Chambers," I laughed.

He glared at me, then turned to stare at the massive Ferris wheel with apprehension clear on his face. It probably wasn't helping my case that the ride looked like it had been built about a century ago, with rust staining the metal beams, and bolts that squealed with each rotation of the wheel.

"Okay, fine," I sighed, resigned. "I'll go by myself. You can watch me."

Popping up onto my tiptoes, I pressed a quick kiss to Finn's cheek, before turning and dashing for the entry line. Handing over three tickets to the man at the entrance, I stood on the platform at the base of the wheel, waiting for my turn to be loaded into one of the passenger cabs. I'll admit, I was a little disappointed that Finn had refused to ride with me, but I wasn't going to miss out on my favorite ride just because I had to fly solo.

I'd always loved the Ferris wheel.

Since we were about sixteen, each fall Lexi and I had made it our mission to find a local fairground where we could pet goats and llamas in the petting zoo, overload on sugary cotton candy and funnel cakes, and ride the rickety, structurally-questionable carnival rides until we were ready to throw up. I'd always loved the rush of adrenaline an amusement park ride or roller coaster brings; they were almost as thrilling as my late-night motorcycle rides.

I couldn't remember the first time I'd ridden a Ferris wheel. I knew my love of the contraptions dated back further than my trips with Lexi to the fair, but for the life of me I couldn't recall the exact details of that maiden voyage up into the air. I'd been young, I knew that much.

I'd always just assumed I had been with my mother.

Regardless, the prospect of getting back on one was too tempting to pass up, with or without my – *sissy* – boyfriend with me. And, despite my disappointment, I couldn't possibly be upset with him after everything he'd done for me today.

I'd woken later than usual; the sun streaming through my windows was bright, indicating that it was well into midmorning. The first thing my half-asleep mind had registered were the rose petals scattered across the pillow next to my head, their drugging floral scent seeping into my consciousness and pulling me fully awake.

Pink, red, white – there'd been petals everywhere, strewn in a pathway that led across my bedspread, down onto the floor, and out through my doorway. Stumbling from my bed and rubbing the sleep from my bleary eyes, I'd followed the trail of petals out into the hallway and finally to the kitchen beyond.

The room had been utterly transformed.

Hundreds of multicolored balloons had been strung up from the ceiling and blanketed the hardwood floors. Red and white streamers had hung from one corner of the room to the other, so thick I couldn't quite make out the skylights above my head. A huge sign was taped across the wall opposite the stove, reading 'HAPPY BIRTHDAY BROOKLYN' in a familiar, sloping masculine hand. The kitchen island had been piled high with boxes, sloppily wrapped in striped blue paper with clumps of translucent tape sticking out in every direction – a clear sign that they'd been wrapped by a man's unpracticed fingers.

An unstoppable, incandescent grin had spread across my face at the sight, even as tears began to prick at my eyes; it was more than anyone had ever done for my birthday.

"Happy birthday, princess."

He'd been standing by the stove, leaning casually against the kitchen island. His smile had nearly matched my own – as if the excitement and near-childlike sense of glee emanating off me was infectious.

"You did all this?" I'd asked, walking toward him.

I knew it must have taken him several hours to put up all the decorations, plus there was the fact that he'd obviously spent time picking out presents and – attempting, at least – to wrap them.

"It's your birthday," he'd shrugged, as if it were no big deal; like it was some kind of given that he'd do all this, simply because one more year of my life had passed. He didn't understand that this was in no way similar to what I'd become accustomed to in the past fourteen years. He was breaking my annual tradition of solitary, semi-drunken celebration – deviating from the norm and turning a day I normally dreaded into something magical and romantic.

He didn't know that my father's idea of a birthday gift was a painfully generic card, stuffed full of empty, meaningless words written by a Hallmark employee, and a hefty check. The years he'd remembered to even scribe his signature on the bottom of the card were the most memorable; usually, he had his secretaries take care of such trivial business, as he couldn't be bothered to deal with unimportant matters like his only child's day of birth.

When I'd moved out of the house last year to come to Charlottesville, I hadn't even gotten a phone call from him – not that I'd really been expecting one. Lexi had bought me a cupcake and a bottle of tequila, then taken me out and gotten me wasted enough to forget why I hated the day so much.

So I'd guess it would be repetitive to say that my expectations, when it came to this year?

Zero, zilch, nada.

I'd figured that twenty-one wouldn't be much different from twenty; judging by the state of my kitchen this morning, though, I'd be pretty comfortable admitting that I was wrong.

"I love you," I'd whispered, glancing around at the room in wonderment, before arching my head back to brush a kiss across Finn's smiling lips.

I was broken from my reverie when a passenger cab finally descended and it was my turn to climb onboard the Ferris wheel. A hand appeared from my peripheral and one of the carnival workers helped up into the compartment.

"Thank you," I said, releasing his hand and turning to face him after I'd settled onto the bench.

"I wouldn't do this for anyone else, you know." At the sound of his voice, my eyes flew away from the safety bar I was preparing to secure my lap to examine his face. To my surprise, Finn was standing there, looking a little green as he stared up at the ride over our heads. It had been his hand I'd grabbed for support.

"You changed your mind?" I asked, trying to subdue my sudden excitement.

"It was the puppy dog eyes," he shrugged, climbing into the cab and settling close next to me. "They get me every time."

I laughed as he pulled the bar tight across our laps, shaking it several times to check that it was securely latched.

"...probably spent about ten minutes total putting this deathtrap together...completely unsafe..." Finn was muttering under his breath about the ride, looking in every direction as we lifted off the ground several feet so the couple in line behind us could board their own cab.

"Hmmm? Did you say something, caveman?" I asked sweetly, cupping a hand around my ear.

"Just how much I love you for convincing me to ride this thing," he replied sarcastically.

I smacked him on the arm.

He laughed, but it was strained with tension. His white-knuckled grip on the security bar betrayed his anxiety, only tightening the further we rose into the air.

"You really didn't have to come," I told him, feeling rather ashamed of myself. "I'm sorry for bugging you about it."

"Don't be," he said, staring at the fairground lights below.

The park really came alive at night. It was sunset now, and most of the little kids had gone home hours ago, replaced by too many couples to count. Country music blared from the speakers of almost every game stand, screams rang out as adventure-seeking fair-goers were spun upside down by the scarier rides on the far side of the park, and food vendors called out their wares to passerby. The myriad of voices blended together into one distinct medley: the nighttime soundtrack of every autumn carnival across the country.

Noisy, bustling, bright; just breathing the air made you feel more alive.

"The view is so beautiful from up here," I sighed.

"It really is," he agreed. When I glanced over at him, though, it was me he was staring at, rather than the carnival spread out below us.

"Corny," I accused, elbowing him lightly in the stomach. Secretly, I was enjoying the rush of warmth his words sent spiraling through my chest. Finn wrapped one arm around my shoulders and tugged me closer, so I was snuggled up against his side.

"You love me anyway, though," he whispered into my ear, his mouth moving lower to press a kiss to the sensitive spot behind my lobe. I shivered at the sensation, tilting my head to give him better access. With his face buried in my neck, he didn't notice the kids in the passenger cab above us, but I did.

There were two small children around eight or nine years old – siblings most likely – in the compartment. The boy was bigger, and he was finding great delight in his sister's fear; he heaved his body backward and forward, until the cab gained momentum of its own and was rocking wildly. His sister was clearly terrified, hanging on to the security bar and pleading with him to stop. He was laughing at her.

It happened so fast.

Sometimes you see change coming. You might not want it, might not be ready to embrace the new course your life is about to set out on, but at the very least you can prepare for it. Adjust your expectations. Formulate a new plan.

Other times, change is so sudden, so unexpected, that it knocks you right on your ass and leaves you wondering how you got to this place – blindsided, with your expectations and hopes and dreams as unsalvageable as an ice cream cone dropped to the ground at the carnival, melting slowly into the dirt road.

Had I known, in that moment, that getting on that goddamn amusement ride would irrevocably change things between Finn and me, I never would've climbed aboard. We were young and in love; we were invincible – or so I'd thought. If I'd known it was all about to be ripped from me, maybe I'd have held him tighter, told him I loved him one last time.

I didn't get that chance.

One minute, I was looking up at the siblings in the cab above us, and the next, I was somewhere deep inside my own head. It was disorienting, how quickly the memory took hold of my senses, dragging me back exactly fourteen years in a single instant.

Our foster mother, Eva, had agreed to take us to the Fall Festival, and the eight of us kids divided into two minivans, with the oldest fighting for the front seats. There were two chaperones with our group – women I'd never met before – but they kept mostly to themselves, talking to each other rather than the kids. I think they were Eva's friends – sometimes they hung around with her at our group home – but I wasn't really sure.

As usual, my scrawny frame was shoved into the back row, between two of the bigger kids. I kept my eyes closed for the majority of the ride, retelling myself the legend of Andromeda over and over in my head to shut out the noise in the van and the uncomfortable, cramped backseat.

The boy sat in the row ahead of me and didn't look back. A part of me wished he would, but I knew it was for the best – we never talked to each other in front of the other kids. As far as they knew, I was still the little mute girl who kept to herself.

The back porch at night – that was our *place, the one space in the house I ever felt safe enough to be myself. Safe enough to speak. Every day I feared one of the other kids would discover us out there, and learn my secret. But for now, on my way to a carnival with the promise of sugar and fun hanging in the air all around me, I pushed my fears away and determined to have a good time. It was my birthday, after all.*

I was seven. I didn't feel any different – I didn't look any bigger, either.

I hadn't told anyone it was my birthday, not even the boy. My foster mother had given me a rare, unexpected hug when I'd walked into the kitchen for breakfast this morning, but other than that there had been no recognition that I was one year older.

If my mom had been here, there'd have been cake and presents and so much laughter my sides would ache for the next three days. The fact that it was my birthday and she wasn't *here made it seem more real, more final than ever before – she was gone, and she was never coming back.*

Even with my eyes pressed closed, I could tell we were approaching the fairgrounds. The other kids' voices got louder as they talked about which rides they would go on and pointed at different attractions through the windows as our car rolled slowly into line for the parking lot.

Squeezing my eyes shut even tighter, I made a birthday wish. It wasn't done over a cake, and I hadn't blown out any candles, but I hoped it would count anyway.

I didn't wish for presents. I didn't wish for my father to find me. I didn't wish to be adopted. I didn't even wish for my mother back.

Instead, I wished on every star in the night sky, on all those constellations the boy had taught me to find and name, that we wouldn't be separated. That, whatever happened, we would stay together. Because the boy with the sad eyes? He'd become my *brightest star; the one who led me to safety every night, when the nightmares and the grief became too much. He'd guided me from the darkness – my North Star in the never-ending shadows.*

And I didn't want to lose him, not ever.

Our foster mother parked the van and the rest of the kids immediately jumped out and sprinted for the park entrance. I trailed slowly behind, knowing I would never be able to keep up

242

anyway. When we were handed our tickets and allowed into the park, the group splintered off in every direction.

The older girls I shared a bedroom with, Mary and Katie, took off for the food stands on the other side of the park. A pack of the older boys ran for the giant thrill rides that flipped upside down and made you throw up. The rest headed for the ring toss and dart throwing games.

I didn't see where the boy had gone.

My foster mother and the other two chaperones were busy with Bobbie, the three-year-old toddler who'd arrived at the house two weeks ago. He was the youngest by far, and he used up almost all their attention. The rest of us had been given an allowance of twenty tickets each, and sent off to spend them however we wanted. I think Eva was just happy that she didn't have to deal with the other seven of us for the next few hours.

I decided to stick by myself, rather than chase after a group of older kids who didn't want me tagging along anyway. I wandered around for a few minutes, taking in the sights and smells, and eventually parted with three of my tickets in return for a lump of cotton candy so sticky I had to suck on each of my fingers for several seconds to get them clean.

When I saw the Ferris wheel – shiny red and lit up with hundreds of tiny glowing lights – it seemed magical, like something out of a storybook. It was enchanting, utterly unlike any ride I'd ever seen before, and I instantly wanted to ride it up, up, up into the sky. I knew the view of the stars from the very top would be incredible.

I got into line and tried to ignore the three boys standing several feet ahead of me. They lived in the group home, and I knew from experience that they would tease me mercilessly if they discovered me standing anywhere near them. I should have gotten out of line as soon as I saw them – I almost did – but the lure of the Ferris wheel was too strong, and I figured there was a pretty good chance they wouldn't notice me anyway.

I was wrong.

We were nearing the front of the line when Eugene, the oldest – and meanest – of the boys turned and spotted me. About thirteen, with blond hair and a tall frame, Eugene was a bully. I'd always thought it was because he hated his dorky name so much, he felt like had to prove how tough he was every minute of the day.

"Hey, freak!" he yelled, the excitement and malice clear in his eyes.

I, as usual, didn't respond.

"What, cat gotcha tongue, freak?" Eugene sneered.

The other boys turned to look at me as well, laughing and joking amongst themselves. I wrapped my arms tightly around my chest, trying to hold myself together as I did my best to ignore them.

Don't let them see you cry, Brooklyn. Never let them see weakness.

The boy had told me that several weeks ago, after a particularly brutal day of teasing at the dinner table when Eugene had "accidentally" bumped into me, causing my entire plate of chicken nuggets and mashed potatoes to fall to the ground. Eva had blamed me for being clumsy and sent me to bed without supper as punishment.

A target who doesn't fight back, who won't even defend herself with words, is the easiest victim in the world.

"Riding alone?" Eugene asked, reaching out a hand to grab my upper arm roughly. "We can't have that. I am your big brother after all – obviously not by blood. As if I would be related to such a loser," he laughed hysterically.

The other boys snickered at his words.

"Come on, Brooklyn. We'll ride together. Just like real siblings."

This was no innocent suggestion; I could hear the threat buried within his words. The last thing I wanted in the world was to ruin the magic of the Ferris wheel by riding with Eugene, but I didn't seem to have a choice.

What I did *have was a bad, bad feeling about this.*

I glowered at him and tried to tug my arm away from his grip, but he was so much bigger, stronger, tougher – you name it – than me. It wasn't a fair fight; but then, it never was when it came to Eugene.

Before I knew it, all my remaining my tickets had been ripped from my hands and I was being herded onto a Ferris wheel cab with Eugene hovering at my back. The other boys were standing behind us, waiting to board their own cab and blocking the exit; any escape attempts would be stopped before I made it two feet. I tried to catch the eye of the man checking our safety bar, but he didn't look in my direction once.

And then it was too late; we were up in the air.

Eugene hooted loudly, victorious, and the boys in the cab below answered with cheers of their own. I made myself small, squeezing as far away from him as possible within the tiny compartment.

When we were about halfway up, he started the rocking.

Leaning his body forward over the bar, then slamming it abruptly against the backrest, Eugene made the whole cab swing back and forth dangerously fast. Within seconds I grew dizzy and began trembling in fear; a few times we tilted so sharply I was sure I'd slide right out from under the bar and fall to my death on the hard ground far below us.

I didn't scream, I didn't cry; I refused to give him that much satisfaction.

But I was scared out of my mind, wailing internally at the injustice of this. He'd taken away any and all excitement I'd had when I'd first spotted this awful ride. By the time we finally returned to the ground, I was not only ready to throw up my cotton candy, but had vowed I'd never ride a Ferris wheel again, as long as I lived.

The boys left me – ticketless, nauseous, and alone – at the base of the ride. They laughed as they sprinted off, high fiving one other and planning which rides they'd go on next. I sat in the dirt and tried very, very hard not to pity myself.

It was there that the boy found me.

"Hey, Bee," he said, extending one hand down to help me to my feet.

"Hi," I whispered, my voice small.

"Are you okay?" he asked.

So, he'd seen what Eugene did. I nodded.

"Don't let them get to you. Not on your birthday."

I looked up into his face, surprised he'd even known it was my special day, and he winked at me. "Come on," he said, grabbing my hand and pulling me back toward the line for the Ferris wheel. He paused when he felt my resistance.

"I don't want to go back on there," I insisted, tugging my hand away.

"That's exactly why you have to, Bee. Haven't you ever heard the phrase, 'get back on the horse that threw you?'" he asked.

I shook my head no, looking at him questioningly.

"Well, it's the truth. Don't let an idiot like Eugene ruin Ferris wheels for you. I saw your face earlier, when you first got in line… You looked so excited. Weren't you?"

"Yes," I admitted. "I did really want to ride, before. But now…" I trailed off.

"It will be different, Bee. I promise. Don't you trust me?"

I thought about it for all of a second. "Of course."

"Then let's go."

We waited in line for a short time, and the boy shared some of his tickets with me since Eugene had taken all of mine. I was nervous when we first climbed on board, but soon enough I realized that the boy had been right – it was *different this time.*

The only thing the boy hadn't *mentioned was that he was terrified of heights, which I figured out about twenty seconds after we left the ground. He was breathing heavier than usual, and his skin looked pale and clammy with fear.*

When the wheel stopped turning, we were perched at the very top of the park and I could see the whole galaxy lit up like a million tiny frozen fireflies in the night sky. I started to point out constellations to the boy, naming them easily now, after weeks of practice, and even retelling some of their stories out loud.

I think that calmed him somewhat, because his grip on the safety bar loosened up and he turned to look over at me as we began our descent back to the ground.

"Happy Birthday, Bee," he said, squeezing my hand with his own.

I thought again about my earlier birthday wish, and prayed even harder that it would come true.

"Thanks, Finn," I replied, smiling back at him.

Chapter Seventeen

Breaking Point

"Bee? Bee, what is it?" Finn asked. He'd pulled his head up from the crook of my neck, and was staring over at me with a concerned look on his face. "What's wrong?"

His voice snapped me back to reality. Our cab was poised at the top of the wheel, no doubt offering a breathtaking panoramic view of the fair below and an incredible sunset – a fiery ball of red making its descent in the western sky. At the moment, though, it was all a blur. I stared straight ahead, unable to look at him. Completely unwilling to believe what my mind had just revealed to me.

My first instinct was to reject it outright. Utter denial. Because there was just no possible way that the sad-eyed boy who haunted my memories was Finn. *My* Finn. It was too ludicrous to even contemplate.

My next thought was that this was all some kind of coincidence; a grand cosmic joke, played out by fate or destiny or whatever gods exist up there. Maybe one day they, in all their infinite omnipotence, were bored enough to reach down and stir the pot; to mess with us mere mortals here on earth, so that by the time we finally caught on to what was happening, it was too late. Then, when we were running around like chickens with their heads lopped off, trying desperately to do damage control on our messy lives, they could just kick back and watch, unapologetically entertained by our lack of power and foresight.

I quickly rejected that idea, partly because I liked to think I had at least a semblance of control over my own destiny and secondly because that would be one hell of an unlikely coincidence.

That left one final option – the only true explanation there'd ever really been. I didn't want to face it. I didn't even want to think it. All I wanted to do was rewind the clocks back fifteen minutes, to before I'd climbed on this goddamn Ferris wheel and everything had changed.

Was it only fifteen minutes ago that everything had been perfect? That I'd been happy? That I'd believed that I, for once in my life, was lucky?

It seemed a distant memory now, superficial and fleeting; disappearing with the wind on gossamer wings, so quickly it was as if it had never been real at all.

The truth was, though, a part of me had suspected all along that this, that *he*, couldn't possibly be meant for me. Deep down, I'd known I wasn't meant for good things – for lightness and love. It just wasn't in the cards for me, and what a fool I'd been, if only for a brief span of time, to think otherwise.

Even with that knowledge firmly in my head, it wasn't any easier to accept it as the truth. And, against all logic, I desperately wished for any other explanation.

Because if it were true, it meant that not only were Finn and the sad-eyed boy one and the same…it also meant that Finn was a liar.

He'd known exactly who I was from the moment we'd met.

He'd known about my past.

He'd known about my mother.

And he'd used that knowledge to break me apart and put me back together again just the way he wanted. He'd infiltrated my life, inserted himself into each and every facet of my existence, until I fell so deep in love with him I didn't know where he ended and I began anymore.

And he'd never said a goddamn word.

I'd *trusted* him; that was monumental for me. Worse, I'd let all my walls crumble, and for what? Some boy who'd charmed his way into my good graces and then wormed his way into my heart and my pants.

What was I to him? What was this mockery of a relationship? Some kind of fucked up retribution for our shared childhood?

Did he really think he could just saunter back into my life and…what? *Fix* me?

Did he even love me?

How could you truly love someone if everything you'd ever told them was a lie?

There were endless questions, and no simple answers. But the bottom line was that he was twisted.

He was a liar.

And he definitely, unquestionably, was not the man I'd thought I knew. The man I'd thought I loved.

I'd never before understood the term breaking point. People always talk about how they've been pushed to that place where the stress and fear are so intense your mind simply can't handle it anymore. I'd thought it was a load of crap, a concept thought up by people who are either too emotionally unequipped or too cognitively lazy to sort through their mental messes and face reality.

I understood it now.

I could literally feel my mind breaking apart – splintering into pieces as it tried desperately to reconcile the things I thought I knew about Finn Chambers with what I had just discovered. It was kind of like looking at a Picasso – all the essential parts were there, but damned if they weren't fucked up and put completely in the wrong places.

My mind wasn't alone though, because my heart – my stupid, blind, unprotected heart –was fracturing into pieces too.

"Bee?" Finn repeated, worry apparent in his tone. "What's going on?"

I didn't answer, but I'm sure the horrified look spreading across my face as the realization sunk in and took hold of me spoke volumes.

I couldn't do this right now – I wasn't about to hash things out here, on a freaking Ferris wheel hovering forty yards above the ground. In fact, I didn't think I wanted to hash things out at all. Ever. I just wanted to run away and forget the past three months of my life ever happened. But first, I needed to get away from him. And I couldn't let on that I'd remembered, that I *knew*,

250

or he'd never let me leave without talking things out.

And I definitely didn't want to talk. I wanted to flee. I wanted to punch him in the face, then sleep with every beautiful man who walked across my path until his scent and his touch were permanently removed from my memory. I wanted to whitewash my walls, burn my bed to ash, and throw my guitar in a gutter somewhere.

Hold it together, Brooklyn.

"I feel sick," I lied through my teeth, my tone flat and utterly devoid of emotion. "I forgot how much I hate Ferris wheels." That part, at least, was true – after this, they'd be forever ruined for me.

"Aw, I'm sorry, princess," Finn's voice was gentle, understanding, loving; listening to it felt like he'd thrown salt in an open wound. "You had me worried."

When he wrapped his arms around me, I couldn't help myself – I went completely tense. It took everything I had not to pull away.

"Bee?" Finn's questioned, confusion evident in his voice.

I was really fucking up my plan to act like nothing was wrong; I needed to pull it together. One muscle at a time, I forced my body to relax in his arms.

"Sorry. I'm really okay," I swallowed the lie. "Just trying not to throw up."

Unfortunately, that second part was true. I'd been fighting nausea since I'd returned from my involuntary jaunt down memory lane, but it had nothing to do with motion sickness or heights.

"Don't worry," he told me. "We're almost back on the ground."

He was right; we were the next cab to unload. I still hadn't looked at him, for fear of what he might read in my eyes.

I couldn't look at him.

Hell, I would barely be able to stomach looking *myself* in the mirror.

I felt used, dirty, lost, betrayed. But, worse, I felt like a child. Completely beguiled and naïve. And those were words no one had ever, in the history of my existence, used to describe Brooklyn Turner.

The emotions were threatening to overwhelm me, and I knew if I started crying now, I might never stop; I needed to be far, far away from him when the levies inevitably broke.

Hold it together, Brooklyn. You can do this. Just a little longer.

When we touched down and climbed out of our cab, I immediately sidestepped Finn so I was standing several feet away. He noticed my distance immediately – how could he not? In the months since we'd met, even when we weren't officially dating, we'd always fully invaded each other's space, gravitating so close to one another that we were near-touching at all times.

"I have to go to the bathroom," I said, turning to scan the crowd for the nearest restroom. When I spotted the dull green concrete building several yards away, I turned on my heel without another word and began striding toward it. I made it about halfway there before Finn caught up with me, grabbing my arm to bring me to a halt.

"Hey, do you need me to come in with you? Hold your hair back or…something?" His voice was a mix of confusion and concern, the sincerity in his words burning my ears like acid.

"No," I said, yanking my arm away roughly. "I need to throw up, Finn. Girls don't like their boyfriends—." I nearly choked over the word "–seeing them like that, okay? So let me go. I'll be fine. But if I stand here another moment, you're going to be covered in regurgitated fried dough and cotton candy."

"Okay…I'm sorry," he said quietly. "I'll wait for you outside. Just…let me know if you need me." He sounded upset, and for a moment I felt sorry that I was being so nasty to him; only for a moment, though, because I quickly remembered that he was a lying bastard who'd been toying with me for god only knew how long.

As I raced for the bathroom, alone this time, I had an even more terrifying thought: What if Finn wasn't just a liar…what if he was psychotic?

Here I'd been, worried that all those phone calls and scary

instances were the work of a stalker or some kind of unknown sociopath who was out to get me. But what if I'd been closer to my attacker than I ever thought possible…so close, I'd invited him into my bed and thrown down a freaking welcome mat at the doorstep of my heart?

I rejected that thought so fast it barely had time to fully form, expelling it from my mind with a violent forcefulness that surprised even myself. No matter what – *who* – Finn Chambers was, he would never hurt me. I knew that as clearly as I knew that sun rose every day in the east, that my middle name was Grace, and that seven shots of Cuervo were enough to make me forget what year it was.

I'd never had a broken heart before, but now I totally understood the term. It isn't just an emotional pain, it's a physical one – as if someone has literally reached inside your chest and ripped your heart out, leaving an aching, open cavity behind that you know has no hope of ever fully healing.

Glutton for punishment that I am, when I reached the doors to the bathroom I turned back for one final look at Finn, knowing that, in all likelihood, it was the last glimpse I'd ever have of him. The tears I'd been holding off finally broke free, building in my eyes and spilling over as I found him in the crowd. He was standing exactly where I'd left him; eyes turned to look at that damn Ferris wheel with a contemplative look on his face, as if he were seeking the answer to a particularly difficult equation.

He was perfection, from the roots of his messy dark hair down to the slightly scuffed toes of his favorite black motorcycle boots. And, even though I was supposed to hate him, in that moment all I could do was drink in his image – like a woman dying of thirst in the middle of a desert, staring at the oasis she would never reach.

When the tears had begun running too fast to see straight, I turned and ran into the bathroom. Pulling my cellphone from my pocket, I dialed Lexi. Thankfully, she answered on the second ring.

"Brookie! How's your birthday going, babe?"

"Lexi." My voice was broken. I had nothing left – no

more will to even pretend I was remotely okay. "Please. I need you to come get me."

"Okay," she agreed immediately, no questions asked. That in itself spoke volumes about the shattered desperation she heard in my voice. "Where are you?"

I told her, and she agreed to meet me by the side entrance in ten minutes. When I made her promise not to tell Ty where she was going, I knew she was catching on that this concerned Finn, but she didn't say anything.

I slipped out the back door of the restrooms, looking over my shoulder to make sure Finn hadn't spotted me, and disappeared into the crowds. As I lost myself in the mob of joyful fair-goers, slowly winding toward the east park exit, I let my tears fall to the ground and wished, with everything I had left in me, that I could forget Finn Chambers and move on with my life.

I'd probably have had better luck wishing for a lifetime supply of calorie-free chocolate or an all-inclusive trip to the moon and back.

***

He was much faster than I'd anticipated.

The calls had started almost as soon as I'd hung up with Lexi. I'd turned my phone off, unable to even see his name appear on screen without feeling sick.

I'd been home all of five minutes when the pounding on the front door began, loud enough that it could be heard behind the closed door of my bedroom. Lexi stared at me with a bewildered expression when I walked into the kitchen and told her in no uncertain terms that she wasn't allowed to let him in. I didn't care what he said, what he did – under no circumstances did I want to see or talk to him.

"Bee!" he yelled, his fists slamming against the wooden door so hard it shook in its frame. "What the hell is going on?"

I leaned against the kitchen counter for support.

"Tell me what I did." His voice was desperate, shattered. Lexi stared from me to the door and back, a horrified look on her face.

"Brooklyn! Please!"

254

I closed my eyes so I didn't have to see her judgmental expression.

"Princess, just talk to me. We can fix this, please, just don't shut me out."

It went on like that for nearly an hour, until his voice grew hoarse and he'd run out of air. When he finally gave up, I opened my eyes, took one look at Lexi, and hightailed it from the room.

"Not so fast!" she yelled, racing after me and throwing out her arms to stop me from shutting my bedroom door in her face. "You owe me one hell of an explanation. First, you make me pick you up from the fair, in tears and barely breathing, and now Finn is here, banging on our door like a lunatic, and I can't let him in?" She stared at me, eyes wide. "What. The. Fuck. Happened. Today?"

"He's not who I thought he was, okay?" My voice sounded like a stranger's.

"Uh, no. *Not* okay," Lexi said, pushing my door all the way open and forcing me to back up from the doorway as she stormed into my room. She sat on the bed, crossed her arms over her chest menacingly, and leveled me with her best glare. "Now explain, or I'm not helping you anymore. Which means, I can answer the door for *whoever* comes a'knocking."

I glared at her.

She tapped her foot impatiently.

"He lied to me. About how we knew each other, about how we'd met. About everything. He's been lying to me since that day I tripped over the fire hydrant, Lex. And I can't talk about it," I said, my voice cracking as I pleaded with her to understand. "Not because I'm being a bitch, and not because I want to shut you out. Because I literally *cannot* talk about it. It hurts too damn much." I took a deep breath and tilted my head upwards to fend off the building tears.

"Oh, Brooklyn," Lexi whispered, tears filling her own eyes. "Come here." She pulled me down into a bone-crushing hug, and suddenly, I was weeping in her arms, gasping for breath as I swam upstream in a tidal wave of grief and heartbreak and betrayal.

I don't know how long we sat there on my bed, both crying our eyes out, but when I eventually ran out of tears it was pitch black outside my windows; full night had fallen hours ago. Lexi kissed my cheek and said goodnight, wiping her eyes as she headed out into the hallway. When the door closed behind her, I collapsed on my bed, curling up in a ball of misery.

I must have drifted off to sleep at some point, exhausted from my crying jag.

I jolted awake at the sound of my window sliding open. Sitting up on my bed, I grabbed for my cellphone on the nightstand and frantically pressed the button to turn it back on. I could hear someone maneuvering through the window just as my phone blinked alive.

I was halfway through dialing 911 when I saw that the feet descending through my open window were stuffed into familiar black motorcycle boots, their scuffed toes apparent even in the dark room.

Resignedly, I switched off my phone screen and stowed it back on my bedside table. I sat on the bed, arms crossed, and watched as Finn tumbled through the window, losing his balance and nearly face-planting in the process.

When he righted himself, his eyes instantly cut across the room and locked on mine.

"Hi," he said, stuffing his hands into the pockets of his jeans, and making no move to approach me.

"What are you doing here?" I asked, my tone unwelcoming and my demeanor frigid.

"Well I climbed the tree–" he began.

"I asked *what* not *how*," I said, cutting him off.

"I had to see you, Bee," he said, staring at me with a desperate look in his eyes. "I don't know what's going on. It's not fair that you're clearly so angry, when you haven't even told me what I did to piss you off."

"Not fair? *Not fair?*" I asked, my voice scathing. "That's rich – *you* talking about what's fair."

"What?"

"Don't play dumb, Finn. If you're going to be here,

wasting my time, the very least you can do is be honest."

"Brooklyn…" He held his hands out in surrender, as if he was trying to calm me. As if I could be calmed, at this point.

Is he freaking kidding me?

I'd thought I had it under control, thought I could get through this confrontation without losing it, but it was just too much. Seeing him here like this…still lying to me, still pretending…

I snapped.

"*Tell me a story*, Finn," I said, my voice bleak. His face drained of color as the familiar words registered with him, and he realized that I knew.

That I'd remembered.

I walked across the room, approaching him where he stood utterly still. I could see the vein in his neck throbbing with each heartbeat, his neck and shoulders straining with tension as he held himself immobilized. His eyes were slightly narrowed, filled with wariness, indecision, and what looked a lot like fear as he waited to see what I would do.

When I reached him I got right up into his face, pushing aside my pain and channeling every swirling emotion inside me into one singular feeling: betrayal.

"*TELL ME A STORY*," I screamed in his face, my control shattering to pieces.

He flinched, but otherwise remained still and silent, with his gaze locked on mine.

"Fine," I said, my breathing labored as I looked into his dark eyes. They were heavily guarded, concealing whatever he was feeling from me. "Then I'll tell *you* a story. It's about a little girl who lost everything, who had nothing left. Nothing and nobody to call her own. Until she met a boy, and for a while *he* became her everything." My voice broke on the last word and I cursed inwardly, determined to hold myself together through this.

There were things that needed to be said, and since he'd forced this confrontation, they were going to be said right freaking now.

Hauling a breath into my lungs, I forged on. "But that

boy, the one who gave her back a piece of herself? He's a liar. He's a manipulator. So even though that little girl, who wasn't so little anymore, had trusted him to glue back together her broken fragments...even though she thought he could make her believe in happy endings again...even though she thought he would be the one to erase all her scars..."

Tears were leaking from my eyes now, and my voice grew shakier with each sentence I forced out.

"The little girl was wrong. The boy couldn't be trusted, any more than all the other men in her life who'd let her down. He'd spun deceit and deception until she couldn't tell reality from the lies anymore; until she knew there would be no happily ever afters for her. Not ever.

"Because she was broken, irreparably, for the second time in her life. That glue the boy had used to piece her back together wasn't strong enough, wasn't true enough, to hold her together. It slipped and crumbled, and all her pieces fell and shattered worse than they'd been in the first place."

I'd lost all control by this point; tears were streaming down my face and Finn looked like a shadow of the man I'd come to know; he looked as haunted as I felt inside.

"I suppose I should thank you," I said, a bitter laugh slipping through my lips.

He held his silence for a beat, then whispered, "Thank me?" His voice was rougher than I'd ever heard it, devastated and lacking any of his typical self-assurance.

Good. He should be broken too.

"I thought that I was strong, that my walls were impenetrable, until you came into my life and proved just how weak I really was. I actually thought I was safe with you," I laughed mirthlessly, looking up at the stars painted across my ceiling. "So *thank you*, Finn, for showing me my own fragility. I'll be sure not to make the same mistakes in the future."

"Bee–" he started.

I cut him off. "Don't. You don't get to call me that anymore."

His eyes were glassy with unshed tears, full of hopeless resignation.

Nodding, he took a step back, out of my space, and turned his eyes to stare at the floor. "I'm sorry, Brooklyn," he whispered. "You have no idea how many times I tried to tell you...how close I came–"

"Close only counts in hand grenades and horseshoes, Finn."

"I know that," he said, reaching up to run his hands through his hair. "But how do you find the words for something like that? How do you tell someone that you've spent your whole life looking for them?" He laughed, a bitter sound escaping his lips. "Brooklyn, since we were separated as kids, I've been trying to track you down. I begged my adoptive parents to go back for you, to let me call you or even write to you. By the time they relented and I called the group home, you were already gone. Eva wouldn't tell me anything. Your case files were sealed; I never thought I'd actually find you. And then, one random Tuesday afternoon two years ago, I typed your name into a Facebook search engine and *bam*! There you were."

I thought about the long-dormant social media account Lexi had insisted on setting up for me when we'd been accepted to the university. She'd posted a photo of the two of us wearing new matching college sweatshirts that advertised the university logo in proud orange across the front. I wondered if that was how Finn had tracked me down.

Since I'd never really used the site, I'd assumed it would deactivate after such a long period of inactivity. Apparently, all that preaching my professors did about permanent Internet footprints really was true after all; Facebook is forever.

"I knew it was you immediately – you were beautiful as a little girl, and you're even more gorgeous now... those eyes, that smile. There was no denying it was you." Finn continued. "But I still needed to see that you were okay, Brooklyn. I've worried about you for years. You have to understand, when I got adopted, when I left you...I felt like I'd abandoned you. And I knew I'd never put that to rest until I'd seen you again, face to face."

"So, when you found me, what then? Was the plan to screw me back to normal? To fix me with the sheer will of your penis?" I bit out. "You could have checked on me and walked away, without speaking one single word to me. I was *fine* before I met you. The only thing you've done is fuck me up even worse than I was before."

"It wasn't like that, Brooklyn," Finn said, anger infusing his tone. "I never planned on this – on us. I didn't want to fall in love with you, any more than you expected to fall for me. I transferred here when I learned you'd be attending last fall. But did you see me at all, your entire freshman year? No. I didn't approach you. I didn't mess with your life. I was just there, in the off chance that one day you'd need help – that you'd need *me*. I wasn't about to fail you again, regardless of whether you even knew I existed."

I didn't know what to say to that. He'd transferred here *for me*? That was crazy. Not the good crazy either – the stalkery, obsessive kind of crazy I wanted nothing to do with.

"I think you should leave now," I said, backing away from him.

"Bee...Fuck!" He buried his hands in his hair. "Please don't be scared of me. I'm so fucking sorry I didn't tell you sooner. I tried, so many times. I just couldn't find the words. That day, when you fell over that hydrant and hit your head – it seemed like fate. You were right there in front of me, injured and needing help. I thought maybe I could get close to you, just to be your friend. I swear my intentions never went further than that.

"But I fell in love with you, Brooklyn. I can't pinpoint the exact moment I realized that you were everything that was missing in my life, but I knew – just like I had when I was a ten year old kid – that I couldn't be without you anymore. Still, I tried to push you away, tried to keep boundaries between us when I realized that you didn't remember me...But I just couldn't stay away from you."

"Finn, this...it's just so messed up," I whispered, at a loss. I was way, way out of my emotional depth. I wasn't just in the deep end, here – this was the freaking Mariana Trench.

"I know that, okay? I know how fucked up we are. With you, it's one step forward, and three monumental fucking leaps back. But I also know that you can be incredibly sweet when you aren't too busy slapping me, or glaring at me, or hating my guts."

At that, I glared at him and crossed my arms over my chest.

"You don't want anyone to take care of you – I get that. I respect it, even," he continued, heedless of my glare. "But sometimes, behind that icy, impenetrable front you show the rest of the world, I catch a glimpse of that fiercely vulnerable, heartbroken little girl who still needs me. And I like that I'm the only one who gets to see her and protect her.

"I know this is a lot to think about – I know you probably hate me. And maybe it makes me a total bastard, but you should know that I don't regret a single second of our time together, Brooklyn. With or without the lies, this relationship has been – and always will be – the most important, beautiful, goddamned sacred part of my life. And I'll wait for you – as long as it takes, I'll wait."

I've already been waiting forever. He'd said those words before and I hadn't understood them at the time, but I comprehended them perfectly now.

"I need time, Finn," I said. "I feel broken, betrayed, confused, and frankly just…exhausted by this. I don't want to lie to you or give you false promises that everything is okay between us. None of this is okay – *I* am not okay." I dragged a deep, calming breath in through my nose. "I need to be alone right now."

"I can understand that," he said, nodding. I thought I saw a flicker of hope flash through his eyes as he stared at me.

"I'm not saying this to hurt you because, as insane as it sounds, I believe your story. But that doesn't change anything. For right now I don't want to see you. I don't want to hear from you. And I can't promise that I will *ever* be ready to be with you again."

He nodded, his jaw clenched tight and the hope in his eyes extinguished.

"Goodnight, Finn," I said, walking over to my bedroom door and opening it. "Use the front door this time, will you? Your hands are torn to shreds."

Between the pounding he'd given my front door earlier and scaling the rough bark of the giant maple outside my window, he'd wreaked havoc on his palms and fingers; the knuckles were swollen and bloodied and at least two were turning an angry bruised-purple color, which meant they were likely broken.

He made his way to the door, pausing in the frame for nearly a full minute. Keeping his back to me, he whispered into the dark hallway so quietly I could barely make out his words.

"I love you, Brooklyn Grace Turner. I always have, and I always will. It took me nearly thirteen years to find you; I'm not about to lose you now. And if you decide you never want to see me again, I'll try to live with that decision; but you should know that the way I feel about you? It's been the one constant in my life. This is permanent for me. *You* are permanent for me."

With those words hanging in the air, he disappeared out into the hallway. I listened until I heard the front door click closed, then headed across the room to lock my window.

I'd thought I cried out all my tears earlier, but as I climbed in bed and hugged my pillow to my chest, I found there were still more to be released.

CHAPTER EIGHTEEN

100% GUARANTEE

Rock bottom: I thought I'd hit it the night Finn left.

Isn't it funny that when you think it's simply not possible for life to get any worse – that, no matter what else life throws at you in the future you'll be able to handle it, because there's just no way it could ever be as bad as the pain you're experiencing at this very moment – life takes one good look at you and says, *"You idiot, don't you know by now? Things can always, always, always get worse. Watch, I'll prove it."*

Days passed with an excruciating slowness that made me feel like I was losing my mind.

I left my room only for trips to the bathroom and kitchen. I skipped my classes, cancelled my sessions with Dr. Angelini, and refused to talk to Lexi when she came in to check on me. I had no appetite. I didn't even bother to shower. Worse, though, I wasn't sleeping.

As in, not at all.

I was afraid I'd see him in my dreams, whether as a little boy or as the man he'd become, and that prospect alone was enough to keep me awake for the rest of my life. After two full days without sleep, though, my body had different ideas. I had to be on guard at all times – if my mind wandered even for a minute, I'd find myself on the brink of unconsciousness, forced to pinch or slap myself back from sliding down into dreamland.

I became obsessed with alarm clocks – my own personal bastions against the threat of sleep. I spent hours on my laptop, reading about sleep cycles and REM stages. A concession to my body's needs, I became the master of naps, nodding off in exact ninety minute intervals before I could fall into the deep sleep where dreaming occurs.

At some level, I knew that none of this was rational or remotely healthy, but I didn't really care. As soon as Finn had walked out my door that night, I'd accepted the fact that my heart would never be the same; all I could do now was try to stitch the tattered shreds of my soul back together – and if it took weeks of reclusive, Howard Hughes-like behavior to get there, so be it.

I kept waiting for the moment when things would start to get better. It couldn't go on like this forever, I reasoned; people every day, all over the world, got out of bed and faced their own heartbreaks. One day, they woke up, opened their eyes, and decided that the pain had lessened – maybe not a lot, maybe not even enough to make a tangible difference in the devastation clinging to them like a dark cloud, but enough to give them hope. Hope that one day, in weeks or months or years or decades, the pain would dissipate to the point that it no longer pulsated like a physical wound, with every aching heartbeat a reminder of what had been lost.

Maybe, if I lay in bed long enough, staring at the constellations he'd left behind on my ceiling, I'd finally feel better.

Or worse. It was a toss-up, really.

That first morning I'd woken up without him, as soon as I'd opened my eyes and caught sight of the ceiling I'd leapt out of bed and driven straight to the nearest Home Depot. I threw the first can of white paint my hands had landed on inside my cart, wheeled it to the counter, and purchased it without a second thought.

When I got home though, I sat on my bedroom floor staring at that can of whitewash for almost two hours unable to even crack the lid. With a frustrated scream, I eventually just shoved the unopened paint into the back of my closet along with Finn's leather jacket, where I didn't have to look at them anymore.

For the first day or so, I tried not to think about him at all. Then I realized how insanely useless and counterproductive *that* was, so I gave up and started acting like a girl – or, in other words, I began obsessing over everything he'd ever said or done in the months since we'd met.

I began to realize that, in many ways, Finn actually had tried to tell me – maybe not with words, but certainly with actions…

The night he took me out to look at the fireflies by his lookout point.

His strange song dedication when he sang at The Blue Note.

How he'd always, from the very start, called me 'Bee.'

How protective he'd always been.

Even the way he'd phrased certain things…

There's never been anyone real for me except you.

It's always been you.

You're so different from what I expected.

I love you, Brooklyn. I always have.

The list went on and on, until my eyes were swimming and I forced myself to stop searching my memories.

I think it was day seven post-Finn when the door to my bedroom was abruptly thrown open, slamming against the opposite wall so hard the photos hanging there rattled and threatened to come crashing down. Lexi stormed in, her blue eyes flashing with determination, and walked up to the bed where I was huddled under a mountain of blankets. With one jerk of her arm, she ripped the comforter from the bed and tossed it to the floor.

"Brooklyn Grace Turner. This is pathetic. Look at yourself!" She demanded, pointing at my ratty sweatshirt and ripped pajama shorts. "More importantly, though, *smell* yourself. Seriously, can you even remember the last time you showered?"

My lips twitched traitorously in the beginnings of a smile.

"Get up!" Lexi yelled. "Right freaking now!"

"Go away, Lexi," I countered wearily, rolling over to face the wall. I was definitely not in the mood to play nice.

Suddenly, my bed shifted as the weight of a body landed solidly on my mattress. Startled, I rolled over to see Lexi standing over me on the bed, hands planted on her hips. I opened my mouth to ask what the hell she thought she was doing, but it snapped closed, clacking my teeth together painfully, when she began to jump up and down like a crazy person.

The whole mattress was bouncing, and me with it – each time her feet made contact with the bed, I was launched several feet in the air, clutching frantically at the frame so I wouldn't be bounced right onto the floor.

"I SAID GET UP!" Lexi yelled, jumping even harder. When her feet came dangerously close to landing on my internal organs, I had no choice other than to abandon ship.

I dove to the ground, scurried several feet away from the bed, and spun around to face the madwoman that was my best friend. She'd stopped jumping as soon as I'd cleared the bed, but remained standing up there, fuming at me.

Without saying anything, she hopped off the bed, strode across the room, and backed me into a corner until I was pressed tight against the wall. Leaning in, she trapped my face between her palms and looked me in the eye.

"It's been seven days, Brooklyn. I gave you a full week to wallow. And, trust me, its been hard to watch." She made a disgusted face. "I know you're going through a hard time right now. I get that it's the hardest thing in the world to even fathom getting out of bed in the morning and pretending that everything is normal. I've been there."

I started to interrupt, but she cut me off before I could get a word in.

"But this isn't you, Brooklyn. I don't care what he did – no boy is worth subjecting yourself to this."

Was this *Lexi* talking?

"I know what you're thinking. Who am I, queen of the ever-revolving door of boyfriends, to tell you anything about relationships, right?"

Wow, that had been almost my exact thought.

"And you'd be right; I *have* had more than my fair share of boyfriends and unhealthy relationships. But because of that, I've also had my share of heartbreaks." A sad, small smile graced her lips. "If there's one thing I'm really good at, it's getting over assholes and moving on with my life. Maybe I don't move on to the right people, but that's not the point… Thing is, Brooklyn, that's really all you can do – you just go on. In spite of the pain, in spite of everything, you keep breathing. And one day, I promise, it will get better."

I supposed she had a point.

"Do I really smell that bad?" I asked in a quiet voice.

"Literally, I could smell you from the kitchen," Lexi giggled. "I think you're starting to mold."

"Ew!" I said, crinkling my nose. "I am so not that bad."

"Whatever you say." She rolled her eyes. "Just shower, would ya? We've got places to go, people to see."

"Where?" I asked.

"Just trust me."

***

"Okay," Lexi grinned over at me. "You can thank me now."

"Off the record?" I hedged.

"Uh-huh, whatever you say."

"Fine, I admit it. You were right."

"That's all I get? After the shitstorm you kicked up over this?! Not even a 'Thank you Lexi, for being the most wonderful, thoughtful, stunningly beautiful, amazingly insightful – *and did I mention good looking?* – best friend on the planet, and for forcing me, against my will, to get such an incredibly sexy new haircut?'"

I rolled my eyes and walked toward the car without her.

"Oh, lighten up!" She said, racing to catch up with me. "It really does look great, though."

As much as I hated to admit it, Lexi had been right about the haircut; it was exactly what I'd needed to shake off the gloom that I'd been drowning in for the past week. The stylist had been lectured thoroughly by Lexi for fifteen minutes before even so much as lifting a brush – in fact, I was surprised Lexi hadn't just grabbed the scissors and started hacking off clumps of my hair herself.

Thankfully, it didn't get that far and her micromanaging hadn't escalated to actual maiming.

The stylist, following Lexi's instructions to the letter, had chopped off several inches of my long hair, leaving it just long enough to brush the tops of my breasts. She'd added layers and trimmed the pieces around my face to better accentuate my features. Lastly, she'd threaded caramel-brown high- and low-lights throughout my hair, a look I'd never before attempted with my dark locks.

I'd originally been worried about how it would turn out, but as soon as I'd seen the finished product in the mirror, I'd fallen in love with it. The cut was flattering, showing off my small features and framing my face in a way that made my mouth look more supple, my cheekbones higher. The new color offset the deep green of my irises, making them stand out more prominently and flattering my skin tone.

In short, I looked – and felt – like a new woman.

After our stop at the hairdresser, I learned that it had been only the first on a long agenda of activities Lexi had planned for the day.

Next, we drove across the street to Lexi's favorite nail salon, where we were manicured, buffed, and top-coated to perfection. Then we hit the local strip mall for some quality retail therapy, each buying a few new dresses and tops. I even found a gorgeous vintage pair of Chanel heeled boots in a second-hand shop of designer cast offs, scooping them up for a fraction of their original price.

After our shopping spree I thought for sure we were done, but instead of heading home, Lexi steered us toward the local movie theater. We ate stale popcorn with too much butter and laughed ourselves silly at the on-screen antics of our favorite female comedy duo.

By the time we finally pulled in at the house, it was well after midnight and I was exhausted from a jam-packed day of girltime. We sat in the driveway, staring at the Victorian, and I realized I'd barely thought about Finn all day – Lexi had kept me too busy.

It had been so good to laugh – to get out of that room, away from all the memories. I almost didn't want to go back inside to face everything.

"Hey," Lexi said, breaking the silence. "There's one more thing on our itinerary."

"What?" I asked.

"Sleepover. Just like when we were thirteen; we'll eat ice cream from the carton and talk about how I'm going to marry Lance Bass and you're going to have seventeen babies with Justin Timberlake. Except now we have the added benefits of vodka."

"Firstly, we are never revisiting the 'NSync phase, no matter how drunk you get me. Secondly, Lance Bass is openly gay, so good luck with that plan of yours. And thirdly, thank you."

"*Moi*? Whatever for?" Lexi grinned.

"For being you," I shrugged. "We don't have to do the corny hug-it-out thing, right?"

"But…" Lexi winked, then burst into song. "*IT'S TEARING UP MY HEA—*"

"Stop!" I interrupted her. "There will be no singing, either!"

Two hours later we were both half in the bottle, singing Backstreet Boys at the top of our lungs into hairbrush microphones.

When we finally fell asleep, spooning like little girls in Lexi's bed, a solitary tear slipped from my eye and rolled across the pillow. I thought I'd lost everything when I lost him, but I'd been wrong. I still had Lexi. And, more importantly, I had myself.

It had been a tough week, but I knew deep down that Lexi had been right – it doesn't matter that you get knocked down.

It's how you get back up and carry on that matters.

***

After that day, I forced myself to start living again. Eating regular meals, sleeping semi-normal hours. Piece by piece, I picked up the discarded fragments of my life and tried to find myself within the chaos.

I threw myself into my schoolwork, which was a good thing considering how many classes and assignments I'd missed during my week of hibernation. I had a lot of ground to make up academically, especially with finals and the end of the semester approaching. At least my professors had been understanding.

Dr. Angelini was a different story.

To say she was frustrated with me would be an

understatement. Not that she showed it, or anything –outwardly, she appeared as calm and collected as always. But the storm of emotion raging behind her eyes gave her away.

So, to appease her, I told her everything.

"I found the trigger," I said as soon as I sat down in her office.

"Pardon me?"

"The trigger. It was Finn." I swallowed. "He's the boy of my dreams."

"Finn is the little boy from your dreams?"

"That's what I just said, isn't it?" I asked, growing frustrated.

"No, you said, 'he's the boy of my dreams,' which has an entirely different connotation."

"So help me god, doc, if you even *think* the words 'Freudian Slip' I will leave this office and never come back," I grumbled.

Dr. Angelini hid a smile behind her coffee mug before taking a sip.

"So Finn is the trigger," she prompted, gesturing at me to continue.

I told her everything, then – about the dreams I'd had, the memories I'd uncovered on the Ferris wheel, and our breakup afterwards. I glossed over my activities of last week, apologized for skipping our sessions, and prepared to leave. When I stood, Dr. Angelini stopped me.

"So that's it?" she asked, as close to incredulous as I'd ever seen her.

"What's what?" I was confused.

"You're just going to give up on Finn? On all the progress you've made? On yourself?"

"What do you mean?"

"Four months ago, if you had a problem, you'd bury your head in the sand like an ostrich, and either wait for it to go away on its own, or run like hell until it was a tiny speck in your rearview," Dr. Angelini said. "Isn't that exactly what you're doing now?"

270

"Did you seriously just equate me to an ostrich?" I asked.

"Look, I'm probably overstepping my bounds as your therapist here, but I can't help but feel that you are going to regret it for the rest of your life if you don't deal with this. That moment people look back on when they're lying in their deathbeds, wishing they'd chosen differently? *This* is that moment."

"He lied to me!" I pointed out defensively.

"I know that, Brooklyn," Dr. Angelini said quietly. "But aren't there things you've kept from him as well?"

Of course there were, but I wasn't about to own up to it.

"Humans are flawed creatures – selfish and cowardly most of the time. We lie, cheat, and steal better than we do almost anything else. We hurt each other with words, actions, and omissions," Dr. Angelini sighed. "There is a one hundred percent guarantee that the people we love most will let us down. That's the risk you take, when you open up your heart." Dr. Angelini paused for a moment and leaned across the coffee table to look at me intently.

"But at some point, you have to decide which ones matter more than the pain, and forgive them for their mistakes." She placed one hand on mine. "So, if you love him, I guess the only real question you have to ask yourself, the only question that matters is, at the end of the day, is he worth the suffering?"

***

For the rest of the day, I wandered in a daze, thinking over Dr. Angelini's words. I drove out to the lookout point Finn had taken me to in August, sad to see that it had been overtaken by winter. Frost clung to the fronds and grasses near the riverbed, and the stream was flowing sluggishly under a thin sheet of ice. There were no fireflies; there was no life at all, here – not anymore. It was difficult to believe the hard, frozen ground would ever bring forth new flowers; that the trees would blossom again; that the animals would return to this barren place.

I wasn't sure what I'd been looking for when I decided to come here – answers, I guess – but I definitely hadn't found it.

I'd turned to go, depressed by the much-changed landscape, when a cardinal – red and majestic, defying the wintery chill in the air as it soared between deadened trees – burst from a nearby bush, startling me. Clutching a hand to my chest, my eyes tracked the bird's flight and a genuine smile bloomed on my face. It felt odd, unnatural on my lips after weeks of frowning, and probably looked more akin to a grimace than an actual grin – but at least it was there.

There was life out here after all.

Even in the most desolate place, when it appeared nothing would ever be the same – there was hope.

I pulled out my phone and scrolled through my contacts to a name I hadn't pressed in weeks. Typing out a quick message, my fingers quickly went numb in the chilly air.

Do you remember when we were kids, and you told me the story of Princess Andromeda? How her parents sacrificed her to the sea monster to save their country?

His response was instantaneous, as if he'd been waiting by his phone.

Of course I do.

I typed back quickly, afraid if I didn't say this now, I'd never find the courage again.

I never understood how Andromeda could forgive her parents so easily for that, after Perseus saved her. All my life I've thought about that myth, thinking it didn't make any sense and wondering what I was missing. But I think I finally get it now.

Get what, princess? he asked.

Holding my breath, I hit send.

When you love someone, truly *love them – more than your pride, more than yourself, even – you can forgive them anything, no matter how much they've hurt you. And maybe I'm an idiot, but I still love you. I've loved you since I was six years old.*

My phone rang.

"Hi," I laughed into the receiver.

"I'm coming over," Finn said without hesitation, his voice demanding. I could hear noises in the background, as if he were pulling on his boots and jacket.

"Don't," I told him. "Not right now anyway. I'm not home."

272

"Well, where are you? I'll meet you somewhere. Anywhere." Hearing his voice was a balm to my desperate soul; I let the sound wash over me, reveling in it like some kind of addict who'd been denied her fix for far too long.

"I'll be home tonight. Come over later – let's say eight? We can talk then," I said. I could hear the smile in my own voice.

"But it's only three, now," he grumbled.

"It's been two weeks," I shrugged, though he couldn't see it. "Are a few more hours going to kill you?"

"Yes," he said immediately. "I'll be pacing my living room for the next four hours and forty seven minutes."

"Not that you're counting," I laughed. "And don't pace – you've got nice carpeting. It would be a shame to ruin it."

"I'll see you soon, princess. Don't make any other plans. Tonight, you're mine." His voice held a dark promise that sent a thrill rushing through me.

"Counting the minutes," I breathed, before hanging up.

I raced back to the Victorian, eager to shower and clean the apartment a bit before Finn's arrival. I stopped on the way home to grab some groceries for dinner, feeling light and happy for the first time in weeks.

I couldn't wait to see him. Sure, there were things we still needed to discuss. But now that I'd decided to forgive him, everything seemed easier – like a giant weight had fallen from my shoulders and clattered to the ground at my feet.

I walked through the front door, whistling under my breath with my arms loaded full of groceries. The apartment was quiet – Lexi and Ty were spending the weekend skiing with another couple at a mountain range three hours away. Conveniently, Finn and I would have the apartment to ourselves to get reacquainted. I blushed in anticipation, hoping all the stories I'd heard about the wonders of make-up sex were true.

I didn't notice anything out of the ordinary. I didn't have a sense of foreboding, or a gut feeling that something was deeply wrong. I was happy, with a goofy smile pasted on my face, when I walked into my bedroom.

I took two blissfully unaware steps into the room, before

the images in front of my eyes registered and I came to an abrupt stop.

Horror – that's the only word I can use to describe what I felt as I stood frozen in place, scanning the walls of my bedroom.

There were photos covering every surface of the room. They plastered the walls, a morbid collage of images; they hung from strings on the ceiling; they littered the floor and the surface of the bed.

And every single one was a photo of me.

There were snapshots taken from far away, as I made my way to class or ate at the campus student center. Here, an image of me laughing with a classmate as we entered our Criminal Justice lecture hall. There, a photo of me sitting under a tree on the quad, munching an apple as I studied for Media Law.

There were close-ups of my face, multiple shots taken from every angle and in every light. His lens had captured each emotion – happiness, joy, sadness, grief, frustration, doubt, anxiety, fear. He'd gotten photos of expressions I hadn't even known my face could make.

None of those were as scary as the ones that had been taken from inside this very apartment. I wasn't sure how he'd gotten in without Lexi or me ever taking notice, but there they were – unquestionable proof that he not only had access to our living space, he'd made himself fully at home.

There were shots of me cooking, singing along to the radio as I stirred pasta or checked the oven. There were images of Lexi and I taking shots of tequila. Laughing as we put on makeup and got ready for to head out for the night. Hugging tightly, with matching smiles on our faces.

They only got worse, the more I looked.

Hundreds of shots of me naked, as I changed clothes in my bedroom. More images than I wanted to count depicting me in the shower, fully exposed and vulnerable.

I had been the unknowing and unwilling subject of every image captured by his camera lens.

The most terrifying photos were the ones of Finn and me. In each of those, Finn's face had been harshly scratched over with

274

sharpie or cut out with scissors. Several of them showed his face with a huge gun-sight target drawn over his face.

In a daze, I pushed the hanging photographs out of my way as I walked over to the bed, my feet sliding as they searched for traction on the slippery photos covering the floor. There was a box sitting on top of my comforter amidst a pile of images, wrapped in shiny black paper. The lid was fixed with a matte black bow; I tugged on it lightly and it tumbled loose with ease.

I reached out to lift the lid of the box, bracing myself with the knowledge that whatever was inside was probably even more horrifying than the Brooklyn-collage on my walls.

I held my breath as I flipped back the lid, eyes scanning the contents disbelievingly.

He'd planned this carefully, no doubt wanting it to have maximum impact on my emotions. To simultaneously terrify me and confirm that all my suspicions had been correct.

He succeeded.

The box was full to the brim with black rose petals. Resting atop the sea of macabre flowers, there was a note. It had been written in formal calligraphy, the flowing black lettering beautiful in an archaic, timeless sort of way. It had been scribed on a piece of thick off-white cardstock, the kind used by the wealthy in the days of old when they'd send out handwritten invitations to their balls and galas.

It felt heavy in my hand as I lifted it from the box and read the slanting message.

A gift for you, since I ruined your last one.

Beneath the note and the petals, there was a beautiful dress folded inside the box. I recognized its green bodice and elegant beading immediately; this wasn't any dress, it was *The Dress.* An exact replica of the one I'd worn the night I was attacked outside Styx – newly purchased and, terrifyingly, the correct size.

I glanced back at the note; it was signed in the bottom right corner with only two initials:

E.S.

And then I knew.

There it was, in black and white. Undeniable.

He'd come back for me.

I turned to face the door, to find my phone, to do something, *anything*, to stop what was about to happen. But I knew, even as I spun and caught sight of him in the doorway – his face, the face of my nightmares, unchanged by time or years behind bars – that it was far too late for that.

The table was set, first course had been served.

Somehow, I didn't think I'd make it to dessert.

Chapter Nineteen

Revelations

I'd struggled.

He must've hit me with something that knocked me out for a time, because when I woke up I was no longer in my bedroom. My arms ached, pins and needles shooting through my fingers due to a lack of circulation.

I thought that was odd, until I realized *why* the blood wasn't flowing to those limbs: my hands had been bound together with a thick, coarse rope, and strung up above my head. The rest of my body dangled in the air, with my tiptoes barely grazing the ground and taking a meager fraction of my weight off my wrists.

There was duct tape across my mouth, blocking my airway and my screams for help. Wherever I was, it was completely quiet. I didn't move for several minutes, hoping that I was alone, and taking stock of my bodily inventory.

I was still wearing my jeans and my dark green sweater from earlier, but my shoes had been removed; my bare toes scraped against the rough, cool cement floor. I could no longer feel the weight of my cell phone in my back pocket. My hair fell like a curtain in front of my face, blocking my view of the room around me. Unable to use my hands to push it out of my eyes, I tilted my head up toward the ceiling and tossed it in either direction until the hair draped back over my shoulders.

"Good, you're awake." He'd been here all along, standing on the far side of the room watching me slowly reenter consciousness. His voice may have held the dispassionate courtesy one might use when discussing opposing political views over tea, but his underlying hostility was visible beneath the mask of composure he wore.

Ernest "Ernie" Skinner, in the flesh.

His face had more lines now and his muddy brown hair had some grey strands mixed through it, but the eyes were the same. Dark, fathomless pits of brown-black, they stared back at me, tauntingly victorious. The one difference was that now they weren't glazed with the aftereffects of too much cocaine – they were completely lucid and full of cool triumph.

I stared at him warily, unresponsive. My mind was reeling as I tried to piece together where I was, and how I was going to get out of here. The alternative, that I wasn't going to escape, was too terrifying to even consider.

The walls were dull gunmetal gray, and looked to be made of concrete or some other thick material. There was no furniture, with the exception of a set of metal folding chairs and a matching rusted table. Chains hung from steel rafter beams in the ceiling; I had no doubt that my hands were tied to the one running directly above my head. One bare light bulb swung from a wire, illuminating the dark room in a dim yellowish hue.

If I had to guess, I'd say I was in a basement somewhere.

"It's good to finally see you, Brooklyn. Face to face, that is," he laughed, a harsh unnatural sound coming from his lips. "Now that you've seen my little gallery, we both know I've been *seeing you* for quite a long time."

He'd been standing about ten feet away from me, but now he began to circle closer with his arms clasped behind his back. I tugged at my wrists, trying to maneuver away from him, but the ropes binding my arms had been tied so tightly I couldn't swing more than a few inches.

"You know, Brooklyn, you don't look very comfortable." He smiled. "I would cut you down, but something tells me you'd be less receptive to our little chat if I did."

He stopped directly in front of me, an unruffled smile pasted on his lips as he reached up a hand to tenderly stroke the side my face. I tried to jerk my head away from his touch, but his hand clamped around my jaw with a bruising grip, stilling me. His sudden show of violence was at complete odds with his calm demeanor.

Now that he was closer to me, I could see he had a gaping cut on his forehead, just above his right eye. It was scabbed over, as if it had been healing for about a month, and I knew

278

immediately that it had been put there by my stiletto heel that night in the alleyway.

With one hand still wrapped around my jawbone, he brought his other up to savagely rip the duct tape from my mouth. I yelped as the adhesive tore at my lips, splitting the bottom one open and sending a trickle of blood leaking down my chin. As I gasped for air, I watched his pupils dilate in excitement – he definitely enjoyed the sight of me hurt.

His thumb brushed at the wound, smearing the blood all over my chin and lips before he released me and took a step back. He looked down at the bright streaks of red staining his fingers and smiled softly.

I whimpered in fear.

As soon as he backed off, I began screaming for help, praying that someone above ground would hear me and send for help. His smile remained in place as my cries grew desperate, my frantic voice hoarse with use. He was serene – unhurried and unconcerned, as if he had all the time in the world to toy with me. That in itself told me numerous things: either he was crazy enough not to fear discovery by neighbors and passerby, or we were in a spot so isolated, so far removed from civilization, that no one could hear me for miles.

"Go ahead, Brooklyn," he said. "Scream all you want. There's no one around to hear you."

A chill raced down my spine as my suspicions were confirmed.

I was alone. Help wasn't coming.

"Lexi." My voice sounded weak; clearing my throat, I tried again. "Lexi will notice if I don't come home," I said, trying to reason with him. "If you let me go, I promise I won't tell anyone about this. It'll be our secret."

"Oh, Brooklyn," he said, shaking his head in a show of disappointment. "I wish you hadn't lied to me. There's a price for lies, you know."

"I'm not lying," I whispered.

Abruptly, his arm flew out from behind his back and he backhanded me across the face. The force of the blow rocked my whole body backward, it's motion only stopped by the rope tether binding my hands. Stars swam in front of my eyes and tears leaked down my face as pain ricocheted from my smarting cheekbone to my ravaged wrists and back again. My wrist bones had nearly snapped under the strain of the hit; the skin felt raw beneath the ropes, chafed, bloodied, and stinging painfully.

"There's a price for lies," he repeated flatly, returning his hands to their clasped position. "Now, where were we? Ah, yes. I was just about to discuss our plans for the afternoon. You didn't have anything scheduled, did you?" He chuckled.

I didn't respond.

"I assume you didn't, given the fact that Lexi is off with her boyfriend for the weekend and you've put an end to your own dalliance with *Finn*." He sneered Finn's name with contempt, the most emotion I'd yet to see from him; even when he'd struck me across the face, he'd seemed only clinically interested, his impassive nature untouchable.

He spoke with immaculate annunciation and diction, his grammar perfect and his tone practiced, as if he'd rehearsed these words countless times. *He probably has,* I realized. *He's been planning this for years.*

"I must say, Brooklyn, it made me very happy when you broke off that relationship."

Well, he might've thought he knew everything about me, but at least he didn't know Finn and I were back together.

Wait...Finn!

I'd been so preoccupied, what with being abducted and strung up by a psychopath, that I'd completely forgotten he was coming over at eight. Hope flared to life in my chest. I had no idea what time it was now, though I suspected it was midafternoon; eight was likely still hours away, but if I could just hold on till then...

Why hadn't I agreed to let him come over right away? I lamented internally, hating myself for telling him to wait. By the time he got to my apartment, saw the photos, realized that I'd been taken, and called the police, it may well be too late for me.

Plus, there was the fact that I didn't even know where I

was.

The hope dwindled to embers, then died out.

By this point I'd realized that he hadn't simply been watching me or spying on me; he'd been listening, learning, picking up every scrap of information he could find. He'd probably bugged my apartment with listening devices and cameras – it would certainly explain where he'd gotten the photos of me in the shower and my bedroom.

What I didn't understand was *why*. So I asked him.

"*Why?*" he echoed, as if the question was incomprehensible to him. I could see, beneath that veneer of calm, that I'd thrown him off balance. I didn't understand; it should have been the simplest question in the world for a normal person to answer.

That's when I realized: I wasn't dealing with a normal person.

I was dealing with a sociopath.

This wasn't a revenge mission, driven by passion or vengeance or nearly two decades of anger. It was a cool, calculated meting out of justice; his way of evening the score. And he would eliminate me as easily as a king taking a rook off the chessboard – with meticulous concentration and well-planned moves he'd thought out far in advance.

My sense of hopelessness grew as I realized what that meant.

He likely hadn't been sloppy when he'd put this plan together, insuring that nothing was easily tied back to him. Emotions didn't drive him, and therefore couldn't be used to manipulate him into making mistakes. And he would have no qualms when it came time to kill me.

"Can you believe I only served twelve years before they let me out? I see from your face that you can't." He laughed. "You've gotta love that trusty old California legal system. Good behavior gets you a long way with the guards. And when I went before that parole board with tears in my eyes and told them all about how I'd found the Lord and Savior Jesus Christ, and he'd guided me from the dark path of substance abuse and violence, out into the light? Well, I must say, just about every damned one of them got misty-eyed."

I stared ahead impassively, trying to show no reaction to his words.

"I should've gotten a damn Oscar for that performance," he said, smiling at the memory. "Instead, I got paroled and sent back out into the world, a *changed man*. That's what they want to believe, you know – that prison fixes us, takes out all the bad tendencies and swaps 'em for goodness and a healthy respect for authority. It's what they have to believe, otherwise they wouldn't sleep at night – but it's not the truth."

I swallowed nervously, watching as he approached me once more.

"The truth is, sweet Brooklyn, that all time in the slammer does is offer you plenty of time to think," he whispered, his breath hot on my face. "Can you guess who I thought about?"

I began to tremble.

"That's right," he said softly, tracing one finger down my cheek, across my collarbone, and into the cleavage revealed by the v-neck of my sweater. He stopped midway down my chest, his finger skimming slowly back and forth across the swell of my breasts. "I thought about you."

***

He disappeared for a while, leaving me alone with my thoughts.

Arms aching, I hung with my back bowed against the strain and tried to imagine I was anywhere else in the world. Closing my eyes, I mentally erased the concrete walls around me, and pictured a different night – the night I was supposed to have.

Finn would arrive, stepping through the door and into my arms. He'd hold me, kiss me, and everything would be all right in my world again.

I think about an hour passed. It must have been close to dinnertime by now – around six or seven most likely – because my stomach had begun to rumble with hunger.

When Skinner returned, emerging from a stairwell located somewhere behind me, he was holding the green dress in one hand. A large, wickedly sharp kitchen knife was clasped in the other. He approached me and a helpless, involuntary mewling noise burst from the back of my throat. I'd begun to tremble as soon as he'd appeared.

"Now, now, Brooklyn," he said, making a *tsk* sound. "I'm not going to hurt you before dinner. That wouldn't be very polite."

As if social niceties are a factor when you've got a girl hanging from your basement ceiling. He really is crazy.

"We're going to be together for a long time, my dear. All that nasty business can certainly wait until after we've eaten."

My mind raced as I wondered what constituted a "long time" in his warped brain. Minutes? Hours? Days? *Years?* I could barely survive the mental strain of three hours with the man – if he made me his plaything, keeping me here for weeks on end…

Well, let's just say, I think I'd sooner choose the quick end with the sharp knife.

True to his word, he used it now only to cut me down. The bonds around my wrists remained fastened tight, but at least they were no longer forced up above my head. As soon as he severed the rope holding me up, my legs gave out and I crumpled to the hard ground like a rag doll.

My arms felt as if they were on fire as feeling came rushing back, like physical flames were licking up my arms along with the returning blood filling my vessels. I knew this was the moment – you know in all the movies, how the heroine finally gets her chance to run away, to save herself, to fight back?

I felt that moment slip away as I lay on the cement, incapacitated and utterly unable to fight for anything except the shaky breaths I struggled to drag into my lungs.

"Come now, dear, you don't look at all excited for dinner." His voice was quietly amused. He stood over me, enjoying the sight of me defeated. Twice, I tried to push myself up from the ground; each time, my arms gave out beneath me and I fell back to the cement floor.

He let me struggle for five minutes or so, before reaching down a hand and roughly yanking me upright. Looping an arm around my back, he dragged me over to the metal chairs in the corner of the room and threw me down onto one. When he released me I nearly slipped back to the floor, but managed to steady myself with my bound hands at the last minute.

He sat down in the other metal chair, watching me as I tried to rally the little strength I had left in my body. My breathing eventually slowed and my limbs began to regain most of their feeling. I was wiggling my fingers and toes, testing out the sensation in them, when he abruptly stood and pulled me to my feet.

"Come."

We walked – thankfully, I didn't need his help this time – through the basement and up a set of wooden stairs tucked against the far wall. Emerging into a dimly lit kitchen, I was shocked to discover that I knew exactly where I was.

The layout was a little different, but all of the appliances, woodwork, and furniture were the same. Hell, the walls were even painted in that unmistakable jaundiced yellow.

This was the first floor apartment of the old Victorian.

We were directly under my apartment – I'd bet my life on it. Had he been living here all year, so close to me all this time? The thought made me shiver.

He led me through the kitchen and into the living room. This was clearly his lair: the walls were covered not just in photos of me, but also in newspaper clippings. The headlines were varied, spanning years and occasions, but all centered around one thing: Me.

Local Woman Killed in Car-Jacking, Daughter Lives to Tell the Tale

Seven Year Old Gives Condemning Testimony in Court
Car-Jacking Killer Sentenced to 25 Years in San Quentin
Captain Brooklyn Turner Leads Varsity Field Hockey Team to Victory

UVA Freshman Brooklyn Turner Makes Dean's List

He hadn't just been following me for months – he'd been watching me for years. I forced myself to stop looking, but my eyes soon locked onto something even more disturbing. There were at least six computer monitors set up along the wall, with each screen divided to show several camera angles. They were live feeds, streaming video from inside my apartment upstairs.

Every room had been bugged.

I tried to ignore the monitor on the far left, which was dedicated to my bedroom. Or, more specifically, to my bed. There was a camera trained on every side, capturing every angle. When I thought about all the times Finn and I had been together there, all the things Skinner had witnessed, I had to choke back the vomit that was working its way up my throat. He'd violated a space I'd thought was sacred, completely private, and I had the unbearable desire to shower – as if I could scrape myself clean of the feeling of his eyes on my skin.

I felt dirty, vulnerable.

He eventually pulled me away, a smug smile on his face. He'd wanted me to see this – to understand just how deeply he was embedded in my life. To know that he'd seen everything, heard everything.

"Aren't you going to ask how I did it?" he said, his tone anticipatory.

This is what he gets off on, I realized. *He's an egomaniac. He wants – he needs – to impress me. To frighten me. To think he's the master puppeteer, pulling my strings and controlling every facet of my life.*

That's his weakness, I thought. *Pride.*

"No," I said, making my voice uninterested just to goad him.

He fumed silently for a minute, then continued as if I hadn't spoken.

"Isn't it amazing what the Internet can do nowadays? You'll never guess how easy it was to find your little Facebook page and to track down your apartment address through the university directory. Everything I needed to know about you was right there at the tips of my fingers – not to mention how easy it was for me to order all this helpful electronic equipment. Free, two-day shipping for these babies," he laughed, gesturing toward his elaborate setup of computer monitors. "No background checks or identification required."

I stared at the wall, trying to block out his words.

"There are YouTube tutorials for everything; there's even a how-to guide for bugging someone's house with cameras, right there online for anyone to watch." He laughed maniacally, nearly giddy with his own success.

He marched me into the adjacent dining room. The table had been set for two, and I would have laughed if I'd had the stomach for it: a crisp white tablecloth glowed under the warm, ambient light of several tall taper candles. Red cloth napkins, folded into graceful triangles, sat atop gold-filigree plates. Fresh roses – red, this time – were arranged in a gorgeous crystal vase. Several warming platters sat in the center of the table, covered by silver lids.

He'd created the perfect romantic atmosphere for a dinner date for two.

Rather than leading me to my chair at the table, he pushed me toward the small settee in the corner of the room. When I landed on the plush cushions, he threw the green dress onto my lap.

"Change for dinner," he ordered, setting his knife on the table. He didn't need to wield like a mad man – its presence alone was an implied threat, and enough to keep me complacent.

I looked down at my bound hands. "I can't."

He slapped me across the face so hard my head snapped back. At least he'd hit the other cheek this time; *I'll have matching bruises*, I thought, rather dazedly. Blinking away the dark spots dancing in front of my eyes, I looked up at him.

"You'll do whatever I say without question, bitch," he said, his voice strained. The thought that I'd disobey was nearly enough to unhinge him.

"Of course," I agreed, trying to infuse my voice with humility. "I just wondered if you would be kind enough—" I forced out the words. "—to untie my hands first."

His face was stony, contemplative.

"Just for a minute," I added hastily. "So I can put on the dress. It's beautiful."

The last thing I wanted to do was strip bare in front of him and put on some dress he'd bought for me, like we were playing some sick, twisted game of house. But with my hands bound, I didn't stand a chance at escaping.

If I can get my hands on that knife…

I tried not to think that far in advance. I was taking this one careful step at a time, feeling out his weaknesses and playing it smart.

"You like the dress?" he asked, skeptically.

"I love it," I agreed immediately. "Thank you for getting it for me."

He nodded. "I'll take off the ropes while you change. But I will stay in the room the entire time, and if you do anything foolish there will be consequences."

I could pretty easily guess what he meant by 'consequences,' watching as he picked up the knife and advanced toward me. He quickly cut my bonds, allowing the rope to fall to the floor beneath the settee, and retreated back across the room. Sitting down on one of the chairs at the table, he kept the knife in his hand and his eyes on me.

Trembling, I cast my eyes down to the floor and peeled my sweater up over my head. I stood and shimmied out of my jeans, watching as they hit the floor. I resisted every urge I had to cover myself from his eyes, to put a stop to this depraved and degrading strip tease, knowing he would be angry if I did.

With shaking hands, I pulled the dress fabric over my head and settled it around my body. Smoothing down the skirt with my palms, I did up the side zipper and surreptitiously hiked up the neckline to cover as much cleavage as possible.

When I was done, I looked up and met his dark eyes across the room.

He looked both aroused and empowered by my immodest show, his gaze following my every movement.

"Sit," he said, gesturing toward the chair to his left. "You can eat without your hands tied, for now."

A small victory, but a victory nonetheless.

I sat and watched as he spooned a helping of chicken and potatoes onto both of our plates. It smelled good, but the thought of eating anything turned my stomach – anything I consumed would likely just come right back up again.

"Eat," he ordered, lifting a forkful of potatoes to his mouth.

I reached for my glass of water.

We both stilled, my hand frozen midway through its reach and his fork poised in the air, when the indisputable sound of a motorcycle engine roared down the street and came to a stop outside the house.

Our gazes locked and I could tell we were both thinking the same thing.

Finn was here.

CHAPTER TWENTY

CHOOSE ME

Skinner was up and around the table in a flash, with one hand covering my mouth and the other holding the knife tight against my throat.

"Shhh," he breathed in my ear.

We listened as the engine cut off, and the sound of footsteps echoed on the stairs going up to my apartment. We heard Finn banging on my front door for several minutes, calling out for me. I imagined him standing there, confused and wondering where I was.

Lexi's car was in the driveway. I wasn't answering my cellphone.

He'll know something is wrong. He'll call the police.

My assurance was quickly overtaken by a flurry of doubts: what if Finn thought I'd changed my mind about meeting him? What if he thought I didn't want to get back together? What if he gave up and left, without ever going inside the apartment?

Then, I realized that this was *Finn* – he didn't take no for an answer. I'd been surprised he'd even conceded to giving me a week's worth of space; shocked that he'd agreed to wait until eight to come over tonight. When that boy wanted something, he went after it with everything he had.

And he wanted me.

I fought off a smile when I heard the undeniable sound of my apartment door being kicked in. *Such a caveman.*

Skinner cursed, dragging me up out of my chair and walking me into the living room, with the knife still pressed to my neck. He watched the monitors as Finn entered the apartment, scanning the kitchen for anything out of place. Finn walked over to the bags of groceries I'd abandoned on the counter earlier, a speculative look marring his brow.

Reaching one hand into the bag nearest him, he took

out the block of cheese I'd purchased and held it in his hand for a minute. At first, I didn't understand what he was doing, but I quickly put it together – he was gauging its temperature, trying to see how long it had been left unrefrigerated.

From the anxious look on his face I assumed it was now lukewarm, which told him I'd been gone for quite some time. Placing it back on the countertop, Finn walked through the apartment and checked every room, moving from the kitchen, through the living and dining areas, into Lexi's room and, finally, into my bedroom.

I could spend hours trying to describe all the emotions that filtered across his face when he walked into my room and saw not only the collage of photos, but also clear signs of the struggle that had taken place. My desk chair was overturned, my bedspread was askew, the pictures littering the floor were disturbed and bent where I'd eventually fallen to the ground.

He looked shocked, horrified, angered, and terrified all at once.

Skinner was talking under his breath, clearly unhappy with this turn of events. Grabbing a roll of duct tape off the shelf, he ripped off a piece and pressed it over my mouth. He pulled my hands in front of me, hastily wrapped duct tape around them, and shoved me down into the straight-backed desk chair facing the screens.

Whirling back around to check the monitors, Skinner watched as Finn took out his cell phone and dialed 911.

"Fuck!" he snarled, leaning close to the screen and staring at Finn as he spoke rapidly into his phone. "I'm gonna fucking kill that asshole."

It wasn't a threat; it was a promise. His earlier control had evaporated along with his carefully laid plans. With Finn's arrival, Skinner's focus had shifted away from me, and I knew he wouldn't stop until either Finn was dead, or he was.

Skinner spun around to face me, his eyes wild, the knife flashing dangerously in his grip. "Stay here," he barked. "I'm going to go deal with this."

This was the man who'd taken everything from me.

Who'd killed my mother in cold blood, as I'd watched. Who'd haunted my every nightmare for years. Who'd made me afraid to love, for fear that it could be ripped away from me again.

He'd taken my innocence. He wasn't about to take the love of my life, too.

As he began to run from the room, I reached up with my bound hands and used the tips of my fingers to rip off the duct tape covering my mouth.

"Stop!" I yelled after him.

He paused in the doorway, listening, but didn't turn to face me. He wasn't a stupid man – he must've realized that he didn't have enough time before the police arrived to deal with both of us.

If I wanted Finn to live, I had to make Skinner choose me.

I knew I wouldn't survive if I went through with this; I understood it with an unshakable clarity. I could see exactly how my death would play out in the next few minutes and, though I didn't exactly like that picture, it would be worth it if Finn lived.

I couldn't save my mother, but I would save him.

"Is this really the best you could do?" I mocked Skinner. His ego was at the heart of every decision he made – maybe, if I pushed the right buttons, he'd lose all restraint and turn his rage on me. "You had fifteen years to plan tonight, and this was all you came up with?" I forced a laugh and got shakily to my feet.

I watched his spine stiffen, his muscles tense; it was working. I was getting to him.

"I thought you'd do better, *Ernie*." I made a disapproving *tsk* sound, as he'd done earlier – purposefully baiting him. He spun to look at me, red faced and panting with anger.

I could hear sirens approaching now. A glance at the monitors showed Finn making his way back through the apartment, heading for the front door so he could greet the arriving officers.

"What did you say to me, little girl?" Skinner snarled.

"Don't forget it was this *little girl* who sent you to prison, Ernie. It was this *little girl* who caused that car to crash and steered us straight into the arms of the police," I said, desperately trying to keep my voice steady and hold my tears at bay.

He took a step toward me, holding out the knife.

"Shut up, bitch," he screamed. "I know what you're trying to do."

"It's me you want," I reminded him. "It's me you've watched all these years, obsessed over, fantasized about. It's me you've tried to frighten, to destroy. But you know something, Ernie?" I asked, backing away from him so the table was between us. "You *failed*. I lived, and loved, in spite of you. I'm *happy*. And that's certainly more than I can say for you, old man."

That did it.

He launched himself at me with a primitive scream, the knife held high over his head as he prepared to strike me. Anticipating his attack, I threw out my taped hands, grabbed the top of the chair in front of me, and threw it in his direction. It didn't go very far but it did land in his path, slowing him down.

He chased me in circles around the perimeter of the table – a deadly game of cat and mouse. On one of my passes, I managed to grasp a dangling edge of the tablecloth and yank it roughly. The abrupt movement sent the dishes and platters flying, clattering to the floor loud enough that the noise hurt my ears. The vase of roses fell and shattered, sending millions of razor-sharp shards of glass exploding in every direction. I heard Skinner yelp as they sliced at his feet and lower legs.

I turned in time to see him trip over one of the loosed serving dishes and fall to the ground, his knife clattering across the hardwood floors and coming to a stop beneath the desk on the other side of the room.

I looked frantically to the door, hoping I could run to safety, but immediately discarded that plan when I saw that Skinner was clamoring to his feet in the space between me and the exit. Even in his unarmed state, I couldn't fight him with my hands bound.

Out of ideas, out of options, out of *time* – I dove for the knife.

As I fell to my knees, arms outstretched and reaching for the handle, time seemed to slow down, as if everything had suddenly shifted into slow motion. I heard Skinner yell, his footsteps loud as they pounded across the room to reach me.

My fingers closed around the handle, and I gripped it tightly between both hands. It was uncomfortable with my wrists still taped together, but it was the best I could do at the moment.

Everything happened at once.

I flipped over onto my back at the exact moment Skinner jumped into the air, hoping to tackle me from behind. I think he knew, as soon as his feet left the ground, that he was going to die. It was there in his eyes when he saw the knife in my hands, suspended over my stomach and pointing up toward the ceiling.

He tried to pull back, to change his course midair, but it was too late. His weight landed on me, knocking the breath from my lungs, and I felt the pressure of the knife as it slid into the soft flesh of his abdomen, slashing deep into his vital organs.

He gasped at the pain, his face inches from my own. His eyes bored into mine, burning with hatred, and when he opened his mouth to speak, a foamy red spittle flew between his lips and landed on my cheeks.

"You fucking bitch!" he screamed, lifting his hands up to close around my throat. He was dying, his strength waning as the lifeblood slipped from his veins, but he was going to use the last of his energy to take me with him. His hands grew dangerously tight as he choked the life out of me, cutting off my air supply completely. My hands, bound and trapped uselessly between our bodies, were helpless to stop him.

Things started to go dark. Skinner's face was fading in and out of focus as I stared up at him, at times unable to make out his features. I thought I heard the distant sounds of a door crashing open, a man's voice yelling, and footsteps thundering across floorboards, but my mind was too hazy to be sure of anything.

I thought about Finn, in those last moments. I closed my eyes so I didn't have to look at the dying man above me, and instead focused my thoughts on the man I'd do anything for.

There he was – one dimple popping out in his right cheek, as he threw his head back and laughed at something I'd said;

his dark hair disheveled, and the beginnings of a scruffy beard darkening his jawline. Those eyes, so blue and full of emotion, staring at me – seeing straight into my soul.

My head was swimming with the lack of oxygen, and I knew I had only a minute left – maybe less – before I lost consciousness. I used those precious seconds to live the life we should have had together.

I watched him graduate, grinning proudly and cheering until my throat was raw, as he crossed the stage and received his diploma.

I threw my arms around him and screamed YES! when he got down on one knee in a puddle, pulling out a ring on a rainy street corner one drizzly afternoon.

I floated down the aisle, dressed in a cliché white gown and clutching my bouquet like a lifeline, as I walked, smilingly, into my future.

I grinned tiredly in the delivery room, watching as Finn held his baby son in his arms for the first time.

Image by image, I lived out our life, even as I felt my own slipping away. I couldn't feel Skinner's hands on my throat anymore; I couldn't feel much of anything anymore.

I'd gone numb.

Somewhere deep down, it registered that someone was shaking me, saying things to me, but I was too far-gone to feel and long past hearing. My eyes slivered open and the last thing they saw was Finn's face, his expression frantic as his lips mouthed my name over and over.

I tried to smile at him, to let him know that it was okay, because he'd lived – he'd have a future, even if I weren't around to share it. I tried to put the I love you into my eyes, before the dark embraced me.

He clutched me to his chest, his tears falling like rain onto my face.

And I died.

Epilogue

Life doesn't always turn out the way we think it will.

It isn't a fairytale, and there isn't always a happy ending. Sometimes, there isn't a happy beginning or middle, either.

But here's the thing: it doesn't matter.

Because when you're lying there, asphyxiated and lifeless, your life doesn't flash before your eyes like a running movie reel of regrets. It's not the big picture you see – all the things that went wrong, all the mistakes you made, all the experiences you missed out on.

What you see are *moments*.

Flashes of time, no matter how fleeting, when you were happy.

What you see are *faces*.

Glimpses of the people who gave a shit, who loved you in spite of all your crap.

What you see is *yourself*.

The things you did right. The times you were proud meet your own eyes in the mirror. The moments you knew exactly who you were, and where you belonged.

So, I guess when it came down to it, my story was really a love story. Not the one you'd expect – not the one about Finn and me.

It was a story about a girl falling in love with herself. It was about me learning to accept the woman I'd become, flaws and all. Because everybody's a little bit fucked up – that's life. And maybe there aren't any happily ever afters, or white knights who ride in on valiant steeds to save the day. Maybe, in real life, Prince Charming isn't always perfect –he's just as flawed as everyone else in the tale.

And that princess, alone in her tower? She's not perfect either. Birds don't braid her hair every morning, she can't serenade wild forest creatures into servitude, and she doesn't even own a ball gown. But she's also smart enough to know not to accept poisoned apples from strangers, or prick her finger on deadly spindles.

She doesn't wait around for a prince to charge in and slay the dragon. Maybe she saves herself and in the end, rides off into her own goddamned sunset.

I don't know, it's just a theory.

And thankfully, I don't have to have it all figured out yet; I've got my whole life ahead of me to do that.

When I woke up in the hospital, Finn was there. I'd been out for almost 24 hours, and for a while they'd thought I might never regain consciousness. Finn had saved my life, doing CPR until the paramedics arrived.

My heart stopped twice that day; I was lucky to be alive.

Ernie Skinner wasn't so lucky.

The knife wound had sliced deeply, rupturing too many internal organs to fix. He'd nearly bled out by the time the paramedics arrived, and had been pronounced dead at the hospital.

Since I'd woken, I'd had a near-constant parade of visitors, starting with the police. Officers Carlson and O'Callahan took my statement, thanking me on behalf of the Charlottesville PD for my service to the community in removing not only a parole violator, but also a dangerous criminal from the area. On their way out the door, Officer Carlson had wished me a speedy recovery, adding, "Brooklyn, for your sake, I hope this is our last meeting."

I laughed and waved goodbye, sharing his sentiments completely.

Lexi and Ty had returned early from their ski trip as soon as they'd heard about what happened. Lexi's face was the first I'd seen when I woke up; I'd find out later that she and Finn had nearly come to blows over who would get the seat closest to my bed – apparently, she'd won. I couldn't say I was surprised by that, though.

She asked me if I wanted to call my father, and I think she was surprised when I said yes. After bringing me her cellphone,

Lexi, Tyler, and Finn moved toward the door. I told them to stay, though, knowing this would be a brief conversation.

His phone rang three times before he picked up.

"This is Daniel Turner," he said, his stern voice unchanged.

Why can't he just say 'hello' like a normal person?

It had been nearly two years since I'd spoken with my father; I didn't know where to begin.

"Hello? Is anyone there?" His voice was impatient.

"Hi, Dad."

"Brooklyn?" he asked, surprise coloring his tone. "What's happened? Have you been expelled?"

"Why is that always your first question?" I asked, annoyed and already preparing to hang up.

"Because the last time you called me, you'd been expelled from your third boarding school for sneaking boys into your dormitory."

Okay, I guess that was a valid point.

"Well, I'm not in trouble." I took a deep breath. "I'm in the hospital."

"Do I need to send a check?" he asked, his tone accusatory. No questions about *why* his daughter was in the hospital. No parental concern for my wellbeing.

"That won't be necessary," I bit out, clenching my jaw to keep from screaming. "I just need you to answer one question, and then this can be over."

"Yes?" His voice was weary, as if a two-minute conversation with me every two years was enough to tire him out completely.

"Did you know?" I asked, my voice breaking on the last word. "Did they call and tell you that he was released? I couldn't figure out why I hadn't been informed by his parole board, until I finally realized – I was a minor at the time. I was still living under your roof."

I took a deep breath and squeezed my eyes shut so the tears couldn't escape.

"So, Dad, I'm asking. Did you know that Ernie Skinner,

the monster who killed my mother in front of my eyes, had been released early from his sentence, and actually choose not to tell me about it?"

There was a charged silence over the phone. I thought he wasn't going to answer but he finally did respond, and his voice was more strained than I'd ever heard it. "Yes. I knew," he admitted. "They called three years ago to inform me."

"How could you not tell me!?" I exploded.

"I made a judgment call. You were struggling with your studies, already. It—it wasn't something you needed to be concerned with."

"Not something I needed to be concerned with," I echoed bitterly. "That's perfect."

"Brooklyn, I– If I made a mistake, I'm sorry," he said, rather haltingly. My father was not a man who apologized – not ever – and he didn't suffer it well.

"He almost killed me. That's why I'm in the hospital," I told him, my voice impassive. "So I killed him, instead – drove a knife right into his gut and watched him die."

"My God, Brooklyn…what can—"

"Save it," I said, cutting him off. "I don't need anything from you. I certainly don't *want* anything from you. I just had to know. And as far as I'm concerned, you and me? We're done."

I hung up the phone.

When I opened my eyes, Finn, Lexi, and Tyler were looking at me with identical expressions – a unique mixture of sympathy and apprehension.

"I'm fine," I lied. "Can we go home now?"

***

As it turned out, I wouldn't be allowed to go home for another 48 hours. They were keeping me under strict observation. Nurses came in to check on me at regular intervals, and occasionally the doctor would return to give a report.

When Dr. Angelini walked through the doors holding a bouquet of flowers, I smiled.

"Did they move me to the psych wing during my nap?" I asked.

A brief grin crossed her face, but quickly faded as she got a better look at me. I knew the colorful bruises on each cheekbone were clearly visible, despite Lexi's masterful attempts with the concealer this morning.

Sitting down in the chair next to my bed, Dr. Angelini deposited the flowers on the bedside table, took my hand in her own, and squeezed tightly.

"Whoa, doc, aren't you violating some kind of doctor-patient, no-touching-allowed boundaries right now?" I joked, trying to make her laugh.

"Oh, just shut up, Brooklyn, will you?" She said, tears filling her eyes. "And call me Joan, for god's sake." I laughed and returned her hand squeeze.

And for once, we didn't talk. She just held my hand in silence, looking at me the way I'd imagine a mother looks at a daughter who's been injured.

When she left, she dropped a kiss on my forehead and wrapped her arms around me. Thankfully, it was less awkward than our first attempt at hugging, several weeks ago.

I had a feeling we'd get better at it as time passed.

Finn, who'd gracefully stepped out when Dr. Angelini – *Joan* – had arrived, came back into the room. It was the first time we'd really been alone together since everything had happened; Tyler had finally dragged Lexi out this afternoon, insisting that she eat and sleep, at least for a little while.

I knew she'd be back before long.

Even though visiting hours were ending, Finn had somehow charmed the nurses into allowing him to stay the night. Closing the door to my hospital room, he kicked off his shoes and climbed into bed with me. Moving gently, so as not to disturb any of my IVs or wires, he settled me against his chest and wrapped both arms around me.

"Are you okay?" he asked, his mouth against my hair.

"Now I am," I said, leaning back into him.

"I love you, you know." His mouth ducked down to kiss my exposed shoulder where the hospital gown had slipped. "When I thought I'd lost you—" He broke off. "You *died*... you died in my arms. I don't think I'll ever be the same after that."

I nodded, knowing exactly what he meant. I'd never be the same either.

"Don't ever do it again," he growled against my ear.

I laughed. "I'll do my best," I promised. "And Finn?"

"Yeah?"

"I love you too."

I relaxed against his chest, listening to the beat of his heart beneath my ear. I could feel my body approaching sleep, still exhausted after everything that I'd been through in the past few days.

Few weeks.

Few months.

It had been a hell of a ride, since I'd met Finn Chambers. And I didn't regret a minute of it.

"Finn?" I asked, my voice slurred with sleep.

"What is it, princess?"

"Tell me a story?"

I felt his lips curl into a smile against my hair.

"Once upon a time, there were two little kids, who fell in love…"

As I drifted off into sleep, Finn's voice a lullaby, I dreamed of the young girl who'd thought she'd lost everything, until she met a boy who showed her that love is the one thing that can never be taken away.

ACKNOWLEDGEMENTS

I could probably fill another novel with thank yous alone, but a page or so will have to suffice for now.

Firstly, to my parents for their unending support and love.

Mom – Since I was a little girl, you've been showing me what it means to be a true woman. Every day, you've proved that Supermom really does exist. Thank you for your constant – sometimes unsolicited – advice on all matters big and small, and for always, always, always having my back. Not many people are lucky enough to be able to call their mother "friend," let alone "best friend." You are my inspiration. I love you.

Dad – From my preschool days on, you instilled in me a love of reading and writing. Thank you for supplying me with a slew of the classics, until I was old enough to ride my bike to the library unsupervised. Through the years, you've been my sounding board, stalwart friend, and trusted advisor. I love you.

To my big brother, Zack, for setting the bar so goddamn high with your own successes and giving me a truly wonderful role model to live up to. You've never been afraid to go after your dreams – thank you for inspiring me to do the same.

To my family and friends – thank you for believing in me.

To Arlene Lammy, for helping me with the editing process and being my personal cheerleader throughout this journey, I am eternally grateful.

To every self-published author out there – thank you for being brave enough to share your stories with the world, and for giving me the courage to share mine as well.

And lastly, to Sara Bareilles, for writing the song Gravity, and leading me back from the throes of writer's block more times than I could count.

ABOUT THE AUTHOR

Julie Johnson is a twenty-something Boston native, suffering from an extreme case of Peter Pan Syndrome and an obsession with fictional characters. When she's not writing, Julie can most often be found daydreaming, drinking too much coffee, or striving to conquer her Netflix queue.

You can find Julie on Facebook or contact her on her website www.juliejohnsonbooks.com. Sometimes, when she can figure out how Twitter works, she tweets from @AuthorJulie.

Playlist

Music is an important theme throughout *Like Gravity*. These are the songs that most inspired Brooklyn and Finn's story:

Crash Into Me – Dave Matthews
Head Over Feet – Alanis Morissette
Blackbird – The Beatles
The Scientist – Coldplay
The Only Exception - Paramore
In My Veins – Andrew Belle
Skinny Love – Birdy
Love, Love, Love – Of Monsters and Men
Home – Edward Sharpe & the Magnetic Zeros
I and Love and You – The Avett Brothers
Can't Help Falling in Love – Ingrid Michaelson
Fix You – Coldplay
The One The Got Away – The Civil Wars
Slow Dancing in a Burning Room – John Mayer
Same Old, Same Old – The Civil Wars
Gravity – Sara Bareilles